MW01602868

How would YOU face the End of Days?
For Kathryn,
And now... the EPIC
conclusion to Mars!
All the best

[signature]

OTHER NOVELS BY KYNAN WATERFORD

AVAILABLE NOW
Jupiter - Illusions of Faith
Pluto - Secrets Within
Mars - Twin Prophcies (Book 1 of 2)

COMING 2017
Earth - Singularity

MARS

End of Days

BOOK TWO OF TWO

A System Series novel

KYNAN WATERFORD

FUTURE FANTASY PUBLISHING

Mars - End of Days

Cover art by: Kynan Waterford

Contributing artists:
Angryfly, Turbosquid 3D artist - created ships on the back cover
Cover images of Mars and Earth courtesy of NASA www.nasa.gov

National Library of Australia Cataloguing-in-Publication data:

Waterford, Kynan (Kynan Stewart), 1978- author.

Mars : End of Days / Kynan Waterford

ISBN 978 0 992 56556 5 (pbk.)

Science fiction.
Prophecies--Fiction.
Mars (Planet)--Fiction.

Dewey Number: A823.4

www.kynanwaterford.com.au

Email: kynanwaterford@gmail.com

Printed by Lightning Source

For my wife, Cass.

You make everything about my life better.

If the world was coming to an end, no matter what planet we were on, I'd want to spend my last few moments with you.

Oh... and our new son, Rowan, of course.

STAGE 4: SOLAR FLARE APPROACHES JUPITER
June 7, 2147 - 3.15 pm

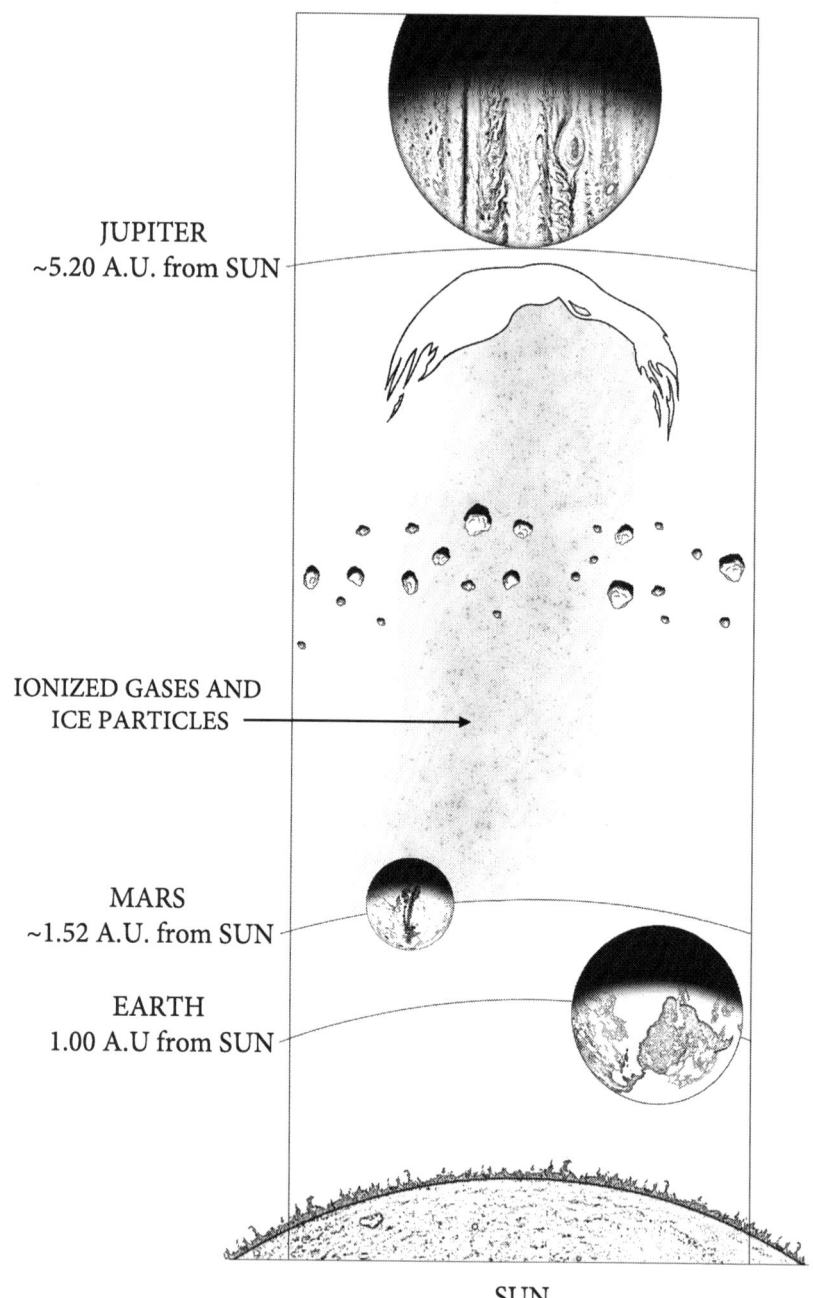

JUPITER
~5.20 A.U. from SUN

IONIZED GASES AND
ICE PARTICLES

MARS
~1.52 A.U. from SUN

EARTH
1.00 A.U from SUN

SUN

1 Astronomical Unit (A.U.) = ~149.6 x 10^6 km

MIANA RAIKEN – DISGRACED LYNT CITY DETECTIVE – was glad Kurt had convinced her to sleep in the presence of the assassin. Travelling through the deep volcanic cave system with a prisoner in tow was more laborious than she expected and, despite nearly a full night's rest and regular breaks, it was gradually wearing her down.

She looked at Kurt, her many-talented companion, and wondered if his ability to continue on without rest was a learned skill or if it was the result of some kind of surgical enhancement.

From what little she knew of his profession, adventurists had no problem upgrading themselves, but such an unnatural advantage didn't seem like something Kurt would go for. He was a man driven by a lust for new experiences and he seemed to master new skills purely for the purpose of searching out more of them. Taking shortcuts would only lessen this satisfaction and so it didn't fit his personality.

Of course, Miana had only known him for a few days now and, despite her intuitive nature, she was well aware that thinking she'd worked him out already would only get her in trouble.

"*I'm just glad he's with me,*" she thought to herself.

1

As they began to scale another steady, uneven slope, Miana turned her attention to the assassin and her mood immediately darkened.

They were currently following the map the assassin had used to find them after he'd destroyed the cave's main entrance. So far, the assassin had been willing to walk where they told him, but Kurt refused to let him climb under his own power. Each time they encountered a cliff-face, Miana had to watch the assassin while Kurt climbed to the top and secured a winch. He then rappelled back down, attached the rope to a complicated harness he'd tied around the assassin's torso and winched them both back up.

Miana didn't know what she would have done without Kurt's rope-handling skills. The assassin had tried to free himself twice now, but both times, Kurt had simply pulled on a rope and the harness either tripped him up or immobilized him in seconds. The few lessons had so far proven extremely effective and Miana doubted the assassin would try again.

The knowledge of Kurt's resilience should have helped her mood, but it wasn't working. Along with being physically tired, the question of what they were going to do when they reached the surface was weighing on her mind.

Since regaining consciousness, the assassin had remained stubbornly silent, which Miana didn't mind at all. She wasn't ready to interrogate him yet. Her first instinct had been to return to Lynt City and hand him over to her old Captain, but that would only result in Captain Farraday demanding an explanation.

Miana shuddered. There were so many problems with that idea that she might as well save them all the trouble and inject herself with an anti-psychotic drug right here and now.

Then there was the matter of the assassin's connection to Loc Breeden. She already knew Loc had enough influence to stop any legitimate investigation in its tracks. His army of lawyers would have the assassin freed before they'd even finished taking his statement, and that was assuming Loc wouldn't simply use his psychic powers to make the assassin kill himself.

But what was the alternative? She couldn't just kill the man, no matter how many problems that might solve. She couldn't risk letting him go either. He was a professional assassin, for one thing, and now that he knew Loc's secret, he was in as much danger as she was. If they let him go, his only real option would be to kill Miana and Kurt so he could pretend ignorance.

Miana clenched her jaw in frustration. At least there was an advantage knowing the assassin was now under threat as well. Perhaps she could use it to persuade him to help them? But even if she did, how could they trust him? And how could he help them anyway?

"What do I really want to happen here?" she thought. *"That's the real question I need to answer."*

Miana knew in her heart that Loc Breeden would never see the inside of a jail cell. Even without his psychic powers, his diplomatic immunity and position within Cosmotech Defence made him untouchable. But that didn't stop her sense of justice from burning bright. It was the same thing that stonewalled her career in law enforcement. She knew some people were too powerful to convict, but something inside her refused to let that stop her pursuing them. And Loc Breeden was the worst culprit of all.

"You're not going to get away with this," she promised him.

Bringing her focus back to the cave, Miana saw that Kurt had stopped at the top of a rocky slope. When she looked at him, he motioned for her to join him and so she did, glancing warily at the assassin as she passed.

"We're not far from the surface," Kurt said quietly when she reached him. "We'll need a plan to deal with him by the time we get there."

"I'll have one," she assured him.

Nodding silently, Kurt pulled on the rope tied to the assassin and continued on.

Miana took a moment to catch her breath and studied the assassin as he passed.

3

He didn't even acknowledge her and Miana was almost glad. She could feel the looming decisions like the approaching edge of a sandstorm and it frightened her more than it should have.

The fear made her uncomfortable and she found herself once more considering allowing Kurt to use his newly acquired psychic powers.

"But should I let him use them again?" she wondered.

After experiencing their effects first hand, she felt disgusted even contemplating it, but it would be foolish not to at least consider how they might be of help.

And it was that point of logic that scared her most. Using the power would be so convenient. So *easy.* And yet, once they started down that path, they couldn't know where it might lead them or what they might eventually decide was a necessary evil.

With a shiver, Miana started moving again and looked at Kurt's back. She already knew he would use the power again, whether she allowed him to or not. He was a risk taker and a free spirit who reacted to stimuli as it appeared.

It was probably what made him so attractive and yet, at the same time, Miana couldn't deny that she resented it a little. Her whole life had been devoted to maturity and prudence. To understanding consequence down the smallest detail so she could follow forensic evidence back to a crime's perpetrator. And had it been worth it? Was it pointless now that she knew what men like Loc Breeden were capable of? And after what she'd seen in the alien cave, did anything she'd ever done have any meaning at all?

"We're here," Kurt said, interrupting her thoughts.

Mentally pulling herself back to the present, Miana saw daylight streaming in from an entrance not far ahead of them and felt an almost primal sense of relief. After trekking through the darkness for so long she was looking forward to bathing in a little sunlight, even the weak kind they got on Mars.

"Wait there," she said to the assassin, motioning him toward a boulder that was just inside the entrance.

The assassin moved to where she indicated and Miana kept a careful eye on him as Kurt climbed a tall rock just outside and pulled out some binoculars to confirm the assassin's vehicle was nearby.

"It's an X-3 sand skipper," he said, lowering the binoculars and turning to Miana. "But it looks modified."

"Modified how?" she asked.

Kurt glanced at the assassin before answering.

"Not sure," he admitted. "The cabin looks different and there are panel variations that could be hiding anything. Weapons most likely. What do you want to do?"

Miana frowned. There was no avoiding it any longer.

"I think negotiations are in order," she said firmly. "And I think you should know before we start… we may have to let him go at some point."

"What?" Kurt said, jumped back down. "You can't be serious."

"I am, Kurt," Miana said, looking him in the eye to prove it. "We're not going to kill him so our options are either hand him over to someone who will, or let him go."

"I could kill him," Kurt said, flashing the assassin a poisonous look.

"You don't mean that," Miana said with a frown.

Kurt looked back at her, his face grim, but after a few seconds some of the anger fell from his face.

"No," he said quietly. "Of course I don't. But I wish I did."

"You don't mean that either," Miana said, putting a hand on his arm. "Look, Kurt, I know what he deserves, but you saw the same thing I did down in that cave. There's something much bigger going on here."

"Don't worry," he said, gently removing her hand. "I get it. But it doesn't mean I have to like it."

At his words, Miana felt a slight pain in her chest, but she knew there was nothing she could do about his anger. Not now, anyway.

Turning away from her, Kurt approached the assassin.

"Take a seat," he said in a menacing tone.

The assassin did as he asked, sitting on the boulder behind him. Miana studied his face for a moment, looking for any indication of what he might be thinking. He wasn't afraid of her, that was immediately clear, but neither was he aggressive or antagonistic. If anything, he seemed calm, as if he were simply waiting for her to speak.

"Can your vehicle fit all of us?" she asked calmly.

"It can," the assassin replied simply.

"And do we need to trek over there, or can you bring it to us?" she added.

"I can fly it here. But I'll need to access my survival suit's computer."

"Not likely," Kurt growled. "He could blow the thing up if he wanted to, or have it attack us."

The assassin remained silent at this and Miana thought about it for a moment. If he was going to help them, they would need to work out some kind of arrangement. Trust was going to be hard for both of them, but they weren't going anywhere without it.

"You know what Kurt can do," she said after a moment. "You experienced his mental control first hand."

The assassin's gaze remained steady.

"He could do it again," she continued. "He could make you tell us anything we want to know. He could make you *do* anything we want you to do, but I'm going to be honest with you. I don't like psychic powers and I don't want to use them if I don't have to."

She paused for a moment to let that sink in.

"I believe you're a smart man," she continued. "An extremely smart man. I think you know what I told you down in the cave is true. Loc Breeden is also capable of controlling people. In fact, it was an example of Loc's abilities that led me to him in the first place. I investigated a man who was forced to carve symbols into his own flesh. Every part of his body that could be reached was covered with shallow cuts and when that was done, he was made to cut out his own eyes."

Again, Miana paused to let the information sink in.

6

"His blood toxicology showed he was awake during the trauma, meaning he felt all the pain that it caused him and yet was unable to stop what he was doing. Another man was made to sit in his home office while the apartment burned down around him."

The assassin didn't give any indication he cared about either situation.

"The reason I'm sharing this with you," Miana continued after a moment, "is because I'd like to emphasise another conclusion that I'm sure you've already made. Loc Breeden has a vested interest in keeping his abilities secret. When he finds out that you know about him, I doubt your situation will be any better than ours. Except, of course, you don't have these abilities yourself."

Miana could see the assassin's mind ticking over now and she paused to let him finish.

"You make some interesting points," the assassin said after a moment, "but if I'm going to believe you, I will require proof."

"Proof?" Miana said carefully. "You've already experienced it first-hand."

"And it could have been a fluke," the assassin replied, "or some kind of chemical weapon I'm unaware of. Perhaps Kurt is a gifted hypnotist."

"It was no fluke, chemical, or mental trick," Miana assured him. "Kurt took control of your mind and body."

"So you say," the assassin replied calmly, "but I want to see it again. Make me tell you something I don't want to. Show me the extent of Loc's power and perhaps I'll consider helping you of my own volition."

Miana felt a wave of anxiety, but was careful not to let it show. This was the last thing she wanted and, she suspected, the very reason the assassin was asking for it. She needed him to believe Kurt could control him at will, but was it worth letting Kurt use those powers again, even just once?

"Just once," Miana thought grimly. *"There's no such thing."*

But how else could she convince him to help them? Torture? Would that be morally better or worse? It was an argument Miana really didn't have the patience for right now and so she decided there was only one option open to her.

"Very well," she said, before reluctantly turning to Kurt. "Make him tell you about the sand skipper."

Kurt gave her an apologetic look, aware she didn't want this, but when he turned to the assassin, his expression became serious and more than a little contemptuous. He didn't speak, he simply stared at the assassin for a long moment, and Miana waited for a sign that something was happening. There was nothing to see, however. Not until a glint of red light flashed across Kurt's eyes and he spoke firmly into the silence.

"Stand up."

The assassin did so immediately.

Miana felt an urge to remind Kurt he shouldn't use the powers any more than was necessary, but decided to hold her tongue. There would be plenty of time for warnings later.

"Now, tell me all the security measures you've installed in your X-3 sand skipper," he said slowly.

"The locking mechanism is synced with my biological signature," the assassin replied in a monotone. "The cabin is tamper-proof. Anyone attempting entry without authorisation is treated as a hostile combatant. The skipper's on-board computer is capable of recognising biological signatures, weapons, and armour. Once a target has been analysed it is incapacitated with either an electric shock, an anaesthetic dart, a concussive blast, or a lethal projectile. Notification systems immediately alert me of the attempted entry. Should the counter-measures prove ineffective, the skipper detonates a small nuclear warhead imbedded in the nose producing a primary blast radius of fifty metres."

Kurt glanced at Miana.

"I've gotta say," he said, "that was easier than I expected. He's an arrogant bastard, isn't he? Are you happy with what he's told us?"

Miana hesitated. It *had* been easier than she expected. And despite her convictions, it seemed foolish to let this opportunity go to waste.

"No," she said firmly. "Ask him how he planned to escape."

Kurt raised his eyebrows briefly and then returned his gaze to the assassin.

"How were you planning to escape?"

"The skipper is capable of distinguishing between my biological signature and others," he replied. "When I convinced you to give me access to my survival suit's computer, I was planning to activate a preset program. The skipper would then strafe our position, using our biological signatures to kill both of you and leave me unharmed."

"Told you," Kurt said, offering Miana a wry look. "Need any more?"

Again, Miana felt an internal struggle as she thought of all the information they could extract, but the mere acknowledgement of a struggle was enough to firm her resolve.

"No," she said quietly. "Release him, Kurt."

Kurt looked a little disappointed, but he did as she asked.

Miana watched the assassin's expression as he was released. It flickered through relief and then fear for a second, before settling into another calm poker face.

"I believe you," he said simply.

"Good," Miana replied. "Then the negotiations can continue. In the interest of saving time, I won't ask Kurt to verify everything you say as you say it, but he will use his power at the end of our discussion to make sure you haven't lied to us. If you do, we'll know you can't be bargained with and we will be forced to hand you over to the L.C.P.D."

"And straight into Loc Breeden's hands. I understand." the assassin said with a nod. "What are you offering?"

"Your freedom," Miana said simply. "A chance to disappear, no ropes attached."

The assassin glanced at Kurt's improvised harness and then returned his gaze to Miana with a raised eyebrow.

"Very droll," he said. "And what do you want in return?"

"First, I want to be certain you're not going to kill us as soon as we let you go."

"I can only give you my word," the assassin replied simply.

"Not good enough," Miana replied.

"It will be when you confirm I'm telling the truth," the assassin said.

Miana thought about it for a moment, her instincts unhappy with the logic.

"The contract to hunt you down is still valid," the assassin added. "If I killed you, I might be able to convince Mr. Breeden that everything went as planned, but I know too much to risk contacting him again. If he uses his powers to interrogate me, I'm a dead man. All things considered, I'd prefer to entrust my life to you."

"Then say it," Miana prompted, "and we'll find out if you're telling the truth later."

"Once I'm free, I will not attempt to kill you, or Kurt."

"Okay," Miana said with a nod. "Now for the second condition of our agreement. I'm well aware Loc Breeden is beyond the reach of any Lynt City law. He'll never be brought to justice in the way I'd prefer."

"I could kill him for you," the assassin offered. "A solution that would suit us both."

"No," Miana replied firmly. "That is not an option."

"Very well," the assassin said with a shrug.

Miana looked at him hard for a moment. Should she make him swear he wouldn't kill Loc? Or anyone else for that matter? But even as she thought it, she knew it was a slippery slope that would require them to use psychic powers more and more, and so she decided to let it go.

"I may not be able to arrest Loc Breeden," she continued, "but it doesn't mean I have to sit by and let him go about his business as usual. What I need is information. Information about what he's planning and, more importantly, who he answers to. To that end, I'd like you to help us break into the Cosmotech facility in Lynt City and steal every computer file they have."

"Hmmm…" the assassin mused for a moment. "Not an easy task, but not impossible. I believe it would be in my power to fulfil the terms of such an agreement."

"Then if you agree to help us break into the Cosmotech facility, steal their information, *and* help us avoid getting caught, we'll release you right here and now."

Miana saw Kurt take a step forward at this, clearly not happy with her terms, but he thankfully restrained himself and remained silent.

The assassin glanced at him before speaking again.

"In the interest of trust, I should tell you that I'm finding it hard to commit to this contract without thinking of ways to betray you. I don't know if it will affect your psychic truth test, but you should at least be aware that it may do so. However, given my options, I agree to your terms and assure you that I honestly intend to honour this agreement."

"Very well," Miana said. "Kurt, please verify the truth of our negotiations."

Kurt gave her a look that communicated all the protests he'd kept silent and then reluctantly turned to the assassin. The process of establishing psychic control was just as quick as the first time.

"Do you actually intend to help us break into the Cosmotech facility in Lynt City?"

"Yes."

"Have you lied to us at all during the negotiations?"

"No."

"Are you planning to betray us?"

"Yes."

Kurt looked at Miana with his eyebrows raised.

"I told you," he said. "We can't trust him."

11

"He said he couldn't help thinking about it," she replied carefully. "And you asked him if he was *planning* to betray us. That could mean he's just thinking about it. Ask him if he is actually going to betray us."

Kurt gave her another reluctant look and then turned back to the assassin.

"Will you betray us?"

"If I'm given the opportunity, yes."

Again, Kurt turned to Miana with an 'I told you so' look on his face.

"We can't do this without him, Kurt," Miana said with a frown. "He's only going to betray us if we give him an opportunity."

"And you promised to untie him," Kurt replied meaningfully.

"We have to trust him at some point," she replied, frowning deeper.

Kurt turned away from her with a frustrated growl and then seemed to think of something. When he looked back at Miana, he had a devious look on his face.

"I think there might be another option," he said, before turning back to the assassin. "Do you have Raze implants in your skipper?"

"Yes," the assassin replied.

"Ha!" Kurt said with a grin. "That will keep him honest."

"What's a Raze implant?" Miana asked suspiciously.

"Don't you watch the Epiphany channel?" Kurt asked her. "It's an illegal technology used by the North Koreans back in World War Three to prevent the capture of their own soldiers. You implant a small explosive charge next to the spine that can be triggered by remote. If he tries anything funny, we blow it."

"What? No!" Miana said, shocked that Kurt would even suggest such a thing. "We're not going to threaten his life just to get what we want."

"Then what the hell do we do?" Kurt snapped, his anger finally flaring. "Let him go free and hope for the best? You heard what he just said! He'll betray us if he's given the chance. A Raze implant will make that opportunity non-existent!"

"There has to be another way," Miana replied, her own anger rising.

"There is," Kurt said, folding his arms. "I can psychically control him the entire way. Make him tell us what we need to know and do what we need him to do."

"No!" Miana snapped.

"Then let me use the Raze implant," Kurt said with a shrug.

Miana turned away from him. She hated being backed into a corner like this, but could tell Kurt wasn't going to back down. He obviously didn't like the deal she was offering the assassin and although she doubted he would actually use the implant unless it was absolutely necessary, she didn't want to put him in that position. Particularly now that he had psychic powers.

"Alright," she said finally, her gut sour with reluctance. "Use the Raze implant."

"Thank you," Kurt said, with only a hint of sarcasm.

Miana glared at him as he turned to the assassin.

"I know you heard all of that," Kurt said. "Our deal now includes you being tagged with a Raze implant. Do you still agree to help us break into the Lynt City Cosmotech facility and steal their information without getting caught?"

"Yes," the assassin replied.

"Good," Kurt said. "Then we have an agreement. And just to make sure you don't discover any *opportunities* before the Raze implant is ready, I want you to bring the sand-skipper to us now."

Miana felt a wave of frustration at this and opened her mouth to tell Kurt to let the assassin go, but quickly thought better of it. This was obviously his way of expressing anger and if she forced him to contain it now, it would only resurface later.

And besides, it was a prudent decision. The assassin may be willing to help them, but the less opportunity for betrayal they gave him, the better.

13

"*I just hope we get this done soon,*" she thought coldly. "*I don't think Kurt should spend any more time in this man's presence than he has to.*"

FAYINA – ANYA POLOVSKI'S STRONGEST AND MOST violent personality – strode through Lynt City with a purpose.

No one got in her way. Whether it was the expression she wore or the new outfit she'd acquired, something warned them to stay clear.

Fayina liked it. For the first time she could remember, she was in complete control of her body and she wasn't going to waste this opportunity.

The first thing she did was get out of Anya's flimsy clothes and into some heavy boots, black Kevlar pants, and an armoured sports jacket. It made her feel so much more like her *real* self. She'd never understood Celia's love of different colours and styles. Clothing had a purpose: to cover your naked body and protect you from cold or injury. Beyond that, any embellishment was just superficial waste.

Sneering at the thought of Celia judging her clothes, Fayina imagined punching the useless twit in the face. She'd been uncharacteristically quiet since Fayina had wrestled control of her body from the others. Ianka and Dr. Haig too.

Fayina had expected them to offer more ongoing resistance and had actually been looking forward to it, but their silence was more than a little disconcerting.

15

Were they sulking? Celia certainly would be, but Ianka didn't sulk and nor did Dr. Haig. Their intellectual and – Fayina often thought – *arrogant* personalities would not permit such childish behaviour.

No. If Fayina wasn't mistaken, they were plotting something. Waiting for an opportunity to retake control and send her back to the depths of Anya's guilt-scarred mind.

"Fuck that!" she roared, causing a skinny man that was passing her to recoil in alarm and crash into a hedge that ran along the walkway.

Fayina strode on, ignoring the wary looks that others were now giving her.

It was a frustratingly long way to the Cenovian district. That snivelling coward Sabian had obviously wanted to keep her as far from Isaac as possible. Fayina knew she could easily take a vehicle, but she wasn't going to be taken that way again.

She gritted her teeth as she remembered how easily she'd been captured.

"Anya's a useless fucking idiot," she growled beneath her breath. "I never would have given in so easily."

Whenever possible, she broke into a run and only slowed to a walk when it was clear running would attract too much attention. She'd already stopped to eat and go to the toilet after buying her new clothes and was ready to do whatever it took to bring down this crazy, Isaac-worshipping cult. Whoever they were.

She wanted to believe this was more about getting revenge than it was about helping Isaac, but she could almost hear Ianka telling her not to be stupid. She had a connection with that spineless fool whether she liked it or not and finding out what happened to him was at least part of why she was doing this.

"He's got plenty to answer for," she growled.

When her feet eventually hit the Cenovian district, Fayina started to think about how she was going to get inside Cosmotech offices when she reached them. This wouldn't be as easy as Isaac's rescue in the Valles Dome.

Taking down a bunch of religious nut-jobs without backup was one thing, but dealing with highly trained professionals within a Cenovian district domescraper was something else entirely. If the building's electronic security didn't defeat her then the sheer number of human security they'd have on site eventually would.

"*What I need is a more subtle way in,*" she thought.

Unwilling to access any technology that might give her location away, she'd already memorized a map of the area and knew exactly where to go. When she eventually reached the block that was home to Cosmotech offices, she took up position a few hundred metres away and studied the auras of those coming out the entrance.

It was perhaps the one skill that every personality inside Anya could access and although Fayina didn't like using it, she wasn't so stubborn as to ignore a valuable advantage.

"*There's my ticket,*" she thought as a small woman exited the building.

Her delicate aura flickered like a million butterflies. Colourful, obviously intelligent, but timid as well. She'd be easily coerced by the kind of intimidation Fayina had to offer.

"*Let's go and say hi, shall we?*" she thought with a smile.

As the timid woman turned along the walkway and headed for home, Fayina left her position and began stalking her. She didn't exactly blend in with the crowd around her, but wasn't overly concerned. Her target didn't seem like the kind of person to invite social interaction by looking around.

Fayina followed her for several blocks to make she wasn't planning on meeting anyone nearby, and then quickly cut across the main thoroughfare and ran along a side street to get ahead of her. As expected, the timid Cosmotech employee didn't take any unexpected turns and so when Fayina peaked out from behind a corner made of flowery wall plants, the target was headed straight for her.

"*Time for introductions,*" she thought.

When the woman was only a few metres from the corner, Fayina stepped out to block her path and the small woman was so lost in her own thoughts that she crashed straight into her.

"Watch where you're fucking going," Fayina snarled as the woman stumbled back, tripped, and landed hard on her bottom.

The woman raised her arms in defence, clearly terrified of what might happen next and her aura flickered with bright red and blue slashes, mirroring her sudden change of emotion.

"*Perfect,*" Fayina thought to herself.

"I'm s-sorry," the woman squeaked, peering up at her warily. "I didn't see you–"

"Go fuck yourself," Fayina sneered, before stepping over her and striding away.

The encounter had gone perfectly. This woman was just what Fayina needed and the initial hook of intimidation had been well and truly sunk into her fragile psyche. Now all she had to do was reel her in.

Wasting no time looking back, Fayina once more crossed the main thoroughfare and ducked down another side street so she could double back and intercept her target once again. The short loop brought her back to the scene of their first encounter and she hid behind another flower-draped corner to watch her quarry from a distance.

An old man who seemed to have helped her to get up was hovering nearby, but the woman was assuring him that she was okay.

"*That's it,*" Fayina coaxed her with a smile. "*You don't need his help. You'll be fine. Just keep coming this way.*"

When the woman eventually begged her way free, she looked more shaken than ever and Fayina grinned in anticipation. This was going to be easy.

Her target walked another few blocks before turning down a smaller side street and Fayina used the opportunity to run ahead and wait behind another corner.

This time the tiny woman was more wary and her gaze darted around the street like a mouse searching for predators in the underbrush. It didn't help her find Fayina, however, and it was quite a surprise when she suddenly found herself face-to-face with the woman who'd just knocked her over.

"Oh!" she yelled, placing a trembling hand against her chest.

"Hello pretty," Fayina said with an evil smile.

"I..." the woman replied, hesitating in confusion. "I'm so sorry about before. I–"

"That was nothing," Fayina assured her with a dismissive wave as she took a step closer. "But if you want to make it up to me, I could really use your help with something."

"Oh?" the woman replied, a little quieter this time.

"What's your name?"

"R... Rita?"

"Nice to meet you Rita. My name's Fayina. You work for Cosmotech Defence, don't you?"

"Uh hmm," the woman replied, nodding timidly.

"Well, I don't, you see, and I'd like to get inside."

"But you can't–"

"That's right," Fayina interrupted her, pulling the knife she'd used on Sabian from the small her back. "I can't get in by myself. Not without help."

Rita's eyes locked onto the blade and gradually opened wider.

"Beautiful, isn't it, Rita?" Fayina said in a soothing tone. "So sharp. So clean. I don't like using it actually, because it ruins the shine. But I'm so *good* at using it and sometimes people just don't give me a choice. You wouldn't make me use it, would you, Rita?"

Rita's eyes didn't leave the blade, but her head shook emphatically.

"That's good," Fayina said quietly. "Very good. Now tell me, Rita, do you have authorisation to allow visitors into your office?"

"Y... yes," she stammered, "but... but only up to level three. Beyond that... th... they take circulatory scans. I... I don't have the right level of clearance to bypass them."

19

"Level three is fine," Fayina assured her. "Now, you look like an intelligent and capable woman, Rita, so I really don't think I need to spell this out. But I'm going to anyway, just so we're clear on what's going to happen. Are you listening, Rita?"

Rita's head quickly bobbed up and down.

"I'm going to put this knife away and then we're going to walk back to your office. You're going to make up a story they'll believe so you can sign me in as a visitor. Something that will make sure they don't suspect anything. After that, you're going to take me on a tour of the areas you have access to. No one is going to get hurt. That's an important point, Rita, and I hope you understand it because you're the only one with the power to make it come true. If you do what I say, you, and anybody else we come into contact with, will walk away with all their blood still in their veins. But if you screw this up somehow, well… would you like me to explain what will happen?"

Rita's head shook forcefully from side-to-side.

"Very good, Rita," Fayina said with a smile, before sheathing her knife with a flick of her wrist. "Let's go and visit your workplace then, shall we?"

KURT DIDN'T LIKE BEING SO CLOSE TO THE ASSASSIN. The sand skipper's cockpit was barely able to accommodate three of them and the fit was much tighter than he was comfortable with.

He was, admittedly, excited about their planned assault on Cosmotech Defence, but it was hard to enjoy when he was being forced to trust an assassin who'd recently tried to kill him. Not to mention the fact they had to let him walk at the end of the mission.

Kurt appreciated Miana was simply following her strict moral code and even liked that about her, but he didn't feel so noble himself. In fact, if it was up to him, he would have gladly used his new powers to make the assassin open the cockpit, step out, and plummet to a well-deserved death.

"It wouldn't be the same as murder," he thought to himself. *"At worst, it'd be self-defence, just a little after the fact."*

But he knew Miana would never go for such a weak argument. It was the root of her problem. She couldn't think of a way to ensure Loc Breeden got what he deserved and so she'd fallen back on her investigative instincts. Kurt wanted answers too, of course, but he doubted they'd find any at Cosmotech Defence. Certainly none that would give Miana the satisfaction she craved.

21

In his humble opinion, they were operating well beyond the boundaries of state-imposed justice she was used to and, out here, the only laws that applied were the primal demands of nature. Adapt or die. Kill or be killed.

"Well, I've got no problem with that," he thought determinedly.

Kurt had spent his entire life 'adapting' to different environments in order to conquer them. If he was put in a situation where he had to kill in order to save his own life, he would exercise that primal instinct without any fear of moral judgement.

Of course, he also knew it wasn't that simple. Like it or not, he was beginning to genuinely care for Miana and that meant her morals were important to him. He couldn't just brush them aside when it suited him.

Shaking his head in frustration, Kurt looked out the cockpit window and focused on the view below to calm his nerves.

He loved how Mars looked from this high up. The harsh, rocky landscape was about as unfriendly as things got on the surface, but up here, the same desolate wasteland took on an aura of majesty that only Mother Nature could provide. The intricate detail of canyon and gully twisted through the landscape like life-giving veins and the pastel browns, oranges, and yellows painted the vast expanse like God's personal canvas. It was nothing short of magnificent.

As he stared at the beautiful desolation, Kurt was reminded of the lush forests that covered the alien world they'd seen in the underwater cave. Then how those thriving ecosystems had been destroyed by the biblical column of red fire.

"God, I hope that wasn't real," he thought with a grimace.

Turning his eyes upward, he scanned the horizon again and saw a gleaming strip of reflected light flash into view.

Lynt City. It too looked impressive from this high up, but in Kurt's opinion the achievements of humankind never seemed to measure up to the grandeur of Mother Nature.

The assassin – Mr. Drevit – had told them the only way into Cosmotech was through Lynt City's enormous perimeter dome.

"*But how?*" Kurt wondered. "*It's certainly not as simple as landing on it.*"

Meteorite strikes were more common on Mars than they were on Earth because the atmosphere wasn't thick enough to burn them up. Because of this, Lynt City had defence systems capable of tracking even the smallest potential missile. This meant approaching the city from above without being detected was virtually impossible and, even worse, there was an outside chance the meteorite defences might accidentally blow you out of the sky.

Kurt knew all this because his job occasionally included sight-seeing flights around the city's perimeter and even he wasn't crazy enough to tempt fate by crossing into the airspace above it.

But that didn't seem to be the assassin's plan either. Kurt felt the weak gravity holding them into their seats fall away as they banked toward the city and realised they were descending toward a brightly lit landing zone on the edge of the spaceport.

"*So, the usual way then,*" he mused.

It was strange knowing they were going to re-enter the city so openly and Kurt immediately felt uneasy about it. He accepted that an international assassin would know how to move around anonymously, but to him, this was just another situation where they were being forced to trust a killer.

"How will this work?" Miana asked, clearly no more comfortable than he was.

"I enjoy a level of clearance that is close to diplomatic immunity," the assassin replied calmly. "Upon landing, we will be greeted by a customs officer who will log fraudulent details on our behalf. We will then be escorted inside Lynt City borders."

Kurt shook his head again. In movies, this kind of thing was right up his alley, but seeing it in real life made him feel sick.

"*I really miss that blissful ignorance,*" he thought with a frown.

When they reached a standard perimeter, the assassin allowed the airport computers to take control of the skipper and their landing was fast and smooth.

When they were on the ground, the skipper taxied into a private hanger and the enormous doors sealed behind them to re-pressurise the atmosphere.

It didn't take them long to disembark with their luggage and yet a customs officer was already waiting for them, just as the assassin promised. Kurt expected her to confiscate all personal items for security scans, but instead she simply gave them a cursory glance, spent a few moments entering information into her data pad and then handed it to Drevit.

Kurt was shocked. Seeing this kind of blatant corruption first-hand was more disconcerting than he expected. He turned to Miana in disgust and felt a little better when she appeared as tense as he was.

He wanted to go to her, to massage her shoulders and relieve some of that tension, but he resisted the urge. He didn't want to give Drevit any indication he wasn't alert and ready to do whatever it might take to keep them both safe.

When the assassin seemed satisfied with the information logged by the customs officer, he passed the data pad back without a word. The customs officer then turned toward a door with 'authorised personnel only' written in large red letters. A conspicuous looking camera was mounted above the door, but when the customs officer looked at it, the light beside it blinked off.

"We're clear," she said simply, before holding the door open for them.

Kurt gave her the fiercest look of disapproval he could muster as he passed through, but she simply ignored him.

When they were through, the customs officer led them down several long access corridors and paused only to make sure each camera they encountered blinked off before moving on. Kurt assumed it meant there was another spaceport official following their progress and manipulating the security footage that would otherwise betray their presence.

"*I'll never trust a spaceport officer again,*" he thought.

When they eventually reached an access door that led to the main foyer, they had to wait almost a minute before the camera blinked off. Beyond the door was a security cordon that would normally restrict access to the airport's inner corridors and, beyond that, Kurt could see the crowded main foyer.

The customs officer didn't accompany them through this time. She simply waited for Drevit to nod at her and then closed the door behind them.

"That was easy," Kurt commented dryly.

"Planning is everything," Drevit replied, before gesturing toward the cordon. "Quickly, please. Mr. Breeden is certain to know we've arrived. We need to disappear again, fast."

"Hmm," Kurt grumbled.

He didn't know how the assassin remained so calm with an explosive device implanted next to his spine. It kind of made sense given he killed people for a living, but after all that had happened back in the caves, Kurt didn't like it one bit.

Putting his concerns aside for the moment, he moved through the unmanned security cordon with Miana. Their illegal entrance didn't seem to draw any attention and they were soon just a part of the crowd that moved toward the exits. The steady stream of people was perfect cover and it wasn't long before they were headed toward the pick-up bay that waited beside the entrance.

"*Welcome home,*" Kurt thought to himself as he stared up at the clean, towering domescrapers and brightly lit levels that spider-webbed the spaces between them.

"Come on," Miana prompted, making him realise he'd lost focus for a second.

"Right," he said, feeling annoyed at himself.

As they approached the kerb, a sleek vehicle that would easily fit three silently pulled to the curb and Kurt watched the assassin carefully as he secured their luggage and then took the front seat.

Taking the seat directly behind him, Kurt saw the assassin attach something to the computer display and immediately felt suspicious.

25

"What's that?" he asked with a frown.

"I'm scrambling our output signal," Drevit said without looking up. "Mr. Breeden won't be able to track us through the city."

"Where are we headed?" Miana asked from the seat behind Kurt.

"The lower levels of seven hundred and seven, Gettysburg Avenue," Drevit replied, giving her, at least, the courtesy of a glance. "The building reaches all the way to the dome and connects right under one of the maintenance control towers. From there, we can access the dome repair unit that will take us to the Cosmotech facility."

Kurt felt a rush of adrenalin as they pulled away from the curb.

"Those things travel at five hundred kilometres an hour," he said, trying not to smile.

"And your point?" Drevit asked in a dismissive tone.

"Just... saying," Kurt replied, his excitement doused by irritation. "I've never even thought of riding one of those before. That should be... pretty cool."

The assassin actually looked at him this time, but it was only to offer a sneer of disapproval.

Feeling a little unfairly treated, Kurt found himself battling an urge to touch Miana again and wondered if she needed it as much as he did. She didn't seem the kind of woman to rely on a man's affections, but he was sure she'd enjoy what he could give. If they survived long enough for him to share it, of course.

The rest of the ride went in silence and as their vehicle finally approached Gettysburg avenue, Drevit spoke again.

"There's a service elevator near the rear of the building. The information desk will attempt to verify our identities so you'll need to wear one of these."

He handed each of them a pin-sized device.

"What's this?" Kurt asked suspiciously.

"When the information desk scans us, this will return an active signal that will access the building's security database and randomly assign each of us an identity. It will only choose someone who isn't already present. If, and when, the real person shows up, the double count will be flagged by security, but there's no tracking protocols once we're inside. Even if they don't believe it's a computer error, they'll have no way of finding us."

"Hmmm," Kurt mused, impressed despite his intense dislike of the man.

"Let's go," Miana prompted again as she exited the vehicle.

After retrieving their luggage, the three of them entered the building and once more mingled with the crowd as it moved past the information desk.

Kurt tried to remain casual, just as he imagined an international assassin would be, but at just the moment he assumed he was being scanned, he couldn't help locking eyes with the security guard.

"*Oh shit,*" he thought, his heart skipping a beat. "*He knows.*"

But the man looked away again almost immediately and Kurt quickly breathed a sigh of relief.

"*Damn it, I need to be braver than that,*" he scolded himself. "*This is only going to get more dangerous and second guessing myself will just put us all at risk.*"

As they approached a bank of large, fast moving elevators, the three of them quietly separated from the crowd and headed to the service elevator at the back. The assassin paused in front of the access panel and attached the same device he'd used to scramble their vehicle's signal. Kurt thought he could have hotwired the elevator if he had to, but he wasn't sure he'd be able to bypass any monitoring systems that might have been installed.

Drevit, on the other hand, barely touched the device to the panel before he stood back and the elevator doors slid silently open. Feeling a little less than his usual, confident self, Kurt followed him inside. When the doors had closed behind them he felt several kilograms heavier as it began its descent.

Once more, they travelled in silence and Kurt found himself feeling more uncomfortable by the second.

"Will this pin work inside Cosmotech?" he asked, unable to stay quiet.

"Not in the same way," Drevit replied, not looking at him again. "Cosmotech monitors the location and condition of their staff at all times. These will help us fool the computer systems into thinking we're authorised to be there, but we can't just appear inside the building. First we need to hack the security system from an information node on the top floor and set up a movement history."

"Right," Kurt said slowly. "And you can do that?"

"I can," Drevit replied simply.

"And then what? We just stroll into the server vault and steal what we want?"

"No," Drevit replied, his tone almost bored now. "I can't give us identities with that authorisation."

"So, what do we do?"

"It will depend upon the circumstances we find."

Kurt couldn't believe it.

"You don't know yet? I thought you said planning was everything."

"There will be time," Drevit replied, before turning to Miana. "We may encounter personnel on the maintenance floor we're headed to. I'll need to prevent them from tripping an alarm or the repair units will be rendered inoperable."

"No one dies," Miana said firmly.

"Of course," Drevit replied with a nod. "Sedation is always preferable. I'm simply preparing you for what I'll be doing so you don't feel compelled to act against me."

Kurt received a meaningful glance as the assassin said this and it made his fists clench. He was the one with the power here. He could control and even kill the assassin at a moment's notice. But the way he was being treated made him feel more like an attack dog on the end of Miana's leash.

"*Keep it together, Kurt,*" he thought to himself. "*He's just trying to manipulate you into making a mistake.*"

"Noted," Miana said simply.

When the elevator eventually came to a halt, Drevit motioned them to stand against the wall.

"Give me thirty seconds before you follow," he said simply.

Nodding reluctantly, Kurt stood next to Miana and watched closely as the doors opened onto a wide space. The ceiling beyond was at least two stories up and he could see several heavy-duty robotic systems hanging from a sturdy network of girders. He assumed they were used to maintain the repair droids that serviced Lynt City's dome and felt a traitorous rush of excitement.

"*We're really going to ride one of those?*" he thought incredulously. "*This is going to be wild!*"

Returning his attention to Drevit, Kurt watched the assassin stride confidently out of the elevator and, a few moments later, heard him talking to someone. A woman's voice answered in an enquiring tone, but Drevit didn't say anything else.

Suspicion flashed to life in Kurt's mind and he pictured the assassin pressing a gleaming blade against the throat of a beautiful woman. He knew it was stupid, but something fired inside of him and before he knew what was happening, he was sprinting out through the elevator doors.

Caught in an adrenalin-fuelled rush, he saw Drevit standing in a glassed-off section of offices beside a woman who was turning toward him with a surprised expression. She wasn't anywhere near as beautiful as he'd imagined and, for some reason, it made him realise his mistake. But before he could do anything about it, the woman's eyelids slid shut and she slumped unconscious against the desk.

Feeling like an idiot, Kurt slowed down and stared at the woman as he stepped inside the small office.

"What did you do to her?" he demanded.

"I told you, thirty seconds," Drevit replied sharply. "She saw your face before the sedative kicked in."

"She saw your face too," Kurt said reproachfully, the energy that had propelled him to action sinking into a pall of embarrassment.

"The first thing I plan to do when this mission is over is change my face," Drevit said. "I didn't assume you were willing to do the same."

"Well… I…." Kurt stuttered.

"Is she alright?" Miana interrupted, entering the office behind him.

"She'll be fine," Drevit assured her as he strode past Kurt and headed for the maintenance drone.

Kurt felt a sudden urge to punch him in the face, but Miana laid a hand on his arm just in time. He turned to look at her and saw understanding along with a hint of warning in her eyes.

"I'm sorry," he said quietly. "I just… I'm finding it hard to trust him."

"It won't be for much longer," Miana assured him.

"I hope you're right," Kurt replied with feeling.

Giving Drevit a glowering look, he moved over to check the woman's pulse. Her heartbeat was steady and strong.

"She's okay," he told Miana.

"Good," she said with a nod, before turning to follow Drevit. "So, how is this going to work?"

Drevit was working methodically on one of the drones and he didn't look around as he answered.

"The dome has several layers with different sized spaces between them. The first is the only one wide enough for us to move through. It's a five metre thick airspace filled with Sulphur Hexafluoride."

"The heat cap," Kurt offered.

Drevit glanced at him for a moment, but otherwise didn't acknowledge his contribution.

"You'll need to put your survival suits back on," he said. "The rest of your luggage will have to stay here. I'll be bringing a few extra items with us, but there's no room for anything else."

Kurt felt irritation gnawing at him again. The heat cap was Lynt City's lifeblood and he'd explained it to clients on countless occasions.

Sulphur Hexafluoride was a colourless, odourless, non-toxic and non-flammable greenhouse gas, two-thousand-nine-hundred times more powerful than Carbon Dioxide. It sucked in the heat provided by Mars' weak sun with a voracious appetite and drove the massive network of turbines that created a large portion of Lynt City's electricity. It also helped regulate the atmospheric temperature inside the dome.

It annoyed him that Drevit clearly wasn't impressed that he possessed such knowledge, but despite an urge to explain it all to Miana, Kurt remained silent. He refused to acknowledge the feelings of inadequacy that Drevit inspired in him.

As he pulled on his survival suit, he ran his eyes over the repair drone that the assassin was working on. It was larger than he expected and rested on a rail-like set of tracks that terminated against some heavy-looking doors. He assumed there was an airlock beyond that would transition between the breathable atmosphere of the maintenance level and the superheated layer of Sulphur Hexafluoride. It was something he never expected to see outside of a documentary and he wished there was someone with them who could explain its engineering.

By the time they were finished suiting up, Drevit had joined them and was quickly pulling on his own.

"There's only enough room for one person in the cockpit," he said. "I suggest Miss Raiken takes that and we attach ourselves to the left-hand side."

"The top would be easier to hold on to," Kurt commented, eyeing the drone critically.

"Not enough clearance," the assassin told him simply. "You'd be crushed within a few hundred metres."

"Will you need me to do anything?" Miana asked as she moved to the open hatch.

"No. I've programmed our journey already and will have access to the controls if anything happens en route. I'm sure I don't need to ask you to refrain from touching anything."

"No," Miana replied.

Kurt wondered where she got her patience from. He could certainly do with some of it.

Once the assassin's survival suit was fitted and his helmet was back on, he helped Miana into the cockpit and showed her how to strap herself in. He then joined Kurt at the left side the drone.

"There's only two tether points," he said, indicating the ring-bolt Kurt had already found. "One at the front, one at the back. Once we get moving, there'll be too much wind to move in any meaningful way. Just relax and I'll let you know when we're close."

Kurt tried to ignore the fact he was being forced to trust the assassin *again* and simply lay down next to him in the small recess in the drone's side.

When they were both clipped in place, the assassin activated the computer on his wrist and, in response, the large doors opened ahead of them. The drone then moved into the cramped airlock beyond. Inside, there was barely enough clearance to accommodate both of them and Kurt had to shuffle uncomfortably close to the assassin as the doors closed behind them and a loud *hissss* assaulted the air.

Sulphur Hexafluoride was now being pumped into the airlock and Kurt imagined the heavy gas washing over them like water. Without his survival suit, he knew it would fill his lungs and make his voice sound a full octave lower than normal – the opposite to what lighter gases like Helium did – but the innocuous fact would have been lost on the assassin and Kurt didn't want to embarrass himself by trying to tell Miana.

After about half a minute, the doors ahead of them began to open, signifying that the airlock was full. Then the superheated gases from inside the dome rolled over them. Kurt wasn't ready for the intense exchange of heat and was immediately glad for his survival suit.

"*Here we go,*" he thought, smiling despite himself.

He could feel the drone humming beside him and took in a slow, steady breath, ready for the ride to come.

But all his preparations were for nothing when the drone suddenly accelerated out of the airlock without warning.

Eyes wide and abruptly breathless, Kurt revelled in the acceleration that wrenched them forward. He was acutely aware that his harness was the only thing keeping him secured to the drone and his survival suit was the only thing keeping him from being shaken until his bones broke.

When the initial shock of acceleration eventually dissipated, Kurt was able to turn his head and stare out across the dome's vast inner space. It was just as amazing as he'd anticipated.

The slightly curved panels stretched away in graceful arcs that were split only by the frames that held them together. The whole thing shimmered as convections within the superheated gas warped the filtered sunlight and the way it distorted his vision reminded him of taking Peyote as a young man – a psychoactive cactus eaten in spiritual ceremonies by ancient American Indians.

Beside him, he could feel the drone accelerating, faster and faster. The speed was incredible and the enormous dome panels soon whipped past them in a furious blur. For a moment, he wondered what would happen if he was somehow unhooked and a sudden jolt of anxiety washed through him. If the assassin wanted to get rid of him, now was the perfect *opportunity*.

He quickly focussed on the man tethered beside him, but there was no sign Drevit had any such plans. Of course, an assassin of his calibre wouldn't give anything away until it was too late.

Kurt's paranoia urged him to carry out a pre-emptive strike and unhook the assassin first, and he eyed the safety catch next to his own. It would have been so easy. And yet... as much as he wanted to do it, his good sense firmly kicked him in the rear. If Drevit died now, they wouldn't know how to get back to the maintenance level, let alone have any idea how to get into Cosmotech Defence.

Being once more reminded of their vulnerability made Kurt's irritation spike and he gritted his teeth in anger. He shouldn't feel like this when he had the power to control people. He shouldn't feel like this because of a man who had tried to *kill* him.

For a moment, all Kurt could do was stew in his unpleasant emotions, oblivious to the amazing view all around him. It was only when the assassin reached up to unhook their harnesses that he was pulled out of it.

In an explosion of panic, Kurt grabbed Drevit's hand just before he could unhook the harness.

"We have to get beneath the drone as soon as it stops," the assassin spoke into his helmet intercom.

Kurt looked into his eyes, searching for the lie and unwilling to let go. He didn't know why Drevit hadn't warned him earlier, but again, he suspected the assassin was playing games with him.

"You can feel the drone slowing," the assassin said patiently.

And Kurt realised he was right. He could feel their speed draining fairly quickly now. But it still took all the courage he could muster to release his grip on the assassin's hand.

As soon as he did, the assassin nimbly unhooked himself and, when the drone came to a smooth halt, swung down to the dome's lower surface. Kurt quickly followed and was soon lying on the dome beside him. Drevit pointed to the drone's undercarriage and a metal skirt around its base began to descend around them. The outer edge suckered to the dome's smooth surface and they were soon sealed inside an area about three metres across between the drone and the dome.

"Move as close as you can to the skirt," the assassin said, pressing himself against the metal barrier on his side, "and don't look at the laser."

Kurt did as he was asked, but despite the assassin's warning, he couldn't help watching what came next.

Between them, six robotic arms swung down from the underside of the drone and attached themselves to the dome in a regular pattern. Then an intensely bright laser blazed downward and Kurt would have been blinded if his survival suit didn't automatically filter the extra light out. For the next minute or so he watched in amazement as the laser cut through the dome in a grid, leaving each robotic arm holding a thick cube of material that it then folded back into the repair drone.

"Miana," the assassin said when it was done, "if you activate the hatch panel beside you – it's a yellow icon – you'll be able to join us."

Kurt looked from the assassin back up at the drone and saw a panel open next to the robotic arms. Miana slid out onto the slim area of dome that remained next to Kurt and he held her close for a moment.

"I'm fine," she said, giving him a quick smile.

"Follow me," the assassin said, before rolling into the hole that had just been cut in the dome.

Kurt peered down into the space beneath them and saw the top of a building only a few metres away.

"You go first," he told Miana.

"Thanks," she replied, before nimbly following the assassin.

When she was down, Kurt dropped through himself and then turned toward the assassin.

"Where to next?"

"Step aside," the assassin said, tapping his survival suit computer. "This will take a little longer."

Taking a hesitant step back, Kurt was surprised again when the repair drone's laser blazed into life once again. This time, however, it was cutting through the roof of the Cosmotech building instead of the dome.

Realising what the assassin was doing, Kurt felt another traitorous rush of excitement and looked at Drevit with a grudging respect. This plan may not be brilliant, but it was both simple and effective.

It took a few minutes for the drone to cut through the tougher material of the roof and when all the pieces had been pulled back up into the repair drone, they could see a small room below. The drop was a little deeper this time and so once the assassin was inside, Kurt grabbed Miana's hand and lowered her in before entering himself.

There was a bank of computer servers lining one wall of the room and its blinking blue lights illuminated a complicated fibre optic junction on the opposite side. Drevit was already half out of his survival suit and he gestured to several Cosmotech uniforms he'd brought with him.

"Put them on," he said simply. "I'll work on the security system."

There wasn't much space to change inside the small room, but they managed it with a little cooperation and, soon enough, were dressed in their new disguises.

When Kurt returned his attention to Drevit, he found the assassin working on the information node with a serious look on his face.

"We have a complication," he said after a short pause.

"What do you mean?" Miana asked.

"Do you know this woman?" Drevit asked, handing her a data pad he'd pulled from the information node.

Kurt looked over Miana's shoulder and saw the picture of a pleasant-looking woman alongside a name and other information. Anya Polovski. A psychiatrist, interior decorator, research academic, black belt in four martial arts… the list was long.

"I don't know her," Miana said, handing the data pad back to him. "Why?"

"Cosmotech Security are running a local sting on her. I'm not sure what they believe she's intending to do, but there are twice the usual number of security personnel in the building. They've ordered all classified information on the main servers to be deleted."

"Shit," Kurt swore. "We're screwed before we even begin."

"Not necessarily," Drevit said quietly. "It will take them some time to complete the deletion and their attention will be entirely focussed on this woman. I'll find another way to get what you need, but that involves a new plan and time is short."

Kurt could feel the advantage slipping away from them and turned to Miana for a lead. She too seemed to be thinking hard, but the determination on her face hadn't gone anywhere.

"What do you want to do?" he asked her.

Miana looked at him for a moment and then said, "I think we should help this woman."

"Help her?" Kurt said, genuinely surprised. "Why?"

"If Loc Breeden is worried about her then she might know something we can use."

"That wasn't in our agreement," Drevit told her calmly.

"I'm not asking you to take any risks," Miana replied, "and I'm not asking you to save her. I just want you to warn her. If nothing else, she might provide a more effective diversion than she already seems to be. Do you think you can do that without revealing our presence?"

Drevit thought about it for a moment.

"Perhaps," he replied.

"Then I think it's in our best interests," Miana finished. "Don't you?"

Again, Drevit paused before answering.

"Very well," he said after a moment. "But it is quite likely this woman is going to be captured and possibly killed. In the interest of trust, you should know I will not risk my own freedom in any attempt to save her."

"You're not free yet," Kurt reminded him.

"Soon," Drevit said, as if it were a promise.

"That's acceptable," Miana said firmly. "Let's not waste any more time. Get working on your new plan."

"Already on it," Drevit said as he returned to his manipulations.

Kurt looked at Miana. He wasn't sure he liked how this was going, but it wasn't like he had much of a choice.

"*I just hope she knows what she's doing,*" he thought to himself. "*I really don't like the idea of getting caught by Loc's security.*"

LYNT CITY STREETS - June 7, 2147 - 5.24pm

RITA SNUCK A PEAK AT THE TERRIFYING WOMAN A FEW
steps behind her.

Fayina noticed her looking and offered Rita a malicious smile in
return. Rita quickly turned back around.

Fayina was perhaps the most intimidating person Rita had ever
met. Anger radiated off her like fog and it left the promise of violence
hanging in the air like a bad smell.

Rita didn't like violence. Even the fake kind made her squirm. But
she had no doubt Fayina would carry out her threat if she didn't get
what she wanted.

"*There's something seriously wrong with this woman,*" she thought
with a shiver.

The icy ball of fear in her stomach grew heavier as she approached
Cosmotech and she had to try hard not to cry. There were so many
things going through her mind that it was hard to think straight and
she really, *really* needed to think straight. Fayina expected her to
come up with a believable lie to get her inside Cosmotech, but Rita's
mind kept returning to the same pathetic questions.

Why was this happening to her? What did she do to deserve this?
Was this the day she was going to die?

"Stop it, Rita," she thought, clenching her tiny fists. *"You have to make this work. No excuses! Or do you want to die like the pathetic little girl you are?"*

The words sounded like her mother and Rita winced in shame. She knew she wasn't as useless as she felt, but it wasn't easy to prove when you were being shadowed by a homicidal maniac. Not to mention the consequences she'd be facing if she actually managed to get Fayina inside Cosmotech Defence.

What did she plan to do once she was inside? How much blame would be placed on Rita? Would they expect her to fight back? To alert security? To do something different?

"Your life is in danger, Rita," she thought firmly. *"She's not giving you a choice."*

But the words sounded hollow and would look even more pathetic on an official incident report.

Rita had always strived to be a devoted and loyal employee, even to the detriment of her own comfort and sanity on occasion. If someone asked she would have sworn she would never betray her employer, but she couldn't get an image of that gleaming knife out of her mind and the comfort that came from keeping her head down at work seemed insignificant against the possibility of real, physical harm.

"No," she thought firmly. *"Today, I intend to do exactly what this woman wants and damn my corporate obligations."*

The determination felt good... for a moment. But when Rita realised they'd almost reached the front entrance, she started to panic. She still hadn't come up with a decent explanation. Her heart danced to the rhythm of time running out and her kidnapper's presence began to feel like a gathering storm cloud that was blocking out the sun.

Once more, Rita found herself focussing hard on not crying and could only hope that her weak bladder wouldn't give the game away before it had even begun.

"*Think, you idiot, think!*" she pleaded as they stepped through the revolving entrance.

But the words only reminded Rita of her disapproving mother and, as if barracking for her death, her heart picked up the pace.

This was it. She was inside now and the security guard had already seen her. It was now or never.

She self-consciously wiped her damp hands on her thighs, cleared her throat, and swallowed as they approached the security desk.

"*Oh no,*" she thought.

She knew the officer on duty and he wasn't going to be fooled easily. They never hired stupid security personnel at Cosmotech Defence.

"Hi Wendell," she said, wincing inside at the obvious tremble in her voice.

"Didn't you just clock out?" he asked with a glance at Fayina.

"Yes," Rita replied, feeling sicker with each second. "I… I just had to meet up with… with Sandia, here. I was… was hoping to show her around Cosmotech. Uh… the bits I'm allowed to, of course."

She gave him a desperate smile, trying to make the last point sound like a joke, but Wendell clearly hadn't brought his sense of humour into work today.

"What interest does Sandia have in Cosmotech Defence?" he said with a serious expression.

"I… uh… well," Rita spluttered, her mind racing.

"What's the matter?" Wendell said, his forehead creased in suspicion. "Why are you so nervous, Rita?"

She tried to think of something that would steer the conversation back to a more casual tone. Something that wouldn't end in blood. But she could already feel herself falling apart.

Terror ripped through her struggling mind and she realised she wasn't going to think of anything in time. She was useless. She was going to die right here and now, just as she feared, and all she could think about was her mother's disapproving glare and all the disappointed things she'd ever said to her.

What's wrong with you, Rita? Why don't you have more friends? Why don't you smile more? No man is ever going to want to marry a shy little sad-sack like you. Do you even like men, Rita? Are you one of the gays? Is that it?

Suddenly a bolt of inspiration shot through Rita's panicked mind and she looked Wendell square in the eye.

"Actually, this is kind of a prelude to our second date. Sandia's my new girlfriend."

"Oh," Wendell said, his suspicion turning into confusion.

Rita wasn't sure if it was the revelation itself, or the way she'd delivered it so confidently, but it was clear Wendell had been knocked off balance. The small but substantial triumph sent relief flushing through Rita and, with it, she felt the unexpected thrill of excitement.

"I just haven't told anyone yet," she continued, giving Wendell an embarrassed smile. "So... could you maybe keep this to yourself?"

"Uh... yeah, of course," Wendell said, well and truly on the back foot now. "We're required to keep all personal information confidential, anyway. Just remember to update the relationship status on your profile if... tonight goes well."

At this point he winked and Rita realised he was imagining something *quite* embarrassing. Her face flushed with heat, along with something much lower down, and a mischievous urge to embellish her story took hold.

"After I show Sandia where I work, we're going to grab some dinner at *Zyriab* and then hit the entertainment district," she said with more confidence than she'd ever thought possible. "You know, have a few drinks, maybe a dance or two. Then..."

"Yes?" Wendell asked, his expression as eager as his voice.

"Well... we'll see," Rita said, averting her eyes in very real embarrassment this time.

"Riiight, okay then," Wendell said with a lecherous smile. "Better sign Sandia in then. Visitor access closes in twenty minutes."

"Sure thing, Wendell. Thanks."

Rita felt a little out of breath as she tapped in Sandia's name and signed her bio-signature, but she noticed her hands weren't trembling anymore.

When Wendell handed 'Sandia' a visitor's pass, Rita beamed at him.

"Thanks Wendell," she said with feeling.

He gave her a final wink as she turned away and Rita felt another flush of not-entirely-unpleasant embarrassment as she left the security desk.

"You did really good," Fayina said behind her. "He was close to getting you both killed."

A shard of fear pierced Rita's buoyant mood, but it didn't deflate it entirely. She was still alive and, better still, she felt as if she'd won an important battle. She knew she'd be in serious trouble when Cosmotech found out what she'd done, but where she would usually be worrying about what her mother might say, now she honestly didn't care.

"Where's the internal security hub?" Fayina asked her quietly.

"On one of the higher floors," Rita said hesitantly. "But I told you before, I can't take you there."

"Which floor? Where is it in relation to us now?"

"Uh… the fifth floor, I think. There's not much else on that level. I've only ever been to the induction area near the lifts, so I'm… not sure what's beyond that."

"Good," Fayina said in a purring voice that made Rita wonder if something was wrong.

She turned to look at her captor, but there was no indication anything was different. Until Fayina spoke again. This time her voice was weak and yet at the same time gruff.

"Give me access to a computer terminal. I'll find Isaac for you."

"Um… okay?" Rita replied, even more confused now. "Who's Isaac?"

"What makes you think I need your help?" Fayina snapped, her voice back to normal.

"Uh… didn't you just ask–?" Rita stammered, but Fayina cut her off with an entirely different voice.

This one was harsh and biting, just like Rita's mother.

"Don't be ridiculous! Of course you need our help."

"I… I don't know what you mean," Rita pleaded, but Fayina just continued talking over the top of her, as if she was having a conversation with herself.

"I got in here fine," she snarled.

"And what happens when you start tearing this place apart?" the disapproving mother's voice replied.

"I don't need you!" Fayina snapped.

Rita recoiled in confusion. What was going on here? She already assumed Fayina was mentally unstable, but this suggested something far, far worse.

The next voice Fayina used was weak again and Rita heard a distinct rattle when she drew in breath.

"I can find the information we need without drawing attention."

"We shouldn't draw attention," an entirely new voice added, this one as timid as Rita's. "I don't want to get Rita in trouble."

Rita nodded quickly, not sure if it would make any difference, but willing to give it a try.

"I can deal with it," Fayina growled in her scary voice.

"No one is disputing that," the motherly voice added. "But don't be foolish, Fayina. If there's an easier, *quicker,* way to find Isaac, where is the logic in ignoring it?"

"Maybe this isn't about that little trouble maker," Fayina snarled.

"Oh, for pity's sake," the mother's voice snapped. "You can't lie to us, Fayina. Your stubborn nature may be an asset during violent physical encounters, but it does you no service in this situation. Let us help you."

"Argh!" Fayina grunted in obvious frustration.

For a long moment, she said nothing and Rita felt as if things were finally about to get either better, or much, much worse.

She held her breath, hoping for the best, and only let it out when she heard the frail, older voice speaking again.

"Once I've found Isaac, I'll give you the location of the security hub and attempt to subvert any systems between us and them. You'll have complete access and all the time you need to take this place apart, if you so wish."

"Fine," Fayina snarled. "But don't get any ideas about stealing back control. I'm not going away again. Do you hear me?"

"Of course we do," the motherly voice replied.

"What about Rita?" the timid, younger voice asked.

Rita jumped at the sound of her name and felt a flush of embarrassment when she realised there were tears rolling down her cheeks.

"Please don't hurt me," she said in a voice that was surprisingly strong and didn't tremble as she expected it to.

"I need you to log in to the local computer network," Fayina told her firmly. "Are there any private terminals nearby?"

"Yes," she said, even more willing to help than before. "Follow me."

She led Fayina into the small office she shared with her team and said a silent prayer of thanks when she found the room was empty. She then sat at her work station, pulled her employee data pad from her purse, and placed it in on the connection icon that glowed softly on one side of the transparent desk.

The screens immediately blinked to life and when her data pad synced with the network, a keyboard lit up on the desk.

"It's ready," she said, turning around. "You now have access to everything I do."

"Thank you for your help," Fayina said in her older voice.

"Uh… what are you going to do with me?" Rita asked.

"Don't worry," Fayina said, her voice scary again. "I'll be gentle."

Rita flinched as Fayina darted forward and the next thing she knew there was an arm around her throat, squeezing hard against her neck.

She grabbed at it weakly, trying in vain to breathe through the immense pressure, but it was impossible. Her heart beat louder as it was slowly starved of oxygen and Rita felt Fayina's breath against her ear as she spoke one last time in her timid voice.

"I'm sorry about this, Rita. I would have liked to get to know you better. You're... you're quite beautiful, you know."

The compliment registered with a confusing warmth that seemed to rise up from the arm at Rita's neck and a white mist gradually stole the world from view.

No longer fighting now, Rita's chest muscles convulsed once more in vain then the white mist faded to black and her panic fell away.

For a second, she felt more content than she'd ever felt before, and in the moments before her oxygen starved brain finally shut down, Rita's lips stretched in a smile.

Fayina gently lowered Rita to the floor and made sure she was breathing again. Her timid little hostage had done better than she expected.

The security guard had been close discovering their ruse and Fayina was seconds away from taking matters into her own hands, but Rita made it unnecessary.

Fayina smiled. She didn't quite understand why, but there was something about Rita's success that pleased her. And it wasn't just that it suited her goals. It felt like she'd just witnessed the birth of rebellion in this woman and seen it awaken a strength in Rita that she didn't know she possessed.

"*Classic maternal issues,*" Ianka said dismissively.

"*I can relate,*" Fayina growled.

"*She simply pushed beyond the limitations that self-loathing has imposed on her life,*" Ianka finished, ignoring the remark.

"*We shouldn't delay,*" Dr. Haig added.

Fayina growled beneath her breath and sat down at Rita's work station.

"Do what you have to," she said, before reluctantly taking a mental step back and relinquishing control of her body to Dr. Haig.

Without hesitation, his fingers began to fly across the keyboard. It took him no time at all to access the local Cosmotech network and scan through the information folders Rita had access to. Most were related to a form of propulsion technology designed to function in the depths of a gas giant and Fayina could tell Dr. Haig found it interesting, but he also knew it was irrelevant and so he quickly moved on.

In minutes, he'd hacked his way past the internal security net and gained administrator access, which allowed him to scan through personnel movement files. Given the fact Isaac didn't seem to exist in any official databases, Fayina thought it was unlikely there would be any actual reference to him, but she had to agree it was at least worth a look.

Fayina waited impatiently as Dr. Haig searched through the information and quickly began to get restless. She tried to be patient, to give him the time he needed, but the lack of control was making her anxious.

"Hurry up," she warned him.

"I'm going as fast as I can," he replied calmly. "Give it a little time, Fayina."

She wanted to. She really did. She wanted to be patient and give him all the time he required. But each passing second soon felt like an eternity and her desperation to regain control of her body grew ever stronger. Her anger quickly boiled to match her rising fear and she was about to swear at Dr. Haig when a message appeared on the screens in front of them.

Anya Polovski, they know you're here.

"What the fuck is that?" she snarled, snatching back control from Dr. Haig and pushing away from the terminal.

They won't let you find what you're looking for.

"Who are they talking about?" Celia asked, obviously frightened.

Cosmotech Security is surrounding your location.

This time, along with the words, a security screen appeared beside the message window and Fayina saw an image of the room she was currently standing in. The view then expanded into a virtual map and she saw more than a dozen security beacons moving into the corridors around her. Alongside each beacon was a list of the weapons and equipment each officer was carrying. Flash-bang grenades, tazer sticks, tranquiliser pistols, disruptor rods. All of them were non-lethal, but it didn't make Fayina feel any better.

Her mind raced.

"*I need more information*," she thought, before speaking directly to hey mysterious messenger. "Can you hear me?"

The message beside the security feed disappeared for a moment then a new one appeared in its place.

Yes.

"Who are you?" Fayina demanded.

A friend.

"Bullshit. I don't have any friends."

I'm offering help. Do you want it, or not?

"How do I know I can trust you?"

You can't know, but if you stay where you are much longer, it won't matter.

Fayina bared her teeth. She didn't like this at all. How did this 'friend' have access to the security network? And, more importantly, why did they want to help her? What was in it for them?

"Why are you helping me?" she demanded.

Take the data pad. It will remain connected to the network. Use it to open any locked doors you encounter. They're close.

The map showing Fayina's location zoomed in again and she saw that several Security officers were now right outside Rita's office.

"Fine," she said, snatching the data pad from the desk, "but you'll answer my questions eventually. I don't like being controlled."

Shoving the data pad into a pocket, Fayina leapt over the transparent computer desk and upended it with a grunt of effort. It was heavier than she expected, but she still managed to manoeuvre it in front of the doorway, blocking the entrance.

Just as the desk fell into place, the officers outside cracked the door and launched several flash-bang grenades into the room. As Fayina had hoped, the desk's clear resin fooled them long enough to prevent them from holding fire and the grenades bounced straight back into the corridor.

Turning away from the inevitable blinding flashes, Fayina waited for the sharp *BANG! BANG!* of detonation and then turned to slip through the gap between desk and doorway. The officers outside had anti-flash gas masks that prevented them from being blinded, but their surprise allowed Fayina long enough to kick two of them to the ground, relieve the third of his mask and fire a smoke grenade from his weapon down the corridor.

Three more officers coming round the corner were met with an unexpected explosion and as they recoiled from the plume of rising smoke, an apparition they weren't prepared for emerged through the fog.

In seconds, the trio were sprawled across the corridor, unconscious or too injured to get back up.

Standing over them, Fayina snatched the data pad from her pocket and quickly checked the security feed again. The remaining security teams – and there were a lot of them – were now scrambling to fill the gap she'd just punched in their perimeter.

"Not likely," she growled, before sprinting down a side corridor and away from the nearest group.

"*Idiots thought they could take me that easy?*" Fayina thought with disgust. "*Fucking insult.*"

"*They would have if we weren't warned,*" Ianka assured her.

"*Who saved us?*" Celia asked.

"*And why?*" Dr. Haig added.

49

"*Who cares,*" Fayina snapped. "*If this is how they want it, this is what they'll get.*"

"*Fighting will only get us so far,*" Dr. Haig warned. "*We should determine the extent of our advantage before re-engaging.*"

"*What are you talking about?*" Fayina snarled. She hated not knowing things.

"*Dr. Haig is referring to our link with the security network,*" Ianka answered for him.

"*Yes,*" he confirmed. "*We're being fed information directly from the network. If you can find us a few moments of safety, I might be able to work the link in reverse and find the information we came for.*"

"*Will our new friend like us doing that?*" Celia asked timidly.

"*We'll see,*" Dr. Haig replied simply.

"*Even if they don't give a shit,*" Fayina added as she smashed through a doorway to avoid the firing line of an incoming security team, "*you could still get us captured or killed. I'm not risking that for anything.*"

"*Oh, don't be ridiculous,*" Ianka snapped. "*We can easily keep track of security through the link and if circumstances change you can do what is needed. How else do you propose we accomplish anything of worth here, Fayina?*"

Fayina's temper flared again and she wished there was a way to silence Ianka for good. The woman's tone cut like a knife.

"*Fine,*" she relented. "*Give me a few minutes and I'll find a place we can risk your plan.*"

"*Thank you,*" Dr. Haig said.

"*Some sense at last,*" Ianka added sourly.

"*I hope this works,*" Celia finished.

COSMOTECH DEFENCE, LYNT CITY - June 7, 2147 - 5.47pm

MR. DREVIT RAISED AN EYEBROW IN ADMIRATION. LOC Breeden was right to be concerned about this Anya Polovski. She was skilled and clearly dangerous.

"She's been assisted," he said, turning to Miana. "I believe we've done all we can for the moment. I'm going to return my focus to the Cosmotech servers."

"Right," Miana replied with a nod.

Given the circumstances, Mr. Drevit should have been concerned. His life could be snuffed out with the touch of a button, he was under threat of being psychically controlled by a man who clearly wanted him dead, and he was stealing from an organisation more powerful than any in the history of humankind.

But concern was not an issue. The danger did provide more motivation than usual, but what he really felt was *energised*. Being forced to rely on his wits like this was exactly why he'd pursued a criminal career in the first place. He liked knowing he was better than others in so many ways.

And besides, the truth of the matter was that he needed this information just as badly as Miana did. Now that he was aware Loc Breeden could enslave him with a look, he needed considerable leverage if he wanted to survive long enough to obtain the intriguing power for himself.

It was a shame he'd blocked off the caves that apparently bestowed this ability before being made aware of their significance. But he would find a way to open them again. It would become his first priority after completing his current objective.

Glancing at his captors, Mr. Drevit wondered if it would be that simple. He had no doubt Miana would keep her promise to free him, but Kurt was another matter. Thankfully, however, he appeared smitten with the former detective and Mr. Drevit expected it would be enough to ensure he stepped into line when the time came.

He held no grudge against the man. That didn't mean he wouldn't kill either of them if the opportunity presented itself, but he couldn't risk something so dangerous with the Raze implant ready to sever his spinal cord. Of course, patience was a virtue that he held in limitless reserve.

Returning to the task at hand, Mr. Drevit quickly worked through the options available to him.

There were no offices directly adjacent to the server rooms. The only way inside – without boring directly through titanium walls nearly a metre thick – was via the access corridor. And that could only be accessed with legitimate authorisation. He could easily neutralise the guards at that point, but their vital signs were linked with the security system and if anything happened to them, the system would go into lockdown and all external connections with the vault would be severed.

The only way to steal the information was to have someone remove it for them.

"Of course," he said with a smile.

"What?" Kurt asked in a distrustful tone.

Mr. Drevit looked at him, enjoying that fact Kurt felt so threatened despite the immense power he commanded.

"There's no way to get the information directly from the servers," was all he volunteered before turning away, knowing it wouldn't satisfy him.

"And?" Kurt asked impatiently.

Mr. Drevit smiled inside.

"So we get someone to do it for us," he finished simply.

"How do you plan to do that?" Miana asked, her questions always straight to the point.

Mr. Drevit turned to her and looked her in the eye before answering.

"Organisations like Cosmotech rarely delete information stored on their servers without some kind of backup or transfer procedure. For whatever reason, Ms. Anya Polovski has changed that. She poses a significant enough threat for Loc Breeden to order no such backup or transfer. I believe this break from tradition will allow me to convince a Cosmotech technician to create a physical backup."

"How exactly?" Miana asked.

"They will believe I'm Loc Breeden," Mr. Drevit replied. "And when the backup has been created, I'll have them transport the data out of the secure server room to a place we can intercept it."

Miana's eyelids closed slightly as she paused to think the plan through.

"Good enough," she said after a moment. "Let's do it."

That was another thing Mr. Drevit liked about Miana. She obviously had experience in situations where time could not be wasted and knew how to make decisions when they were needed.

With a quick nod, he returned to his work, artfully creating the necessary codes and identification checks that would convince the computer systems his order was coming directly from Loc Breeden. He then opened a programme that would create a near perfect avatar of Loc Breeden on the Cosmotech technician's screen. This computer model would be linked to several key points on his own face, allowing it to mimic his expressions and make the forgery look more real.

"I'm ready," he said, turning to Kurt and Miana. "You'll need to remain silent while I put the call through."

They both nodded, Kurt with a scowl on his face, and Mr. Drevit initiated the call.

"Yes, sir," a female security liaison answered, her serious but pleasantly symmetrical face appearing on Mr. Drevit's data pad. "How may I help you?"

"I need you to create a back-up of all Alpha level information files," he said in the smooth, arrogant tone Loc Breeden was so good at.

"Of course, sir," the woman answered promptly, just as Mr. Drevit expected.

Cosmotech employees knew better than to second guess Loc Breeden.

"Once you've created the backup, transfer it directly to security station four," he added. "I want three security officers escorting the package at all times. Further instructions will be waiting at the security station."

"Right away, sir," the woman answered.

"I assume you're aware of the security sweep being run as we speak?"

"I am, sir."

"What you don't know is that I've received intelligence indicating the target is not alone. So, I want your actions kept off the security grid. Do not allow anyone outside your own team to know what you're doing. Do you understand?"

"Yes, of course, sir," the woman replied promptly.

"Very well," Mr. Drevit finished. "Expect further instructions when you've reached security station four."

He cut the transmission without any formality, as he knew Mr. Breeden would, and then smiled. There was a distinct pleasure in impersonating such a powerful man. Particularly when he knew this would be his one and only opportunity to do so.

When his ruse was discovered, Mr. Breeden would make sure it could never happen again.

"It's done," he said, letting his smile disappear as he turned to Kurt and Miana. "When we leave here, if we come into contact with anyone let me do the talking. Only speak if it's absolutely necessary."

"Fine," Kurt said with a frown.

"Understood," Miana added.

Mr. Drevit nodded again and then turned to the door and quickly checked his data pad. He could see exactly what was being displayed on the Cosmotech security monitors and so he waited until the cameras covering the corridor outside cycled into a low priority viewing pattern before opening the door.

The three of them slipped outside into an empty corridor and Mr. Drevit set off at a brisk pace. Having studied the layout of the building whilst he was inside their systems, he had a clear route in mind. He also knew where the Cosmotech staff still on duty were located and so it was a simple matter to minimise any direct contact.

They occasionally saw people at the other end of the corridor or through a transparent wall or doorway, but it was only for a few seconds and they were always either moving through a door themselves, or just about to disappear round another corner.

When the three of them eventually reached an elevator connected with the lower levels, Mr. Drevit activated the call button and quickly checked the security logs again. Cosmotech Security were still scrambling to catch up with Anya Polovski and their incursion had gone completely unnoticed.

"*Excellent,*" he thought to himself.

When the elevator arrived there was an older man waiting inside and Mr. Drevit felt Kurt stiffen behind him. He ignored the reaction and joined the unexpected passenger, before turning to enjoy the discomfort on Kurt's face.

He wasn't worried about the man in the elevator. Cosmotech Security was so tight that once you were inside people assumed you were meant to be there. Even if Kurt pulled a weapon, the man probably wouldn't have reacted. He did look at them askance when Kurt coughed to hide his anxiety, but he didn't say anything.

When the doors closed again an awkward silence was left hanging in the air and Mr. Drevit enjoyed it immensely. A few moments later, the elevator stopped and he noticed Kurt breathing easier as soon as the Cosmotech employee exited the lift.

"Not as brave as you think, adventurist," he thought.

When the doors closed again, he quickly linked his data pad with the elevator's computer so he could ensure they had authorisation to access the floor where security station four was located. It took a little longer to hack the authentication systems this time, because he didn't want anyone to know they were coming, but when he was done, the elevator smoothly transitioned past the ground floor and took them to the lower levels.

"Security will identify our presence as soon as we exit the elevator," he told Miana and Kurt. "I can make sure the intrusion isn't logged on the wider network, but the officers on this level will be using an independent system I don't have access to."

"How are we going to avoid them?" Kurt asked.

"We aren't," Mr. Drevit answered bluntly, before handing them both an ear piece. "Take this and put it in your ear. I'm going to use the same device I used on you back in the caves. When the security officers attempt an arrest, stay behind me and do everything they order you to. Anything else and I can't guarantee your safety. When it's safe to do so, I'll activate the device."

They both put the device in their ears, Kurt frowning again.

"Do you understand what you have to do?" he asked when they were ready.

"Yes," they answered together.

Mr. Drevit could see that despite his mistrust, Kurt was excited. He already knew from the man's profile that he was an adrenalin junkie.

"Well, you're about to get one of the best adrenalin hits of your life," he thought to himself.

Miana, on the other hand, looked sick, but determined. A much truer indication of courage.

"Alright," he said when the doors opened again. "Follow me."

They exited the elevator together and Mr. Drevit led them down the corridor at a casual pace. He knew the security officers wouldn't believe they were there by accident, but he didn't want them to think he was dangerous. Not before their concern became irrelevant.

As expected, when they approached the first corner three officers appeared in tight formation. One knelt behind the corner with only his weapon showing, while the others advanced aggressively with weapons drawn.

"You are not authorised to be in this area," the first said in a sharp, no-nonsense tone. "Get down on your knees and place your hands on your head or you will be fired upon. Lethal force has been authorised."

Mr. Drevit did as he was asked and saw Miana and Kurt doing the same. One of the officers quickly moved behind him and restrained him with a simple zip-lock band. He stayed silent and didn't move until the officer turned his attention to Miana. Then, he slowly crossed his fingers, which activated a pressure switch imbedded in the metatarsal of his index finger.

In response, the officer heading for Miana stumbled awkwardly and hit the corridor wall with a *thump* before clattering loudly to the floor. The other two quickly followed suit and Mr. Drevit rolled onto his side and manoeuvred his legs in front of him so he could sit up.

"My hands," he said to Kurt, who was back on his feet and grinning like an idiot. "Do you know how to open zip-lock cuffs?"

"Sure," Kurt said.

True to his word, Kurt retrieved a key from the fallen security officer and opened the cuffs quickly.

As soon as he was free, Mr. Drevit got to his feet and moved to the nearest collapsed officer. He took a sedation stick from the officer's belt and easily brushed aside a half-hearted attempt to stop him.

He then removed the officer's armoured neck cuff and pressing the baton against exposed flesh.

As soon as the shock snapped through officer's body, his erratic movements ceased. In seconds, his eyes were closed. Mr. Drevit turned to do the same to the others, but Kurt and Miana were already taking the initiative.

He wasn't surprised. They knew what it felt like to be under the influence of his sonic incapacitator and clearly didn't want the officers to suffer longer than necessary.

Turning his attention to the local security system, Mr. Drevit saw that an alarm had been tripped. He checked to make sure the firewall he'd set up was still isolating them from the rest of the building. It was.

"*Excellent,*" he thought. "*We should be safe until someone else arrives in person.*"

"How are we doing?" Miana asked from behind him.

"There are three more officers at the security station ahead," he replied, "but they'll be expecting reinforcements so they'll stay put for now. And if they make a move, I'll know it. The alarms are otherwise contained to this level so once we've changed costumes, we can just wait until the package arrives."

"Changed costumes?" Kurt said.

"Grab that one and drag him round the corner," Mr. Drevit told him, pointing to one of the sedated officers. "Miana, help me with this one."

Working together, they soon had the officers laid out in a row so they couldn't be seen from the elevator.

"Kurt, that one looks close to your size. I'll take this one. Miana, take him. Don't worry if the outfit's a little large, as long as the insignia are showing, you should be fine."

It took them several minutes to extricate the sedated officers from their armoured uniforms and put them on. Then, when they were dressed, Mr. Drevit checked his data pad and saw that the security detail transporting the back-up copy of Cosmotech's servers was almost there.

"You won't be able use their weapons," he told Miana and Kurt, "but take one anyway. We need to look the part when the transfer team arrives."

"What about the other officers already on this level?" Kurt asked, clearly worried.

"They're blind and waiting for re-enforcements," Mr. Drevit said with a wave of his hand. "If they decide to attack, we can just stop them the same way we did the others. Now get ready. We do this the same way as before."

Kurt glanced toward the security station, but he stayed silent and Mr. Drevit put the adventurist out of his mind. This was it. The end game. Time to finish this mission so he could focus on his future.

"*Apologies, Mr. Breeden,*" he thought with a smile, "*but I'm afraid my resignation is about to be made irreversibly official.*"

FAYINA LEAPT DOWN ANOTHER FLIGHT OF STAIRS AND kicked open the door at the bottom. The security forces were closing in fast and she wanted the next encounter to happen at a place of her choosing, not theirs.

Dr. Haig and Ianka were still whining for her to stop so they could search the security network for Isaac's location, but she wasn't going to risk everything just to find something she didn't even believe was there. Not yet, anyway. First, she had to make it through the next security team that was close to catching up with her.

Grabbing one of the concussion grenades she'd taken from the first officers she'd dealt with, Fayina approached the next corner and flicked the arming switch.

"*Only one chance to get this right,*" she thought with gritted teeth.

She waited a second for the timing fuse to shorten and then threw it round the corner. A moment later an intense flash lit up the corridor and a loud *BOOM* assaulted her ears. Fayina knew the officers would be expecting this, so she didn't wait before ducking round the corner and launching herself at the nearest one.

As she slammed a foot into his head, a sharp pain pushed against her left shoulder, but she ignored it and spun toward the next officer.

In the confusion that followed, she kicked, levered, and elbowed every one of them to the ground, one by one, and was soon left standing amidst seven unconscious officers, breathing heavily.

"Your shoulder is bleeding," Ianka said firmly.

"It hurts," Celia whined.

Fayina looked down at the offending shoulder and gently probed the bloody gash with her fingers.

"Hmmm," she mused. The satisfaction of violence still buzzed through her system and she barely felt it. "It's just a flesh wound, but I'll need to seal this up. This fight is far from over."

"Let me," Dr. Haig offered.

"You'll pass out in a second," Fayina growled as she kneeled and roughly searched one of the fallen officers.

She soon found a medi-kit strapped to his waist and pulled a tiny spray bulb from inside. When she used it on her wound, the liquid foamed into a rapid seal that stung with antibiotics, but the pain was brief and it soon fell to a dull ache.

"Alright," Fayina said, taking a mental step back, "you can have a few minutes, Haig, no more."

"Thank you," Dr. Haig said as he once more took control.

Using the data pad they'd brought with them, Dr Haig quickly accessed the security logs and searched for any reference to Isaac. There was a lot of useless information, but since Isaac couldn't have arrived earlier than the day before, there was at least a limit to what they could check.

"There's no mention of Isaac," he said eventually.

"Sabian lied to us," Fayina growled.

"Why would he do that?" Celia whined.

"He didn't lie," Ianka said firmly.

"Then why the fuck can't we find anything?" Fayina snarled.

"He doesn't exist, remember?" Ianka answered. "Without any official identity, there would only be a record if they chose to create one. Apparently they didn't."

"Then what do we do now?" Fayina growled, impatient to retake control.

"Find the man who left the precinct with him," Dr. Haig replied, beginning another search.

They knew approximately what time he would have returned with Isaac and so it was easy enough to find a person that looked just like the man they were after.

"Loc Breeden," he said after a moment.

"He's hot," Celia offered.

"He's too old for you," Ianka said quickly.

"Oh, get real," Celia said with a pout.

"He left less than an hour ago," Dr. Haig continued, "with a small group of people. One of them could be Isaac."

"Where?" Fayina demanded.

"The security log has them departing for the space port," Dr. Haig replied.

"The space port?" Celia added. "Where could they be going?"

"Who cares," Fayina said. "We've found what I came for. Give me back control so we can get the hell out of here."

"I don't think it will be that easy," Ianka said.

"What?" Fayina snarled. "Give me control, now!"

"Not that," Ianka replied sharply. "I mean there's more security coming."

Fayina wrestled control from Dr. Haig and quickly tapped through the data pad herself. Ianka was right. There was more security closing in. A lot more.

"How are we going to get out of here?" Celia asked, sounding scared.

"We go right through them," Fayina said with a growl.

"No, wait," Dr. Haig said quickly.

"What?" Fayina snapped.

"I think I can hack the emergency systems through this link."

"So what?" Fayina said, running along the corridor. "That's not going to help us."

"It will if we set off the building's containment protocols. I can trick it into thinking there's a fire and we can use their safety procedures against them."

Fayina clenched her jaw in frustration. She hated giving away control like this, but with a wounded shoulder, her risk of being captured was much higher than it was before. And capture was simply *not* an option.

"Fine," she said, relinquishing control once more. "Just hurry it up, alright? We don't have all day."

PILSA STONE PASSED THE MEMORY CARD TO THE DUTY officer, Yaunis, and waited patiently as he confirmed her authority to remove it from the server room. She didn't know what had prompted the deletion protocol in the first place, but she felt much better now that Mr. Breeden had ordered her to make a back-up. Without it, there would be no way to retrieve any of the sensitive information they were purging.

Pilsa was in the unenviable position of being responsible for the data stored on Cosmotech servers and letting it be deleted without a contingency plan went against everything she'd ever learned. She'd also been given full authority over her security escort and could tell it hadn't gone over well with the ranking officer, Gabriel Weltz. He would do as he was told, of course, but he was making it abundantly clear that he didn't like the arrangement.

"Put this on," he said, offering her a small ear piece.

"Yes, I'm aware of security protocols, thank you," she replied, snatching the ear piece from him.

"Good, because I plan to follow them to the letter," Weltz said firmly. "Cosmotech is under a level-five lock down, ma'am. When it eventually lifts, my actions will be scrutinized to exacting detail."

"As will mine, officer Weltz," Pilsa added, before turning away.

She knew it wasn't his fault, but her edgy mood had to be taken out on someone and if he couldn't handle it, he didn't deserve to be employed here.

"One woman," an officer said as Pilsa approached the elevator. "How can one woman take out so many of us?"

"Not our problem," Weltz told him firmly. "We don't get involved."

"The way she's going through us, we might have to," the officer replied.

"They'll get her," Weltz assured him, "and even if they don't, she's nowhere near us. Now get your head in the game. We've got our own mission. Get moving."

Pilsa waited for her escort to enter the elevator and then followed them inside. She watched Weltz punch in the codes that gave them access to sub-level four and the elevator immediately whirred into life.

As they rapidly descended, Pilsa focussed on the floor indicator beside the doors. The sooner she reached security station four and could leave these meatheads behind, the better. Every second she was in their company meant the data she was escorting was under threat, meaning her career was also on the line.

"No one deserves this kind of pressure," she thought.

Thankfully, the floor indicator changed quickly enough and Pilsa was just beginning to feel her confidence returning when the lights suddenly blinked red and an alarm sounded.

"What the hell?" one of the security officers growled.

"What's going on?" Pilsa demanded, her heart racing.

"The fire alarm's been tripped," Weltz said.

"Fuck is on fire?" asked the same officer.

Weltz took a moment to check his data pad.

"There're spot fires on three upper floors. They shouldn't be affecting this area, but the elevators have shut down for some reason."

"Well get them moving again!" Pilsa snapped.

Weltz worked on his data pad for a moment then he looked up with a grim expression.

"I can't," he replied firmly. "The error that caused us to stop has locked me out of the system."

"That is *not* acceptable!" Pilsa hissed. "If I don't get to sub-level four, I guaran*tee* every one of you will be lucky if all Cosmotech does is demote you to opening doors instead of guarding them."

"Understood, ma'am," Weltz replied sourly, "now please step back."

Allowing herself to herded into the corner, Pilsa watched as one of Weltz's officers knelt down and manually opened the elevator doors. Most of the space beyond was simply wall, but there was a gap at the bottom easily big enough for them to get through.

"Is that sub-level four?" Pilsa asked hopefully.

"It is," Weltz replied.

Pilsa sighed in relief.

"Then let's go," she added, before starting forward.

"Not yet, ma'am," Weltz said, stopping her with a brisk gesture and then turning to the officer who'd opened the doors. "Pricey, get out there and secure the corridor."

"Done," the first officer said as he slid out the gap with his weapon ready.

Pilsa's impatience increased steadily as they waited for the officer to return and she had to continually bite back an urge to demand they get moving. Eventually, however, a familiar voice spoke over the alarm.

"Clear!"

"Right," Weltz said firmly. "Stent, join Pricey and cover the package while she disembarks."

"Package?" Pilsa said, immediately offended.

"Standard operating language, ma'am," Weltz offered with a token baring of teeth.

Pilsa didn't feel at all satisfied with his response, but she didn't waste any time exiting the elevator. She didn't want to be stuck in there with this irritating fool, or the information she was transporting, any longer than was absolutely necessary.

As the officer stated, the corridor outside was completely clear and Pilsa was soon surrounded by her security detail once more.

"Security station four, come back," Weltz said into his comm.

A moment of silence passed, then a voice spoke clearly into Pilsa's earpiece.

"This is security station four."

"We have the package. Barely reached your floor. Have you heard anything about the fires?"

"The target that's tearing through the building somehow got a hold of incendiaries. No threat to us, but the emergency system down here has been tripped as well."

"Right. Are we clear to proceed?"

"You're clear."

"I really hope they smack that bitch up," one of the officers growled.

"Can we get moving?" Pilsa said briskly.

"You heard the package," Weltz stated. "Get moving."

Pilsa glared at him as they began moving down the corridor and jumped in surprise when a new voice spoke in her ear piece.

"-walking into an ambush! Do not, I repeat, do not bring the package to security station four!"

"What?" Weltz said, bringing them to a halt. "Who is this?"

"This is officer Hills, identity code four-oh-seven-seven-two. We've been breached, we–"

As Pilsa tried to process what she was hearing, the signal suddenly cut off and the first voice spoke into the silence.

"This is officer Garnet, identity code eight-four-four-eight-two. Disregard previous message. The security system on this level has been breached. I repeat, the security system on this level has been breached. Transport the package to security station four for lock down immediately."

"Shit," the officer known as Pricey swore. "What the hell's going on? Both codes were legit."

"Stay cool," Weltz said sharply.

Pilsa felt a cold stab of fear in her stomach,

"We cannot allow this information to be captured," she said, trying not to sound desperate. "Your lives won't be worth spit if something happens to this memory card... or me!"

"Be advised," the voice added after a moment, "we are sending back-up to your position. Engage any non-security personnel on sight. Lethal force is authorised."

"This is bullshit," Pricey said nervously. "What do we do?"

"I believe the call is yours," Weltz said to Pilsa.

Pilsa clamped her jaws in frustration. She had no idea what to do. The information stored in her memory card represented hundreds of millions, if not billions of dollars' worth of Cosmotech research. If the deletion protocol was proceeding as scheduled – and there was no reason to believe it wasn't – then this was the last and only copy. In any normal situation she was meant to destroy the card here and now, but what would Loc Breeden do if she made the wrong decision?

Pilsa's career and perhaps her entire future on Mars was suddenly hanging in the balance and there was no one to help her make the decision.

"Head for the security station," she said, deciding she would just destroy the memory card at the first sign of trouble.

"Right, you heard her," Weltz said firmly. "Weapons hot. We're heading for the station. Stay alert and take out anyone not in a Cosmotech security uniform."

At his command, the team headed down the corridor and the chill in Pilsa's stomach grew colder. They were moving quickly by the time they reached the first corner, but they pulled up abruptly when a security officer appeared on the other side.

"Identify yourself!" Weltz barked, his weapon raised.

"Officer Draden, identity code eight-four-four-nine-one," the officer replied with his own weapon raised. "I'm your backup. Don't just stand there, move your asses!"

Weltz hesitated a moment before gesturing to his officers and barking an order.

"Get moving!"

Pilsa felt a wave of relief as two more Cosmotech uniforms appeared around the corner and almost managed a smile.

"Just get me out of here," she told them firmly.

"You got it," one of them replied with a wink.

Pilsa wasn't sure what it was, but something about the posture of the two new officers made her hesitate.

"This could be the ambush they warned us about," she realised with horror.

She turned to Weltz and saw that he'd picked up on it too and was already raising his weapon. The staccato of gunfire shattered the silence and she instinctively ducked and scrambled to hit the self-destruct on her memory card, but before she could reach it, the ground suddenly skipped out from under her feet.

She hit the ground hard, confused and desperate to reach the memory stick, but for some reason her arms and legs weren't working properly. Every time she tried to move, her body would simply jerk and spasm helplessly, disobeying her completely.

The officer who'd met them appeared above her and Pilsa tried one last time to get control of herself and initiate the memory wipe, but, again, her body refused to respond. She could only watch in horror as he leaned down and plucked the memory card from her belt.

"Thank you," he said, before a sedation stick appeared in his hand.

Pilsa felt another surge of panic and tried to scream, to explain what would happen to this person, to *her*, if they took the memory card, but she couldn't make a coherent sound.

A life flashed before her eyes, but it wasn't the one she'd already lived. It was the hard, dirty, and pointless life she would be condemned to when Loc Breeden found out she'd lost the only copy of Cosmotech's entire Lynt City data base.

It was the worst nightmare she could imagine and when the sedation stick snapped its incapacitating bolt into her neck, Pilsa almost cried with relief. Anything was better than the horrors of a future without job security.

MIANA FELT CONFLICTED. SHE SHOULD HAVE BEEN GLAD they now had what they'd come for, but after investigating the bloody aftermath of many criminal deals gone wrong, she knew that would be dangerously naïve.

They still had to get out of there, they still had to free Mr. Drevit, and they still had to find a way to use the information they'd stolen against Loc Breeden. None of it was guaranteed to go without a hitch and Miana certainly wasn't ready to celebrate just yet.

Kurt, on the other hand, was enjoying himself immensely. He was exhibiting the same youthful exuberance Miana had witnessed in many graduate police officers and she hoped it wouldn't make him reckless. They didn't need any complications.

She turned to watch Mr. Drevit, who was holding up the memory card he'd just taken from the woman lying on the floor.

"This will be encrypted," he said.

"Can you decrypt it?" Miana asked him.

"I can, but that wasn't part of our deal."

Miana felt a familiar tension in her throat. The complications had begun.

"What are you talking about?" Kurt said, his tone hard. "You agreed to get us the information."

"And it's all here," Mr. Drevit replied, offering the card to Miana. "Take it."

She looked him in the eyes and could tell he wasn't bluffing. He'd done what he'd agreed to and he'd been completely honest about it.

"What do you want?" she asked slowly.

"I want a copy of what's on here," Mr. Drevit said simply.

"What do you plan to do with it?" she asked.

"I don't know," he replied, looking at the memory card. "It depends on what's on it. But my main goal will be to gain leverage over Loc Breeden. As I pointed out prior to our agreement, when he finds out I helped you steal this, he'll want me dead as much as you. And he has considerable resources to make that happen, believe me."

Miana thought about it. She knew this man would go straight back to killing once they set him free. Would he do more or less damage with Cosmotech's information? And was there another way to de-crypt the data if she refused him?

She'd done deals with criminals in the past and it had never been easy. But necessary was never the same as easy. And given all that had happened, the thought of losing their advantage now was almost too much to bear.

"*We don't have a choice,*" she told herself.

The best she could do was promise herself she would devote time to finding Mr. Drevit in the future, or at least pass on what information she had on him to the authorities. She wasn't foolish enough to believe it would make a difference, but it was at least enough to bring her to a decision.

"Alright," she said after a moment. "Hack the encryption and make your copy. Just be aware I plan to have Kurt question you again before we set you free. I'd advise against trying any technical deception."

"Understood," Mr. Drevit said with a nod.

Miana watched as he plugged the memory card into his data pad and went to work.

A moment later, Kurt appeared next to her and spoke in a quiet voice.

"Do you really believe it's encrypted?"

"We have to assume it is," she replied calmly. "He wouldn't risk lying to us when he knows what you can do."

Kurt remained silent for a moment and then spoke again.

"You know he's going to use that information for something... unsavoury."

"I do," Miana replied, "but we need that information more than we need to protect his future victims. I have to find out what Loc is planning and who else is involved. What we saw in the caves..."

Her voice trailed off as she contemplated the terrible vision they'd shared.

"I get it," Kurt said quietly. "I just don't like it, Miana."

She turned to him and saw that his excitement had disappeared beneath a cloud of concern. She should have been feeling the same, but experience assured her it would do them no good. The decision was made and she would have to live with the consequences, no matter what they might be.

"Done," Mr. Drevit said, handing her the data pad. "The files are decrypted. You can access them under the primary memory bank like any other."

"I'll check it," Kurt offered, snatching the data pad from him.

Miana let him do so gratefully. She knew enough to check it for herself, but wasn't confident she would recognise any problems.

She peered over Kurt's shoulder as he worked.

There were hundreds of folders, all with reference names she didn't recognise. Kurt seemed to choose one at random and it expanded to list dozens of sub-folders and different file formats. He opened several and took a moment to scroll through the information. One was clearly financial, another was a structural blueprint for some kind of mining vehicle, and the last was a detailed map of an area Miana didn't recognise.

Kurt closed the files and opened several more – all technologies Miana wasn't familiar with – then he ran an interrogation program. From what she could make out, it was a search for any locked or encrypted files. It found none.

"Looks fine to me," he said after a moment, "but I think we should–"

Before he could finish, a *hisss* from somewhere above interrupted them. Miana looked up to see a thick door sliding down from the ceiling and although her muscles twitched in shock, they did nothing useful.

Her mind provided a gruesome, split-second image of what would happen if the door closed on top of her then she felt a strong grip on her wrist that pulled her to the floor. Pain bit into her elbow as she landed and she heard Kurt's panicked voice call her name once before a loud *thoom* blocked it out.

The bulkhead had closed right next to her and Kurt was on the other side.

"Quickly," Mr. Drevit said, helping her to her feet, "you have to disable the Raze implant."

"What? How could you–"

"This is not a betrayal of our contract," Mr. Drevit continued quickly. "Anya Polovski has managed to trip the building's containment protocols and all the fire doors have been activated. I can't override it without direct access to the network. You know as well as I do what Kurt is going to think. He'll kill me if you don't disable the implant. You have to do it, now!"

Miana's mind reeled in shock. This was happening too fast. She knew Mr. Drevit was probably right, but without the threat of Kurt's psychic control, what would happen if she released him?

She also wasn't certain Kurt would even use the Raze implant. He might have been the one who'd insisted on using it in the first place, but she didn't believe he'd use it lightly.

Of course, she also knew that anyone could make a bad decision in the heat of the moment.

"What do I need to do?" she asked reluctantly.

Mr. Drevit picked up a stun baton from one of the security officers and changed the setting before handing it to her and removing his jacket.

"Press the end against the entry scar and zap me continuously for three seconds."

"What? That could kill you," she said.

"It's a possibility," Mr. Drevit agreed, "but less of a risk than Kurt deciding I've betrayed you. Please, Miana, you must act quickly."

Staring at the stun baton, Miana took a moment to steady herself and then looked up and pressed it firmly against the scar at the base of the assassin's neck. When she pulled the trigger a sharp *TSZZszszszszzz* split the air and Mr. Drevit arched his back and gasped in pain. Miana held the baton against his skin, making sure the contact was continuous, and counted down in her mind.

"*Three, two, one...*"

When she released the trigger, Mr. Drevit fell to the floor, still twitching, and Miana knelt to check his pulse. It was strong.

"Can you hear me?" she asked, "are you alright?"

"Freeze!"

Miana looked toward the new voice and saw a security officer at the far end of the corridor with his weapon pointed right at her.

"Put the weapon down and slide it toward me," the officer barked.

Miana did as she was told quickly.

"Lie on the ground with your hands behind your head," the officer ordered.

Again, Miana did as she was told.

"I don't know who you are, but you're going to pay for fucking with us," the officer growled as he roughly placed her in cuffs.

"*Come on, Mr. Drevit,*" she willed in her mind, "*use the disruptor.*"

The officer dragged her to her feet and Miana felt a blow land hard against her head. It dislodged the earpiece that protected her from the disruptor and she watched in dismay as it bounced across the ground.

"*Oh no,*" she thought, a moment before the ground was suddenly whipped out from beneath her.

Mr. Drevit had done just as she'd hoped, but without any protection, Miana was vulnerable to the disruptor's incapacitating influence as well. She rolled onto her side, trying not to vomit as the corridor spun around her, and hoped desperately that this wasn't the opportunity Mr. Drevit had been waiting for.

"Interesting," she heard him say from somewhere behind her. "I lied to you, ex-detective. I could have opened the fire door easily, but I saw an opportunity and I lied."

Miana felt the chill of fear settle over her shuddering body.

"It's interesting because I intended to honour our agreement," he continued casually. "Your interrogation methods were foolproof. I couldn't lie to Kurt and although I told you I'd betray you if the opportunity arose, I still wasn't sure if I would actually do it."

"Don't…" was all she could manage to say.

"It is an interesting situation, wouldn't you agree?"

Miana tried to speak again, but could only spray spittle across the ground in front of her.

"Yes, I know you do," Mr. Drevit added with a disturbing laugh. "And just so you know, I don't plan on looking you in the eye. You know the old saying – fool me once, shame on you, fool me twice, shame on *me.* I don't know if you have psychic powers, Miana, but I'm certainly not stupid enough to risk it."

Beyond her randomly contracting muscles, Miana sensed movement behind her and a moment later heard a grunt and a loud *crack!*

"*The security officer,*" she thought helplessly.

"I appreciate your professionalism, ex-detective," Mr. Drevit said, his voice getting closer. "My respect for you will not make this easy, but I feel it is in my best interests to kill you now. And Kurt, of course, although I'll need to be extra careful with him."

Miana felt the same panic she'd felt back in the caves.

"And don't worry about Mr. Breeden. After I return to the caves where Kurt was gifted with his unique abilities, I'll hunt him down and end this case of yours once and for all."

A moment later, Miana felt herself being lifted off the floor and then an arm closed around her neck. The sudden certainty of death caused a whole host of emotions to rush forward – fear, regret, anger, guilt – and as they quickly overwhelmed her, a strange sensation joined them.

Miana didn't know if it was the sonic disruptor or just a side-effect of her imminent death, but suddenly she couldn't feel her body. In a panic, she tried to move again, desperate for anything that might confirm she still had a connection with her body, but something else happened instead.

First, there was a momentary rush of blurred light and then she was looking down on the assassin. He had his arm locked around the neck of a shuddering woman and it took Miana a moment to realise who it was.

"*That's me,*" she thought with a strange sense of calm.

She should have been terrified, but being disconnected from her physical body seemed to mute her ability to feel emotion.

Then a single thought entered her mind.

"*Stop.*"

As Miana watched. Mr. Drevit's serious eyes suddenly went blank. She didn't know how this was happening, or where the thought had come from, but it didn't seem to matter.

"*Let go.*"

The second thought came as clearly as the first and, again, Mr. Drevit did as it commanded. Miana saw her shuddering body fall limply from his arms.

"*Turn off the disruptor.*"

This time Miana was certain the thought wasn't her own, but it worked just as the last two had. Mr. Drevit made a motion with his right hand and her shuddering body became still.

A suspicion took hold in Miana's mind, but before she could act on it a flash of movement caught her eye and she turned to see a security officer standing at the end of the corridor.

Suddenly, the stutter of gunfire filled the air.

Crack-ack-ack!

Something hot bit into Miana's non-corporeal leg and the strange light she'd seen earlier blurred around her. She blinked in surprise and found that she was no longer looking down on herself. Now, she was staring across the corridor floor at the slumped form of the security officer Mr. Drevit had killed.

"*I'm back in my body,*" she thought.

Before she could move, something else entered her vision from above and it hit the ground between her and the dead officer with a *thud.* Miana blinked once again and saw that it was Mr. Drevit, his eyes wide and blood streaming from his mouth.

"*They shot him,*" she thought numbly.

His eyes locked onto hers for a moment, gleaming with accusation, then the life seemed to fade from them and Miana knew he was dead.

A wave of guilt washed over her.

"*Did I just use psychic powers?*" she thought, before her detective mind added, "*or did someone... someth*ing *use me?*"

As the questions rolled through her mind, Miana barely noticed the fire doors retracting behind her, but she recognised Kurt's voice as soon as it spoke.

"Hold your fire," he barked.

She turned her head toward the officer who'd just shot at them, and saw that his weapon was pointed directly at her. But at Kurt's command, the officer immediately relaxed and his weapon lowered.

Miana managed to roll onto her back, overwhelmed with pain and exhaustion, and the next thing she knew, Kurt was by her side.

"Are you okay?" he asked quickly.

"I've been shot," she said weakly, "through the leg."

"I can see," he said gently. "Lie still. I'll get us out of here. Hang on."

She saw Kurt stand up and a wave of vertigo washed over her.

"Where's the nearest first aid?" he said, his voice sounding far off.

The officer's reply was too muffled to make out and Miana realised what was happening.

"*I'm going into shock,*" she thought. "*God, I'm tired.*"

Kurt appeared above her again and she felt something press hard against her leg.

"Argh…" she gasped.

"This will help with the pain," Kurt said. "I'm going to patch you up then we're getting out of here."

"How… did you get through the fire door?" she asked as a woozy feeling crept over her.

"Hot-wired," Kurt said with a smile. "What? I may not be an international assassin, but I've got a few tricks of my own. I wasn't going to leave you alone with him."

"I… killed him," Miana said, a tear sliding down her face.

"Doesn't look like it to me," Kurt said, glancing away for a moment. "Unless you found a way to get those security weapons to work."

"I used the power, Kurt," she said, her voice trailing off in a whisper.

"Don't worry about that now. You can explain everything later."

"Don't… leave the data pad," she finished, closing her eyes as the world closed in around her.

"I won't," Kurt assured her. "You just sleep now, okay?"

And Miana decided that was the best advice she'd ever been given, so she did.

ANYA WATCHED HELPLESSLY THROUGH HER OWN EYES as Fayina steered her body down another corridor. From the moment the man who called himself Sabian had taken control of her, she'd been locked away at the back of her own mind, unable to take control of her body.

It was a cruel irony, but Anya didn't think her personalities – particularly Fayina – had ever experienced her control over them as she did now. But what if they had? The thought made her feel sick and embarrassed. It was no wonder Fayina, who she suppressed more than any of them, was so angry all the time.

At least Dr. Haig's suggestion was working. Whatever he'd done to hack the building's emergency systems, Fayina was using it to successfully confuse Cosmotech Security and there was a chance they might actually open a clear path out of there.

Anya only hoped the Security officers would lose some of their enthusiasm once she'd left the building. It was clear they were prepared to go to great lengths inside Cosmotech offices, but Lynt City authorities would surely respond to this kind of activity once it spilled beyond Cosmotech's 'sovereign territory'.

Of course, the people trying to capture her weren't stupid. They knew Fayina was trying to escape and any officers not trying to get her directly were already marshalling near the exits.

"I need another way out," Fayina growled, sounding slightly tinny from Anya's mentally chained perspective.

"Why don't we ask our new friend?" Celia asked in a sing-song voice that also reverberated strangely.

"I don't need anyone's help," Fayina snapped.

"Well, that's a lie," Ianka broke in with a snort. "We've all recently witnessed several examples to the contrary."

Anya could feel her muscles tightening as Fayina replied.

"I'm not trusting anyone I don't have to."

"How about trusting us for a change?" Ianka said sharply.

"Fuck you," Fayina snarled.

Anya could feel Fayina's tension growing, just as it always did when Ianka spoke to her, but she couldn't do anything about it. She'd been trying to communicate with her personalities since Sabian had locked her away, but they didn't seem to notice her attempts on any level.

"Celia's suggestion is a good one," Dr. Haig said with his usual diplomacy.

"Really?" Celia said, sounding excited.

"I agree," Ianka replied firmly. "What about you, Fayina? Are you going to trust us and try contacting our mysterious helper again?"

Anya felt a flush of heat roll through her face and knew Fayina's temper was flaring. She didn't like the others ganging up on her.

"If it will shut you up, then fine," Fayina snarled, coming to an abrupt halt. "Just make it quick."

Before giving up control, Fayina re-activated the fire door they'd just passed through and it closed, sealing them within a short section of empty corridor. She then mentally retreated, allowing Dr. Haig to take control of her body.

Anya felt her muscles relax and infuse with the familiar ache of old age. Her now slightly unfocused eyes fell to the device in her hand and her fingers input a complicated program that would back-trace the signal that had been guiding them.

"This won't take long," Dr. Haig said quietly.

"Let me talk to them," Ianka demanded.

"Don't push it," Fayina growled.

"I don't think your skill set extends to negotiation, Fayina," Ianka replied.

"And yours does?" Fayina snapped. "Your condescending tone will alienate them in seconds."

"Being sensible is far from condescending," Ianka replied curtly.

"Your version of sensible is exactly that," Fayina growled.

"I wish Anya was here," Celia chimed in. "She always knows what to say."

At the mention of her name, Anya felt a surge of hope and she pushed harder against the mental barrier that held her in check, but Fayina just snorted.

"That's not–"

But before she could finish, the fire door behind them suddenly began to rise again.

"What did you do?" Fayina snarled, taking back control of Anya's body with a violent jerk.

"I did nothing," Dr. Haig replied, sounding just as surprised. "Our connection with the security systems was severed."

"I told you we shouldn't have messed with it," Fayina snapped.

"Why would they do that?" Celia whined. "They wanted to help us, didn't they?"

"Did you get through at all?" Ianka asked.

"I did," Dr. Haig replied, "but not long enough to get a reply."

"It doesn't matter now," Fayina growled, "so just shut the hell up, all of you."

"I can re-establish the link," Dr. Haig said.

"You've had your chance," Fayina snarled. "Now we do this my way."

"Don't be a fool," Ianka snapped. "We won't make it out of here unless we work together."

"I don't need anyone's help!" Fayina shouted.

"Saying it louder doesn't make it any less of a lie," Ianka replied.

"Please, calm down," Dr. Haig added, forever the diplomat.

"Don't shout," Celia whined.

"Fuck you all!" Fayina screamed.

Anya could almost feel the point at which Fayina's temper snapped. She'd always been hostile toward the other personalities, but this time was different. It was clear now that Fayina was an embodiment of Anya's hatred for herself, which explained why she was so violent and reckless in a way that precluded any thought for her own safety.

Throwing the useless data pad aside, Fayina ran toward the still-opening fire door and, at the last minute, dropped to her hip and slid through the widening gap.

The security officers beyond weren't ready for this and Fayina ploughed into them in a whirling fury, slamming several of them aside and lashing out at the others with deadly accuracy. The officers quickly rallied and tried to fight back, but they weren't prepared for Fayina's reckless violence.

Anya watched, helpless in her own mind and body, as the battle continued. It was brutally one-sided. Fayina ripped through the officers just as she had all the others, but even as Anya started to become confident they would make it through the attack, she noticed something Fayina didn't.

There was an officer at the back of the group who'd just thrown a large grenade-like device into the middle of the action.

At the last moment, Fayina seemed to notice the grenade and she spun on her heel, whipping the other foot up and batting the grenade back toward the officer who'd thrown it. She then grabbed one of the falling officers she'd just smashed in the temple and pulled him into place like a shield.

Then the grenade detonated.

A sharp *CRACK* filled the corridor and a nimbus of blue light exploded outward. The pulse of energy passed straight through the struggling officers, even the one Fayina was using as a shield, and Anya felt a sizzling pain roll across her skin.

The officer Fayina was holding fell from her suddenly numb fingers and Anya saw the corridor ceiling tip into view as her legs gave way beneath her. She expected to hear Fayina swearing as she fought the paralysing energy that had sapped her strength, but she remained completely silent. So did Dr. Haig, Ianka and Celia.

Anya wasn't sure what had happened for a moment and then she realised they'd been knocked out by the grenade, leaving her the only one still conscious.

The security officers must have decided that the only way to subdue her was to sacrifice themselves as well. It was clear that whoever was behind this assault didn't want her harmed, but the knowledge didn't reassure Anya at all.

She could hear the officers falling to the floor around her and wondered how long it would be before another team would come to take her away. But with no control over her body, all she could do was watch from the back of her own mind and wait for the inevitable.

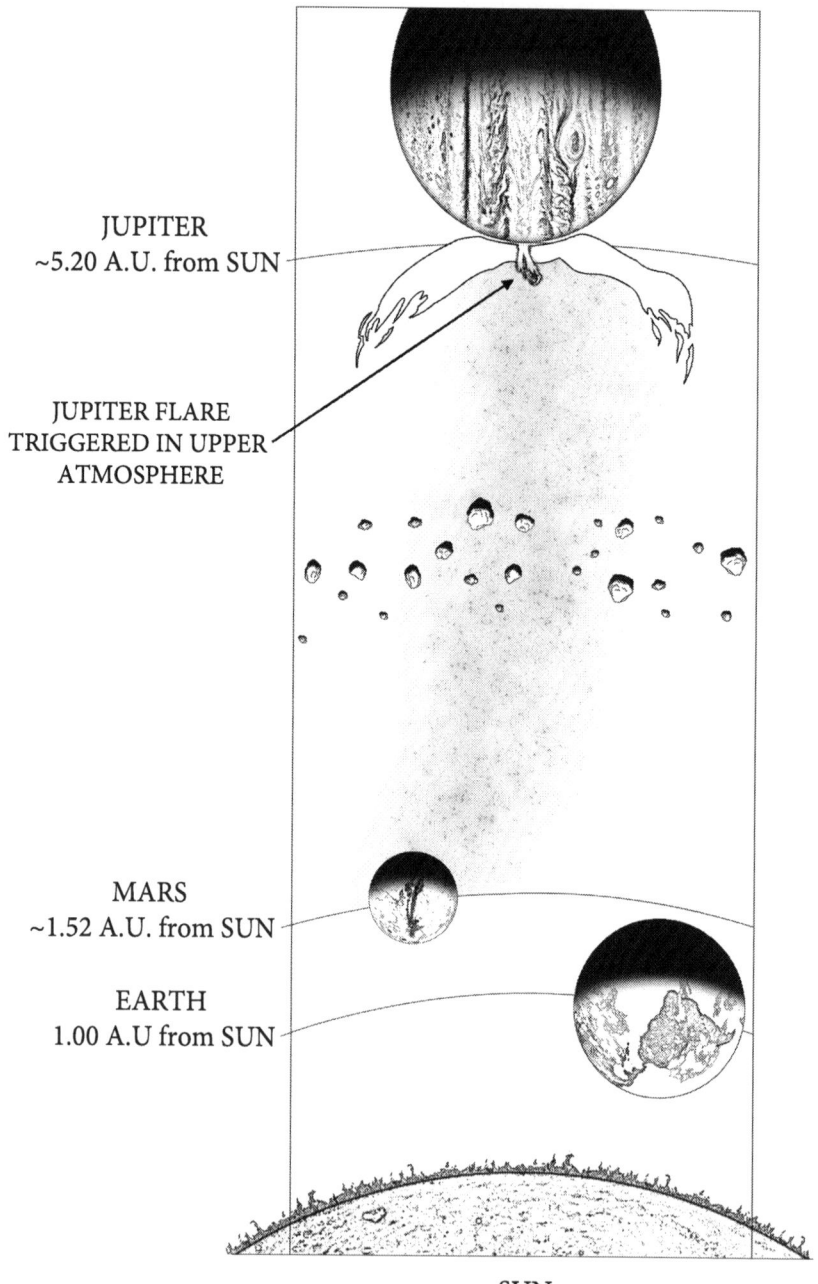

STAGE 5: SOLAR FLARE REACHES JUPITER'S ATMOSPHERE
June 7, 2147 - 6.30 pm

JUPITER
~5.20 A.U. from SUN

JUPITER FLARE
TRIGGERED IN UPPER
ATMOSPHERE

MARS
~1.52 A.U. from SUN

EARTH
1.00 A.U from SUN

SUN

1 Astronomical Unit (A.U.) = ~149.6 x 10^6 km

MARS UPPER ATMOSPHERE - June 7, 2147 - 6.40pm

ISAAC TAYLOR WAS STARTING TO WONDER IF HE WAS looking at everything wrong. It all seemed so real. So *vivid*. He could touch things, feel heat, cold, even pain. He could smell things, taste them, *see* them clearly. But was it all in his head? Had their psychic experiment backfired and somehow made his dreams come to life?

The longer he thought about it, the more reasonable it sounded. Especially given the alternative.

"*Parallel universes,*" he thought, shaking his head.

Multiple realities had long been theorized, but moving between them was a fantasy at best. And what about the religious cult that claimed Isaac was their Messiah? That was even less believable in some ways. Accepting that he was meant to save them from some rapidly approaching catastrophe was just ludicrous.

But whether he was stuck in a waking dream or an alternate reality, Isaac couldn't seem to change the fact that he was currently strapped inside a craft he'd never heard of and headed for a mega-scraper that didn't exist in the world he'd allegedly come from.

"*The Bas Quirat.*"

Neither Dr. Grayson or Loc had told Isaac anything about the Bas Quirat and that worried him.

He wanted to ask Loc a few questions, but since boarding the ship, he'd quarantined himself behind a soundproof screen and seemed to be working on something important.

Dr. Grayson, on the other hand, was lost in another of his strange, absent-minded trances. Isaac found the scientist's erratic behaviour to be a strange dichotomy. He could be so engaging and passionate when discussing the science behind Isaac and Jason's experiment, but every once in a while he'd become agitated, as if his thoughts were getting too loud for him. When that happened, he usually wandered off, mumbling or hissing to himself and completely ignored Isaac along with whatever it was they'd been talking about.

Shaking his head again, Isaac looked around unfamiliar craft's cabin. He was near the front and had a pretty amazing view of the terrain rolling over the horizon ahead of them. The entire front of the cabin acted like a virtual window and so it displayed the view from the front of the ship in incredible detail.

The seats behind him were full of Dr. Grayson's bodyguards and Loc's security team. Isaac could have asked them for a bit of local knowledge, he supposed, but none of them looked very approachable. He also got the feeling they were watching each other very carefully and wouldn't appreciate the distraction.

With a sigh, Isaac absently turned to the controls on his arm rest. He wasn't sure what they did, but when he touched one of them, a large virtual screen appeared in the air in front of him. He reached out a hand instinctively and was pleased when his touch caused the screen to scroll through some entertainment options.

"This reality isn't so different," he thought to himself.

There were all the usual interactive movies and mind-numbing games, which Isaac was genuinely curious about, but he didn't stop scrolling until he found a familiar icon.

"I hope that's what I think it is."

Activating the icon with a touch, Isaac felt a small thrill of triumph when it turned out to be a search engine for some kind of planet-wide internet.

The controls were fairly intuitive and so it didn't take him long to work out how to search for information on the Bas Quirat.

"*That's odd,*" he thought when the results arrived.

There didn't seem to be anything available on the world inside the Bas Quirat, but where it came from was almost a legend in itself. Apparently, three decades ago, the wealthiest Islamic countries on Earth put aside their differences and banded together to build a Marsian city on the consensus it would be run as an Islamic democracy that was strictly controlled by Sharia law.

The proposal had caused quite a stir in the international community, but the amount of money being invested dwarfed any international concerns and construction began immediately. Since then, it appeared the Bas Quirat had been an unexpected success, both socially and economically. The number of ongoing births was more than adequate to keep their estimated seven million strong population stable and shrewd political handling, along with strict labour laws, kept the populace employed and productive.

There was, however, a quite serious level of exclusivity involved. If you were not born within the Bas Quirat's towering walls, the only way you were allowed entry was through a long, arduously bureaucratic process that kept migration to a minimum and the introduction of any alternate dogmas virtually impossible. But Quiration officials considered it a weak criticism given the unprecedented success of their mega-scraper city.

And the Bas Quirat was truly immense. Given Mars' weaker gravity and the latest architectural technologies, the Bas Quirat was constructed many times higher than any equivalent structure on Earth. Soaring a colossal three kilometres into the dusty Marsian sky, it was heralded as a modern day pyramid. Its vast base was spread across dozens of square kilometres and its sides stretched upward in a spectacular network of intricately connected towers.

At its centre and peak, a single spire as large as the tallest skyscraper on Earth rose into the heavens and was rumoured to house the most ancient Islamic families.

The rest of the Bas Quirat spilled out below this empirical structure in delicate swathes of cascading domes and sparkling ziggurats.

One of the articles explained that, as with Islamic cultures on Earth, much of the architectural design was focused on the inner space, but Isaac couldn't find any record of the internal structure. Apparently the world beyond the Bas Quirat's sparkling exterior was a closely guarded secret and anyone caught trying to share such information automatically lost their citizenship.

"*I wonder how it could possibly be any more ornate than the exterior,*" he thought in amazement.

"Isaac," Loc interrupted him.

He looked up to find the screen surrounding Loc had slid into the ceiling.

"Pull your head out of those unworthy approximations and marvel at the real thing," Loc said with a wide grin and a flourish toward the front of the cabin.

Isaac closed the virtual screen that blocked his view and caught his first glimpse of the famous Bas Quirat.

"Welcome," Loc added, "to the third and arguably most spectacular wonder of the new world. The Bas Quirat."

"Wow," Isaac said in amazement.

Despite all the impressive facts and figures he'd been reading, none of it prepared him for the reality of what loomed before them now. The Bas Quirat straddled the Marsian landscape like a mountain made of organic steel and glass, and yet its familiar, human-made facade made it appear far more immense than any natural formation.

In the dusky light of early evening, the immense structure glittered with millions upon millions of reflections and the intricate design of spires and ziggurats gave it an unreal complexity that only added to its incredible size.

As they gradually flew closer, Isaac felt the pull of gravity and realised they were slowly banking up toward the central spire that topped the enormous construction.

Seeing it rise before him was perhaps the most impressive sight of all. It was nothing like the spire he'd studied atop the three dimensional model he'd found on the internet, and as it filled the cabin's virtual screens, he felt a shiver of awe run through him from head to toe.

Their ship climbed and climbed, and then climbed some more, and still the top seemed far away. When they finally came within sight of the ultimate peak, Isaac noticed several small craft detach from its side and fly out to meet them. Each had wide triangular wings that gave them the look of predators and beneath their sleek undercarriages, several menacing-looking weapons glistened in the rapidly fading light.

This was the third time in as many days that dangerous technology had been aimed in Isaac's direction and his awe quickly gave way to anxiety.

"They know we're coming, right?" he asked nervously.

"Of course," Loc replied, turning from the console he'd been studying for the entire trip. "That's just our escort coming to greet us."

"You are honoured," Dr. Grayson added, apparently back from wherever his inner voices had taken him. "We will find no aggression here."

As he said this, the ships coming toward them split apart and circled around until they flanked the transport on either side. Isaac felt a little better knowing these dangerous-looking ships were simply an 'escort', but his reassurance faded when he saw the battery of anti-aircraft missiles that flanked the hanger they were headed for.

As they glided smoothly into the gaping space, Isaac couldn't help noticing that their Quiration 'escort' remained hovering outside, as if waiting for a signal to open fire.

It was only when they landed with a gentle bump that the menacing ships turned and flew off immediately, presumably returning to the perches they'd just alighted from.

"You'll need one of these," Dr. Grayson said, pulling Isaac's gaze from the world outside the hanger.

He looked at what was being offered to him and saw a small, curved device he didn't recognise.

"It's just an ear piece," Loc said helpfully. "For translation. English is considered barbaric by the majority of Quirations and is even forbidden in some parts. Arabic is seen as the one true language of Islam and, by Quiration law, all residents must use it."

Isaac remembered seeing something about that in the articles he'd skimmed, but he still found it confronting. English was by no means the dominant language on the Mars he'd come from, but neither was there any discrimination between cultures. Not when it came to language at least. A universal translator quite similar to the one Dr. Grayson had handed him had dealt with that problem a long time ago.

"Now," Loc said, putting an arm around Isaac and leading him toward the cabin's exit, "this will mean you can understand the Quirations, but there's no guarantee they'll be wearing one of these as well."

"So they won't understand me?" Isaac asked.

"Not unless they want to," Loc replied. "Their cultural tolerance is somewhat... limited when it comes to those who live outside the Bas Quirat. But I'm sure it won't be a problem. Just try not to speak unless they talk to you directly. We're guests here and privileged ones at that, but there's a strict adherence to Sharia law within the walls of the Bas Quirat. Unless you know what those laws are, you could unintentionally get yourself, or someone else, into very serious trouble. Oh, and don't stare at their women."

"Their women?" Isaac said weakly.

But before Loc could say anything else, the door opened with a *hisss* of escaping air and Isaac was surrounded by a cordon of large men that ushered him down the gangplank.

When they reached the bottom, his burly escort parted and Isaac was surprised to see a double line of Quirations stretched out before him, all wearing long ceremonial robes of blue and purple.

He stared at them in amazement and wondered where they'd come from. Every one of them wore a burka that covered everything but their eyes and when Isaac saw long eyelashes and the glint of sparkling makeup, he quickly looked away.

"*They're all women,*" he thought with a sinking feeling.

"Don't be afraid," Loc said, grinning as he put a hand on Isaac's shoulder, "they're just the welcoming committee. You won't offend anyone here."

A long, brightly coloured carpet stitched in intricate detail lay between the waiting lines of women and Isaac stayed close to Loc as the small group walked along it. At the end of the carpet, a delegation of richly-dressed men waited in front of a larger group that wore unfamiliar uniforms and looked like soldiers, or perhaps police.

As their small group approached, the richly-dressed men bowed simultaneously, as if on cue, and when they rose once more, one of them spoke in perfect English.

"Welcome, greetings, and salutations," he said, holding his arms wide. "My name is Sirun Abdullah. I will be your humble liaison while you grace the Bas Quirat with your presence."

"Aasalaamu aleikum," Loc said, bowing low himself. "It is truly an honour to be welcomed into your great city, Sirun Abdullah. My name is Loc Breeden, honoured representative of Cosmotech Defence. May I present to you, Doctor William Grayson, our most respected scientist, and this is Isaac Taylor."

Sirun nodded as Loc introduced himself and Dr. Grayson, but when he indicated Isaac, he bowed lower than before and spoke facing the floor.

"I do not have adequate words to describe this honour, blessed one," he said quietly.

Isaac frowned in confusion and glanced at Loc for guidance, but he merely gave him a shrug and said nothing.

When he looked back at Sirun, he saw the man had thankfully straightened again and was now stepping aside, just as the men behind him were doing. Sirun then gestured toward the space that had opened between them.

"Please," he said, still not making eye contact with Isaac.

Isaac wasn't sure what was going on, but it seemed clear they wanted him to walk through the gap. He turned to Loc for guidance, but he just nodded and so Isaac tentatively began to walk through the opening.

From the corner of his eye, he saw Loc move to follow him, but one of the uniformed Quirations stepped forward and firmly barred his way. Isaac hesitated as the Cosmotech Security detail tensed in readiness, but Loc held up his hand and took a step back, bowing low.

"I would like to remain at Isaac's side," he said to Sirun.

"He is to meet the Prophet," Sirun said, as if this explained everything. "He alone has been summoned. In the meantime, our leaders are anxious to converse with you, Loc Breeden, and our scientists are eager to discuss matters with you, Doctor William Grayson."

Loc looked at Isaac for a moment, as if contemplating his options. Dr. Grayson was talking to himself quietly, or arguing in a whisper by the sound of it, and so he didn't even seem to know what was going on.

"I'll… be okay," Isaac said uncertainly. "Won't I?"

Loc looked at him a moment longer then he nodded in capitulation.

"You'll be fine," he said, before glancing meaningfully at Sirun. "I'm sure I'll see you again soon."

"Please," Sirun said to Isaac, ignoring Loc's comment and gesturing once more through the gap.

Turning to give Loc a final shrug, Isaac moved on and couldn't help noticing that each man he passed was lowering his eyes in deference.

The colourful carpet beyond them continued out through a pair of enormous, ornate doors at the back of the hanger, before turning abruptly into a short corridor. No one followed Isaac as he walked warily along it and he eventually found an archway at the end draped with thin, filmy curtains.

The curtains silently moved aside when he came within a few metres and a small, grandly designed chamber was revealed beyond. As Isaac reluctantly stepped through the archway, he saw dozens of intricately carved columns arrayed around the circular chamber. All of them were draped with colourful hangings and they matched the beautiful patterns that flowed through the tiled walls. A magnificent marble floor cast polished reflections, filling the grand space with light, and it seemed to pull Isaac's focus to the centre, where a three-stepped dais led up to a large, throne-like chair.

The carpet Isaac was following led to the base of the dais and three waiting women. Two stood either side of the throne and were covered from head to toe in a jet black material that revealed only their piercing eyes. The third was much taller and she wore light blue robes that left her face uncovered. Her cheekbones were high and smooth, just like her alabaster skin, and a small red ruby hung at the very centre of her forehead. It was held by a thin, white-gold head chain that emerged from her grey, almost white hair, and that hung over her left shoulder in a long, intricate braid.

But what really drew Isaac's attention was her eyes. They were almost as white as her hair, clouded from edge-to-edge with cataracts, and although they stared into the distance, clearly unable to see anything, Isaac felt as if they were looking straight at him.

As he tentatively approached them, the women in black knelt gracefully and the older woman said something in Arabic.

"Tarhib, Isaac Taylor. Laqad kunt tantazir waqtaan tawilaan jiddaan limuqabalatik."

The device in Isaac's ear translated the words with a smooth tone and inflection that matched the woman's voice perfectly.

"Welcome, Isaac Taylor. I have been waiting a very long time to meet you."

"Uh… hi," he replied, feeling a little out of his depth.

The woman smiled, making her handsome face soften, and when she spoke again her words were translated in his ear almost as soon as she spoke them.

"Aismi Hani'ah Nazari. 'Ana maeruf litilk alty dakhil qirat bas muqaddas mithl alnnabi walmustashar al'awwal lilmurshid Quiration alssamia."

"My name is Hani'ah Naziri. I am known to those within the sacred Bas Quirat as Prophet and first advisor to the Quiration High Leader."

Isaac could tell this woman was important, even without her titles, but he wasn't sure how he should reply.

"Um… nice to meet you," he offered, feeling a little lame.

"Do you know why you're here?" she asked him abruptly.

Isaac was a little thrown by the question. He had no idea how much this woman knew about what he was doing with Dr. Grayson or if he was allowed to tell her anything. He doubted Loc would let him come here if the Quirations didn't already know something, but he couldn't be sure. Particularly after he'd seen Loc barred from accompanying him.

"No, not really," he answered, deciding to wait for confirmation before he volunteered anything.

"You cannot guard your thoughts from me, Isaac," Hani'ah added casually, as if it were a friendly piece of advice.

"I didn't realise I was trying to," he replied with a frown.

"You were," she confirmed, her vacant eyes boring into him. "Now, please tell me. Do you know why you are here?"

Isaac paused. He didn't want to say anything that might hurt the people who'd brought him here, or himself for that matter, but it didn't seem like he had any option but the truth.

"We're… trying to recreate an experiment I ran with my twin brother, Jason," he said reluctantly.

"And it's purpose?"

"To… create a rift between this reality and… the one I came from."

Hani'ah smiled at this and Isaac wondered if she was laughing at him. Just because it was true didn't mean she was going to believe it.

"Very good," her translated voice spoke in his ear. "But that is only what you are here to accomplish, Isaac. Do you know why it must be done?"

"So I can be reunited with my brother?" he said hesitantly.

"Of course," Hani'ah agreed, "but there's more at stake than returning home, Isaac. You have heard these words from another already, have you not?"

"What?" Isaac said, his mind instinctively returning to his kidnapping in the Valles Dome.

"I can see that you do," Hani'ah said with another smile. "Your captor was a man misguided by faith, but his message was based upon truth. You are destined to save us."

Isaac took a step back. He thought he'd left this madness behind him. Did Loc know what this woman believed? And how did she know what he was thinking anyway?

"Allah took one form of sight from me," Hani'ah said, touching a hand to her eyes, "and replaced it with another," she added, moving the hand to her forehead.

Isaac glanced at the ruby that glinted in the centre of her forehead and wondered if she was pointing to that or if she was referring to some kind of mystical third eye. Then Hani'ah spoke once again.

"*Kunt 'aerif ma 'atahaddath eanh, Isaac.*"

This time the translator didn't change her words to English and it took Isaac a moment to realise she'd spoken directly in his mind.

"You're psychic?" he gasped.

"Ana."

"I am," the translator responded this time.

At the news, a surge of hope broke through Isaac's confusion.

"Then you're going to help me recreate the experiment?"

"Yes," Hani'ah replied, "just as you are going to help us."

Isaac frowned. He would do anything to get back to Jason and his own reality, but he wasn't sure he would be doing himself any favours if he went along with some apocalyptic fantasy.

"I don't know about that," he said carefully.

"Destiny has marked you, Isaac Taylor. Do not turn from it simply because another has tainted this sacred purpose with his madness."

"I don't believe in destiny," he added defiantly.

"And yet, here you are, at the prophesied time," Hani'ah replied.

"What are you talking about?"

Hani'ah remained silent for a moment then she began to slowly move down the dais steps.

"What I am talking about cannot be explained, Isaac. It must be shown. Will you allow me to show you?"

Isaac hesitated. He really didn't like where this conversation was headed, but refusing this woman didn't seem to be an option.

"Okay," he said slowly.

Hani'ah nodded reverently at this and the two women in black were suddenly standing on either side of Isaac. He jumped in surprise, but they simply lowered their heads and held out a white silken robe between them.

"What's this?" he asked, feeling a little woozy.

"A ceremonial robe more befitting your status," Hani'ah replied.

Isaac held out a hand to touch the material and the women in black slipped it smoothly over his arm and round his back. In moments, they had his other arm inserted into a sleeve and the robe was tied securely round his waste with a thick sash.

"Thank you, Isaac," Hani'ah said with a smile, before turning away from him. "Now, please, follow me if you will."

Hani'ah glided across the marble floor as if she was on wheels and Isaac followed her without thinking. From the corner of his eye, he saw the women in black close in behind him and instinctively quickened his pace. Whereas Hani'ah's eyes stared into nothing, these women seemed to take in everything and their gaze was disturbingly intense.

He wasn't sure if he should be walking beside or behind Hani'ah and so for an awkward moment he found himself almost stumbling in indecision. Hani'ah, on the other hand, continued on as if he wasn't there and so he eventually settled on walking just behind and to her right.

A pair of doors recessed into the chamber's delicately tiled walls slid open as they approached and Hani'ah stepped inside a small, golden elevator before turning and beckoning him inside.

It was disconcerting seeing a blind woman acting so aware of her surroundings and he tried to avoid Hani'ah's stare as he joined her. The women in black quickly followed him inside and the golden doors closed without a sound.

As the elevator descended, Isaac tried not to think any negative thoughts. He didn't want to offend or upset Hani'ah and yet he had plenty of opinions on her beliefs that were likely to do just that.

It was a relief when the elevator finally came to a halt, but when the doors opened again, Isaac felt a distinct change in the atmosphere. It was charged with something he couldn't quite identify and there were voices coming from somewhere nearby. Lots of voices.

He peered out past Hani'ah, but could only see a large open space and a short transparent walkway that ran directly out of the elevator. It ended in a circular platform near the centre of the open space, but the platform had no railing or any obvious attachment with the far wall.

Without hesitation, Hani-ah moved out onto the walkway and the voices fell to a sudden, expectant silence.

The women in black stood either side of the doors and it seemed to Isaac that he was expected to follow Hani'ah, but he hesitated. He wasn't quite sure he wanted to leave the relative safety of the elevator.

He watched Hani'ah glide out to the circular platform with an otherworldly grace and flinched when she turned toward him and spoke into the loaded silence.

"Min fadlik, walaindimam li, Isaac Taylor."

"Please, join me, Isaac Taylor."

The original Arabic version of her words echoed loudly through the large chamber and it sent a rush of anxiety through him.

"*Who's listening?*" he thought.

Hani'ah didn't answer his unspoken question this time, whether she heard it in his mind or not, and so Isaac summoned all the courage he could muster and slowly stepped out of the elevator. He avoided looking down for a few steps, not sure he wanted to see what was below the transparent walkway. Then his curiosity pulled his gaze downward.

"*Oh God,*" he thought incredulously.

Far below the walkway, filling the bottom of the tall, dome-like chamber, were thousands upon thousands of faces. And every one of them was staring upward. Toward Hani'ah. Toward *him.*

"*What is going on?*" he thought in a panic.

"Waqad tamm fi aintizarikim, Isaac Taylor."

"They have been waiting for you, Isaac Taylor," Hani'ah answered, this time happily reading his thoughts.

Isaac looked back up as the Arabic echoed around the chamber and had to battle an urge to run back to the elevator.

"Please," she said, raising a hand, "join me."

Swallowing a lump in his throat, Isaac stared at her hand for a moment and found that the gesture seemed to feed him strength.

He let it build until he was able to continue forward again and soon found himself standing next to Hani'ah.

It was strange seeing her on the small, transparent platform they now shared. If she took even one wrong step, she would plummet to a certain death far below, and yet Isaac got a sense that would never happen.

He looked down at the crowd again and realised they'd grown even more silent, as if they were holding their collective breath.

"I don't understand any of this," Isaac whispered so only Hani'ah would hear him.

"That is why you are here," Hani'ah said, her voice unapologetically loud. "To understand how important you really are."

At her words, Isaac felt a wave of vertigo wash over him and closed his eyes for a moment.

This was madness. He wasn't important. He was just a guy... who was psychic... and had somehow engineered a device that allowed him to travel between realities. Okay, maybe he was a little unique. But he was certainly no *Messiah!*

Opening his eyes again, he saw that Hani'ah seemed to be waiting patiently and appreciated the fact that she hadn't commented on anything he'd just thought.

"Okay, fine," he said at last, feeling faint again. "Show me."

Hani'ah gestured upward and Isaac looked up.

"Woah..." he gasped with an all new amazement.

The entire ceiling was missing. Or it looked as if it was missing. But Isaac knew there had to be something there, because the winds this high in the Marsian atmosphere would have been howling through the chamber otherwise.

Where the ceiling *should* have been was the night sky, glistening with a clarity he'd never experienced.

It was spectacular. The stars of the Milky Way, distant galaxies and nebulae, all stretched across the sky in a glistening river that sparkled brighter than Isaac had ever seen. And, almost as soon as he looked up, something bright red flashed into existence near the very middle of the cosmic tableau.

The enormous crowd at the bottom of the chamber gasped in unison and Isaac felt a shiver run through him.

"What just happened?" he asked, glancing down at them.

"You have witnessed the final sign, Isaac Taylor," Hani'ah replied solemnly. "And, as it has been prophesied, it did not appear until the one who comes to save us looked to the heavens."

Isaac stared at her with his mouth open.

"Are you saying I… caused this somehow?"

"You did not create this end," Hani'ah said, shaking her head, "but you have been sent here to stop it."

The people below them were talking again, but this time they weren't whispering. They were clearly frightened and Isaac could feel the tension rising in the chamber like static electricity on his skin.

He returned his gaze to the night sky above and saw the flash of red was now a small ember that glowed and flickered in the darkness. It also consumed the light of nearby stars in a way that Isaac found hauntingly familiar.

"You have seen this before," Hani'ah said. "As have I."

And Isaac knew she was right. It was one of the visions he'd seen when his experiment had gone terribly wrong. This was the image Anya, or Dr. Haig – her older, male personality – had analysed for him back in the Valles Dome.

"It's nothing," he said, his voice hoarse, "it's just a Jupiter flare."

"It is the final sign," Hani'ah replied.

Isaac tore his gaze from the glowing red spark to look at her.

"A sign of what?" he asked, not really sure he wanted an answer.

"The end of all things."

Isaac's eyes opened wider.

"What are you talking about?" he asked. "I told you, it's just a cosmic phenomenon. A lightning bolt of plasma created by the ionization of gases produced in the wake of an asteroid."

"And if that cosmic lightning bolt were to reach Mars?" Hani'ah asked calmly.

As Isaac let the scenario play out in his mind another shiver ran through him.

"It is the time of Armageddon, Isaac Taylor," Hani'ah continued. "The end of all things has come."

Isaac stared at her in terrified disbelief. Was it even possible for a Jupiter flare to reach Mars? Surely it couldn't travel that far through space, but... what if it did?

"What am I supposed to do about it?" he asked helplessly.

"Do you still believe it is a coincidence that you are here, now, when the final sign has appeared?" Hani'ah asked him.

He didn't know how to answer. Someone below had begun singing some kind of hymn and as more people joined the haunting chorus, Isaac looked down to find many of them swaying in unison with their hands stretched upward.

"What are they doing?" he asked weakly.

"They are praying, Isaac. Praying to their new Prophet. To their new Saviour. They are praying to you."

Isaac felt another wave of vertigo wash over him.

"I… don't know what you expect me to do," he said wretchedly.

"Only what you came here for," Hani'ah said calmly.

He looked at her again and his desperation growing.

"How is my experiment meant to stop a lightning bolt of plasma more than five hundred *million* kilometres long?"

"I don't know," Hani'ah said with a smile, "but I have faith we shall find out together."

Isaac studied her calm, trusting expression, but his vertigo only got worse. This was all too much. He didn't care anymore if this was real or a dream. He just wanted it to stop.

"I feel… a little…" he whispered, bringing a trembling hand to his forehead.

The chanting that now filled the chamber seemed to steal the last of his strength and Isaac's mind sparked with panic. He couldn't lose control now. Not here. If he stumbled and fell from this precarious platform…

But as the chamber began to spin around him, all he could do was picture himself falling from the platform and plummeting down, down, down to the swaying, singing people far below.

"Isaac," Hani'ah said quietly, her voice drawing his eyes back to her. "I know the burden you now carry and I understand your reluctance to believe. But there is no need to be afraid."

"Mm… tired," Isaac slurred.

"Then sleep, Isaac Taylor. There will be time to meet your destiny when you are rested."

And as her words registered in the tiny translator in his ear, Hani'ah's blind, staring eyes and the glinting red stone above them seemed to fill his vision.

A warm sensation spread through him and he let it come, hoping it would wash away the absurdity of this dream and take him home, or at the very least drag him to the depths of another world beyond this one. But as the strange sensation swamped his other senses, the impossible chamber with its chanting crowds and portentous night sky began to fade, carrying Isaac into a deep, welcome sleep.

GREAT BALLROOM, BAS QUIRAT - June 7, 2147 - 8.05pm

LOC TOOK ANOTHER SIP OF EXQUISITELY FINE NON-alcoholic wine and smiled at the pompous Quiration delegate who was patiently explaining another pointless cultural tradition. The Quiration's were proving to be infuriatingly good at wasting his time.

He would never normally attend a function like this without knowing every man and woman present, along with a hefty amount of background information on each of them, but necessity and the Triumvirate had thrust him into the fray, unarmed and unprepared. His only advantage seemed to be that the Quirations didn't want to upset him. That, and the fact his finely tuned political senses were screaming that something was wrong.

The tension in the room was palpable. These men didn't want to be entertaining an arrogant foreigner any more than the arrogant foreigner wanted to be entertained. Something far more important was occurring elsewhere.

"But what?" Loc asked silently.

Given their self-imposed economic isolation, the Quirations had previously held little interest for Loc, but that didn't mean Cosmotech hadn't gathered useful information on them.

He knew, for example, that despite public claims the Quirations were a fiercely united people, there were actually several serious divisions within the Bas Quirat. In fact, he'd seen irrefutable evidence that a full-blown religious war had been going on for months.

From what his sources had provided on the journey over, it appeared a significant minority were refusing to believe the word of Allah as translated by their Prophet, the mysterious Hani'ah Naziri. It was a shocking revelation to most, but didn't surprise Loc in the slightest. War seemed to be religion's default setting.

He laughed politely as the Quiration delegate completed another tedious anecdote and took another sip of wine.

"Tell me," he said in flawless Arabic, before the man could launch into yet another pointless story, "have you managed to capture the Quiration heretics yet?"

To the delegate's credit, there was only a flicker of hesitation in his eyes before he responded.

"I do not understand," he said with a polite frown.

"Please, forgive me," Loc said with a smile, "I'm not sure what you call them. Only, I heard there were subversive elements within the Bas Quirat preaching alternative scriptures."

"That is quite an offensive accusation," the delegate said, his expression now exuding serious concern. "I would like to know who speaks such lies."

"Yes, I'm sure you would," Loc said lightly, enjoying the man's acting, if not his answers. "But I severely doubt they would thank me for making the introduction. And besides, something tells me you may already possess this knowledge."

At this, the delegate's face clouded with affront and Loc knew it wasn't fake this time.

"You have been afforded a great honour, Loc Breeden of Cosmotech Defence," he said, echoing the words of almost every other person Loc had spoken to. "Let us not sully the moment with talk of treason."

MARS - END OF DAYS

"An honour I welcome," Loc replied smoothly, "but I'm ashamed to admit, I do not fully understand the extent of that honour. Please, tell me more about our gracious host, Hani'ah Naziri."

"Ah," the delegate said, clearly warming to this less controversial subject. "The Prophet Naziri is a wise and blessed host. I believe she will be here to answer your questions presently."

"I'm to be granted an audience?" Loc said, honestly surprised.

"Of course," the delegate said, his tone just a little gloating.

"And do you know when this audience will occur?"

"When Allah wills it," the man said with a mysterious wave of his hand.

"Then may he will it soon," Loc said, hiding his irritation and imagining the fool puncturing his own throat with a cheese knife. "Please, excuse me."

He bowed slightly before leaving the delegate's side and then headed for his security detail. They were standing by the room's grand doors and were matched by an equal number of Quiration ceremonial guards – both a diplomatic and yet firm statement about whose sovereign territory they were currently standing on.

Loc knew it was provocative to insist his security detail remain with him, but he'd be damned if he was going to give an inch when he knew so little about why they were even here. He trusted the Triumvirate – how could he do anything else – but he sure as hell didn't trust the Quirations.

At least he now knew he would be meeting Hani'ah Naziri, which made this political charade even more pointless.

He was looking forward to the 'honour'. Hani'ah Naziri was notorious for being illusive, even by Loc's standards, and Cosmotech had very little intelligence on the woman. All he knew for sure was that she was the Quiration's religious leader, their 'Prophet' as they liked to call her, and the real power behind their sham of an Islamic democracy.

109

There were no official links between Hani'ah and the consortium that originally proposed and funded the Bas Quirat, but there were many who believed it was built at her request. Or, to be fair, at the request of Allah who spoke through her.

Loc would have grimaced in disgust if he were in private. Even more so when he considered just how far the Quiration's insanity went. To those who believed, the Bas Quirat was considered their new Holy Land – something promised thousands of years earlier by another Islamic prophet – and was meant to replace the much-embattled Jerusalem of Earth.

It was all ludicrous, of course. Not for the clearly delusional religious context, but because Loc knew just how difficult it would have been to part the Islamic consortium from their money in the first place. Yes, the Bas Quirat had turned out to be an economic success on many levels, but there was no way they could have anticipated that at the time of building. Those with the money and power to make it happen would have required much more than religious promises to take such an incredible leap of faith.

"*Is that where the Triumvirate come into the picture?*" he thought, politely declining another pointless conversation as he made his way toward his security detail. "*Are they perhaps part of the consortium themselves? The First certainly looks the part. Did they perhaps groom this Hani'ah Naziri as they did me and then feed her information so she could fool her followers?*"

It made a lot more sense than the promise of a prophet thousands of year's dead. The barriers that had been raised to those outside the Bas Quirat also suggested Triumvirate intervention. Just as Loc did, they coveted control above all else and the underlying racist aversion to 'outsiders' that characterised so much Quiration legislation was perfect for controlling both their people and their economy. Quirations did not need, nor want, anything from anyone outside the Bas Quirat's glittering walls.

"*But that control is being challenged now,*" Loc thought to himself, "*thanks to the volatility of religion.*"

110

He held a great deal of professional admiration for the manipulative power of religion, but when it came to his own audience of business leaders and politicians, he much preferred logic and argument – along with a little psychic push on occasion. Yes, he used metaphors and yes, he tended to apply a heavy dose of political spin to any argument, but he very rarely spouted outright lies.

Religion, on the other hand, distributes fantastical stories like candy and yet still manages to convince otherwise intelligent people to ignore logic and apply no rational thought to their beliefs. As far as Loc was concerned, *faith* was simply the point at which 'true believers' stopped thinking for themselves.

But what annoyed and frustrated him more than anything else was religion's unfailing success rate. There seemed to be an instinctual switch inside people that made them *want* to be deceived. History was certainly littered with hundreds of wars in which humans killed each other in vast numbers and endlessly inventive ways simply for the right to say that their delusion was better than their enemy's.

And yet, no matter how ensconced a religion seemed to be in a society there was always another charismatic leader ready to rise from the latest generation and rally those experiencing the most despair into revolutionary action.

"*But who's causing trouble now?*" Loc asked silently.

Finally reaching his security detail, he carefully turned the Captain's back so none of the delegates or ceremonial guards could read their lips and then he spoke in a quiet voice.

"Have you contacted Lynt City?" he asked.

"Yes, sir," Captain West replied, his voice also low.

"And have they found them yet?"

Loc knew the Captain would be aware he was talking about Miana Raiken and Kurt Jones.

"No, sir," West replied. "They–"

"I'm not interested in excuses," Loc interrupted him quickly. "Have we coordinated with Lynt City Police?"

"Yes, sir," West continued, "but they're being... uncooperative. The primary target's former Police Captain, Simon Farraday, has requested a formal list of charges and access to the evidence supporting them. The process is taking longer than expected."

Loc's eyes narrowed.

"That idiot should know better than to get in my way," he said. "Leave it with me then. I'll get things moving as soon as I get a chance. What about our other concern?"

"She's stable, heavily sedated, and on her way to the orbital platform, as instructed."

"Good. Ensure your officers maintain strict information control whilst inside the Bas Quirat, Captain. Consider this hostile territory."

"Yes, sir," West finished.

Loc felt a new frustration settle over him. It appeared Miana's former employer had discovered a hidden reserve of political courage. Well, Loc would make certain he paid for that little mistake. Until he could get at Miana, he would have to be content with destroying anyone unwise enough to help her.

At least they'd managed to capture Anya Polovski. It should have been a satisfying victory, but when taken in conjunction with Miana's brazen theft of Cosmotech's entire Lynt City database, there was little to be happy about. There was no legal way she could use the information to attack Cosmotech, of that he was certain, but he also knew better than anyone that knowledge was power and Miana now had more than enough to create serious problems.

With that thought, an unfamiliar tension settled in Loc's jaw. He still couldn't work out how Miana had convinced Mr. Drevit to work for her. There was some consolation knowing the assassin had paid for the betrayal with his life, but Loc would have preferred to question and punish the traitor himself.

In any other circumstance, he would have admired Miana's scheming. She'd accomplished what no one had managed before her. In fact, it would have even been a welcome distraction if the Triumvirate weren't so unforgiving.

Running a hand through his immaculate blonde hair, Loc turned to face the delegates once more and was surprised to find them all bowing low.

He turned to where they were bowing and saw a tall, regal-looking woman in light blue robes standing between two shorter figures that were covered completely in black.

"*Hani'ah Naziri,*" he guessed.

She was taller than Loc expected and her clouded eyes held more confidence than a blind person had any right to. She was also quite beautiful, but her face was unadorned with makeup and she wore only a modest, white-gold headchain that held a small ruby at the centre of her forehead.

"The blessings of Allah be upon you all," she said in strong, clear Arabic. "I will speak with Loc Breeden alone."

Loc turned to look at the delegates and gauge their reaction, and wasn't particularly surprised when they obeyed their prophet like well-trained pets. There were no glances his way and no hesitation whatsoever. They simply bowed low and left in an orderly fashion via the chamber's enormous doors.

At the same time, the Quiration soldiers formed up around Loc's security detail, making it clear they were meant to leave the chamber as well.

"Wait for me outside," he told Captain West, seeing no reason to be concerned.

"Yes, sir," Captain West nodded smartly.

Loc waited for the two groups to leave and then turned to approach his host.

"Hani'ah Naziri," he said in his best Arabic. "You do me great honour by receiving me in person."

Hani'ah seemed to stare straight through him for several seconds and Loc couldn't help but notice the two black clad figures were eyeing him closely.

"Loc Breeden," she said eventually, adding no welcoming words. "I trust all your needs have been catered for?"

"Your hospitality is impeccable," Loc said, bowing low in a perfect imitation of the Quiration delegates.

"Very good," she said, ignoring his bow and sweeping past him, "and now, I would like to know about Miana Raiken and Kurt Jones."

Loc was momentarily stunned into silence. How did she know about Miana?

"*The Triumvirate*," he concluded. "*They may be coaching her after all.*"

Hani'ah turned to him and smiled in a way that made Loc reconsider her blindness.

"What would you like to know?" he asked calmly.

"What do they know of Isaac Taylor?"

Loc didn't see the connection, but neither did he see any harm in answering truthfully.

"They know nothing about him."

"And what is their interest in you?"

Loc paused. He didn't like Hani'ah's arrogant tone, but decided it would be unwise to antagonise the most powerful person in the Bas Quirat.

"Miana Raiken was, until recently, a forensic detective with the Lynt City Police Department," he told her honestly. "She attempted to link me with the suicide of Doctor Naseem Indari, a geologist from Lynt City. After suffering the political consequences, she's been hunting for more evidence on her own."

"Why is she still alive?" Hani'ah asked, not batting an eyelid.

"There were... complications," Loc replied slowly, not wanting to admit any of the details. "Forgive me, but why do you want to know this?"

"What do they know about you?" she continued, ignoring his question.

Loc's jaw muscles tightened. This was no way to treat an honoured guest, let alone a man of his power and influence.

"Nothing of importance," he replied.

"Then she is unaware of your psychic abilities?"

Loc glared at her in confusion.

"What do you know of–"

"The question was," Hani'ah interrupted him smoothly, "what does Miana Raiken and Kurt Jones know about you?"

Loc stared at her for a long moment and then intentionally relaxed his muscles. This so called 'prophet' had clearly been supplied with more information than he anticipated, but it didn't mean he had to submit to being manipulated.

"Miana is aware of my... abilities," he said calmly. "By now, Kurt is likely aware of them too."

"And they have access to Cosmotech's entire database of information," Hani'ah said with a hint of disapproval.

Loc felt his temperature rising again. How could she know all this if not by some connection with the Triumvirate? For a moment he contemplated using his psychic powers to confirm it, but wasn't sure if they would even work on someone who was blind.

"Your powers are nothing compared to the sight of Allah," Hani'ah said, interrupting his thoughts.

Again, Loc was thrown, but suddenly he had the answer he was looking for.

"You're psychic as well," he said.

"Clairvoyant," Hani'ah corrected him. "Your mind is open to me, Loc Breeden, as are all others."

The admission seemed to pull what little advantage Loc still had out from under him and he finally allowed himself a frown.

"Why are you interested in Miana and Kurt?" he asked carefully.

"They will come to the Bas Quirat," Hani'ah replied.

"What? How do you know?"

Loc could think of no reason Miana would follow him here. There was certainly no information on the Cosmotech server that might tell her where he'd gone.

"They will follow the path you left for them," Hani'ah replied in an accusing tone. "It will lead them here."

Loc felt another wave of frustration and his temper strained against the shackles of his better judgement.

"You seem to have mistaken me for one of your devoted followers," he said in a cold, deliberate tone. "I don't know how this information came into your possession, but if there is a point to your accusations then, by all means, please get to it."

Hani'ah's dead eyes bored into him, the ruby on her forehead glinting angrily.

"They are not coming for you, Loc Breeden," she said, ignoring his tone. "They seek a man linked to Naseem Indari. A man they must not find."

Loc's eyes narrowed. He'd thought Naseem Indari's case was closed and certainly wasn't aware of any link to an outside party. Could this man she spoke of be the source of Hani'ah's information? The Triumvirate had mentioned Miana made contact with a 'heretic' of some sort. Could it be that whoever was leading the rebellion within the Bas Quirat was one and the same?

If that was the case, Loc knew less that he anticipated and it made him wonder what else the Triumvirate was keeping from him.

"You know all you need to," Hani'ah said, as if answering his thoughts again.

"Stay out of my head, prophet," Loc hissed, his temper giving way. "I'm not one of your devout puppets and I have no allegiance to the Bas Quirat. You would be unwise to make an enemy of me."

"And yet you are essential to our prophecies," Hani'ah replied, as if it were a shame.

"Don't give me that," Loc snapped. "Your scriptures have no hold over me or my future."

"Your ignorance is immaterial," Hani'ah assured him with a smugness that made his jaw muscles twitch again. "You will believe in time."

"Why are you even telling me this?" he asked, trying to steer things in a different direction.

"As I said, you are crucial to the fulfilment of the sacred prophecy," Hani'ah replied with an impatient wave of her hand, "and you should be aware that your role is being threatened."

"If you truly believe that then do something about it," Loc countered. "Close down your borders. Make it impossible for Miana and Kurt to get into the Bas Quirat."

"The disruption will not make their path any harder than it already is," Hani'ah replied, "and the attention will not suit my goals."

"Attention?" Loc sneered. "Ah, yes. Your weak-willed congregation has been misbehaving, hasn't it? Is the man they're looking for the one leading your heretics, perhaps?"

At this, Hani'ah's expression firmed and Loc realised he'd finally hit a nerve.

"You have what you need," she said coldly, turning away from him. "Now I must go. I will contact you when Miana Raiken and Kurt Jones have been killed."

Loc felt an urge to call her back so he could capitalise on his petty victory, but he knew it would only make him look weak and so he simply glared at her as she glided away with her two black-clad servants in tow.

"Good luck with that," he called after her in English. "You're going to need it."

But Hani'ah didn't give him any indication she'd heard him before disappearing through the archway she'd entered through.

"*Sanctimonious bitch,*" he thought, enjoying the possibility she may still be close enough to read his mind.

He knew he shouldn't allow his temper to rise so high, but he wasn't used to feeling ignorant and the way Hani'ah had spoken to him had gotten under in skin.

Spinning on his heel with a growl, Loc headed for the exit and decided it was time to regain a little ground of his own.

"We'll see who ends up killing who, prophet."

SCIENCE LEVEL 12, BAS QUIRAT - June 8, 2147 - 1.13am

DR. GRAYSON WORKED FEVERISHLY ON THE INTERFACE
that linked P.A.T.R.I.C. – Isaac's ingenious psychic transmutation
device – with the containment systems he'd designed to control the
incredible energies it was capable of producing.

His work was progressing well. In fact, the Quiration scientists
were quite adequate technicians and their obedience was flawless,
no doubt a result of their cultural expectations. But there was still
so much to be done.

Given the nature of his position within Cosmotech, Dr. Grayson
was used to being pushed for results. Driven and hounded even. But
this time was different. Since Isaac had appeared in this unfortunate
reality, Dr. Grayson's demons had been somewhat… *inconsistent* in
their usual methods of coercion.

At first he assumed the periods of mental silence were a result of
the concentration he was devoting to their insidious goal, but the
ongoing evidence didn't support that assertion.

When his mind inevitably wandered from his work, he should
have been punished. He *needed* to be punished. He didn't want to
think about the terrible conclusion his work was leading toward.

And yet the closer he came to completing his demons' grand design, the more his traitorous mind began to contemplate the same, pointless question.

"*Am I really going to do this?*"

The thought made Dr. Grayson cringe in anticipation of punitive action, but his demons failed to appear yet again and their absence came with a conflicting sense of anxiety and wretched hope.

"It doesn't matter what I want," he hissed, the anxiety quickly winning out.

He knew there was no turning back now. Even if his demons failed to notice his momentary lapse in concentration, they would not be gone forever. No matter what he might wish were true, they were certain to rematerialize eventually and would make him pay for any foolish thoughts of reprieve that still lingered in his mind.

In fact, this was probably some kind of cruel joke. A test of his resolve that could only end with a brutal lesson in obedience.

"I'll do it," Dr. Grayson growled in desperation, "I'm *doing* it!"

But the words went unanswered, just as his dangerous thoughts had done earlier, and it only made his anxiety grow worse.

"*Where are you?*" he thought wretchedly.

Could his demons be somehow distracted? Was there something outside his own mind that needed their attention?

It didn't make sense, of course, but it was all Dr. Grayson could think and it left him feeling angry. In a perverse kind of way he'd become accustomed to his demons and their constant attentions. Along with the promise of pain, the only thing they'd ever offered him was their constant presence. It almost felt like a betrayal that they would abandon him to finish their terrible work alone.

Shaking his head in frustration, Dr. Grayson placed the delicate component he'd been working on back into the connection slot he'd designed for it and carefully clamped the housing shut.

"It will be done," he said firmly, ignoring the slightly puzzled expressions of the Quiration scientists who'd been monitoring his work.

As he continued his work, a traitorous sense of doubt lingered at the very edge of his awareness, but his anger helped him keep it at bay. It was a trap. He knew it was. His path was already set and the end his demons had forced him to engineer was the only escape he could hope for.

And with that thought, Dr. Grayson's concentration returned.

"Not long," he mumbled to himself. "Not long at all."

MIANA DREAMED. SHE KNEW IT WAS A DREAM BECAUSE she was back in the caves far beneath Mars' surface and yet she was wearing no survival suit and felt no cold.

There was someone walking ahead of her, leading her toward the cavern where they'd found Dr. Naseem Indari and, whoever it was, they were wearing a Mylinric life-suit.

The innocuous fact sparked something in the back of Miana's mind, but it didn't take hold and she was left with an uneasy feeling.

"Who are you?"

She drifted along behind the figure until they reached the cavern and stopped just inside the entrance, then she drifted past until she was able to turn and see through the helmet of the person she'd been following.

"Loc Breeden," she thought in surprise.

It was Loc without a doubt, wearing a thunderous expression that didn't look quite right. His eyes were also focused on something deeper in the cavern and Miana turned to find someone in a survival suit crouched beside some complex mechanical apparatus set up next to the cavern's pool.

"Doctor Indari," she thought in realisation. *"Is this... really a dream?"*

She felt herself drifting sideways and was soon able to see both Loc and Dr. Indari at the same time.

"Traitor," she heard Loc say in a voice that quivered with anger.

Dr. Indari looked up from his work and slowly rose to his feet.

"How did you find me?" he asked calmly.

"Blasphemer," Loc replied, ignoring the question.

Dr. Indari dropped the knife he'd been stripping wires with and walked forward a few steps.

"It has been so long, my brothers," he said. "Do you not wish to know how I still live?"

"Desecrator," Loc growled in reply.

At this, Dr. Indari lowered his gaze and sighed. Then he turned to look at Miana.

"You must have questions," he said, as if he was talking to her.

Miana felt a chill, unsure if she was meant to answer.

"Outcast," Loc spoke into the silence.

"I have seen beyond the end," Dr. Indari continued, still looking at Miana. "I have seen the truth and it is unacceptable."

"Your sight has been cursed," Loc added. "You see nothing but lies."

"Would you like to see the truth?" Dr. Indari asked, his eyes drilling into Miana.

She nodded hesitantly, not sure what was happening, and then gasped when a shadowy form appeared behind Dr. Indari. It loomed over him, almost half again as tall and twice as wide. She couldn't make out any detail beyond the suggestive curve of a back and the bulge of a limb, but it was hard to focus on anything other than two glistening red eyes that glowed near the top of the shadowy mass.

"Your truth is a delusion," Loc snarled, and Miana turned to see that he too was now accompanied by shadowy figures.

Unlike Dr. Indari, there were five figures instead of one, all crowded in a tight semi-circle. Their eyes also blazed with red light, but rather than looking at Miana, they were focused on the figure behind Dr. Indari.

"Who are you?" Miana asked, addressing her question to the one that appeared to be looking at her.

"I am the one who remained," Dr. Indari said solemnly.

"You were abandoned," Loc disagreed. "Discarded for your lack of worth."

"I don't understand," Miana said.

"You have seen what I have seen," Dr. Indari told her.

"We have seen only the one truth path," Loc replied, as if the words had been directed to him.

"I saw..." Miana said slowly, "I saw this planet covered in life."

"One truth, yes," Dr. Indari replied. "The sacred truth we were sworn to protect."

"You are not one of us!" Loc snarled. "You are tainted. Cursed!"

Miana heard Loc's words, but she wasn't listening. Her mind was full of the horror she'd witnessed in the alien cave.

"I saw... red fire," she said slowly.

"The end came for us all," Dr. Indari explained. "The red fire spared no one."

"You know nothing," Loc spat. "The red fire will be tamed."

Miana turned to look at Loc for a moment and then moved her gaze back to Dr. Indari.

"I saw it destroy my people," she added. "On this planet... as it is now."

"The time approaches," Dr. Indari said with a nod.

"Your traitorous lies will not survive to taint the Saviour," Loc said, his voice firm.

"Who is the Saviour?" Miana asked.

"He is the only hope you have," Dr. Indari replied.

Miana felt her confusion growing as Loc snarled another reply.

"Hope is a mere fiction created for the purpose of control. The Saviour *will* prevail, as we have seen it."

Miana stared at the hulking figure that shadowed Dr. Indari.

"Is there a way to stop it?" she asked. "What do I do?"

"Take me with you," Dr. Indari said solemnly. "Deliver my sight to the Saviour and let the entire truth be known."

"Blasphemer!" Loc snarled. "Outcast! Your cursed sight is nothing but lies and you will *never* be one of us."

Miana saw the figures crowding behind Loc rise up and felt terror tighten its grip on her heart.

"I don't understand," she said desperately, returning her gaze to Dr. Indari. "This is just a dream… isn't it? Are you even talking to me?"

"It is and I am," Dr. Indari said with another nod, "and my dreams must be heard."

"Enough, desecrator!" Loc snarled. "You are nothing but a twisted abortion of the sacred power. Feel the sanctity of truth flow through your tainted soul and do as we command. Pick up the knife."

Miana saw Dr. Indari turn to pick up the knife he'd dropped to the cavern floor, all the while keeping his eyes on her, and realised what was about to happen.

"No!" she said desperately. "You have to fight it! You can't give in!"

"I have seen beyond the end," Dr. Indari said solemnly, "and what dwells there must not come to pass."

Miana tried to rush forward, to stop Dr. Indari from hurting himself, but she couldn't move. She could only watch in horror as he broke eye contact and turned to walk toward the habitat where she'd found his broken body.

"No!" Miana shouted, sitting up suddenly.

"Woah, woah, woah," Kurt said from right beside her. "Calm down, Miana. It's okay. You're okay."

Miana blinked in confusion and looked around the strange room she was in.

Panic clung to her like an icy robe and, despite Kurt's touch, she couldn't stop shivering.

"Hey," Kurt spoke softly, pulling her into his arms, "it's alright."

Miana resisted for a moment, the fear holding her muscles tight, then she buried her face in his chest and began to cry. The sobs broke out of her as if the banks of an emotional dam had been broken and slowly, with each jerking breath, the panic and fear bled away.

"It's over," Kurt said quietly, gently stroking her hair. "You're safe."

Miana knew she was stronger than this. A career in law enforcement and murder investigation had made her hard in more ways than one. But she'd been holding on to too much and knew if she didn't let some of it go she would sink into depression and be unable to continue. And so she let it gush out of her. She let it go until she was light enough to pull herself together and gently push Kurt away.

"Where am I?" she asked, wiping her eyes and looking around the strange room once again.

"A unit in the Cenovian district," Kurt replied, "not far from Cosmotech offices."

"Cosmotech?" Miana gasped, her other memories pushing to the fore. "What happened? How did we get out of there?"

"I... got us out," Kurt said, sounding guilty.

"How?" she asked, afraid she already knew the answer.

"I used the power," Kurt replied, not looking at her.

"On who?" Miana asked sharply.

"Does it matter?" he answered, his expression angry.

"Of course it matters," Miana replied, her own anger pushing forward. "You do realize Loc has been killing people to keep his dirty secret, don't you? You may have unwittingly condemned whoever you controlled to death!"

"It was the only way," Kurt snapped, getting up so he could pace the room. "Drevit was dead so there was no way we were getting back to the dome. The only way out was through doors that required authorization, and we didn't have any."

At the mention of Drevit's death, Miana felt her own rush of guilt and realized there was another reason she was so angry and it had nothing to do with Kurt.

"I did what I had to," he continued. "What do you think they would have done to us if I'd surrendered?"

"Look, I'm… sorry," Miana said, finding the words hard to vocalise. "I didn't mean to snap at you, I just…"

She turned away, not wanting to look him in the eyes.

"Let's just forget it, okay?" he said, sitting down beside her again. "We've both been through a lot and you were seriously fatigued."

Miana knew she couldn't blame him for doing what he thought was best in a dangerous and stressful situation. She'd seen it many times before and knew there was rarely an obvious right or wrong way to react.

"How many people did you…?" she began to ask, but was unable to finish.

"Only two," Kurt said quickly. "Once they told me how to get out, I made one of them give me the authorisation I needed and then told them to forget everything that had happened today. I even told them to lie down and go to sleep."

"Forget?" Miana asked.

"Hey, you said it. Loc has been killing people to keep his secret. If they start talking about being controlled, how long do you think they'll survive?"

Miana turned to look at him and felt a new level of respect settle alongside a touch of embarrassment.

"Do you think it will work?" she asked.

"Honestly, I have no idea," he replied with a shrug, "but I had to try."

Miana managed a smile, but it disappeared when she heard a gentle knock on the door.

"Who's that?" she asked in alarm.

"Ah… that's my friend, Yasmin," Kurt told her quietly, before speaking a little louder, "come in."

Miana frowned with concern. How could Kurt drag anyone else into this mess? She also assumed Yasmin was a woman's name and it touched off something inside of her that only got worse when the door opened to reveal one of the most painfully beautiful women Miana had ever seen.

"I heard you… talking and thought I'd bring Miana something to eat," she said, her plump lips curved in a tentative smile. "You must be famished."

"Uh… yes," Miana said carefully. "Thank you."

"I'm Yasmin, by the way," she said, entering the room with a sway that made Miana feel old and awkward. "Just in case Handsome hasn't told you already."

"Handsome?" Miana said, turning to give Kurt a questioning look.

"Just a nick name," Kurt said, with an embarrassed laugh. "Yasmin was born in the Bas Quirat and came to Lynt City looking for adventure. We've shared many."

"And I thought *my* people were modest," Yasmin replied, raising an immaculately traced eyebrow.

There was something about the way she looked at Kurt that rubbed Miana the wrong way, but she kept her expression neutral. She seemed to be this woman's guest, after all, and Yasmin had unwittingly put herself in considerable danger by helping them.

Turning her attention to the plate of food placed in front of her, Miana's jealousy and concern quickly took a back seat to hunger. She was famished.

Attacking her breakfast with gusto, Miana couldn't believe how good it tasted. The fruit was amazing and the yoghurt was even better, but it was the tea that made the last of her irritation melt away.

"This tea is delicious," she said. "What is it?"

"A lily and mandarin infusion," Yasmin said, blushing slightly. "I make it with home grown ingredients."

"It's wonderful, thank you."

"You're welcome," Yasmin said with a demure smile. "Now, if Handsome hasn't already told you, there's a bathroom through that door there. I've put some fresh towels on the sink. Please, feel free to use any of the toiletries. This is the guest room so they're all new."

"That's great, thanks," Miana replied.

"I'll go and select some clothes that should fit you and leave them on your bed."

"Oh no, I couldn't-" Miana began.

"I insist," Yasmin replied firmly. "I have more than enough and from what Handsome has been telling me, you don't have the luxury of returning home for your own."

Miana gave Kurt another look, wondering just how much he'd told her, but he just shrugged.

"Okay," she said, returning her gaze to Yasmin. "Thanks, Yasmin. We really appreciate your help."

Yasmin nodded once in reply and then left in a swirl of flowery perfume.

When the door closed again, Kurt wore an apologetic grin.

"Handsome, huh?" Miana said mildly.

"She's just a friend," Kurt assured her, "and I only told her enough to make sure she knew not to tell anyone else we were here."

Miana ignored him for a moment and took another sip of tea before speaking again.

"My leg feels fine, by the way."

"It was only a graze in the end," Kurt said. "It healed up well."

"How long have I been asleep?"

"Nearly twelve hours."

"Twelve hours?" Miana said, a little shocked.

"You were exhausted," Kurt explained, "and after everything that happened... well, I didn't want to disturb you."

Miana knew it was the only sensible thing to do, but she still felt miffed. Things were getting even more serious, if that were possible, and time wasn't a luxury they had to spare.

"What about the information from Cosmotech? Did we get it?"

130

"We got everything stored in their servers," Kurt replied with a nod, "but I don't know if any of it's useful. I've spent several hours going through it already and found nothing that helps. There's just too much of it. Cosmotech are running thousands of projects, Miana. They also employ millions of people, here, on Earth, and in a dozen space stations spotted around the solar system. I don't think we're going to find what we need unless we narrow the search."

"I think I can help with that," Miana said as Dr. Indari's words came back to her. "But first, I've been asleep a long time and I really need to pee."

"Oh, sure," Kurt said, getting up quickly. "Take your time. We'll work on the database whenever you're ready."

"Kurt," Miana said, grabbing his arm before he could leave.

"Yes?" he said, looking back at her.

She held onto him for a moment, enjoying the feel of his muscles and the warmth of his skin, then she spoke softly into the silence.

"I'm sorry I snapped earlier. I wasn't angry at you."

"You were too," Kurt said with a smile. "But don't worry, I forgive you. Now get to it. We've got plenty of work ahead of us."

Miana smiled as he left the room, but it fell away when her mind returned to what would come next.

"*The time is approaches,*" she thought with a frown. "*And this is one deadline we can't afford to miss.*"

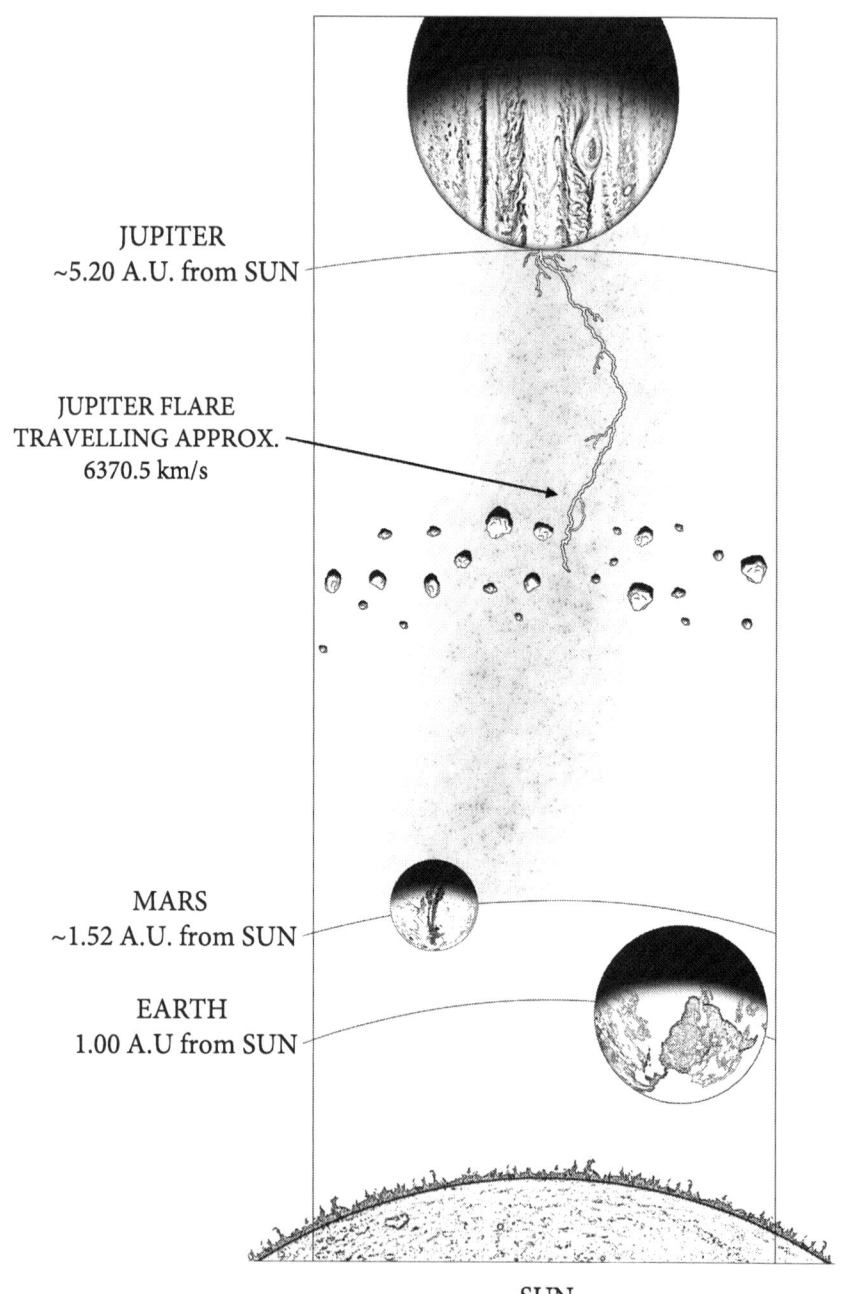

JUPITER
~5.20 A.U. from SUN

JUPITER FLARE
TRAVELLING APPROX.
6370.5 km/s

MARS
~1.52 A.U. from SUN

EARTH
1.00 A.U from SUN

SUN

1 Astronomical Unit (A.U.) = ~149.6 x 10^6 km

VIP GUEST QUARTERS, BAS QUIRAT - June 8, 2147 - 6.00am

ISAAC WOKE WITH A START, HIS BODY SLICK WITH sweat. He'd been dreaming the same dream again – red fire burning him in the darkness of space.

He took in several deep breaths, waiting for the terror to fade, then he gradually relaxed his grip on the sheets and took in his surroundings.

"Wow," he said in amazement.

Rich colours filled the space and polished gold trim traced every edge, weaving intricate patterns through the colours like eighteen carrot spider webs. From his huge four poster bed, he could see a living area with four lavish couches laden with dozens of intricately patterned pillows. The walls surrounding the enormous space were covered in large paintings and finely woven dioramas, and it was these that reminded Isaac where he was – the Bas Quirat.

"Oooh…" he groaned as reality sunk its claws into his brain.

In the last few days, he'd woken in far too many unfamiliar places. Admittedly, two of those places had been luxurious beyond imagining, but it was hard to enjoy given the circumstances.

He turned to haul himself out of bed and jumped when he saw a robed figure standing next to him.

"Sabah el kheer, blessed one," the man said with only a slight Quiration accent.

"Mmm…" Isaac grunted, feeling a little annoyed. "Who are you?"

"I am Hakim Bukhari, blessed one. Please, consider me your most humble servant. I am here to assist you in any way necessary. If you would like anything, anything at all, you need only ask."

Isaac hopped off the bed, not sure if he liked this kind of attention. Hakim simply bowed low and touched the wall behind him. In response, a line of hanging garments slid out of the wall next to the bed.

Isaac blinked in surprise. He glanced at Hakim for a moment and then chose the first thing he saw – a silken dressing gown – and quickly slipped it on before walking into the bathroom.

Hakim walked in quietly behind him and Isaac hesitated a moment. He'd grown up with a twin brother and so he was used to doing his business in front of someone else, but this wasn't quite the same.

"Uh… do you mind waiting outside, Hakim?" he asked.

"Of course, blessed one," the servant said with another bow. "Please, do not hesitate to call me if you require anything."

Thankful he didn't have to fight for his privacy, Isaac waited for Hakim to step outside and then stood before the sparkling toilet and let his bladder do its thing. When he was done, the toilet flushed itself and Isaac contemplated having a shower.

"I'd better if I'm going to see Hani'ah again," he thought to himself.

There was something about the Quiration prophet that exuded cleanliness and he didn't want to embarrass himself. Of course, that might not be possible now that he'd officially been declared a Messiah.

Rubbing his face in exasperation, Isaac stepped into what he assumed was the shower and paused when he couldn't find any kind of shower head. There weren't any obvious taps either.

"What the hell…" he thought with a frown.

He didn't want to ask Hakim to come back in and so he kept searching until he noticed some red and blue tiles about halfway up one side. He touched one of the red tiles and jumped in surprise when the shower's entire ceiling erupted with warm water.

He held a palm up to the water and smiled.

"*Perfect temperature,*" he thought.

Knowing time was probably short, Isaac slipped off his dressing gown, pulled his silken boxers down and stepped under the water. It was like standing in heavy, heated rain. It felt wonderful. The terror from his dream was washed away in an instant and the amazing lotions he found on a small inbuilt shelf made it hard to bring the shower to an end.

Reluctantly, however, when he was as clean as it was possible to get, Isaac sighed in resignation and stepped out from under the water.

With another touch of the red tile, the water stopped flowing and Isaac turned to dry himself with one of the softest towels he'd ever touched. He saw some freshly washed and neatly folded undergarments waiting beside the towels and put them on before striding back into the bedroom to look for his clothes.

When he emerged from the bathroom, he found Hakim waiting with several other Quirations – all men – who each held a piece of clothing he didn't recognise.

"Uh… hi," he said uncertainly .

"If we may impose, blessed one?" Hakim said with an apologetic smile. "We have ceremonial robes made just for you."

"Oh," Isaac said, remembering the robes Hani'ah's companions had put on him the night before. "Sure, I guess."

"Many thanks, blessed one," Hakim said with a bow, before ushering the others forward.

Isaac tensed a little, unsure what was expected of him, but the Quirations were both gentle and efficient. In a few short minutes, he was standing in front of a large mirror and admiring a long silken robe that was secured around his waist with a thick white sash.

Running a hand through his unruly hair, Isaac heard a familiar mumbling and turned to find Dr. Grayson seated on one of the colourful couches.

"Good morning, doctor Grayson," he said, feeling a warmth for the strange man that he knew was a little desperate given they'd only known each other for a day or so.

"Isaac," Dr. Grayson said, looking up from the couch as if surprised to see him. "It is good to see you."

"And you," Isaac said, walking toward him and sitting on the couch opposite. "Everything's been a little... strange since we arrived."

"Yes," Dr. Grayson agreed. "And now there is much work to be done. Please, eat something and we will depart."

Isaac wasn't sure what Dr. Grayson was talking about, but a moment later the grand doors to his room opened and a procession of people holding large covered dishes walked in. As he watched in slightly detached amazement, they began to fill the table between himself and Dr. Grayson with a veritable feast of breakfast foods. There were steaming dishes of soup and freshly sliced meats alongside breads and dips of all colours. There were also several mounds of exquisitely carved fruit that looked almost too good to eat.

Isaac stared at it all for a long moment, not sure where to start.

"This is... incredible," he said, glancing at Hakim.

"Your reaction pleases me, blessed one," Hakim replied with a smile. "We would have the Messiah well satisfied on this fateful day."

Hakim's words brought the reality of his situation back into focus and Isaac frowned. Did he really have time for such luxuries when the world was about to end?

But before he could decide otherwise, Isaac's stomach growled a definitive answer and he gave in to its demands gladly.

Each morsel of food he chose brimmed with flavour and seemed somehow fresher than the last. He chose several meats, some sliced vegetables and broke apart and devoured an amazingly soft and crusty bun. He then tried several of the dips which were spicy in a way he'd never tasted before and finished with a large coffee that lured him in with a rich and promising aroma.

When he was finally done, Isaac chose a whole pear that sat on one side of the incredible fruit platter and rose to his feet.

"I'm done," he said to Dr. Grayson with a smile.

"Not yet," Dr. Grayson said, rising to his feet and shuffling toward the doors.

Isaac shrugged, conceding that he was probably right, and then followed the doctor out of the room.

"So," he said as they joined the large entourage of body guards that had, for once, waited outside. "Did they tell you about... the end of all things?"

"And your role in it," Dr. Grayson replied. "Quite fascinating."

"And you believe it?" Isaac asked incredulously.

"Belief is irrelevant," Dr. Grayson said with a wave of his hand. "There is evidence of an approaching disaster and our work, although seemingly unrelated, may indeed prove to be connected."

"So... you don't believe it," Isaac reasoned carefully, "but you think there could be another explanation as to why they think I'm... so important?"

"Truth is a subjective creation, Isaac," Dr. Grayson replied with a mysterious smile. "That pear you're eating remains a pear even if I believe it is an apple."

Isaac stared at the pear for a moment and then took a large vindictive bite out of it.

"I just..." he said between chews, "I just don't know what they expect from me."

"You will do what you will do," Dr. Grayson assured him, as if that helped.

"But what happens if I don't do what they *think* I'm going to do? There are thousands of people depending on me–"

"Millions," Dr. Grayson interrupted him absently.

"Right, thanks," Isaac said with a frown. "And who are they going to blame if I don't perform this miracle that they're expecting?"

"Miracles are even more subjective than belief," Dr. Grayson replied. "Do you not consider your passage into this reality a miracle?"

"That's just science gone wrong," Isaac protested.

"And what about when we get it right?" Dr. Grayson asked with another mysterious smile.

Isaac understood what he was saying, but it didn't change the powerless feeling at his core. He was – by someone else's definition – holding the lives of millions of people in his hand and yet he had no idea how he was meant to save them.

"I don't know," he said with a sigh. "It would just be nice to have some control over my life again."

"And you will," Dr. Grayson assured him. "Now come, let me show you what we've accomplished while you slumbered."

Isaac took another bite of his pear in resignation. No matter what crazy beliefs the Quirations attached to his work, at least he had a very real chance of finishing it and maybe even getting back to his brother Jason. If that also meant saving the world in the process, well... that clearly wasn't up to him.

"*I'll do what I do,*" he said, quoting Dr. Grayson with a shrug. "*If that isn't good enough, then I guess I won't be alive long enough to suffer the consequences.*"

KURT WATCHED MIANA AS SHE CAME OUT OF THE bedroom. Now that she'd had a shower and, by the looks of it, washed and brushed her hair, she looked more relaxed and in control.

Not surprisingly, she'd chosen one of the more practical outfits Yasmin had offered her and Kurt couldn't help thinking that she looked beautiful. She didn't have Yasmin's figure, or her glamorous looks for that matter, but there was something about Miana that made his libido sit up and take notice.

"Right, let's get started," she said in her usual straight-forward manner. "Where's the database."

"Right here," Kurt said, motioning to a seat at the table. "Would you like to do the honours?"

"Definitely not," Miana said, sitting down beside him. "Technology and I don't get along."

"Okay," Kurt said with a smile. "So, where do you want to start?"

"Did you find anything about Loc Breeden?"

"Not much, I'm afraid," he replied, bringing up the files he'd found earlier. "Most of it's just public relations garbage. He obviously holds a lot of power within Cosmotech, but he's only ever listed as a consultant."

139

"Damn," Miana said with a frown. "I was hoping to place him in the chain of command, at least. Did you find anything about what he's been working on?"

"Not a thing," Kurt said reluctantly. "It was kind of annoying given the huge number of projects Cosmotech has running at the moment."

"Alright," Miana said, with less disappointment than he expected. "We obviously won't find what we need that way."

She stood up again and, with a familiar expression, began to pace the room. Kurt knew better than to interrupt her whilst she was thinking and so he waited until she returned and put her hands on the table.

"Do you know what kind of file types the M.G.C. uses?"

"Mars Global Communications?" Kurt asked, not sure where she was headed. "You mean, like, video links?"

"Video links, audio files, anything like that, yes."

"Well, sure," he said, tapping a few file extensions into the search browser. "I'll see if they have… wow."

The screen had filled in an instant and the file indicator at the bottom of the screen was still ticking into the millions.

"What?" Miana asked.

"There's… a *lot* of them," Kurt replied, wondering how many people this must represent.

"That's good. Have they got time references on them?"

Kurt highlighted a file at random and a small list of metadata popped onto the screen.

"Yeah. Date and time stamp, location, file length… and plenty more. Why?"

"Look for a file marked August fifth, last year, time stamp oh-eight-four-two."

Kurt did as she asked.

"There's something there," he said. "A whole thread of files actually. But none of them look large enough to hold video."

"What's in them?"

Kurt opened a file at random and the image of a man appeared on his screen. He was wearing a dark blue turban and looked old – in his sixties or seventies at least – but his dark eyes were intense and beneath a large, regal-looking nose, he sported a thick black beard that had two grey streaks running from the edge of his mouth down to its neatly manicured corners.

"This one used to be a video file, but they've deleted everything except a single frame," he told Miana. "I think this is the guy that received the call."

Miana studied the face for a long moment.

"Can you find out who called him?" she asked.

"Let's see," Kurt said, opening the complete file extension.

An information profile for the man in the image was attached, but there was nothing on the person who made the call.

"Nothing," he told Miana, "but… hang on."

He paused. The information profile was much larger than he expected.

"What is it?" Miana asked.

"Everything," Kurt said slowly. "I mean, everything on the man who took the call. Saadi Khalil. I can tell you his family tree going out and back almost a dozen branches. I can tell you his psychological profile, his eating habits, his favourite media programs… who is this guy? And why do they have so much information on him?"

He looked up and saw Miana wearing a grim expression.

"I think Saadi Khalil is the man Dr. Indari was communicating with before he died."

Kurt looked back at the bearded face on the screen.

"This is the guy you were trying to find?"

"He could be."

"Then he might… he might know something about the alien cave?"

"If he's not already dead," Miana agreed quietly. "They know so much about him, so..."

141

Kurt's heart sank. Of course he'd be dead. After the way Dr. Indari was killed, there's no way Loc would let someone who'd been in contact with him remain alive. He sighed, returning his attention to the man's profile, and something caught his eye.

"Hang on," he said, double-checking the date and time stamp again. "I've got a reference dated only a few weeks ago."

"What?" Miana said, leaning forward beside him.

"There's a whole bunch of them, stretching back almost six months. They're locations, I think. It looks like they've been tracking him. But…"

"What?" Miana prompted.

"The location markers are all in the Bas Quirat," Kurt finished.

"The Bas Quirat?" Miana said, her voice strong again. "No wonder he's still alive. Even Loc's influence can't reach that far."

"And if this Saadi had contact with Dr. Indari… do you think he might have visited the cave at some point? Could he have psychic powers too?"

"I don't know, but we have to talk to him," Miana said firmly.

Kurt turned to look at her.

"Okay," he said slowly. "I get that this is a good lead, a great one even, but he's in the Bas Quirat, Miana. There's no way we're getting in there."

Miana looked at him for a moment.

"We have to find a way," she said calmly.

Kurt wasn't sure if she knew just how exclusive and hostile to outsiders the Quirations were, but he could see the stubborn look in her eyes. She wasn't giving up on this idea.

"Look," he said quietly, "If you're adamant–"

"I am," she interrupted.

"–then we need to talk about using our psychic powers," he finished with a shrug.

Miana's expression firmed, but at least she didn't fly off the handle this time. Kurt still felt a sting when he thought of how she'd reacted to their escape from Cosmotech.

"I don't want to use them if there's *any* other way inside," she said slowly. "That's the problem with this kind of power, Kurt. Every time you use it because you *have* to, you're more likely to use it when you don't."

"I get that, really," Kurt replied patiently, "but I honestly don't think there's another way in. Only citizens are allowed inside and if you're not a direct descendant of their famous 'thousand Islamic families' you may as well not even apply. They do DNA checks on all traffic, in and out."

Miana remained silent and Kurt knew she was thinking about it. It seemed pretty cut and dried to him, but he knew it was a foolish man who thought he could anticipate the mental processes of a woman.

"Okay," she said finally. "I'll admit, I doubt we'll be able to think of another way in, no matter how hard we try. But if we're going to do this, we can only use our powers once, to get us inside."

"That's all it should take," Kurt said, feeling relieved and a little scared at the same time. "But we still have to think about what happens once we're in. They only speak Arabic inside the Bas Quirat."

"We can get earphone translators," Miana said. "We use them all the time in the LCPD."

"Sure," Kurt agreed, "but what happens when they find out you don't speak Arabic?"

"Me? You mean you do?"

"Enough to get by," Kurt said with a shrug. "You'd be surprised how many Quirations visit Lynt City for a little adventure and they love it when you speak their language."

"You know, we're probably going to need a guide of our own," Miana said after a moment.

"A guide? Where are we meant to get one of those?"

Miana glanced at the closed door and Kurt realized she was suggesting they ask Yasmin.

"Oh, no. You can't be serious. Not after you tried so hard to talk me out of coming with you in the first place."

"Things have changed since then," Miana said, calmly holding his gaze. "Drastically. This is no longer just about you or me, Kurt. Or Yasmin."

"Are you talking about what we saw in the cave?"

"Yes," Miana said, looking away for a moment, "and... something else."

"What?" Kurt asked her, his instincts flaring.

"I had a dream."

"A dream, what do you mean?"

Miana looked back at him and began to explain what she'd seen – about Dr. Indari and Loc Breeden; about the strange shadowy figures that had appeared behind them; about the shadowy figure that had spoken to her. The experience had clearly made an impact and when she was done explaining, Kurt felt somehow heavier.

"The time approaches," he said, feeling a little numb. "Shit."

"So you see," Miana said after a moment, "we need to do everything we can to stop it."

"Everything but use our powers," Kurt said, feeling a little childish even as he said it.

Miana gave him a withering look.

"Letting the world know these powers exist could do just as much damage as the red lightning we saw, Kurt. Destroying a civilization can happen in more ways than one."

It sounded like wisdom, but it still left Kurt feeling frustrated. At a time when millions of lives were in danger, he'd been handed a powerful gift that could help save them all and then told in no uncertain terms that he wasn't allowed to use it.

Admittedly, Kurt couldn't predict what would happen if they did reveal their psychic powers whilst saving Mars, but he suspected it wouldn't be pretty.

Knowing someone else might have the power to control you at any time would create a primal fear in the populace that might end up being more destructive than the catastrophe it helped to avert.

"Alright," he capitulated after a long pause. "I'll ask her, but I can't guarantee anything."

"Thank you, Kurt," Miana said quietly, putting a hand on his shoulder. "I know we're putting her in danger and I promise we'll do everything we can to keep her out of harm's way. Do you think she'll agree to help us?"

"I don't know," he replied honestly. "She's about as liberal as Quirations get, but her Islamic faith is strong. I don't know how far she'll go against the fundamental beliefs of her government. All I know is that she trusts me."

"Well, let's hope it's enough," Miana said.

Kurt saw the confidence in her eyes and managed a brave smile.

"It better be," he said. "It looks like we're all the help this world's going to get."

LOC SAT IN THE LUXURIOUS QUARTERS HE'D BEEN escorted to and wondered if he'd ever felt this angry before.

Since his condescending conversation with the 'Prophet', Hani'ah Naziri, he'd been essentially left to his own devices. He'd tried on several occasions to make contact with Isaac, but the Quirations had firmly denied him access. Even Dr. Grayson was being kept out of reach.

Loc had no real concern for the work they'd come here to finish – that was Dr. Grayson's responsibility and failure wasn't in the man's vocabulary – but he would have appreciated seeing Isaac again. He disliked being kept from making regular contact with anyone he may need to influence in the future. Absence may make a lover's heart grow fonder, but it destroyed a businessman's rapport.

And then there was the Jupiter flare. Where in blazes did that come from? And if Hani'ah Naziri had known it was coming, why didn't he?

Loc didn't believe in Hani'ah's prophetic abilities for a second. Access to exclusive information was the real magic behind any claim to clairvoyance. What concerned him was the fact Cosmotech Defence was clearly involved.

147

The 'investment opportunity' he'd been selling to the business community back in Lynt City was clearly linked to the Jupiter flare. Hell, the *Vita Nova* was probably the cause of the damn thing. And yet Loc was only just beginning to realise how far out of the loop the Triumvirate had left him.

He expected this kind of thing from Dr. Grayson and often planned for it, but if the Triumvirate had chosen to keep him in the dark, what did that say about their promises?

He had no delusions of grandeur. He was well aware there were things he wouldn't be made aware of until he joined the Triumvirate's ranks. But all this secrecy was making him nervous. He thought he knew what their end game was, but now it was clear he knew nothing. And that begged the most important question of all...

"Just how much is the Triumvirate keeping from me?"

Since finding out about the Jupiter flare, Loc had been preoccupied with trying to see things from their perspective. He needed to work out what angle would provide them the most profit. Did they intend to use the Jupiter flare as a weapon? Were they planning to decimate some enemy he didn't know about under the guise of a 'natural disaster'? Could Dr. Grayson have found a way to harness the Jupiter flare's energy for some other purpose? Had he created a technology that would ensure Cosmotech's ongoing dominance for decades to come?

"Perhaps the Jupiter flare doesn't exist at all," he mused.

Cosmotech Defence had certainly gotten away with lies on such a grand scale in the past. Of course, such a ruse would also allow Hani'ah Naziri to play out her prophecies, cement her spiritual status with the Quiration people and, if they were involved, allow the Triumvirate to do whatever they wanted with the Bas Quirat and its deluded populace.

It was the most likely scenario Loc could think of and it enraged him. How could the Triumvirate concoct this 'Prophet' Hani'ah and engineer a Jupiter flare to brainwash an entire nation of Quirations without his knowledge?

"Argh," he grunted, swiping a hand across his face in frustration. In the end he knew it was all pointless speculation. Unless the Triumvirate decided he needed to know, the truth was destined to remain out of his reach and pursuing it too rigorously would only lead to more trouble.

In an effort to pull his mind back to something he could actually influence, Loc focussed on the image displayed on his data pad.

"Saadi Khalil," he said beneath his breath. "So this is the man Miana is looking for."

He only knew about Saadi because he'd been actively searching for the trail Hani'ah claimed he'd left for Miana. He knew it had something to do with the Cosmotech data she'd stolen in Lynt City and so he simply looked at the problem from her perspective. She was clearly still locked in her misguided effort to solve the murder of Naseem Indari and so the information had to be linked to the geologist somehow.

Loc was still fuming about the list of encrypted video calls between Naseem Indari and Saadi Khalil. He found it hard to accept the Triumvirate would keep such an important piece of information from him, even if he could see why they might do so.

There was nothing he could have done about it at the time, after all. The Bas Quirat's walls were guarded in every way that mattered. But he was inside its walls now, nestled deep within the very heart of the viper's nest, and this was his opportunity to show the Triumvirate how wrong they were to underestimate him.

"*I'll prove I'm worthy of joining their ranks,*" he promised himself. "*But first I need to deal with Quiration security.*"

He was well aware they'd been monitoring him and his officers since they'd set foot in Quiration territory, but if there was one thing Cosmotech did better than anyone else, it was counter-intelligence. His officers might appear idle to their hosts, but every one of them had been working on the problem since entering the Bas Quirat's hallowed walls.

Loc waved Captain West and one of his officers over – Lexi Sharp, an attractive and sharp witted intelligence expert – and spoke to them in a voice he knew his hosts wouldn't overhear.

"What have you found?"

"The Quirations have been hunting Saadi Khalil for close to six months, sir," Lexi replied. "Obviously without much success."

"How is he still alive? Are they truly that incompetent?"

"Far from it," Lexi assured him. "There's simply a lot of support for Saadi within the Bas Quirat. Many are willing to hide him and that includes some who are heavily involved in local smuggling operations. They've got years of experience circumventing the Bas Quirat's internal surveillance systems."

"So they can't even control their own populace?" Loc asked, genuinely surprised.

"They couldn't if they wanted to, sir. The place is a rabbit warren. Local law enforcement files estimate that nearly eighteen percent of the Bas Quirat's internal structure has been illegally altered since the first residents moved in. Corruption allowed most of it and a willing ignorance on the rulers' part allowed the rest."

"Why hasn't their Prophet asked the almighty Allah for help?" Loc asked bitterly.

"Hani'ah Naziri has spoken about it only once, sir, to denounce Saadi and his followers as agents of the devil. As you can imagine, it only inflamed the situation."

Loc felt the smug warmth of satisfaction. It appeared Hani'ah Naziri wasn't so clairvoyant after all.

"What is Saadi preaching?" he asked Lexi.

"Nothing too controversial. Something about there being more than one truth. But he also says Hani'ah Naziri is no Prophet."

"Oooh, that would do it," Loc said, grinning at the thought. "Well, as much as I'd enjoy helping him cause further mischief, Saadi Khalil needs to die."

He turned to Captain West.

"How do we make it happen?"

"It won't be easy, sir," West replied. "The Quirations have been hunting him for-"

"The Quirations are pompous idiots," Loc cut him off with a wave of his hand, "and we have a distinct advantage."

"Sir?"

"They've so effectively cut themselves off from the rest of humanity that we can do whatever we want. If we make a mess, they'll just clean it up rather than admit their mighty Bas Quirat could be fallible. Do they have any information on residents with links to Saadi?"

This question he directed to Lexi.

"Yes, sir," she replied. "Their prisons are full of them and we've obtained several dossiers on suspected followers that, by the looks of it, have managed to buy their way out of trouble."

"They can keep the prisoners," Loc said with a grimace. "Trying to access them will attract too much attention. And I'd much rather explore the real Bas Quirat anyway. I think it's time we visited some of the locals."

"There are several barriers to reaching the local population, sir," Captain West said uncertainly. "Just leaving this area will be difficult."

"Oh, I think we'll find a way," Loc said with a smile.

He was sick of having his hands tied and his lines of communication cut. This was the perfect opportunity to make up for his failure with Miana and show the Triumvirate what he was capable of. And it wouldn't hurt if Hani'ah Naziri received a lesson in just how prophetic she *wasn't* along the way.

"*It's not often I get to use my psychic powers with impunity,*" he thought with a smile. "*This is going to be fun.*"

"Sir?" Captain West said after a moment.

"Do you at least control the surveillance systems covering the immediate area?"

"Of course, sir."

"Then make sure we have a few hours to work with. We're going for a stroll."

"I'll prepare the team for heavy resistance, sir," West said, a little too pointedly.

"No, I don't think that will be necessary," Loc replied with another smile, "but have them strip down and be ready to receive new uniforms and I.D.s. I'm going to have a word with our Quiration security escort."

Captain West frowned in confusion, but didn't hesitate before saying, "yes, sir."

Loc wondered if the Triumvirate saw him as he saw West now. He was well aware the man didn't know all the details of what was going on and yet he was expected to follow orders without question. It didn't help that he was already considering disposing of the man when the mission was complete, since he would most likely know too much by the end of it.

"Is that what the Triumvirate have planned for me?"

It wasn't a thought he'd entertained before today. He'd been given everything they'd promised him, after all, and amassed more and more power with each passing year. But things were changing fast and cracks were appearing in places he wasn't comfortable with. Had he finally reached the ceiling? Would he be prevented from rising any further, like this Captain standing before him?

"We're going to finish the Quiration's manhunt for them," he said firmly, putting the thought out of his mind. "But before we do, let's go and make sure we look the part."

EN ROUTE TO THE BAS QUIRAT - June 8, 2147 - 11.25am

MIANA SAT BESIDE KURT, RESISTING AN URGE TO scratch her face. Her spray tan – meant make her look more like a Quiration – was itching like crazy. Her eyes, thankfully, were dark enough already, but Kurt now looked a little spooky wearing dark brown contacts. They were the expensive kind with pupils that dilated along with the wearer, but their authenticity only made him look all the stranger.

Yasmin, on the other hand, looked more beautiful than ever. Even dressed in a traditional Quiration burka, she was undeniably alluring. It was so annoying. Miana knew it was unfair to be jealous of someone who was being so kind to them, but she couldn't help herself. Yes, Yasmin was putting her life on the line, but she didn't have to look so damn good doing it. And it didn't help that Miana knew the real reason Yasmin was helping them.

"*She's in love with Kurt,*" she thought reproachfully.

Miana suspected Kurt knew it as well, but didn't think he realised how deep that love went. Otherwise he might have fought harder against letting her help them.

It was sad, but at the same time it was the very thing that made Miana jealous. Her own attraction to Kurt had grown steadily since

153

he'd insisted on joining her, but when she looked at the gorgeous woman sitting across from her now and heard her speak with just a touch of a Quiration accent, when she saw how intelligent, charismatic and confident Yasmin was, it filled her heart with doubt.

"How could a man not interested in Yasmin ever be content with someone like me?" she thought sadly.

Turning to look out the passenger jet's window, Miana chided herself for worrying about it at all. There were far more important things to consider before satisfying her romantic urges and they weren't going to wait for anything.

"The time approaches," she thought grimly.

The catastrophic images she'd witnessed in the underground cave were still fresh in her mind and they had an annoying way of leaping out at her at unexpected moments.

"We're nearly there," Kurt said, interrupting her thoughts.

Miana turned to look at him, grateful for the distraction.

"How can you tell?" she asked.

"They've engaged the auto-pilot," he replied. "Didn't you feel it?"

"No. I'm a bit... preoccupied," she said. "The sooner we get this over with the better."

"I hear you," Kurt replied, before turning to Yasmin. "I think you should go on ahead of us," he said in a quiet voice. "If anything happens on our way in, I don't want you associated with us in any way."

"But I could—" she protested.

"No," Kurt said, holding up a hand. "You've already done enough, Yasmin. I don't want to put you in any more danger than we have to. If everything goes as planned, we'll meet at the Quinari you told us about. Okay?"

Yasmin pouted for a moment, but then nodded.

"Thanks, Yasmin," Kurt said, laying a hand on her leg in a way that made Miana flush with irritation.

She turned to look out the window again, but the glass was gradually fogging up and was soon completely opaque.

"They do that on purpose," Kurt said.

"What?" Miana asked distractedly. "Why?"

"You'll see," he answered cryptically.

Miana frowned. She didn't know a lot about the Bas Quirat, but she was surprised they didn't capitalise on the view visitors would get approaching its international spaceport.

There were no trains between the Bas Quirat and Lynt City, or the Valles Dome for that matter, but their spaceport was legendary. Given their self-imposed isolation, all visitors had to come by air and although they allowed some limited trade with other cities, it never occurred within the Bas Quirat itself. All contact occurred within a large customs installation at the base of the megascraper, which doubled as a shopping mall and tripled as a popular tourist destination.

For everyone not authorized by blood to enter the Bas Quirat, this was as close as they would ever get.

Miana felt a light jolt when the jet landed on the tarmac and saw that the windows were becoming clear again. From down here, there was no view of the Bas Quirat and, again, Miana was surprised and a little frustrated.

As they taxied to the terminal, she saw many other flights either landing or about to take off and wondered if this was normal. There certainly seemed to be a lot of traffic.

The jet didn't take long to enter the terminal and when it had come to a complete stop they waited until the exit lights above them blinked on, indicating the disembarkation tubes were connected.

"Okay," Kurt said quietly to Yasmin. "We'll see you inside."

She nodded demurely as she rose to her feet and then glanced at Miana for a moment before turning to join the departing crowd.

They remained in their seats until Yasmin had moved through the exit then Kurt stood up and offered her a hand.

"Let's get moving," he said with a neutral expression.

The two of them joined the exiting passengers and soon emerged from the disembarkation tubes into a huge, bustling space.

The custom's installation was much bigger and far busier than Miana expected. Considering the Quiration's strict policies concerning traffic in and out of the Bas Quirat, she thought it would discourage many people from making the journey, but that clearly wasn't the case. Throngs of passengers streamed out of at least a dozen tubes that Miana could see and she suspected the tide wouldn't slacken any time soon.

Along with the rest of them, Miana and Kurt were initially funnelled toward an area thick with shops that sold all manner of clothing, jewellery, electronics, food and drink. There was also a rich look to the stores that made Miana suspect the Quirations who travelled regularly were made up in large part by those who could readily afford it.

As they moved beyond a final rank of shops, Miana noticed the spaceport's ceiling had become transparent and she looked up.

"My God..." she whispered in amazement.

Through the glass ceiling, the Bas Quirat towered above them, glistening like a palace made for Gods. It was the most breathtaking view she'd ever witnessed and Miana could see now why their jet's windows had been blacked out on approach. This was how the Quirations wanted people to see the Bas Quirat.

Realising she was staring like a tourist, Miana reluctantly lowered her gaze and tried to resist the temptation to keep glancing up at the incredible view. It wasn't easy.

To keep her mind occupied, she looked around the circular space they'd entered and saw that many more stores lined the vast viewing area. None of them were closed, but most of them looked empty and, for the first time, Miana got a sense that something wasn't right.

She looked around the crowd and saw that most of them were either quiet or grim-faced. Many were talking in hushed voices and although there were a few groups of tourists scattered amongst the throng, the far majority seemed to be Quirations returning to the Bas Quirat.

"What's going on?" she asked Kurt when she was sure no one would hear her speaking English.

"I don't know," he replied in Arabic, the translation coming from the device hidden beneath Miana's burka, "but they're scared."

A cold weight settled in Miana's stomach.

Again, she tried to distract herself by looking around the crowd and caught a glimpse of Yasmin in the distance. A young man was talking to her as they approached the custom gates and she looked upset. Hopefully she would find out what was going on and have some answers for them soon.

When they reached the far side of the hall, the crowd began to sort itself into dozens of queues that eventually terminated at a line of custom gates. This was where the Quirations submitted themselves for DNA identification.

Miana felt anxiety squeeze her chest as they joined the nearest queue and tried to focus on the Arabic conversations that washed over them and tugged at her ears with waves of recognisable cadence. Her translator caught some of it, but as the words registered in her ears, none of it made sense.

"The Saviour has come..."

"...don't know if they'll make it in time..."

"...didn't come back here to fight..."

"The Prophet will save us..."

The only constant seemed to be fear and it echoed within Miana as well. Could they somehow know about the catastrophe she'd witnessed in the cave? Was this Prophet they were talking about the man she was here to find? Was there someone else who might be able to save them?

She burned to ask the Quirations around her some questions, but knew that wasn't going to happen. If her English didn't get her in trouble, she had a feeling her lack of cultural knowledge definitely would.

When they eventually reached the front of the queue, Kurt took Miana's hand and they approached the customs gate together.

Behind a transparent screen, a plump young woman wearing a plain, official uniform and a serious expression sat at a counter. Because Kurt could speak Arabic, they'd already agreed he would do the talking. It also made cultural sense for a man to speak for the woman he was with. They were now effectively inside a nation ruled by Sharia law.

The woman spoke without looking up from her screen.

"Sabah alkhir. Yrja wade yadak ealaa lawhat alhamd alnnawwi."

"Good morning," the translation came inside Miana's ear. "Please place your hand on the DNA plate."

"*Not good,*" Miana thought. Kurt needed to see her eyes to use his powers.

"Good morning," Kurt replied in barely accented Arabic, "beautiful eyes."

The woman looked up with a half-smile and Miana was impressed. She would never have thought of something so simple. She tensed as she waited for what was to come next and imagined she felt a shiver at the moment Kurt made the psychic connection, but all she could see in the woman behind the counter was that she seemed to relax a little.

"Tell me in a quiet voice how long you have before the end of you shift," Kurt said in a whisper.

"Three hours, seventeen minutes," the woman replied in a soft, hollow voice.

"Good," Kurt said, glancing at Miana with a look of relief.

"*That should give us plenty of time to lose ourselves,*" Miana thought, as Kurt turned back to the customs officer.

"Now, tell me how we can pass through your gate without requiring a DNA scan and a passport check."

The woman paused for a few seconds then spoke in the same soft, hollow voice.

"When a system error occurs, I have authorisation to reset the gate. A barrier will close while the scanner is off-line, but I have an access key that will open it."

"How long will the scanner remain off-line?"

"Ten seconds."

"Very good," Kurt said. "Now, the next time I say 'thank you', you will reset your gate, use your key to open the barrier and we will walk through. When we are gone, you will continue doing your duties in the same way you always do, until the end of your shift. Do you understand what I've told you?"

"Yes."

"Tell me, do you know if there is any reason our unauthorised entry will be noticed before the end of your shift?"

The woman paused again, before saying, "no."

Kurt glanced at Miana again.

"Satisfied?" he asked quietly.

She nodded. He seemed to have thought of everything. Or enough to get them inside, at least.

Kurt turned back to the customs officer and spoke a little louder this time.

"Thank you."

The woman immediately turned to her console and a series of metal poles moved out of the scanner, barring access. She then stepped out of her booth and placed her access key against a panel on the other side. A red light above the gate blinked green and the bars began to retract. When they were all the way open, Kurt took Miana's hand and they walked confidently through the gate.

Miana's heart raced as they walked down the short corridor beyond and she almost gasped in relief when the doors at the far end opened automatically for them.

She wanted to look back, to see if the customs officer was serving the next customer as she'd been told, but she firmly resisted the urge. There was nothing she could do if things weren't going as planned and there was no point drawing attention to themselves.

For now, they just had to keep moving.

Beyond the customs gate, throngs of people milled about looking expectantly into the arriving crowd. Families embraced those who'd just returned home, friends talked frantically with friends, and what looked like police officers argued with small groups of young men. The mood in here was no better than the spaceport and, if anything, the sense of fear was more pronounced.

To keep any chance of complications to a minimum they'd decided not to bring any luggage. Apart from their clothes, the only thing they'd brought with them was a few copies of Cosmotech's database, just in case they needed more information.

Ignoring the crowd that waited in the baggage claim area, Kurt led them straight through the crowd and on to the meeting place they'd arranged with Yasmin. Thankfully it wasn't far.

As they approached, Miana picked out Yasmin almost straight away. It was hard to miss such a beautiful face in the crowd.

"You made it," she said to Kurt, looking relieved.

"We did," Kurt replied with a smile, "but let's not tempt fate. I want to get as far from here as we can."

Yasmin nodded once and turned to lead them away, clearly happy to oblige. When they were well beyond the crowds, Kurt turned to Yasmin and asked the question Miana had been wanting to ask since they'd first entered the Bas Quirat's spaceport.

"What's going on? Everyone seems to be terrified of something."

"The Prophet Hani'ah Naziri has declared the arrival of the Messiah," Yasmin replied, giving Kurt a frightened look.

"Who's the Messiah?" he asked, making sure no one nearby would hear him.

"A man named Isaac Taylor," Yasmin replied, also careful not to share their conversation with anyone else. "I don't know any more than you do, really, but they say he's been sent by Allah to save us. Although... she's also saying that only those within the Bas Quirat will be saved."

Kurt looked at Miana and she could feel the question without needing to hear him ask it. Did this have anything to do with what they'd seen?

"Okay," he said, turning back to Yasmin. "There's a lot we still need to know, but I think we should keep moving and clear all this up when we find... the man we came for."

Yasmin nodded, looking like she was about to cry, and they continued deeper into the Bas Quirat.

Once again, Miana had to resist an urge to gawk like a tourist. The inside of the Bas Quirat was like nothing she'd ever seen. The flowing architecture carried her eyes from ornate archway to curved stairway and soaring architrave in a sweeping river of colour. Alabaster columns sculpted with intricate repeating patterns held up the vast ceilings like ceremonial guards dressed in gold and, everywhere she looked, glass and sparkling crystal refracted the vibrant carpets and wall-hangings in graceful, if sometimes garish patterns.

The crowds thinned markedly as they moved deeper into the megascraper, but whenever Miana caught the eyes of a Quiration they simply looked and then looked away, just as they did in Lynt City. There was no suspicion here. In a world without psychic abilities, the Quirations trusted their DNA identification system to keep out any trespassers and had every reason to do so.

The only one of them that got any real attention was Yasmin. As she led them through the Bas Quirat she drew gazes from men and women alike.

"*Oh great,*" Miana thought with a grimace. "*She's just as ravishing amongst her own people as she is in Lynt City.*"

When they eventually stepped into a large, domed foyer that looked a little more formal than the areas they'd already passed through, Miana was surprised to find it crowded again. There were hundreds of people of all ages present and everyone was dressed in religious attire and kneeling in neatly rowed squares that seemed to mimic the tiled patterns on the expansive floor.

161

"This is one of the many Di'jah prayer domes," Yasmin explained as they headed for the ring of elevators on the far side. "Each morning and evening, all citizens stop for prayer. Many congregate at Di'jahs like these, scattered across the Bas Quirat, but some also take prayer wherever they happen to be at the allotted hour. Today, many have chosen to remain in vigil until the Prophet tells them otherwise."

Miana wondered what it would be like for an entire city to stop what they were doing at an allotted hour so they could pray. She didn't believe in a God herself and although she did occasionally pray it wasn't *to* anyone in particular. Nevertheless, she could imagine it would be a powerfully unifying experience to share such a ritual with your fellow Quirations.

Looking up, Miana saw that the elevators they were headed for seemed to operate behind a transparent ring of glass. It stretched around a giant white column that disappeared into the grand ceiling above. The elevators were slightly curved and much wider than any Miana had seen and inside each one was a row of twelve seats along with a ceiling rail that Miana assumed would allow more people to stand if required.

As one of them smoothly slid down the column and stopped at their level, a section of the glass ring slid aside, allowing several people to get out while Miana, Kurt and Yasmin took a seat.

Miana noticed that each arm rest had a small screen to input a destination and she watched as Yasmin chose a floor. A small note appeared on her screen when she was done.

"Three minutes," Yasmin said to Kurt.

The glass doors then slid shut in front of them and Miana felt her stomach sink as the elevator lifted them up the column.

As the D'jah dropped away, she stared down at the neatly praying Quirations and wondered if their silent pleas would make any difference.

"*I hope so,*" she thought grimly. "*We need all the help we can get.*"

When they reached the ceiling, the transparent doors abruptly turned white and a large video screen appeared in place of the view. On it was a well-groomed, heavily bearded man in a tightly wound turban who spoke in the clear, familiar tone of a news reader.

Miana leaned forward to listen.

"Glory to God, the almighty Allah," he began formally. "The Holy Prophet, Hani'ah Naziri, has confirmed that the Messiah, Isaac Taylor, is now among us. As prophesied, the final sign of his coming was fulfilled at seven-oh-two pm last night in front of a crowd of seventeen thousand Quiration citizens. Millions more witnessed the moment via video feed from their own jurisdictions."

As the announcer spoke, an inset window showed a picture of the night sky, glistening with stars. As the video played, Miana saw a red light appear at its centre and felt a shiver of recognition.

"So that's the final sign," she thought to herself. *"I wonder if they have any idea what it actually is?"*

The announcer continued.

"Abdullah Gohar Shahi, Quiration High Leader, had this to say."

The screen changed to another bearded man, this one much older and with the universal look of a politician. Firm, wise, but also slightly false.

"Now is not the time for fear. Today, we must rejoice, for we are blessed. As our Holy Prophet has foreseen, the Messiah has come at the very hour of our need to save all true believers within the Bas Quirat and prevent the coming Apocalypse. Praise be to almighty Allah."

The image then returned to the news presenter and he finished with a typical government statement.

"Citizens are urged to either stay in their homes and await the prophesied time or join their local D'jah congregations and pray for the Messiah's triumph. Praise the almighty Allah. God is great."

163

Just as the screen winked out, Miana wondered what she would do in a similar situation. She didn't really have anyone to go home to, or any family she knew well enough to join in Lynt City either. She suspected she would have spent as much time as she could at the precinct, doing anything that might have helped. Then, at the final hour, she probably would have found the best view available.

As the morbid thought ran to its conclusion, Miana noticed the elevator doors were becoming transparent again and found herself staring at an entirely new area of the Bas Quirat. The public thoroughfare outside wasn't as wide for a start and although the intricate designs and rich colours were still prevalent, they didn't look as clean or as vibrant as they décor they'd left behind them.

"This is one of the residential levels," Yasmin explained as they got up to exit the elevator. "My brother lives here. He should be able to help us."

"We'll wait here," Kurt said, pausing just outside the elevator.

"It's alright—" Yasmin began, but Kurt stopped her with a hand on her arm.

"No," he said firmly. "I won't put anyone else in danger if I don't have to, Yasmin. Please, go to your brother and find out if he knows anyone who can help. Don't let him come back with you, just get a name and a location if he has one."

Yasmin pouted again and for a moment Miana wondered if she really was going to cry this time, but she simply nodded and turned away.

Miana watched her go with a frown. The further this went, the more guilty she felt.

"We may not be able to avoid incriminating her family," she said in a whisper, careful to make sure no one was close enough to hear.

"I know," Kurt said, his own tortured expression mirroring her guilt, "but it doesn't mean we shouldn't try."

As they waited for Yasmin, Miana watched the other Quirations who passed them. Most of them walked as if there was an invisible axe hovering above them, just waiting for the right moment to fall.

She saw fear, confusion, even anger in some, but not much hope. It made her wonder just what it was she and Kurt were trying to accomplish here.

"There she is," Kurt said quietly.

Miana looked down the corridor and saw Yasmin walking toward them with a serious looking man by her side. She assumed this was her brother and it was clear, even from here, that he didn't approve of what his sister had asked of him.

When they got close enough, Kurt bowed low and began to speak, but the man spoke over the top of him in a sharp whisper.

"Why do you seek this man out?"

Yasmin laid a hand on his arm.

"Forgive my brother," she apologised. "His manners are usually better than this. Kurt, Miana, this is my brother, Hamdhi."

"Peace be upon you," Kurt said with another small bow.

Hamdhi glared at Yasmin for a moment before turning back to Kurt and asking again, "why do you seek him?"

"We need his help," Kurt replied calmly.

"He cannot help anyone," Hamdhi hissed. "He brings only trouble."

"Hamdhi," Yasmin said, clutching his arm. "Please, don't. They must talk with him. Just help them."

"You have no idea what's been going on here," Hamdhi snapped, glaring at her for a moment before returning his angry gaze to Kurt. "Any of you. The High Leader would never admit it, but there is a war coming and the man you have come to see is at the very centre of it."

"War?" Kurt said, startled. "What kind of war?"

"A war of belief," Hamdhi replied, lowering his voice even further. "A war between those who believe in the one truth and those who believe in many."

Miana's mind flashed back to the words Dr. Indari had spoken in her dream.

"...*deliver my sight to the Saviour and let all truths be known.*" Hamdhi continued.

"There are many who would show you no mercy if they heard you were searching for this man. And if they find you, they will find my sister and our family as well."

"I know the risks, Hamdhi," Yasmin said angrily. "I'm not a little girl anymore."

"Then why do insist on acting like one?" Hamdhi countered.

"Please," Kurt interjected, "I didn't want to put your sister or your family in any danger, but there was no other way. We must find this man. We must speak to him, or I can assure you this war you speak of will be the least of your troubles."

Hamdhi stared at him for a long moment, his expression suddenly guarded.

"You are talking about the end of all things," he said. "I don't believe in that, or the Messiah."

"We don't know anything about the Messiah," Kurt replied, "but the end of all things might be more real than you want to believe. And the man we came to see will know what to do if it is. You want to keep your family safe? Then please, tell us how to find him."

Hamdhi glowered silently for a long moment then he appeared to come to a decision.

"I know of one of his followers," he said quietly, "but they will not let you see him."

"Why not?" Kurt asked.

"Because he is a hunted man. The Prophet Hani'ah Naziri has publically condemned him. His outspoken beliefs are the cause of the coming war. Unless he already knows you, his followers will never reveal his location."

"If you can get us close enough, we'll be able to convince him to see us," Kurt said with confidence.

"Please, Hamdhi," Yasmin added.

166

Hamdhi turned to look at her and then returned his grim expression to Kurt.

"I will tell you how to find this man on one condition. One that you all must agree to."

"What is it?" Kurt asked.

"Yasmin must not go with you."

"What? No," Yasmin protested, but Hamdhi spoke over her.

"Your part in this will end here, sister, and you will never see these people again. Swear it to me now or I will not help them."

Miana knew it was the right thing to do and she could already see that Kurt agreed, but it was clear this was Yasmin's decision more than it was theirs.

She watched Yasmin look from her brother to Kurt, her eyes filling with tears, and felt her heart breaking. Despite the jealousy she felt, this wasn't what she wanted at all.

But, after a long pause, Yasmin eventually lowered her eyes and spoke in a quiet voice.

"Yes, I will stay with you, Hamdhi."

"And you will never contact her again," Hamdhi said, this time to Kurt.

Miana could see the reluctance in Kurt eyes and knew he was agreeing to far more than leaving Yasmin behind.

"He has feelings for her after all," she thought sadly.

"I swear it," Kurt said after a moment, looking hard into Hamdhi's eyes.

Hamdhi remained quiet for a moment and then he spoke in a quiet monotone.

"His name is Muhammad Singh. You will find him at the Dhal-Sim café, level one-four-six."

"Thank you, Hamdhi," Kurt said with a nod.

"You will not thank me when you are captured," he said, turning away and dragging Yasmin with him.

"Wait," Yasmin said, pulling on his grip.

167

Hamdhi turned and looked at her for a moment as if debating whether to force her to come away with him then he relaxed his grip and let her go.

"Make it quick," he said quietly.

Yasmin nodded quickly and then stepped forward to place her hand against Kurt's face.

"Please, be careful," she said, her large eyes glistening with tears.

"We will," Kurt assured her, placing his hand over hers. "I promise."

They stared into each other's eyes for a moment, sharing something Miana could only hope she would one day experience herself, then Yasmin lowered her eyes, causing tears to fall from her luxurious lashes.

As she lowered her hand, she turned to Miana and then leaned in to kiss her on the cheek.

"And you, Miana."

Miana felt embarrassed at the gesture and wasn't sure what to do, but before she could react Yasmin pulled her into a hug and whispered something in English.

"I know Kurt feels things for you that he will never feel for me. Please, look after him, Miana, and... make him happy."

Miana was so shocked at her words that she couldn't think of a reply before Yasmin pulled away and returned to her brother's side.

"I do not know either of you, " Hamdhi said, his expression grim, "or what it is you hope to accomplish here, but if my sister believes in you then I wish you well."

"Thank you," Kurt said with a nod.

Hamdhi returned it solemnly and then walked away with his sister in tow.

Miana watched them go and felt a pang of guilt when Yasmin turned to look longingly at Kurt one last time before they disappeared round a corner.

"I'm... sorry," she said to Kurt, ignoring a sudden urge to cry.

"I don't know whose fault this is," he said quietly, not looking at her, "but it certainly isn't yours. Come on, let's go."

Without another word, the two of them walked back to the elevator and waited silently as it returned. Kurt did the honours this time, sending the elevator to level 146, and Miana was too preoccupied to listen to the news feed this time, which appeared to be repeating the same official message.

When they eventually arrived on the level Yasmin's brother had given them, Miana was once again confronted with a new version of the Bas Quirat. For whatever reason, this level clearly wasn't as well maintained as the others she'd already seen. The air was thick with a mix of spice, ozone, and humanity and the walls didn't glisten as much as they fumed.

Unlike the frightened atmosphere that kept the corridors on other floors virtually empty, here they were crowded with people. Admittedly, many of them were in heavy discussion and looked just as scared as those Miana had seen on Yasmin's level, but it didn't seem to stop them from selling things to each other.

Wherever there was space, stalls of every description had been set up. Most vendors were too busy having quiet conversations to spruik their home grown foods, spices and gadgets, but it still felt like any other typical marketplace Miana had visited.

As they moved to join the bustling crowd, a man with a scruffy beard and a serious expression blocked their path. He was also holding a rifle and it made Miana wish she'd brought her tazer.

"What is your business here?" he asked gruffly.

Kurt grasped Miana's hand and gently moved her behind him. She let him do so, sure this man would not want to speak to her, and waited to see what he would say.

"Peace be upon you," Kurt said with a nod. "We are here to purchase food, that is all."

Miana kept her eyes lowered, but could feel the man's scrutiny like an itch she couldn't scratch.

"This is not a good time to be grocery shopping," he growled.

"As you say, brother," Kurt replied. "The police are rounding up anyone they see on our level. We were lucky to even make it here."

"And what level is that?" the man asked.

"One-nine-five," Kurt replied without hesitation, the level Yasmin had taken them to. "You see, my foolish sister here forgot to stock up before the Messiah arrived and... well, we do not have any bread left. Whatever might happen in the next few hours, I refuse to meet Allah with an empty stomach."

"Hah!" the Quiration laughed, clearly accepting Kurt's story. "I understand, brother. But do not tarry long if you want to avoid a nasty interrogation when you return home. Hani'ah's pigs will know you have been here."

"Thank you, brother, I will," Kurt replied, smiling as he pulled Miana into the crowd.

"God is great," the man growled as they left him.

As they continued on through the mass of people, Kurt turned to whisper in Miana's ear.

"That was close," he said, "although he didn't look particularly bright. I'm sure any excuse would have worked."

Miana smiled as they navigated their way through the packed marketplace and only paused when Kurt stopped to flag down a passerby.

"Excuse me," he said politely, "do you know where I can find the Dhal-Sim café?"

The man looked at him askance for a moment, then he glanced around him and hissed, "down that way, third on the left. Go to the end and you'll see the sign."

Kurt tried to thank him, but the man moved off almost before he'd finished talking and didn't look back.

"Looks like the café is known for more than its coffee," he whispered in Miana's ear.

"Someone will be watching," Miana agreed. "We need to be careful."

They pushed on through the crowds, moving through an ever-changing collection of scents, and found that the further they moved from the elevator, the thinner the crowd got. The stalls also began to look a little shabbier and the wares weren't as colourful.

They took the third corridor on the left, as instructed, and continued weaving through the crowd until they saw a sign that glowed dark blue above one of the many doorways. There was a large man standing next to it and his bulging arms were folded over a thick, barrel chest.

Kurt didn't slow down as they approached, but when they tried enter the café, the big man took a step to one side and blocked his passage with a hand that could have palmed a gym ball.

"Peace be upon you, brother," Kurt said hesitantly. "We're... here to see Muhammad Singh."

The man eyed them both suspiciously for a moment and then looked away and said something so soft that Miana's translator didn't pick it up.

"Uh... I'm sorry, what did you say?" Kurt asked, but the man ignored him.

He spoke softly again and Miana realised he was having a conversation with someone they couldn't see.

Kurt glanced at her, raising his eyebrows in supplication, and they waited.

After a moment, the large man lowered his hand.

"Back right corner," he said in a deep voice, before stepping aside and gesturing them inside.

Kurt didn't wait for another invitation, he simply nodded, took Miana's hand, and led her through the open doorway.

The room beyond was about ten metres square and it was filled with small round tables that held groups of two or three. Every patron seemed to be drinking, smoking or talking quietly, and although several looked up as they entered, no one's gaze lingered.

171

Miana could feel the paranoia and fear hanging in the air like smoke and tried to use her peripheral vision as much as possible. It was probably bad enough that she seemed to be the only woman in there, but if she started staring at the men, she was sure they'd get in trouble quicker than she could say 'patriarchy'.

Weaving their way carefully between tables, Kurt led her to the back right corner where another round table waited with two empty chairs. He turned to look at her and Miana took the lead by sitting down on one side. Kurt quickly joined her and they both warily looked around the room.

"I don't like this," Kurt said quietly in Arabic.

Miana caught his eye for a moment and reached across the table to squeeze his hand. She didn't like it either, but it was obvious they had no control over the situation. They were in a foreign place trying to contact a wanted man. They wouldn't be here if the stakes weren't already high.

A man carrying a tray with two cups of steaming liquid walked toward them and both Miana and Kurt watched him come.

"Welcome," he said with a small bow. "What do you want with Muhammad Singh?"

Miana was a little surprised at the direct question, but Kurt wasn't rattled and he answered without hesitation.

"We're looking for a man he might know."

"And who is this other man you seek?" the waiter asked, placing two cups on their table.

"Saadi Khalil," Kurt said quietly.

The waiter tried not to react to the name, but Miana sensed an immediate change in his stance. He was now tense and ready for action.

"I do not know that name," he said slowly.

"You're Muhammad?" Kurt asked.

"I don't know you," the waiter said, backing away.

"Please," Miana said in English, grasping his free hand. "I've seen things only Saadi can explain."

The waiter stared at her with wide eyes and Miana realised the room had gone silent. She looked around and saw that every gaze in the room was now locked onto her, fierce and direct.

"He has foretold your coming," the waiter said quietly, breaking the silence.

"Who? Saadi?" Kurt asked.

The waiter turned to him, his face pale, then he glanced around the room and moved closer.

"Drink your coffee," he said quickly.

"What?" Kurt said, frowning in confusion.

"Drink it, quickly," the waiter said. "I will take you to Saadi, but you must drink your coffee first."

Miana looked at the steaming brew in front of her and wondered what was in it. Were they about to willingly drink poison? Were they effectively committing suicide by trusting a man they'd never met?

"Miana?" Kurt asked, looking at her intently.

She looked at him, at the faces of the men staring at them, and finally at the panicked eyes of the waiter.

"We can't control everything," she said quietly, then she picked up her coffee and swallowed it in one bitter draft.

Kurt glanced at the waiter again then reluctantly did the same.

"Very good," the waiter said.

But his voice suddenly sounded as if it were coming from far away. Miana tried to turn and look at him, but her muscles were so tired that she could barely stop herself from falling forward. Her eyes began to hurt and she closed them only to find that she couldn't open them again. Her thoughts began to race as panic set in and she felt something hit her cheek.

"Miana," she heard Kurt say in a slurred voice, but she couldn't reply.

All she could do was hope against hope that she'd made the right choice.

STAGE 7: JUPITER FLARE APPROACHES MARS

June 8, 2147 - 12.07 pm

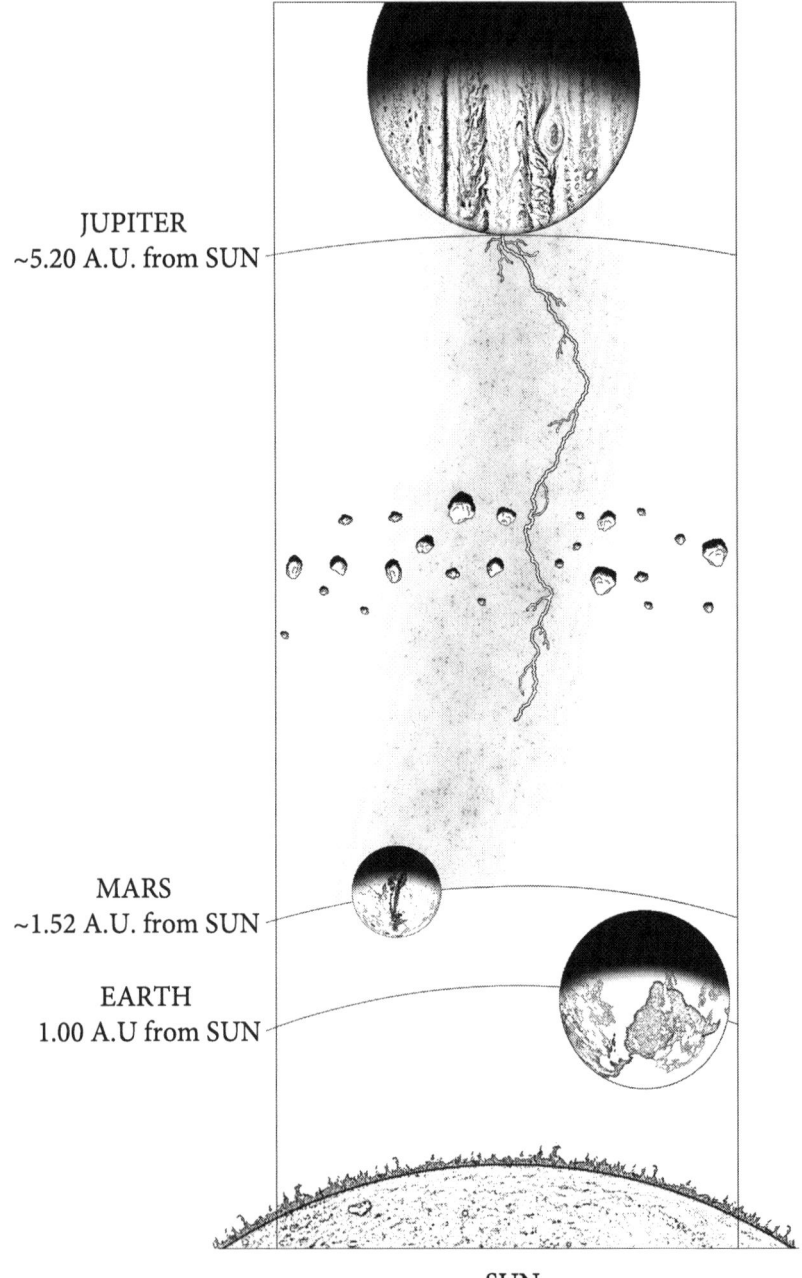

JUPITER
~5.20 A.U. from SUN

MARS
~1.52 A.U. from SUN

EARTH
1.00 A.U from SUN

SUN

1 Astronomical Unit (A.U.) = ~149.6 x 10^6 km

ISAAC WANDERED AROUND THE BUSTLING LABORATORY, feeling a little out of place. Apparently Dr. Grayson and the Quiration scientists didn't need his direct input anymore and so he was simply waiting until Hani'ah arrived for their first and, hopefully, final test.

At the laboratory's core, Dr. Grayson's version of P.A.T.R.I.C. dominated the large space. It was similar to the one they'd constructed back in Lynt City, but had been upgraded in ways Isaac wasn't sure he fully understood.

He'd tried asking about the additions, but it only made Dr. Grayson frown, mumble something unintelligible, and then start arguing with himself. He'd also tried to work it out for himself, but that was easier said than done.

Despite being accepted as their so called 'Messiah', the Quirations didn't like him messing with their equipment. Whenever he approached a machine, several engineers appeared nearby. They didn't actually prevent him from disassembling anything, of course, but if he turned his back for a second they all rushed in and put it back together whether he was ready or not.

It had been annoying at first, but after getting the hang of things, Isaac had decided to make a game of it.

175

His best score so far was five Quirations fixing four different components at the same time.

Isaac smiled to himself. He knew it was immature, but every time he saw the exasperated concern on a Quiration's face, it reminded him of Jason.

As for the equipment's purpose, most of it seemed designed to transfer massive amounts of electrical energy from the Bas Quirat's central power grid into P.A.T.R.I.C. It also connected the entire apparatus to a series of large screens that were placed around the laboratory's perimeter and any Quiration not currently concerned with cleaning up after their inquisitive 'Messiah' was crowded around one.

Isaac paused for a moment to run his eye over the experimental data they were so obsessed with. Not all of it was understandable, but he at least recognised one of the original algorithms Jason had created. It made him smile. It was good to know not all their work had been 'improved upon' as Dr. Grayson so often put it.

Turning away from the screens, Isaac was about to begin another round of 'Tie up the Quirations' when the noise level suddenly dropped. He looked around to find everyone bowing in one direction and wasn't surprised to find their target was Hani'ah Naziri. She was currently sweeping across the floor toward him with her ever-present 'ladies-in-black'.

"Hmph," he grunted.

The Quirations might give their 'Messiah' a measured amount of respect, but they revered Hani'ah like a God.

"Isaac Taylor," she said in warm Arabic, her clouded eyes glistening. "I believe it is time to test your device."

"As far as I know," Isaac replied, before bowing awkwardly and then feeling stupid doing so to a blind woman. "But you know, it's more doctor Grayson's device than mine now."

He glanced toward the man he was trying to compliment, but Dr. Grayson was bent over a work station, oblivious to Hani'ah's arrival and muttering to himself again.

"And yet," Hani'ah added, drawing level with him in a wash of delicate perfume, "it will not work without the Messiah."

"Or you," Isaac added quickly. "I'm really not that special, Hani'ah."

Hani'ah smiled a knowing smile.

"We shall see," she added, before turning abruptly and heading for the chair that had been made for her. "Now let us begin."

Isaac still found it disconcerting that a blind woman could walk around as if she knew exactly where she was at all times. In between frustrating his Quiration hosts, he'd puzzled over how she did it and suspected it had something to do with her ladies-in-black. He watched them as they helped Hani'ah settle into her seat and noticed that they watched everything their Prophet did as well as everything that went on around her.

"*They're seeing the world for her,*" he thought to himself.

As the thought registered in his mind, both of Hani'ah's companions abruptly turned toward him and Isaac heard a voice in his mind.

"*Aladrak jiddaan.*"

Isaac heard the voice only in Arabic this time and so he knew it was Hani'ah speaking in his head. She was, however, smiling, and so he chose to believe his guess had been right and she was merely acknowledging that. He also assumed she didn't want to share that knowledge with anyone else and so he decided not to say anything out loud.

Smiling awkwardly at Hani'ah's ladies-in-black, Isaac moved to his own seat and picked up his trusty skull cap. It was the same one he'd arrived with and the only part of P.A.T.R.I.C. that was from his home reality. Dr. Grayson had wanted to make improvements on it as well, but Isaac flatly refused. He knew it was superstitious, but having something from home with him – unmarked and unchanged – made him feel better about their chances of success.

After taking a seat, he pulled the skull cap into place and then looked up to find Hani'ah's ladies-in-black lowering Dr. Grayson's improved version of his skull cap over the prophet's beautifully arranged hair.

It was a more of a helmet-like device than a skull cap and was attached to a matriculating arm that hung from the ceiling like a vine-laden branch. It also looked a lot more expensive than the device Isaac was wearing.

The crystals that would connect Hani'ah's mind with Isaac's glistened under the laboratory's bright lights like fine rubies and they reminded him of the red fire from his nightmare.

Isaac shivered at the thought and reached out to touch the transparent screen in front of him. It lit up in response and displayed the graphs that were duplicated all around the lab. He checked them for a moment to make sure everything was ready and then glanced at Hani'ah through the screen.

"I am ready," her translated voice informed him calmly.

"Oh," Isaac replied. "Right. So, when we begin, I'm going to create an image–"

"Of a white Maltese terrier," Hani'ah finished for him. "Yes, I've seen your previous attempts, Isaac Taylor. There is no need for explanation."

"Oh... good," Isaac said, wondering how much Hani'ah – or perhaps her ladies-in-black – had actually 'seen'. "Let's get started then."

At his words, the laboratory once more became a bustle of activity. Those Quirations not already in place rushed to their stations and, when the noise eventually died down, Dr. Grayson appeared at Isaac's side.

"You may begin when you're ready," he said, not looking at either of them. "Just as you did with Jason. I will be monitoring."

"Thanks, Doc," Isaac said, smiling nervously at him.

But Dr. Grayson just nodded once and disappeared again.

"O-kay," Isaac said slowly, before turning back to the screen and reaching out to touch it again. "Phase one."

As it had done many times before, P.A.T.R.I.C. powered up and Isaac waited as it calibrated to the two people now connected to it. When that was done, a psychic baseline appeared on the screen. This time, instead of the 2-dimensional line Isaac was used to, the psychic measurement was displayed as a 3-dimensional plane – one of Dr. Grayson's improvements.

As Isaac mentally explored his psychic connection with Hani'ah, it shimmered like a wind-swept pond and he wondered what the third dimension was meant to represent. Dr. Grayson certainly hadn't bothered to explain that part of it and Isaac suspected this was one of the elements Jason would have understood better than him.

"Right," he said when the calibration was complete. "Phase two."

He touched the screen again and it linked P.A.T.R.I.C. with the Bas Quirat's electrical supply. A familiar pressure appeared in Isaac's mind as their psychic energy was boosted and he wondered for a moment just how much was available to them.

"*What would have happened if there'd been enough electricity back home to keep the experiment going?*" he thought to himself.

"That is what we're about to find out," Hani'ah said in answer to his unspoken question.

Isaac looked through the transparent screen at her and smiled. He was never going to get used to that.

All that was left now was The Game.

With a quick thought, Isaac pictured a small, white terrier in his mind and it appeared on the transparent screen before him. He then mentally offered the image to Hani'ah and she accepted it with barely a shimmer of effort.

"Well done," Isaac said, honestly impressed. "Even Jason isn't that quick."

But his admiration was soon replaced with surprise when the little dog's fur abruptly became shorter and darker while the Maltese terrier grew into a large, regal looking canine.

"A Saluki," Hani'ah explained with a hint of amusement. "It is a Persian greyhound and one of the oldest known breeds of domestic dog."

"Impressive," Isaac said, both for the Saluki and for Hani'ah's psychic ability.

The connection they shared was surprisingly strong and although it wasn't quite to the level he'd shared with Jason, Isaac got the feeling Hani'ah had more creative potential than his brother ever had.

When Hani'ah passed the image back to him, he took it eagerly. He wanted to impress her in turn and as he contemplated what to do next, a mischievous thought occurred to him.

With a smile, he focussed his mind and then carefully tweaked the image. Suddenly the large dog was joined by several others and they leapt into motion, racing around a simple, oval track in pursuit of a mechanical rabbit that whizzed along the inside fence line.

Grinning stupidly, Isaac offered the image to Hani'ah and waited to gauge her reaction. He was expecting her to be thrown off by the sudden change in context, but her face remained a picture of calm as the oval track was replaced by a small thicket of trees.

Raising his eyebrows in surprise, Isaac saw the rabbit whizzing along the fence line leap down and become a fox that scrambled through the forest in a desperate attempt to escape the large pack of hunting dogs now racing through the trees behind it.

Isaac nodded slowly in respect. Hani'ah had added, in a single move, more detail than he'd ever got from Jason. She was a natural.

Glancing at the graph glowing at the corner of his screen, he saw there was only a small change in the measure of psychic energy. The electrical consumption, however, was considerable.

"*Jason was right,*" he thought, not at all surprised.

At this point, Hani'ah offered the image back to him and Isaac decided it was time to take things up a notch. With a quick mental stroke, the fox grew into an enormous brown bear and he made it turn and stand up on its hind legs, towering over the hunting dogs.

He then made the Saluki hounds turn to flee, but quickly blocked their path with a large tiger, its glistening coat shining orange, white and black. It bared its fangs and swiped at the dogs, making them head off in another direction, but Isaac once more flexed his imagination and, in quick succession, an enormous crocodile snapped its powerful jaws, a fat rhinoceros thundered into view, and a silver-back gorilla swung into the fray, pounding its fists against its chest.

Each time the dogs yelped and scrambled off in a new direction until, for his grand finale, Isaac created a rearing African elephant that appeared in the only space left and slammed its feet down so hard the hunting dogs were flung into the air.

The pack of regal Salukis fell back to the forest floor in a heap and were left cowering in the centre of the fearsome animals.

This time, when he offered the image to Hani'ah, she hesitated.

"I can simplify it if you'd like," he said with a smile.

"No," she replied slowly. "I just need a moment."

Glancing at the energy meter, Isaac saw that they were now drawing much more power from the electrical grid, far beyond what he'd expected. The psychic indicator had also jumped right up and there was plenty of movement and discussion going on around the laboratory.

When he returned his attention to Hani'ah, she still hadn't tried to take the image from him.

"It's okay if–" he began, but fell silent when he felt her take control.

The image shimmered as she struggled to maintain so many separate items at once. The crocodile blinked out of existence for a moment and then reappeared a lot smaller. The gorilla froze in place and then slowly fell over. The hunting dogs disappeared one by one until there was only one left, but it grew in size, baring its teeth and snarling at the tiger.

Isaac was amazed Hani'ah was able to hold so much of what he'd given her. Technically, she'd just lost The Game, but given they were here for much more than a childish competition, he tried not to think it too loudly.

He could also sense Hani'ah's mind struggling beneath the enormous cognitive load and was about to ask for the image back when he heard her gasp in alarm.

He expected the image to fall apart as she lost control altogether, but instead, a searing column of red energy roared down between them, obliterating the forest and animals in a sea of fire.

Isaac flinched away from the inferno and tried to make it disappear, but when he looked again, the screen between him and Hani'ah was gone.

"What…?" he mumbled in confusion.

In its place was a large, shimmering hole in the laboratory floor.

Through it, he could see a lush, forested landscape far below as if he was seeing it from several kilometres up. He didn't know how it could be possible, but it was almost as if he had x-ray vision and was peering right through the Bas Quirat to the planet's surface… which was now covered by teeming forests and winding rivers instead of barren rock and sand.

"*Is Hani'ah doing this?*" he thought.

His instincts assured him Hani'ah couldn't have created such a vast image on her own and when he looked at her to confirm it, he realised something else was wrong. Hani'ah had the same look of distress he'd seen moments before, but her ladies-in-black were frozen beside her in uncomfortable-looking positions.

Looking around the laboratory, Isaac realised that everyone else also seemed to be frozen in place, as if time had decided to take a short vacation.

He returned his gaze to Hani'ah, hoping she wasn't frozen like the rest of them, and blinked in surprise when a hazy shadow appeared between them. Its edges gradually became solid and the silhouette sparked a familiarity that made Isaac's heart leap with excitement.

"Jason?" he called out, "is that you?"

"*Isaac?*" the shadowy figure replied, his voice sounding much further away than it appeared. "*It's me, bro. But... how are you doing this?*"

"You wouldn't believe me if I told you," Isaac replied with a laugh. "Where are you?"

"*In jail,*" Jason's strange, disembodied voice replied.

"What?"

"*I was arrested for unauthorised access to the power grid. They think... they think I killed you, bro.*"

"What? No!"

"*Listen, Isaac, don't worry about me,*" Jason continued quickly. "*I did some calculations and we used all the power in Lynt City's grid to open the first portal. But... we need more to get you back. More than I think is possible.*"

"How much more?" Isaac asked.

"*More than every generator on Mars can produce,*" Jason replied. "*I mean, even if we added Earth's entire productive capacity, I'm... not sure it would be enough.*"

"But that's..." Isaac said, a chill washing through him. "How am I going to get back?"

"*I... don't know if you can, Isaac,*" Jason said, the despair clear in his voice.

"No," Isaac said defiantly. "We'll find a way. We have to!"

But even as he spoke, Jason's shadow became less distinct and grew smaller, as if it was moving away from him.

"Wait," Isaac called as his brother's image began to fade. "Don't go!"

"*Isaac!*" Jason's distant voice cried, but his shadow continued to fade until it was gone altogether.

"No!" Isaac cried, holding back tears of frustration. "Not again!"

As his blurry vision refocused on Hani'ah, he saw another shadow in the air behind her and the possibility it was Jason rekindled his hope. But as it became more distinct, Isaac knew it couldn't be his brother.

For one thing, there was more than one of them, as if several people were standing there. And they were too large to be human. Each one was hunched in a way that made Isaac feel uncomfortable and as they shimmered in and out of focus, he thought he saw a pair of glowing red eyes near the top of each one.

He blinked again, not sure if what he was seeing was real, and the shapes suddenly disappeared. At the same time, the large hole in the laboratory floor snapped shut and everyone seemed to come back to life around him.

He saw Hani'ah slump down in her chair and her ladies-in-black rushed forward to help. Then several fires sprung to life amongst P.A.T.R.I.C.'s instruments and the Quirations split into two groups that either scrambled to put out the fires or provide assistance to Hani'ah.

Every one of them looked suddenly scared or bewildered.

Reaching up to remove his skull cap, Isaac jumped when a strong hand closed on his arm. He turned to find Dr. Grayson beside him, his face pale and his eyes wild.

"We did it," he hissed, sounding terrified instead of the elation his words suggested.

"Are you... alright?" Isaac asked, not sure what to think.

"I knew it would work, but..." Dr. Grayson said, his voice.

"But what?" Isaac asked.

Dr. Grayson stared at him for a long moment, as if struggling to speak, and Isaac found it hard to meet his wild gaze. He turned to glance at Hani'ah again and saw her ladies-in-black were now carrying her rapidly toward the exit. All the Quiration scientists not battling the fires were also bowing low, clearly frightened for their Prophet.

"Is Hani'ah okay?" he asked, hoping it would snap Dr. Grayson out of whatever mental stasis he was currently in.

"She... overloaded her cerebral cortex," he replied distantly.

"Overloaded?" Isaac said, glancing at Hani'ah again as she disappeared through the laboratory doors. "I think Jason had the same problem."

"You saw him, didn't you?" Dr. Grayson said, squeezing his arm again.

"What? How did you-?"

"My instruments identified a period of localised time distortion," Dr. Grayson replied. "Quickly now, what did he tell you?"

"He said there was a problem," Isaac replied, feeling lost and increasingly worried about Grayson's manic expression.

"And that is?" Dr. Grayson asked eagerly.

Isaac thought back.

"He said the amount of electricity P.A.T.R.I.C. used to get me here was enormous and that we need much more to get back. More than we can possibly produce."

"How much?" Dr. Grayson asked, his frantic eyes gleaming.

"More than the entire generational capacity of Mars and Earth combined," Isaac replied flatly.

Dr. Grayson finally let go of his arm and Isaac noticed that his hands were trembling.

"They were right," he whispered.

"What?" Isaac said with a frown, "Who was right?"

Dr. Grayson stared into the distance for a long moment, as if waiting for something, then he turned back to Isaac.

"We can't do this," he hissed.

"What?"

"We can still stop this," he added, grabbing Isaac's arm again. "You just have to…"

But his voice trailed off abruptly and, a moment later, his eyes rolled back and his head started to shake from side to side. It looked like some kind of seizure and Isaac didn't know what to do.

"Help!" he said loudly, trying to get the attention of one of the Quirations running around the laboratory.

But before anyone noticed him, Dr. Grayson's head grew still and Isaac thought he saw a flash of red light as the man's eyes locked onto his.

"Don't you see?" he said, his tone completely different. "The Quiration prophecy is true! There's more than enough power on its way to Mars, right now! And if we use it to open a portal back to your home, you will *prevent* the oncoming Apocalypse."

Isaac's memories flashed with the red fire from his dream and Dr. Grayson's words suddenly made sense.

"The Jupiter flare," he said quietly.

"Precisely!" Dr. Grayson hissed, his eyes glinting with the same red light.

"That... could have enough power," Isaac said uncertainly.

"And if we convert it into psychic energy whilst returning you to your own reality...?" Dr. Grayson said, pausing so that Isaac could finish his sentence.

"We would save Mars," Isaac obliged in growing excitement.

"Such a beautiful irony," Dr. Grayson said, letting his arm go and clapping them together. "It seems you are destined to fulfil the Quiration prophecies after all."

Isaac stared at Dr. Grayson, dumbfounded at how neatly the pieces were locking into place. His dream of being struck by red lightning; the Quiration 'prophecies'; the experiment that had brought him here in the first place. It was all connected.

Then his mind turned to how they could ever transfer the energy from a Jupiter flare into P.A.T.R.I.C. and his bubble burst.

"But there's no time," he said in despair. "How can you possibly engineer something to convert the Jupiter flare into the energy we need before it gets here? How much time to we have? Twelve hours?"

"Less," Dr. Grayson said with a dismissive wave. "But you don't understand, Isaac. It seems this Quiration prophecy has a way of making sure it comes true."

"What do you mean?"

"Cosmotech Defence owns an orbital platform that I believe will suit this purpose perfectly."

"Really?" Isaac said incredulously.

"Really," Dr. Grayson replied with a disturbing grin. "In fact, it's something I've been working on for the better part of a decade."

Isaac wondered for a moment if all prophecies were meant to work like this, with everything falling into your lap in just the way you needed it.

"Well," he said slowly, "I guess it's worth a try. It's certainly the kind of miracle I can get behind."

"You'll see," Dr. Grayson said, raising a finger. "Now, we must prepare. There is not as much time as it appears."

As Dr. Grayson scuttled away and began ordering the panicking Quirations into a more ordered form of action, Isaac slowly shook his head.

"*He's insane,*" he thought, trying to get an image of the Doc's manic expression out of his mind, "*and yet he's probably right. Which means Hani'ah is as well.*"

It was much easier to believe now that he didn't have to buy into the Quiration's Messiah story. He might actually turn out to be the one who saves them. Of course, it was science that had brought him here and it was science that would ultimately save the day.

"*But what was with that hole in the floor?*" he thought with a frown.

He knew it could have been a random artefact from his own imagination, or even from Hani'ah's for that matter, but it didn't feel like it. It felt more like the visions he'd witnessed when the experiment had gone wrong in the first place.

"*Don't over think it,*" he told himself as he got to his feet. "*Whatever it was, there's an end in sight now. I'll be home before I know it.*"

And that thought alone was enough to make up for the strange things he'd witnessed and even Dr. Grayson's bizarre behaviour.

"*It's only a matter of time now, bro,*" he thought with a smile. "*I'll be back before you know it.*"

187

DR. GRAYSON'S MIND - June 8, 2147 - 12.20pm

DR. GRAYSON COWERED IN DARKNESS. HE KNEW HIS consciousness had been torn from his body in retaliation for what he'd almost said to Isaac.

He was a weak, pathetic fool who should have known his demons would never let him betray them so easily. While he was here, forcibly locked inside his own mind, they would be telling Isaac exactly what he needed to hear and there was nothing he could do about it.

Wherever they had been – if, in fact, they'd gone anywhere – they were now well and truly back and they were furious. He could hear them screaming at him from the shadows. He could see the glint of their blazing red eyes as they slowly circled him, snarling and promising violent retribution for his betrayal.

"No!" Dr. Grayson pleaded. "I wasn't going to tell him anything, I swear!"

But they knew it was a lie, just as he did.

When he'd seen the rift in time created by Isaac's machine, the realisation that the demons' plan would succeed had stirred his long dormant conscience. Their prolonged mental absence may have also

189

played a part, but either way, it had been enough for Dr. Grayson to attempt the unforgivable and try to stop them.

"I'll do it!" he screamed. "I will! Please, you don't have to do this!" But in place of a reply, a harsh orange light appeared below him. Suddenly he was hanging from his wrists, completely naked, with his arms and legs forced out in a wide X.

A searing heat washed over his feet and he looked down to find that he was hanging above a river of bubbling lava.

"No!" he screamed in a panic. "Please! I've done everything you asked of me! I'm just weak! I couldn't help my own thoughts! But they mean nothing! I'll do it! I'll do anything!"

But his demons just mocked and jeered at him from the shadows and Dr. Grayson could feel himself being lowered toward the lava. He squirmed and fought against the invisible grip that held him, but it was pointless.

He knew this wasn't real. He knew it was all happening inside his head. But he also knew that the pain he was about to feel would be worse than reality. Here, he couldn't pass out, or die. Here, there would be no premature end to his torment.

Gritting his teeth in desperate anticipation, Dr. Grayson screamed as the heat boiling off the lava's surface became too much to bear. His muscles shuddered involuntarily, locked in a desperate struggle to escape the fire, but his demons wouldn't relent. When his feet finally made contact with the molten rock, a new sensation joined the broiling mixture of pain and Dr. Grayson's screams took on a whole new level of desperation.

He instinctively looked down at the damage being done to him and saw the flesh, tendons and bones of his feet flash shrivel into twisted lumps of charcoal. The skin further up his legs began to pop and peel, allowing his blood to boil out in dark, sizzling rivers, while the bones beneath cracked one by one, sending splinters of white out through his rapidly cooking flesh.

Dr. Grayson clearly felt parts of him falling off as he was lowered further and reflexively bit his tongue as his organs began to cook inside of him.

He tried to lessen the agony by reminding himself that his real body remained unharmed, but the experience of pain was too visceral and it made no difference.

His screams finally lost their volume when the lava burst his lungs and crackled through his rib cage and it was only when the molten rock flowed past his face and up to the very tips of his fingers that his gruesome descent came to a halt.

With pain now screaming through every part of him, Dr. Grayson felt what was left of him being lifted out of the lava.

Despite the blackened, charcoal pits that had once been his eyes, his demons allowed him to see what had been done to his body. They even allowed him the ability to gasp in air so he could scream once again. He could hear them cackling over his pathetic screeching until the intensity of his pain finally receded and he was left hanging in darkness once more.

"I'm sorry," he thought, taking in several deep, sobbing breaths, certain his demons would hear him. *"I will not fail you again."*

But they only laughed harder. They knew he wouldn't disobey again. They knew everything that would happen. They had seen it already. And Dr. Grayson knew it too. He didn't know why his own mind had betrayed him with thoughts of anything other than the inevitable and he hated himself for it.

"I'll do it," he promised as their laughter echoed all around him. *"I'll do it."*

SHOPPING DISTRICT, BAS QUIRAT - June 8, 2147 - 12.12pm

LOC BREEDEN STRODE THROUGH THE BAS QUIRAT IN the clothes of a common Quiration male – a long white dishdash and headscarf. His security team were also in costume, but they were dressed as Quiration police, and with a little psychic misdirection, the ruse was allowing them to go wherever they wanted.

"Hani'ah Naziri has done her job well," Loc mused.

It was clear from the way they were being avoided that the Quirations feared their police force and were pre-programmed to look the other way at the sight of a uniform. It made Loc's job so much easier. All he needed was a gentle psychic push to prevent anyone from looking closer.

There were other distractions at play, of course. The political undercurrent Loc had noticed with the Quiration delegates was even more potent amongst the general populace. It seemed the religious war was taking its toll and the arrival of Isaac, the Quiration's so-called 'Messiah', had not helped the situation.

On more than one occasion, Loc witnessed small groups either praying together or locked in heated discussion. Those praying did not even seem to notice his police escort, but those simply talking dispersed quickly when they saw him coming.

"That's what religious belief gets you," he thought bitterly, *"division and stupidity in equal measure."*

Eventually, the address they'd stolen from the Quiration's records led them to a large shopping district. Not surprisingly, most of the shops were closed, but their target was one of the few still open for business.

"You can't assist the rebellion if you're not open," Loc thought with a smile.

To avoid spooking his target, Loc stopped his escort at the edge of the district and spoke to Captain West in quiet Arabic, in case anyone was listening.

"Wait here," he said quietly. "And intercept anyone who looks like they might join me inside. This won't take long."

West simply nodded, unable to speak Arabic himself, and Loc turned, walked casually down the row of shops, and then entered the target's store.

Inside, the place sparkled with extravagant jewellery displayed in cabinets of crystal clear glass. Rows and rows of jewels set in all kinds of fittings were arranged next to lockets and watches of gold, silver, and platinum. Expensive-looking rings and bracelets glittered under expertly hidden lights next to ceremonial daggers with sheaths that were embossed with so many gems it was unlikely they would ever be used for the blade within.

"Perhaps today will prove different," Loc thought to himself.

As he crossed the threshold a series of sitar notes echoed through the store and a man appeared through a door behind the counter.

"Salam, good sir," he said in Arabic. "How may I assist you?"

He was shorter than expected and a little plump, but his beard was immaculately groomed and his smile was brilliant enough to rival Loc's finest.

"I have come for information," Loc said bluntly.

"Information?" the man replied with a small laugh. "No, I sell jewellery, sir. The best in the Bas Quirat if my customers are to be believed."

"I'm sure they can be," Loc replied, "but I'm looking for someone who can tell me where to find Saadi Khalil."

The man's smile faltered at the sound of Saadi's name.

"I do not know that name," he said, smiling again, but with a small frown this time.

"I think you do," Loc countered, "but we will see."

"I'm not sure–" the man continued politely, but before he could finish, Loc looked him in the eye and felt the psychic connection click into place in his mind.

As soon as it was made, Loc charged across the mental space between them and smashed into the man's subconscious. His defences were formidable given he had no psychic power, but they lasted only a second before Loc tore through and took control of his mind.

"Excellent," he said with a nod of satisfaction. "Now, what is your name?"

With his brilliant smile gone, the man's plump face looked suddenly haggard. When he spoke, it was in the cold monotone of speech without emotion.

"Farik Sumhah."

"Tell me, Farik, do you know where to find Saadi Khalil?"

"No."

Loc was a little disappointed at this, but it was only a small setback.

"Do you know someone who can tell me where to find Saadi Khalil?"

"Yes."

"Very good," Loc said with a smile. "Now, tell me the name of this person and where I can find them."

"His name is Jemdek Aik," Farik replied. "He runs the Dhal-Sim café on level one-forty-six, section eight, Parvour lane."

Loc felt a small thrill of triumph. It seemed he was destined to finish the Quiration's religious war for them.

195

He could already imagine the look on Hani'ah Naziri's face when she was forced to thank an outsider for getting it done.

"Very good, Farik," he said. "And can anyone visit this café?"

"No. Only those who have heard the words of Saadi Khalil, or been vouched for by someone who has."

"Interesting," Loc said, stroking his chin. "And what do you do to those who do not fit either description?"

"They are killed as spies."

"Of course they are," Loc said with a grin – he enjoyed it when people were so predictable. "Now, one last thing, Farik. Do you believe Hani'ah Naziri is a prophet of Allah?"

"No," Farik replied.

Loc's grin widened. He knew there would be some within the Bas Quirat who felt this way. Many, if the holy war was as widespread as he assumed. But it was still surprisingly good to hear it for himself.

"Excellent," he said. "Now tell me what you really think of her."

"Hani'ah Naziri is a puppet of Satan," Farik replied. "Her prophecies are lies designed to keep us from the truth. She sees one future and accepts it to the detriment of all others. She twists the world to suit her selfish goals. Controls it. Taints it with her arrogance and greed."

Loc was intrigued. If Hani'ah Naziri was working for the Triumvirate then Farik's assessment was surprisingly close to the truth, if a little zealous in its description. Whatever this Saadi Khalil might be, it was clear he was well-informed.

"And what is the truth she is keeping from you, Farik?" he asked.

"That there is no single truth. Allah has, in his wisdom, created a universe where all futures are possible. To force others to conform to a single truth is blasphemy. True enlightenment comes not from selfish control, but from noble action."

Loc sighed. As always, an idea formed from something close to the truth so quickly became the rantings of a child when interpreted through the context of an all-knowing God.

"A naive notion at best, Farik. But I will admit you've made me a happy man. For that, I will grant you a merciful death."

Taking a step back so Farik could move past him, Loc gestured toward one of the display cases he'd admired on the way in.

"Remove your most expensive gem-encrusted dagger from its display," he ordered.

Farik moved out from behind his counter and, after stepping past Loc, placed his palm against one of the glass cases near the centre of his store. His touch disengaged a hidden lock that opened the back of the case and Farik reached inside to pick out a very old, but beautifully crafted dagger.

There were only a few gems on this one and Loc assumed its worth came from its historical significance.

"How much do you ask for this dagger, Farik?"

"Seven-hundred and fifty-thousand," Farik replied.

Loc's eyebrows rose. That was a significant sum of money, even by his standards.

"And what gives it such value?" he asked.

"This dagger was owned and used extensively by the twelfth century warlord, Yusuf Ad-din Shirkuh."

Loc wasn't familiar with the name, but it hardly mattered. Such details were only useful if his clients believed they were and he very rarely dealt with Quirations.

"Impressive in its own way, I'm sure," he conceded. "Unsheathe it."

Farik did as commanded. The blade's edge glistened under the display lights.

"Luck is with you, Farik," Loc said with a smile, "it looks as if your dagger has been sharpened recently. Now, push the blade point-first into your heart."

Without hesitation, Farik brought the knife to his chest and plunged it in deep. The blade slid in easily, avoiding any resistance from Farik's ribs, and when it was buried to the hilt, a blossom of blood appeared in his clean white dishdash. Farik shuddered for a moment as his heart convulsed one final time then he collapsed to the floor.

Loc stared down at the motionless body and watched the puddle of red that slowly spread out beneath it. It only took a minute or so for the psychic tether to disappear from his mind.

Farik Sumhah was now dead.

"I envy you, Farik," he said in English, taking one more look around the glistening jewellery store. "I can only hope my final breath occurs in a place like this."

Walking back to the front door, Loc stepped outside for a moment and gestured to his Captain and his intelligence expert, Lexi Sharp. They quickly joined him inside the store and stopped when they saw Farik.

"Ignore it," Loc told them in English. "The next target is Jemdek Aik. Owner of the Dhal-sim café on level one-forty-six. What do you know of the area?"

Lexi Sharp's gaze lingered on Farik's body for a moment then she pulled herself together and took a data pad out of her pocket. She then quickly tapped through the information they'd stolen.

"That may be difficult," she said after a short pause. "Level one-four-six has been designated rebel territory. In recent months there's been more than a dozen major clashes in the area with fatalities recorded on both sides. Local authorities have attempted to isolate the area by cutting off water and electricity, but the resistance just moves to another level and then comes back after somehow managing to reconnect all utilities."

"So we can't just walk in there with a cohort of Quiration police," Loc said with a frown.

"Not without starting a serious military engagement, sir," Captain West added.

Loc considered it for a moment.

"No, not yet," he said quietly.

"Sir?"

"I think I'll go in alone, Captain," Loc said firmly.

"I don't think–" Captain West protested.

"Yes, you would be a fool not to object, Captain," Loc interrupted him, "but I don't want to hear it. There will be people watching the elevators and I don't want to be seen in the company of a large group of Quiration police."

"Yes, sir," West said, his reluctance obvious.

Turning to Lexi, Loc continued.

"How do I get to level one-four-six?"

"The central elevator atrium, sir," she replied. "The Quirations don't restrict access because they believe it helps them monitor who comes and goes from the area."

"I assume there's a way to stop them from detecting my presence?"

"Of course, sir. Our link to their systems is still secure. I'll monitor your progress myself and delete any security notifications as they're made. No record of your movements will exist long enough to alert the Quirations."

"Good," Loc said, before turning to Captain West. "While I secure the target, have your team get rid of their uniforms and dress as locals. You don't need to be particularly convincing, but I'd like you to avoid any serious confrontations, so make an effort to blend in. Then I want you as near to level one-four-six as you can get. I'll make contact when I'm ready to rejoin you."

"Yes, sir," he replied.

"Right. Get moving," Loc said, motioning them out.

Following them outside, Loc waited until his escort had marched out of sight before setting off in the other direction. He knew this was a dangerous play, but in place of concern he felt excitement. Psychic powers or not, he would need to be careful, but the risk was worth it to feel in control once again.

His progress through the Bas Quirat went quite differently without a police escort. For one thing, people didn't automatically get out of his way and so he actually had to weave around some of them. None of them gave him any undue attention, however, certainly not while his psychic distraction was turned on, and so he made good time to the central elevator atrium.

As with the sections of the Bas Quirat he'd already seen, it was bustling with activity. People were rushing around on whatever business they felt was important given the world was about to end and the air vibrated with tense anticipation.

Loc made his way toward the central column and eventually entered an elevator pod. No one paid him any attention.

"*Time to see what rebel territory looks like,*" he thought.

Using the panel on his armrest, Loc chose level 146, confident his security team would ensure his choice went unnoticed by Quiration security. The elevator then got underway and, one by one, the other passengers departed on different levels. Eventually, the elevator arrived at level 146. Loc was the only one left.

As the new level slid into view beyond the transparent doors, Loc was presented with a very different view of the Bas Quirat. It was more crowded than the levels he'd already seen, which was surprising given its designation as rebel territory, but it was the general condition of things that really set it apart.

The paints used to decorate the hallways were dull, as if stained from smoke, and although what little carpet he could see was as gaudy as ever, it clearly hadn't been cleaned in months and showed several burned and bald spots. There was also less ornamentation along the skirting boards, less paintings on the walls, and less upmarket fashion amongst the residents who crowded the corridors.

As soon as his elevator slid into view, Loc noticed several distrustful looks that he could have taken psychic advantage of, but he left the Quirations to their suspicions. None of these pathetic souls were a threat to him.

"Stop," a rough voice ordered as the elevator doors opened.

Loc turned to his left and saw a scruffy, thick-necked man who looked to be in his forties. His beard was unkempt and his clothing was ragged, but the rifle he held looked immaculately clean and the fire in his eyes promised violence.

"Yes?" Loc asked calmly.

The man looked a little hesitant when his victim didn't show any concern, but he rallied by shaking his weapon.

"What is your business here?" he demanded.

"I come with a message from Farik Sumhah," Loc replied.

The man's eyes narrowed, but he hesitated long enough for Loc to know the war of suspicion was already won.

"And who is this message for?" the man asked.

"Not for you," Loc said firmly.

The man's lips raised into a sneer, but Loc didn't care. He knew men like this intimately. They held no authority of their own, but they enjoyed the illusion of power a deadly weapon gave them. Ultimately, they felt more fear than they ever inspired in others and would not attack unless publically insulted or ordered to do so.

Loc held the man's gaze nonetheless, waiting for any indication the fool was going to make the mistake of actually using his weapon. He could see him thinking slowly through his options and wasn't at all surprised when the man eventually decided the trouble of checking Loc's story was a waste of time.

"Go," he grunted, waving him on.

Bowing his head slightly in acknowledgement, Loc stepped off the elevator and quickly lost himself in the crowd.

It wasn't difficult. There were so many people here that Loc found the need to deflect unwanted attention wasn't necessary. Dressed as he was in a traditional dishdash and headscarf, he was simply another face in the crowd and the people here clearly had more important things to worry about than a possible spy.

The crowded corridor forced him to wind his way through a maze of vendors who sold goods and services of every description. It seemed Hani'ah Naziri needed a lesson in population control.

201

By allowing what he assumed was unsanctioned trade, the rebels were free to avoid any commerce with the parts of the Bas Quirat that were more easily controlled. It would have undermined Hani'ah's authority economically while at the same time depriving her of more subtle ways to manipulate the populace.

"*Amateur,*" he thought, shaking his head.

He suspected Hani'ah's leniency had something to do with the rebels religion, however, and wouldn't be surprised if sending in an assault team to round up the vendors, confiscate goods, and put them in prison would only make the problem worse.

"*Another example of religion undermining effective government,*" he thought to himself.

When he eventually found himself at the hallway leading to the Dhal-sim café, Loc saw three men guarding the entrance. All three were openly holding weapons and much younger than man he'd encountered at the elevator. One seemed to be in conversation with someone on the other end of a video call, while the others were eye-balling anyone who passed the hallway.

Loc smiled. There was no better enjoyment than controlling those who naively thought they wielded power.

Noting the sense of danger he felt when leaving the anonymity of the crowd, Loc walked straight up to the young men and stopped in front of them. The two who'd been watching the crowd immediately raised their weapons and the third ended his call and stepped up to join his friends.

"Who are you and where do you think you're going?" the one in the middle said in a menacing tone.

Loc met his equally menacing stare.

"My name is Abd-al-aziz, and I am here to see Jemdek Aik," he said calmly.

The young man looked him up and down with a sceptical expression.

"Does he know you're coming?"

"Of course," Loc assured him.

The young man gave him a look that suggested Loc was lying through his teeth.

"We'll see," he growled, before glancing at one of his partners.

"No, you won't," Loc replied.

The words made the young man look back at him and the psychic connection clicked into place immediately. Loc rode it straight into his mind and found a twisted mess of fear and righteous anger. The righteous anger resisted his psychic invasion for a moment, but the fear left several openings that were easily exploited. In seconds, the young man's expression went blank.

The other two didn't seem to pick up on what had just happened, but when they moved their uncertain gaze from their comrade to Loc, he took control of them just as easily.

"Now," he said when all three were standing calmly, "you are going to take me to Jemdek Aik. You will hold your weapons ready to fire at all times. If anyone tries to stop us, you will wait for my command. If anyone attacks without warning, you will fire upon them immediately. Do you understand?"

A chorus of agreement came in reply and all three hefted their weapons to their shoulders.

"Very good," Loc said with a smile. "Now, lead me to Jemdek."

In response, the young men turned their blank expressions away from him and set off down the hallway. Even here there were a few people talking quietly in small groups and Loc smiled at the confused looks he received. One older man stepped forward, as if ready to challenge them, but when he saw the look in the young men's eyes, he frowned and quickly stepped back. No one else moved to question them and Loc was a little disappointed. He would have liked an opportunity to make an example.

The only real opposition they received was from a very large man who stood outside the Dhal-sim café. When they approached, he held up a thick-fingered hand and frowned at the young men escorting Loc.

"Aazim, Jamal, Sayf, what are you doing? Who is guarding the hallway?"

"Stop," Loc commanded and the young men did so immediately. The large man's frown deepened at this and he moved his gaze to Loc.

"Who are you?"

Loc smiled as they locked eyes and was a little surprised when he found the subconscious defences on this muscle-bound oaf were actually quite formidable. He held none of the fear the young men did and Loc got the impression he'd long since accepted that his decision to rebel against Hani'ah Naziri would eventually lead to his death. But despite his natural defences, the man's subconscious resolve didn't last long under Loc's psychic assault. It merely held him silent for a few seconds before he inevitably succumbed.

"You're an interesting man," he said when the guard finally relaxed. "I would have enjoyed exploring the source of your strength further, but time is of the essence. Move aside."

The large man did as he was told.

"When we've entered the café," Loc added, "you will not let anyone else through this door. In or out. If you cannot stop them, kill them. Do you understand?"

"Yes," the guard replied in a deep monotone.

Loc allowed this fourth psychic connection to settle at the back of his mind. Holding so many under his thrall weakened his abilities somewhat, but he wasn't concerned. He had more than enough strength to do what was required.

"Take me to Jemdek Aik," he told his young escort.

The inside of the Dhalsim café was louder than the corridors outside, but when the patrons noticed the three young men and their weapons, the noise quickly fell away. Several men rose from their seats and Loc turned to them, ready to make his first example, but a sharp command from the back of the room made him pause.

"Remain in your seats!"

The men who were now standing slowly sat back down.

Loc turned toward the source of the command and saw a man sitting at the back of the café between two much older men in a booth.

"*Jemdek Aik,*" he thought, recognising the man from Lexi Sharp's stolen records.

Because they'd not been told otherwise, the young men under Loc's psychic control continued on through the café until they stopped in front of the booth.

"Jᴇmdᴇᴋ Aik," Loc said, out loud this time.

The name sounded loud in the sudden silence and the men either side of Jemdek tensed noticeably.

"Lᴏᴄ Bʀᴇᴇdᴇn," he replied in a deep, gravelly voice.

At the sound of his own name, Loc hesitated.

"*How does this religious rebel know my name?*" he thought. "*Well, I'll find out soon enough.*"

Jemdek was very kindly looking him in the eyes and so the psychic connection was easily made. All Loc needed to do was reach out with his mind and...

"*Something's wrong,*" he thought in confusion.

The subconscious defences he found behind Jemdek's eyes were different to what he was accustomed to. When he tried to push past them, his efforts were met with an unexpected explosion of psychic energy that flung him back into his own mind.

"You cannot control me, Loc Breeden," Jemdek said in English.

For a moment, Loc was stunned. What Jemdek had just done to him should not have been possible. And yet, if there were others here like him, Loc suddenly realised he could be in very real danger.

"Please," Jemdek said, raising his hands in a placating gesture, "I know why you're here and I know what you're capable of. I do not wish for any blood to be spilled if we can avoid it. Please, sit and drink some tea with us. No harm will come to you, I swear to almighty Allah."

Loc glanced at the young men still under his control and instinctively contemplated ordering them to open fire.

"Not yet," Jemdek said quietly. "Please, let us talk first."

Looking back at him, Loc studied the man's sombre face for a moment and then smiled.

"Why not play along?" he thought to himself. *"I've got plenty of questions to answer and the longer we talk, the more time I have to turn this situation to my advantage."*

Glancing at the young men under his control, Loc spoke once more in Arabic.

"Watch everyone in the room. If anyone stands up, shoot them."

As commanded, the trio turned and raised their weapons, causing a slight murmur of tension to ripple through the café. Loc smiled again and slipped into the seat that had been offered to him, calmly placing his hands on the table.

"You claim to know why I'm here," he said to Jemdek, in English also.

"I do," Jemdek replied, ignoring the young men.

"Tell me why," Loc challenged.

"You are here to find someone, are you not? A man who is spreading a very inconvenient truth to those under the thrall of the false prophet."

Loc noticed the venom with which Jemdek said the word 'prophet'.

"And you know where to find this person?" he asked.

"Of course," Jemdek said mildly, "but you already know that."

Loc paused. Either Jemdek knew more than he realised, or he was pretending he did. Either way, he didn't like it.

"And what might I offer in exchange for this information?"

"You might offer anything," Jemdek said with a shrug, "but all I ask in return is the answer to a simple question."

Loc paused again. What game was Jemdek playing? Was he trying to trick Loc into revealing valuable information? Was he providing a diversion so Saadi Khalil had time to escape? Or was all of this some kind of trap to prevent Loc from leaving?

No one in the café had moved since he'd entered, but that didn't mean there weren't hidden cameras and rebels already on their way to intercept him. And yet, Loc didn't see even the slightest indication Jemdek was lying.

"What question?" he asked, deciding to let things play out a little.

"In time," Jemdek said with a small wave. "First, I need you to agree to this trade."

Loc didn't know what kind of question could be worth the life of Saadi Khalil, but he was finding it difficult to see the play here. And something told him that if there was anyone loyal to this rebel leader, it was the man sitting in front of him.

"Ask your question and we will see," he said carefully.

Jemdek's eyes narrowed for a moment as he considered the counter offer then he spoke in a clear, firm tone.

"Do you know who it is you serve?"

Loc paused. He couldn't immediately see any value in such a question. Was this some kind of reference to Hani'ah Naziri and her illegitimate rule of the Bas Quirat?

"I don't serve your false prophet," he said after a moment.

"She's not my prophet," Jemdek said with another wave of his hand. "And that is not the master I'm talking about. Do you know who it is you *truly* serve?"

Loc paused again. Surely this man couldn't know of the Triumvirate. Not unless he was working for them as well. Which, given the events of the past day or so, wasn't so hard to believe. Could Jemdek be one of their agents inside the Bas Quirat?

"I serve no one," he said after a moment. "Unless you're referring to my contract with Cosmotech Defence."

"Ah," Jemdek said, clasping his hands together, "a simple yet convincing lie. Well done. But you've made an entire life out of mastering this deadly sin, have you not? The very contract you mention requires you to lie for the financial benefit of your employer. And yet, even that contract is a carefully constructed lie."

This time Loc felt a warning chill in his stomach. Jemdek was getting far too close to the truth and it was starting to sound like he was being played.

"You seem to know a lot about me," he said carefully.

"Knowledge," Jemdek said with a shrug. "It can be worth so much and it can be worth nothing. Less than nothing if it false. But what I really want to know is the truth that you, Loc Breeden, believe."

"Truth," Loc said, nodding slowly. "Yes, I've heard about the truth you're fighting over. The one truth. The many. But I'm afraid I have no opinion on either side of this civil war. Your religion means nothing to me."

"Religion?" Jemdek said with a laugh. "I'm not talking about religion. I'm talking about *belief*. And yet, can we not agree that a man's own personal view of how the universe works is essentially a form of religious belief?"

"Not mine," Loc replied coldly.

"No, perhaps not yours," Jemdek said with a thoughtful look. "And yet you still haven't answered my question. Do you know who it is you serve?"

"I told you, I serve no one."

"I don't wish to offend," Jemdek said, raising his hands along with an eyebrow, "but you're full of shit, Loc Breeden."

Loc's jaw muscles tightened at this and he silently promised this man would not die as easily as Farik.

"Very well then," Jemdek said when he didn't respond. "Let me offer you a different question. Who gave you that ring?"

Loc glanced at the red-stoned ring on the middle finger of his right hand. It was strange. He barely noticed it these days and yet it had been with him from the very beginning. It was a gift from the Triumvirate, but he certainly wasn't going to share that.

"No one," he lied easily. "I purchased it on a trip to Egypt, back on Earth, many years ago."

"More lies?" Jemdek said with a shake of his head. "I will honour our agreement, Loc Breeden, but only in exchange for the truth. So let's try this again. Who told you to come to the Bas Quirat?"

Loc remained silent, but his suspicions increased. How much did Jemdek know?

"No? How about… who told you to liberate the Messiah, Isaac Taylor, from the Lynt City Police Precinct?"

Again, Loc was surprised at the information Jemdek had access to, but it only made him more cautious.

"Very well," Jemdek said when he remained silent once again. "Then tell me who told you to kill Miana Raiken."

"*Miana Raiken?*" Loc thought. "*If he knows about her...*"

Suddenly everything made sense. Miana must have come to the Bas Quirat, just as Hani'ah warned, and found her way to Saadi Khalil before him. She then fed them Loc's name and even told them about his powers. Jemdek didn't know anything at all, he was just fishing for information.

"*So, the great prophet got something right, after all,*" Loc thought. "*Miana was destined to find her way here after all.*"

It still didn't explain Jemdek's ability to shrug off his psychic control and Loc was sure Miana couldn't have known about Isaac Taylor, but he would solve both mysteries in time, preferably at the painful expense of the arrogant fool opposite him.

Jemdek smiled when Loc failed to give him an answer.

"I see you've had an epiphany," he said, "and yet you're still reluctant to tell me who it is you serve. But no matter. False names mean little. What I really want to know is how they appear to you. Hmmm... let me see if I can guess."

Loc's confidence faltered. What was Jemdek talking about now? Did he know something about the Triumvirate or not?

"A man of your talents and weaknesses," Jemdek continued thoughtfully, "an expert liar, a manipulative diplomat, greedy and power hungry... yes, I'd say they appear to you as powerful humans able to call upon you at will. They expect you to fulfil your obligations to Cosmotech Defence, of course, but they occasionally have requests that go beyond the petty concerns of business and political intrigue. Am I right?"

Loc's anger grew in the space left by his rapidly retreating confidence, but he refused to give Jemdek any sign of it.

"*How does he know all of this?*" he thought in frustration. "*Is he guessing again? Or is there something more sinister going on?*"

"And what have they promised you?" Jemdek continued. "Riches? Hmm… no, I'm betting your greed goes beyond financial reward. You crave control, don't you, Loc? Power over others. Over *everyone* perhaps? Which means… they must have offered you a place among them. They did, didn't they?"

Loc's temper began to rise beyond his control. There was only one way Jemdek could know all this.

"*He must work for the Triumvirate,*" he thought. "*It's the only thing that would explain the accuracy of his 'guesses' and why I can't control him. But what's the point of goading me like this? Is he trying to make me look bad so he can take my place?*"

It was a chilling thought and one Loc had not considered beyond his rivalry with Dr. Grayson.

"I can see I'm not far from the mark," Jemdek continued calmly, "but before we go any further, I must assure you I have no affiliations with whoever you think you're working for. My guesses come only from what I see in you. You see, it is this same method they use to control many others like you. They give you exactly what you want and tell you exactly what you need to hear so you will do exactly as they say. They deceive you and empower you in equal measure and then have you act in their interests alone. These people you work for are not what they seem, Loc. Not even close."

Loc could feel his emotions being manipulated and was aware of how dangerous it could be to let Jemdek continue. And yet… he wanted to hear more. Something in Jemdek's words resonated with suspicions he'd long held and this seemed like the perfect, and perhaps only, chance he would get to take a closer look at them.

"What are you talking about?" he asked, his voice a little hoarse.

"They're lying to you," Jemdek replied, his expression intense.

"Why would they lie?" Loc asked, not wanting to give anything about the Triumvirate away, but comfortable that his question was safe.

"Isn't it obvious?" Jemdek answered. "Why do you lie, Loc? Why do you deceive and manipulate others?"

"*To control the outcome,*" Loc thought immediately.

And he knew it was true for the Triumvirate as well. They controlled him just as effectively as anyone he'd ever manipulated and yet it was a necessity he'd come to accept. He was born into the control of his parents. They moulded his understanding of the world through punishment and reward, strength and emotion, by expectation and by law. He'd come to learn that breaking free of those bonds required power, emotional stability, intelligence and above all, the right connections.

That understanding had led to his inevitable realisation that the system of control he'd been fighting against for so long was not built to control him, but to control *others.* All he needed to do was reach the top of the pile, where the powerful few made all the decisions that really mattered to the people beneath them.

Given his ultimate goal, his subservience to the Triumvirate admittedly seemed counterintuitive, but it was merely the final step on his path to the top. The Triumvirate controlled everything and everyone, and Loc was willing to do *anything* if it meant he would one day earn a place among them.

And yet here was Jemdek, a religious freedom fighter from a foreign culture, suggesting the Triumvirate were a fraud. Could it be true? Could the Triumvirate be stringing him along, never planning to actually relinquish their control and accept him among their ranks?

The thought angered him. *Enraged* him. How was this pathetic excuse for a rebel leader able to pierce the very paranoid heart of him? Who had given Jemdek the information he needed to manipulate him in this way?

Glaring at Jemdek across the table, Loc contemplated trying to take control of him again. If he ordered the young men under his control to shoot the other patrons and then kill themselves, would Jemdek still be able to hold him off? Could there be another way to get the answers he wanted?

"*I could always answer his question,*" he thought with a frown.

But even as the thought of betraying the Triumvirate entered his mind, Loc felt a warning pain at the back of his neck and gasped in guilty realisation.

"No!" he snarled, slamming a hand onto the table. "Not now!"

He wanted to end this himself. He wanted to finesse the answers from Jemdek or make him watch everyone in the café die. But the Triumvirate were exerting their control at the worst possible moment and there was nothing he could do about it.

The pain of their arrival flashed through Loc's skull like the tip of a rusty metal spike and the room went dark around him. It was as if a hundred living shadows had suddenly rushed in to obscure his vision. All that remained were the three distinct figures of the Triumvirate standing directly in front of Loc with their eyes glowing red in the shadows.

"What are you doing?" he hissed through gritted teeth.

"I think the more pertinent question is what are *you* doing?" the First said in her cold, emotionless tone.

"I was about to find out the location of Saadi Khalil," Loc replied, trying to reign in his temper.

"You were not told to do this," the Third snarled, his sharp white teeth gleaming in the darkness.

"I was using initiative," Loc snapped at him. "Something I do quite frequently, and successfully, I might add."

"This is a dangerous time to be improvising," the Second rumbled.

"Explain to me why," Loc replied. "What information am I missing that will make my actions here such a danger?"

MARS - END OF DAYS

"Enough!" the First said firmly. "If we had known of your actions, do you really think we would not share all the information necessary for success?"

"Not if it helped you control me," Loc growled.

The Triumvirate remained silent for just a moment and Loc wondered if he'd stepped over the mark.

"Control?" the Third rallied with a barking laugh. "You have been given great *freedom*, Loc Breeden. Great power and great privilege. You should know this does not come without sacrifice."

"And when will my sacrifice end?" Loc snapped.

"When you have proven yourself worthy," the First replied in an icy tone. "But that day is not today, Loc Breeden."

Loc shook his head, but felt the anger draining from him. Never before had the Triumvirate stepped in like this with so little warning. He could also tell that, behind their anger, they were also afraid. Whatever it was he'd done here, it went beyond stepping over his bounds of responsibility.

"Despite your critical view of the flow of information," the Second continued, "your ill-considered actions have jeopardized our plans in ways we are not at liberty to explain."

"And now we have to clean up your mess," the Third growled.

With his rage gone, Loc felt the iron grip of emotional control return to him.

"I... apologise," he said carefully. "I was told Miana Raiken was a threat and Hani'ah Naziri claimed she would travel to the Bas Quirat for the purpose of finding Saadi Khalil. Before you... chose to step in, I was about to do what the entire Quiration police force has failed to accomplish despite months of expensive effort."

"And you will be given the chance to complete your mission," the Second assured him, "when we have assessed the amount of damage you have done."

"I understand," Loc said.

The Triumvirate seemed to accept this and, in response, he felt the real world reappearing around him.

Everything looked wrong at first and it took him a moment to realise he was lying on the ground. His nostrils immediately caught a whiff of metal, smoke, and blood and when he pushed himself up, he saw that it was because every person in the Dhal-Sim café was now dead.

He looked for the young men he'd brought with him and saw that they too had been killed. It looked as if they'd opened fire on the entire café and then turned on each other.

Pulling himself back up to the table, Loc wasn't surprised to find Jemdek gone as well, although his end had occurred in a much more brutal fashion. For one thing, his eyes had been gouged out, most likely by his own hands, and their shredded, bloody remains were held in his palms, which rested almost casually on the table.

Behind Jemdek, the Triumvirate stood tall, all immaculately clean in their various outfits and wearing the same grim expressions as a moment ago.

"You disappointed us, Loc," the Second said, shaking his head.

"I did what I could with the information I was given," Loc replied defiantly.

"And it has led us to Saadi Khalil," the Third added with a sneer. "The only reason you were spared the same fate as these rebels."

Loc looked once more around the café and felt a sudden chill. The Triumvirate clearly held more psychic power than he did if they were able to break Jemdek in his way.

"I need to know how Jemdek Aik knew so much," Loc said, aware it was a dangerous question, but determined to ask it anyway.

"Didn't you feel it?" the First said, shaking her head. "He was stealing the information from your mind."

Loc's eyes went wide. Could it be true? If it was, it made him look like a fool.

"No," he said, feeling uncertain all of a sudden. "I... felt nothing."

"He played you like an amateur," the Third hissed, the contempt clear in his voice.

Loc suddenly felt sick.

"Perhaps we misjudged you," the Second added.

"No," Loc replied quickly. "I... can fix this. Let me kill Saadi and Miana for you. I would not have made this error if I knew such a thing were even possible."

The Triumvirate turned to look at each other, as if weighing up his request, then the First returned her gaze to Loc and spoke firmly into the silence.

"Your service has been exemplary until now. For that, you will be given a chance to redeem yourself."

"Saadi Khalil can be found on floor two-eight-seven," the Second continued. "He will be moved as soon as your security team are detected."

"Make sure you do not let him get away," the Third added.

"I won't fail you again," Loc said with conviction.

"We will see," the Third replied with a humourless smile.

And with that, Loc felt another pain in the neck and the Triumvirate were gone again.

A sense of vertigo immediately followed their departure and Loc had to place his hands on the bloody table to how himself steady. His actions today had almost led to him dying in this stinking, smoke-filled café within the rebel-controlled depths of the Bas Quirat, but if there was one thing he knew, it was the greatest reward never came without the greatest risk.

"*I won't let myself be tricked like that again,*" he thought with a cold determination. "*I don't care how many have to die to get this done, I'm not letting anyone threaten my ascension.*"

Then, as he brought himself under control and began picking his way through the corpses that littered the floor, Loc allowed his expression to firm.

"*It's time to do this the hard way.*"

HANI'AH NAZIRI LAY IN HER LUXURIOUS BED, WATCHING images flash past her mind's eye.

The psychic experiment with Isaac had drained her more completely than she expected and she was unable to do much of anything else. At least the ruby on her forehead felt pleasantly cool.

It was astonishing how much detail the Messiah could hold in his mind. He was just an ordinary boy from a culture she did not understand, and yet just as her visions promised, he was destined to save them from the coming Armageddon.

That was, of course, if the foolish pride of one man did not disrupt the divine prophecy. Loc Breeden was proving more volatile than her visions had predicted and he was fast becoming a risk that would soon outweigh his usefulness.

Hani'ah knew this was a situation she should be dealing with herself, but her psychic fatigue wouldn't allow it. All she was currently capable of doing was giving orders from her bed.

She'd already initiated the process of moving P.A.T.R.I.C. – Isaac's incredible machine – from the Bas Quirat to Cosmotech's orbital station and had since called for the head of her police force to discuss how they would respond to Loc Breeden's incursion.

217

As Hani'ah brooded over the problem, one of her handmaidens moved close and whispered in her ear.

"He has arrived, Holy Prophet."

Hani'ah turned her head slightly and her psychic perception moved to what her handmaidens were seeing.

The head of her police force, Faruq Hanif, was standing beside her with his head bowed respectfully. Hani'ah knew him as a hard but loyal man who wore a thick luxurious beard that was as well-manicured as his faith. Up until the point Loc's mission had turned into a violent mass murder, Faruq and his officers had been oblivious to the incursion.

As he approached her, Hani'ah could see the fear and outrage in his body language – one emotion due directly to Loc's behaviour, the other his own negligence in allowing it.

"Holy Prophet," he said, his voice as stressed as his stance.

"Calm yourself, Faruq," Hani'ah told him gently. "A time of great change is upon us and change never comes without turbulence."

"As you say, Holy Prophet," Faruq replied, sounding unconvinced. "What would you have me do about Loc Breeden and his security team?"

"Do not interfere with them," Hani'ah replied carefully. She could not afford to let Loc's actions go unanswered, but she needed to pre-empt any well-meaning attempt to apprehend the fool and make things worse. "Simply monitor their progress. If Loc Breeden is unable to finish what he has started, step in and ensure Saadi Khalil does not escape. I would prefer you to take him alive, but if death is the only way to stop him, then so be it."

"As you command, Holy Prophet," he replied quickly. "And what of Miana Raiken and Kurt Jones?"

"They must not survive to escape the Bas Quirat," Hani'ah replied firmly.

"As Allah wills," Faruq replied, clearly pleased that he would have the chance to aggressively pursue at least some of the foreigners who'd defeated the Bas Quirat's famous security measures.

"Now, go," Hani'ah told him, her voice straining.

Bowing low, Faruq backed away a few steps and then turned on his heel and strode out of her bedchamber.

Hani'ah allowed her second sight to move from her handmaidens and drift back into the future. Things were changing so rapidly now that it was hard to see anything with real clarity. All she knew for certain was that she would be tested before the end.

Hani'ah welcomed the spiritual challenge, despite the fear it created in her. She knew the fate of her people was balanced on a precipice with forces far more powerful than her at play, but if there was one thing she could always rely on, it was the faith she held in her God.

"*Give me strength, almighty Allah,*" she prayed reverently. "*And may your will be done.*"

UNKNOWN LOCATION, BAS QUIRAT - June 8, 2147 - 1.02pm

KURT WOKE SLOWLY, FEELING RELAXED AND CONTENT.
There was a strange taste in his mouth, but it wasn't unpleasant. He
heard a man speaking Arabic in a soft, reassuring cadence and as
his waking mind began to translate the words, he paused to listen.

"There was once an old, American Senator," the voice began,
"who was incredibly rich and incredibly powerful. One night,
he was sitting by his fireplace, drinking the finest brandy
money could buy, when he was surprised to see a dear friend
sitting in the chair opposite him.

"The Senator was so pleased at seeing his friend that he
didn't question how he'd got there. He simply greeted him
warmly, offered him a brandy and a cigar – which his friend
politely declined – and they began to reminisce about happy
memories shared in their youth.

"The stories were joyous and occasionally embarrassing,
and when they'd eventually told them all, the Senator's friend
turned to him and asked: 'are you happy with the life you have
led?'

221

"The Senator thought about it for a moment and then replied, 'Yes, I am. In my career as a policeman, I arrested many criminals. In my career as a prosecutor, I put many of those criminals behind bars. And in my career in politics, I created many new laws that have kept my constituents safe and prosperous. I managed to do all that I set out to accomplish and did some good along the way as well.'

"His friend smiled and nodded, making the Senator feel warm with happiness. Then his friend asked, 'did you lie?'

"The Senator looked at his friend to see if he was joking, but it was clear he was not. The Senator frowned, but cast his mind back and found that it was easier than usual to remember all the times he had, indeed, lied. He remembered lying to trick criminals into incriminating themselves. He remembered lying in court to ensure criminals did not get released due to a lack of evidence. He remembered lying in speeches and press conferences to manipulate his constituents into voting for him, or to turn them against his opponents. He remembered lying to his wife, so she would not find out about his many affairs. And there were many, many more memories of similar circumstances.

"The Senator looked up at his friend, not wanting to admit to so many lies, but he felt compelled to answer truthfully.

"'Yes,' he admitted, feeling guilty, 'but it was always for the good of others.'

"His friend nodded, not smiling this time. Then he asked the Senator, 'Did you cheat?'

"The Senator frowned again, not sure why his friend was asking such impolite questions, but his memory was already taking him back. He remembered times when he'd destroyed evidence that may have exonerated the criminals he arrested, and moments when he'd intentionally kept pertinent information from rival defence lawyers. He remembered searching for dirt on his political rivals and leaking that information to the media, whether it was true or not.

"The Senator didn't like the feelings of guilt that came with each memory, but he couldn't deny them and once more felt compelled to tell his friend the truth.

"'Yes'," he said, 'but I only ever did it for the right reasons.'

"His friend nodded slowly, his face now sad as he asked another question.

"'Did you steal?'

"At this, the Senator became angry, but before he could reply, his memories once more took over. He saw himself taking drug money from crime scenes to help pay his rent and electricity bills. He remembered poaching the most talented young lawyers out from under the noses of rival law firms. He remembered outmanoeuvring his political opponents to secure vast sums of money that would have otherwise gone to them. And when the memories were done, he was again compelled to answer his friend truthfully.

"'Yes,' he said simply, 'but I had to if I wanted to do any real good.'

"His friend nodded once more, his face grim, 'And did you kill?'

"The Senator was shocked at this question and he leapt up in outrage and threw his brandy into the fire. But before he could demand to know why his friend was asking these questions, his memories wrenched him back to criminals he'd shot as a policeman, not all of them in self-defence; to defendants he'd helped send to prison who'd then committed suicide and later found to be innocent; to constituents who'd been poisoned by an industrial accident that occurred after he removed safety legislation as a favour for campaign contributors.

"'Yes,' he said, sobbing now, 'but the needs of the many outweigh the needs of the few.'

"The Senator, his heart now heavy with the guilt of his decisions, looked at his friend and was finally able to speak freely.

"'Why are you asking me these questions? Why are you here?'

"His friend gave him a final, sad look and gestured toward the chair the Senator had leapt out of, 'because you are dead.'

"The Senator turned in horror and saw his body slumped in the chair, his face pale in the flickering firelight.

"He then turned back to his friend and felt the weight of what was happening settle over him.

"'I'm being judged?' he asked.

"'You have been judged,' his friend replied, 'by your own heart.'

"And the Senator wept, for he realised that by ignoring his heart in life – no matter what the justification – he had damned himself in death."

Kurt waited for a moment to see if there was more to this haunting tale, but when the voice remained silent, he opened his eyes and saw that he was lying on a small bed in a small room. The owner of the soothing voice was seated in the room's corner, facing him.

He frowned, looking around for whoever the man had been talking to, but there was no one else there.

"Were you... talking to me?" he asked in Arabic, coughing when his voice came out croaky.

"My words were for you, Kurt Jones, yes," the man said with a nod. "No matter what the justification, you will always know in your heart whether an act is good or evil. All you need do is listen."

Kurt blinked and squinted at the figure as his sleepy eyes focussed.

"Saadi Khalil?" he said in surprise.

He looked just the image from Cosmotech's files – dark blue turban, black, neatly manicured beard with two grey streaks running down from the edges of his mouth, and a pair of dark, intense eyes that made him look much younger than he was.

"Greetings, Kurt Jones," Saadi replied with a small bow from his chair.

Staring with his mouth open, Kurt suddenly remembered where he was and what had happened. This was the man Dr. Naseem Indari had been contacting from his research station deep underground. This was the final 'lead' in Miana's murder investigation.

"Miana," he said as his mind caught up with events, "where's Miana?"

"She is safe and well in the next room," Saadi said quietly. "Come, we will join her and break our fast together."

At this, Saadi rose from his seat and left through the door. Kurt went to push himself up off the bed, expecting to be sore, but apart from a little hunger he felt great.

"*Wow,*" he thought as his memories flashed back to the café where he'd been drugged. "*I should see if I can get a hold of that stuff outside the Bas Quirat.*"

When he joined Saadi in the other room, Kurt found Miana at a table, picking at a plate of food and looking more beautiful than ever. When she saw him appear, her expression lit up.

"Kurt," she said, rushing over and hugging him tight.

Closing his eyes in a mix of relief and pleasure, Kurt gladly hugged her back.

"I'm okay," he said quietly. "How about you?"

"I'm fine," she said, smiling up at him for a moment before blushing and looking away.

It made Kurt feel even better and although he was reluctant to let her go, he didn't want to ruin the moment and so he gently ended their hug and they both returned to the table.

"This looks great," he said, surveying the food.

"It tastes even better," Miana assured him.

Happily tucking into breakfast, Kurt noticed that Miana was watching Saadi as she sipped her coffee. Their host seemed to be waiting for the inevitable questions and Kurt was happy to let Miana start things off.

"You knew we were coming," she said after a comfortable period of silence.

"I did," Saadi replied in English, surprising Kurt enough to drop his bread.

"You speak English?" he asked incredulously.

"I do," Saadi replied, "and many other languages. Communicating with people of all cultures is important to my work and there is no better way to communicate with someone than in their native tongue."

"And what is your work?" Miana asked him.

"I'm a spiritual guide."

Kurt somehow wasn't surprised to hear that. After Saadi's tale of the wayward Senator, it made sense to discover he was in the business of preaching.

"For which religion?" he asked with interest.

Saadi smiled.

"Religion is simply a medium used to experience and develop spirituality," he replied, stroking his immaculate beard. "Personally, I do not subscribe to any one creed or ideology. I am merely a guide who recognises that each person's spiritual journey is unique."

"And you know why we're here?" Miana asked.

"I know you fight to prevent a future that may soon come to pass," Saadi said, turning back to her.

"Have you… seen that future?" Miana asked slowly.

Saadi smiled his mysterious smile again and gave his beard another thoughtful stroke.

"Not the one you are referring to," he replied.

"But you know of it?" Miana prompted.

"I do," Saadi continued. "A dear friend described this future to me in great detail."

Kurt wondered who he was talking about, but Miana made the connection for him.

"Doctor Naseem Indari," she said.

As Saadi heard the name, Kurt saw pain appear in his eyes and knew they must have been close.

"Yes," Saadi confirmed.

"I'm sorry for your loss," Miana added quietly.

"Thank you," Saadi replied with a grateful look, "but Naseem knew his fate long before it befell him."

Kurt was shocked at this and almost dropped his bread again. From what Miana had told him, Dr. Indari's death had been brutally long and painful. If he'd known Loc was coming, why did he choose to remain in the cave system?

"I see you find that hard to believe," Saadi said to him.

"No, I..." Kurt replied hesitantly, "I believe you, I just... why would he choose to die if he knew...?"

"His death is the reason you are here," Saadi said with a wave of his hand. "He was shown the truth, just as you were, and he chose to be an instrument of hope."

"My dream," Miana said, as if that were all the explanation needed.

"What?" Kurt said in confusion.

He remembered Miana telling him about her dream – about the shadowy, red-eyed figures standing behind Loc Breeden and the one that seemed to address Miana directly through Dr. Naseem Indari – but he never once considered it might have actually happened.

"Naseem knew it was the only way to show you what was needed," Saadi said solemnly, "and so he sacrificed himself to protect the future."

"How did he know?" Miana asked, her expression stern.

"That... has a complicated answer," Saadi replied, "but let me try to explain. After living so long and searching for truth in so many places, Naseem learned to see beyond the physical veil that so many choose to view this world from. And, perhaps more importantly, he came to accept that which he could not control. Some of what I am telling you comes from this understanding, some of it was gifted to him in the cave he discovered."

"Are you talking about psychic visions?" Miana asked.

"I am," Saadi replied, before turning to look pointedly at Kurt. "Of course, psychic power comes in many forms, does it not?"

Kurt shifted uncomfortably under Saadi's gaze. The old preacher clearly knew about his abilities and, given his profession, had made his moral judgement.

"I didn't choose any of this," he mumbled in reply.

"Choice is a sacred thing," Saadi said solemnly, "but you cannot choose a gift any more than you can choose a burden, Kurt. And yet life always provides both."

"So which is it then?" Kurt asked, a little sharper than he meant. "A gift or a burden?"

"That, regrettably, I cannot answer," Saadi replied. "What is true for one person is rarely true for another."

"And what about you?" Kurt asked, feeling like a student challenging a teacher. "Do you have any powers?"

"Naseem told me many things," Saadi replied calmly, "and showed me how to defend myself from psychic attack. But no. I possess none of the abilities you are referring to."

"I have more questions," Miana said, clearly wanting to change the subject.

Kurt sat back with a frown and tried to calm down. His anger wasn't going to be of any use here.

"I'll try to answer what I can," Saadi replied, turning back to her.

"Do you know who the Saviour is?" Miana asked.

"His name is Isaac Taylor."

"The one they're calling Messiah?"

"The same," Saadi confirmed. "He is the key to both the future you fear and the one you are fighting for."

"How so?" Miana added.

Saadi paused for a moment, as if gathering his thoughts.

"What do you know of the prophecy of Armageddon?"

"Armageddon?" Kurt said with a frown. "Isn't that meant to be a battle between good and evil before the day of final judgement?"

"Close enough," Saadi conceded. "Although the most important detail may be who is considered good and who is considered evil. In Islamic scripture, the Mahdi – or 'rightly-guided one' – fights for the good of all true believers. Hani'ah Naziri – the self-proclaimed Prophet and spiritual leader of the Bas Quirat – believes she fulfils this role."

Kurt didn't know what to think. He'd never heard this from Yasmin or any of the other Quirations he'd taken on adventures.

"And the Quirations accept this?" Miana asked.

"She has proven herself many times over," Saadi replied with a shrug.

"Proved herself?" Kurt asked. "How?"

"By correctly predicting the future, of course," Saadi replied.

"Huh," Kurt grunted. "After everything we've seen over the past few days, I have a feeling she didn't make those predictions on her own."

"I agree," Saadi replied with a nod, "but it doesn't change the fact that Hani'ah truly believes she is the Mahdi and the one destined to help the other agent of good in the final battle of Armageddon."

"There's another agent of good?" Kurt asked.

"He is known in Islamic scriptures as the Prophet Isa," Saadi explained.

"Prophet Isa," Miana said. "You mean Isaac Taylor, don't you?"

"I do," Saadi replied.

Kurt felt a little overwhelmed now. He knew they'd been thrown in the middle of something that could potentially end the lives of millions, but Armageddon? Really? It sounded more than a little crazy and he wasn't sure if Saadi expected them to believe it, or if he was just explaining what the Quirations believed.

"And who's on the other side of this battle?" Miana asked.

"Ah," Saadi said, sitting back and steepling his fingers in front of him. "That is a very good question. In Islamic scripture, the person you're referring to is the Al Dajaal, or anti-Christ, known for spreading lies and creating misleading thoughts in true believers."

229

"Charming," Kurt said grimace. "And who's the lucky owner of that infamous title?"

"You're looking at him," Saadi replied, sweeping his hands wide.

"You?" Kurt spluttered. "But... how can they possibly believe that?"

"Very easily, I assure you," Saadi said with a tilt of his head. "All I did was speak out against Hani'ah Naziri, but in her followers' eyes that was 'spreading lies' and 'creating misleading thoughts'. In Quiration culture, many who oppose those in power are branded the anti-Christ, but with the Jupiter flare on its way and the Prophet Isa appearing as predicted, many are ready to believe the accusation is more than political spin."

The three of them remained silent for a moment and Kurt looked at Miana, lost for words.

"May I ask you a personal question?" Miana said.

"Of course," Saadi replied.

"What do you believe?"

At this, Saadi smiled his mysterious smile and stroked his beard again.

"I believe the prophecy of Armageddon is not so far from the truth," he said. "I am not the Al Dajaal, of course, and I do not believe Hani'ah is the Mahdi, but Isaac may indeed be the Saviour many claim him to be."

"So who *is* the Mahdi?" Kurt asked, trying his best to keep up. "You?"

"No," Saadi said with a chuckle. "I am merely a man caught in a role he did not choose. Much like yourselves."

"Then who?" Miana asked.

Saadi stared at her for a few seconds before answering and Kurt wasn't sure if he was implying something.

"I don't think even the Mahdi will not know that for sure until the end."

Miana frowned at his response and Kurt wondered what she was thinking.

"That's the prophetic version of events," she said, "but there's more than one truth to this Armageddon, isn't there?"

"Of course," Saadi said with a nod. "Isaac may or may not have been sent by Allah, but he still bears knowledge that is being manipulated to save a world."

"Manipulated," Miana repeated slowly, "you're talking about the beings we saw in our visions, aren't you?"

"The aliens?" Kurt added.

"In a very real sense, it is *we* who are the aliens here," Saadi said to him, "but yes. These shadowy figures are the manipulators I'm referring to. I like to think of them as the indigenous peoples of Mars, but they are known by many different names to many different people. I have come to know them as the Divsek."

"The Divsek," Kurt said quietly, trying the name out for himself.

"What did Naseem tell you about what he found in the caves?" Miana asked.

"He told me of a cave filled with ancient symbols made of red crystal," Saadi replied. "He told me of touching one and seeing the beautiful world that Mars once was. He described the psychic power that one of its native species had evolved and mastered, and how they used this power to help other intelligent species cooperate and thrive. He told me they protected this world for tens of thousands of years."

"It was… a beautiful thing," Miana said, her eyes focussed in the distance.

"But he also told me their psychic powers were not limited to controlling other species," Saadi continued. "Their gift also allowed them to see into the future and they used this power to search for dangers that might threaten what they had created. Eventually, it was inevitable they would find one they could not control or avoid."

Kurt frowned as his memories flashed with the images they'd seen in the caves.

"The Jupiter flare," he said quietly.

"Yes," Saadi replied with a nod. "They were a perfect society who venerated life above all else and suddenly the very planet that allowed it to flourish was under threat."

"What did they do?" Miana asked.

"They searched desperately in their limited future for a way to save their world, but found nothing. The only option left to them was to look beyond the end and so they used their psychic powers to peer further and further into the future of their dead planet. Eventually, they witnessed the arrival of strange robotic beings and saw them move slowly across their dead planet, probing the soil and drilling into rocks."

"The Mars Rovers," Kurt said, unashamedly swept up in the story.

"That's right," Saadi confirmed, "and the Rover's owners were not far behind. That is when the Divsek got their first glimpse of humans – a new intelligent species that had travelled to Mars from another world. They watched us colonise their dead planet through persistence, innovation, and with the help of amazing technology and saw a great potential."

"But then the same disaster happened to us," Miana added.

"Yes," Saadi said with a nod. "The Divsek saw the Jupiter flare return once more, devastating this industrious new species and dashing any hope that humans would provide them with an answer."

"But… we must have shown them something," Kurt said with a frown. "Otherwise they wouldn't be manipulating us now."

"You're right," Saadi agreed with a nod. "Despite witnessing our own terrible destruction, the Divsek did find the key to saving their planet."

"Isaac Taylor," Miana said.

"What?" Kurt said, confused now. "Are you telling me they saw Isaac Taylor stop the Jupiter flare?"

"Not exactly," Saadi said, shaking his head. "In fact, that is where things become a little… complicated. You see, Naseem didn't tell me what the Divsek actually saw, but he was convinced it was enough for them to spend the remainder of their existence planning to make sure that future would come to pass."

"By using people like Loc Breeden?" Miana asked.

"Correct," Saadi confirmed.

"And Hani'ah Naziri?" Kurt added.

"And many, many others," Saadi replied with a nod.

"Alright, hang on," Kurt said, the puzzle not quite fitting together in his head. "I get how Naseem might know all this because of what he discovered, but how did Loc and Hani'ah get their powers? Did they enter the same cave we did? Or are there more of them out there?"

"Not on Mars," Saadi said pointedly.

Kurt paused as the implication hit home.

"Are you telling me the Divsek somehow got to Earth?"

"Not in the traditional sense," Saadi replied, "but their spiritual essence was, effectively, transferred."

"What?" Kurt said incredulously. "How?"

"They made use of the same catastrophic event that ended their world," Saadi explained. "You have heard of meteorites falling to Earth that originated on Mars, have you not?"

Kurt frowned as he tried to picture the journey of a rock starting on Mars and ending on Earth.

"So you're saying… they poured their spiritual essence into Martian rocks," he said slowly.

"Like the red crystal we saw in the cave," Miana added.

"Right," Kurt agreed, "and when the first Jupiter flare hit, some of that rock was thrown into space and eventually found its way to Earth?"

"And was discovered by an early human culture," Saadi finished for him.

"Early," Miana said with a grim expression. "How long have they been among us?"

"Almost as long as they guided the intelligent species of their home planet," Saadi replied.

233

"Tens of thousands of years?" Kurt gasped.

"Apparently so," Saadi replied. "The Divsek have been a part of human cultures for a very long time, showing us whatever we needed to see so they could shape our reality and more effectively control us."

"But… what's the point?" Kurt added incredulously. "Isn't their world already destroyed?"

Saadi looked at Kurt for a moment, as if he wasn't sure how to explain.

"The past is not as set in stone as you may believe," he began slowly. "Time may appear to move in one direction, but only because that is how we experience it. In reality, every choice and action we make creates ripples that can affect both our future as well as our past. We have evolved specifically to understand the shape our actions give to the future, but the ripples moving backward in time are just as real. That is how the Divsek are able to see beyond the present. They perceive these ripples and understand what they mean for the future."

"Okay," Kurt said slowly, "I get how that might help them see into the future, but how is it meant to help them change the past?"

"I'm afraid I don't know," Saadi replied. "All Naseem told me was the Divsek saw something in Isaac Taylor that translated into an opportunity to save their world."

"And… why is that such a bad thing?" Kurt asked.

Both Saadi and Miana turned to look at him.

"Well, even if they're using bastards like Loc Breeden to do it, isn't saving their planet a good thing? What makes them so evil?"

"They're fighting to save the world they came from," Saadi replied. "There's no guarantee that involves saving ours."

"But it might," Kurt persisted. "What if we inadvertently guarantee the Jupiter flare hits us both by getting involved."

"Given what I saw-" Miana began.

"In a dream," Kurt reminded her.

"In a dream, yes," Miana agreed with a disapproving look. "Given what I saw, I don't think we can risk trusting that the Divsek have our best interests at heart."

"But one of them is helping us, right? What's that about?"

"Not all the Divsek agreed that manipulation of the human race was the right thing to do," Saadi replied. "The one who chose to help us instead was... unique. It saw more than the other Divsek and did not distinguish between humans and the species they already cared for. All it saw was life and thus a sacred duty to protect it."

"Oh, come on," Kurt said, "you can't tell me it tried to argue for the demise of its own world?"

"In a way, it did, yes," Saadi replied, "which is why it was immediately cast out of the Divsek's sacred circle. While the other Divsek made plans, the outcast used its own unique abilities to create the cave Naseem discovered and it has been trying to prevent them from succeeding ever since."

"Okay, I get that," Kurt continued, "but who says the Divsek trying to 'help' us isn't on the wrong side of this? What if it turns out we're being manipulated by the real anti-Christ here? I mean, it's possible, isn't it?"

"Are you forgetting what happened to Naseem?" Miana asked him.

"You mean the one man we *know* had contact with the alien you're defending?" Kurt countered.

"Loc Breeden admitted to killing him," Miana shot back.

"So now you're telling me I should trust what Loc Breeden says?"

Miana looked bewildered for a moment and Kurt had to take a mental step back. He knew he was only speaking out of frustration and that his line of argument wasn't helping. He just didn't like it when things got so complicated.

Admittedly, there were times he actively sought out complication, but being told the past wasn't set in stone was making him feel lost in a way he'd never felt before.

"I'm sorry, that was uncalled for," he said, lifting his hands in supplication. "I'm just trying to make sense of all this and, to be honest, it's freaking me out a little."

"I understand," Saadi offered quietly. "Naseem's explanation left me feeling a little 'freaked out' myself. But doubt is a natural reaction to being asked to act on faith. The choice to listen to those doubts, however, is yours and yours alone."

"At least I get a choice in something," Kurt mumbled.

"Did Naseem tell you anything else?" Miana asked, obviously deciding to ignore Kurt's outburst for now. "Did he say anything about us or what we're supposed to do?"

"Not much I'm afraid," Saadi replied, "but I believe you already know what the Divsek helping us wants you to do."

"It wants me to find Isaac Taylor," Miana said.

"I believe it wants him to know the truth," Saadi added, before focussing on Kurt again. "You, on the other hand, Naseem was quite specific about."

"Me?" Kurt replied. "What am I supposed to do?"

"Naseem told me you must walk a different path to Miana if the destruction of our world is to be avoided."

"What does that mean? Are we going to be separated?"

"I can't say," Saadi replied with a shake of his head. "All I know is Miana must find Isaac Taylor and show him the truth. You, on the other hand, must find Hani'ah Naziri and shatter the parts to save the whole. You must fix what has been broken and restore the balance."

This last bit of cryptic information made Kurt feel even more irritated. The thought of being separated from Miana was bad enough, but how was he meant to get close to the Quiration Prophet?

"Do you know the truth I'm meant to show Isaac?" Miana asked before he could say anything.

"Regrettably no," Saadi told her, "but I've come to believe it may simply be to let him know there is a choice to be made."

"Can you help us get to him?"

"And Hani'ah," Kurt added quickly.

"I can, however–"

But before Saadi could finish, the kitchen door burst open and a Quiration with what looked like an automatic rifle stepped into the room. Kurt leapt up, prepared to take psychic control of him, but Saadi was just as quick to rise and he placed a hand on Kurt's chest.

"He is known to me," he said quickly, before adding in Arabic, "what is it Abdul?"

"Holy one," Abdul replied, sounding out of breath, "forgive my interruption, but they are here."

"Who's here?" Kurt asked him angrily.

"They've found me," Saadi said in English, his eyes distant for a moment. "This meeting, as all things do, came with a price."

"Please, Saadi," Abdul said, clearly agitated. "We must go. Now!"

"Yes," Saadi said, before getting to his feet and motioning to Kurt and Miana. "Please, follow me."

Kurt wasn't happy with any of this, but it was clear time was of the essence and so he followed Saadi's lead. Together with Miana, he moved through the door Abdul has just burst through and found several young men outside who were holding weapons and staring at Miana with something approaching awe.

"They will give us time," Saadi told Kurt, before turning to Miana. "Come, we must go."

"Wait," Miana said, pulling up short. "I don't want others to put themselves in danger on our behalf."

"I understand your concern," Saadi replied calmly, "but there is more at stake here than the safety of you and Kurt. If you're to reach Isaac in time to save us all, we cannot delay."

Miana hesitated for a moment, but Kurt could see she was struggling to find a logical counter argument.

"Fine," she said eventually. "Let's go."

With a quick nod, Abdul and Saadi moved to the next room and Kurt was surprised to find an enormous hole had been knocked through one of the walls.

"So this is how the rebels move around the Bas Quirat," he thought.

Abdul quickly led them into an entirely different apartment and another pair of armed men immediately began to close the hole behind them.

Shaking his head in amazement, Kurt followed Saadi into a bathroom where another hole gave them access to a third apartment. This one had a large cylindrical pod in the corner of the living room and it reached all the way to the ceiling. When they approached, a door opened in its side.

"You built your own elevator?" Kurt said in disbelief.

"Many," Saadi replied, motioning them inside. "Without them, we would never be able to avoid Hani'ah's police force."

It was a tight fit with all four of them inside, but Abdul managed to close the door and lock them in. Kurt then felt himself gaining weight for several seconds before the doors opened onto two more people who looked like they'd been waiting anxiously.

Kurt frowned in confusion. One was a man and the other a woman, and they were wearing the same clothes as himself and Miana.

Abdul quickly exited the elevator, but when Kurt moved to follow he felt a hand on his arm.

"Wait, please," Saadi said quietly.

Abdul had a short, whispered conversation with the two who even looked a bit like them, then he turned to nod at Saadi.

"Peace go with you, teacher," he said in Arabic, pressing his hands together.

"And you, Abdul," Saadi replied solemnly.

Kurt wasn't sure what was going on until Abdul moved to close the elevator doors from the outside.

"Hang on, where's he going?" he asked Saadi.

"They will draw them away," Saadi replied simply. "It will not give us much time, but it will be enough."

"They're going to pretend to be us?" Kurt asked incredulously.

"No!" Miana said loudly. "It's too dangerous!"

"They have made their choice with full knowledge of what is to come," Saadi said calmly. "If we pause to argue this point, you will only be putting them in more danger."

Kurt stared at him for a moment, wanting to argue further, but he knew it wouldn't make a difference. He looked at Miana, but even she seemed to accept that there was nothing they could say at this point.

"Thank you," Saadi said quietly as he set the elevator in motion again.

The hum of the elevator sounded loud in the uncomfortable silence and Kurt was relieved when the doors finally opened on another apartment. This one was crowded with people holding weapons and they looked ready to fight.

"Quickly," one of them said in Arabic, the desperation clear in his eyes. "They are not far behind."

Kurt allowed Miana to exit the elevator first and they joined the rebel soldiers who formed up around them and herded them through the apartment's front door. From there they were marched down several empty corridors until they reached another apartment with its own elevator. As they entered the elevator and began their ascent, Kurt couldn't help noticing that their rebel escort had once more stayed behind.

"Are we starting a war here?" he asked Saadi, his conscience prodding him again.

"This war was started a long time ago," Saadi assured him, "but there will be a battle fought here today, yes."

"Why?" Kurt asked in frustration. "Why does it have to be this way?"

"These people wish to fight for their future," Saadi replied. "Knowing what you do now, would you choose to stand aside and let others decide your fate? Or would you take up arms and fight for a chance to save your future and the future of your family."

Kurt's frown deepened. It was a fair point, but he still didn't feel right running away like this when so many others were about to face a danger that was coming for him.

"I understand your reluctance," Saadi said, placing a hand on his arm, "but your battle will come soon enough and you must be there to fight it."

Looking into Saadi's eyes, Kurt wondered just how much this man knew about the future they were trying to save.

"If you say so," he said, feeling a little sick as he said it.

CAPTAIN WEST STARED DOWN AT THE TWO DEAD BODIES at his feet. The glowing genetic markers that silhouetted each one identified them as Miana Raiken and Kurt Jones, but the faces looked nothing like them.

"How did this get past you?" Loc demanded.

Captain West looked up at him. He'd never seen Mr. Breeden this agitated before and it made him suspect there was something he wasn't being told. He was capable of working with less than perfect intel, of course, but given the fact they were deep in hostile territory with no possibility of backup, it was beginning to concern him.

"The rebels are more sophisticated than the Quiration police files suggested, sir," he replied. "These two were carrying DNA signature tags that fooled our sensors along with the local surveillance systems."

"And the real targets?" Loc snapped.

Captain West glanced at the holographic map that hovered in the air in front of him.

"We can't know for sure, but I believe they're using rebel safe-routes with undocumented elevator systems. Given their ability to move rapidly between levels, our chances of keeping up with them are low."

"Unacceptable!" Loc snarled. "I don't care if you have to cut through the Bas Quirat with lasers and bomb the elevator shafts one by one. Find a way to stop them!"

"Yes, sir," West replied firmly.

Waving him away, Loc began massaging his temples and Captain West knew this wasn't going to end well, whether they succeeded or not.

He turned toward his team and quickly joined them. Each of them wore traditional Quiration dress with subtle skin, hair, and iris pigmentation to help them blend in. They also openly held weapons, but Captain West doubted they would be identified as anything other than a rogue, rebel force.

Phelps and Gideon were running the penetrative radar sweep that fed his holographic map and it didn't look good. Captain West certainly didn't like the idea of following their prey into that labyrinthine mess of corridors, private residences, and elevators shafts. If this were Lynt City, he would have advised a retreat and regroup, but Mr. Breeden expected results and he clearly wasn't in the mood for excuses.

Studying the maps carefully, Captain West grimly noted the ambush points and tallied the collateral damage they may have to inflict to move past them. He wasn't particularly concerned with killing civilians – he wouldn't be head of Cosmotech's elite security team if he didn't possess a flexible morality – but he didn't want to complicate things further by forcing the Quiration police to intervene. He suspected they already knew what was going on and had chosen to stay out of it for the moment, but if too many Quiration civilians died...

"*The situation could change fast,*" he thought, before talking to his team. "Give me options."

"Lasers and bombs?" Halley replied with a raised eyebrow.

Captain West knew he was joking, but he answered the suggestion anyway.

"We move forward with the equipment we have on us."

"We could climb the outer walls?" Devril offered.

"Too heavily defended," West replied. "We need to avoid legitimate Quiration forces if we can. I'd also rather not cause an international incident. If we keep things contained to the inside of the Bas Quirat, the Quirations can simply deny anything ever happened."

"Our main problem is tracking *and* following them," Lexi said with a frown.

West looked at her. She was right, as usual, and her observation gave him an idea.

"Okay," he said firmly. "Halley, take Phelps and Gideon and cut back to the central elevator shaft. Keep scanning the structure as you go and travel as high as the elevators will allow. We'll follow the targets into the rabbit warren. By feeding each other intel, we've got a better chance of locking onto their location. If we don't reach the targets first, you three get ahead of them and engage as soon as you get a chance. Any questions?"

All three remained silent and Captain West nodded smartly.

"Right, get moving Halley," he ordered. "Lexi and Devril, clear a path."

Without hesitation, Halley, Phelps and Gideon jogged around the corner and Devril began to rig an explosive net on the nearest wall. They were going to blow their way through to the elevator shaft the targets had just used to leave this level.

"You'll need to wear this, sir," Lexi said to Mr. Breeden, handing him a transparent mask.

Captain West waited for Mr. Breeden to put it on and then reached for his own. The pliable material was imbedded with filtration sacks that would allow them to breathe easy no matter what the conditions and it sucked onto his face, creating an otherwise air and water tight seal around his mouth, nose, and eyes.

"Do it," he said simply.

"Fire in the hole," Devril hissed.

A second later, a loud *WHUMP* smacked into Captain West's body and the wall crumpled inward. The destructive force created a pall of dust and smoke that billowed both inward and outward, but Devril and Lexi didn't wait before charging through.

Activating his team's respective video feeds by glancing at their glowing icons, Captain West watched as they expertly cleared the room.

The few surprised Quiration rebels beyond the wall were clearly outlined in glowing red light and Devril took each of them down with ruthless efficiency – a double-tap to the chest and one to the head.

When the short staccato of gunfire fell silent, West watched Lexi move to the back of the apartment and inspect the glowing green outline of an unofficial elevator.

"The elevator is stationary," Lexi said quickly, her throat mic sending the words straight to his ear. "Six floors up."

"Room is secure," Devril said shortly after.

Captain West turned to Mr. Breeden and motioned him forward.

"We're clear, sir."

Mr. Breeden scowled as he stepped through the neat hole Devril had cut through the wall.

"Where are they?" he said.

"The elevator stopped moving six floors up, sir," Captain West advised him. "I believe–"

"Blow it to hell," Loc said.

"Sir?" West asked, unsure it was such a good idea when they weren't sure how far their targets were ahead of them.

"Do it!" Loc roared.

"Sir!" West replied smartly, before gesturing to Lexi.

Without hesitation, Lexi reached into her pack and pulled out a small, pointed cylinder. Captain West recognised it as a Hex-8 self-guided missile, made specifically for manoeuvring in tight spaces.

By using the penetrative radar sweep Phelps and Gideon had constructed earlier, the missile could target any structural waypoint and guide itself straight to the target.

Lexi placed the small missile at the edge of the open elevator shaft and several small legs sprung from the casing along with three sleek fins. The legs shifted slightly to angle the missile toward the open shaft then Lexi took several steps back.

"Ordinance away," she said simply, before the missile sparked and shot out of view with a sharp *fsssszzz!*

For several seconds there was only the rapidly diminishing sound of its progress then a much louder *BANG* echoed down the elevator shaft. A distant roar quickly followed and flames lit up the shaft in harsh yellow and red light. A screeching sound appeared, growing louder with each second, then the mangled elevator crashed to the apartment floor, sending another plume of dust and smoke into the air.

With her face mask easily filtering the toxic particles from the air, Lexi moved forward and scanned the wreckage.

"Unoccupied, sir," she said quickly.

"Then get us up there," Loc snapped.

Joining Lexi at the elevator, Captain West turned to Devril.

"Secure the upper floor," he told them, "and be prepared for heavy resistance. We'll wait for confirmation before following."

"Sir," they both acknowledged.

Captain West turned to keep an eye on the hole in the wall behind them and watched the video feeds that showed Lexi and Devril firing zip lines up the elevator shaft. Moments after the two rose into the smoky darkness, the sound of gunfire and muffled explosions filtered down the elevator shaft.

It should have been a simple engagement. The rebels were well armed and more organised than Captain West would have expected, but Lexi and Devril were the best in the business. And yet, almost as soon as the shooting began, one of the vital signs glowing at the edge of his vision flashed red.

Captain West focused on the indicator and more information blinked to life next to it. Devril had gone into cardiac arrest due to massive trauma to the left hemisphere of his brain.

"*Shit,*" he thought, gripping his rifle tighter.

There was no coming back from an injury like that. Devril was dead.

More gunfire echoed down the shaft along with some thuds and grunting as Lexi finished off the remaining rebels, then her voice spoke in Captain West's ear.

"Clear."

Ignoring an urge to punch the closest wall, Captain West turned to Mr. Breeden.

"We're ready, sir."

"Then let's go," Loc replied, his impatience clear.

Firing another zip line up the shaft from the motor attached to the underside of his rifle, Captain West hooked himself to the harness hidden beneath Mr. Breeden's clothes and carefully guided their ascent to the upper level. Near the top, they encountered the limp body of Devril – still dripping blood and hanging from his zip line.

Careful not to get any of the blood on Mr. Breeden, Captain West guided them through the elevator doors and into the apartment. Lexi was waiting near the middle of the room beside four more dead bodies. In front of her were two young men on their knees with their arms secured firmly behind their backs.

"They tried to detonate themselves," she said. "One of them tagged Devril on the way up. Firepower's impressive."

Captain West glanced at the weapons Lexi had kicked away from the two rebels. They were high-tech, as good as the rifles used by his own team, and it didn't surprise him they'd been able to end Devril's life.

Moving his focus to the structural map being constructed by the team he'd sent up the central elevator shaft, Captain West noted they'd travelled another twelve floors, but it wasn't enough.

Their real targets had moved through several corridors in the meantime and were already in another illegal elevator. Penetrative radar showed fourteen bodies in the intervening space.

"There's another ambush waiting for us, sir," he said, turning to Mr. Breeden, "and without Devril the likelihood of making it through safely has lowered considerably. I suggest we retreat to a lower level and find another way to follow them up."

Loc's expression soured as he listened to the advice and his eyes burned with something that made Captain West uncomfortable.

"No, I don't think so," he said after a moment. "It's about time we showed these rebels what real power looks like. Stand him up."

Captain West realised Loc was talking to Lexi and saw her haul one the prisoners to his feet. The young man looked like any other young Quiration and he met Loc's gaze defiantly.

"What is your name?" Loc demanded in Arabic, the words translated in Captain West's ear piece.

He doubted the young man would do anything other than spit in Loc's face, but as soon as Mr. Breeden spoke, the young man's scowl fell away and he spoke in a calm, hollow tone.

"Dahli," he replied.

Mr. Breeden turned to one of the dead bodies on the floor and picked up a discarded weapon. He then offered it to Dahli.

Captain West quickly stepped forward to stop him.

"Sir, he'll–"

"He'll do nothing but what I order him to do," Loc snapped.

Loc's expression made Captain West take an involuntary step back.

"Uh… yes, sir," he said hesitantly.

Loc held his gaze for a moment then he turned to the young man and held out the weapon again.

"Take this," he said, in Arabic, "walk out of this room and move to the end of the corridor. Kill every person you see beyond that door."

West frowned in confusion. Did he really think the young man would follow such a reckless order?

But even as he puzzled over the bizarre request, the young man took the rifle and began walking toward the door.

"*Is he hypnotised?*" West thought in confusion. "*But... that's not how hypnotism works... is it?*"

Unsure what was happening, Captain West watched in disbelief as the young rebel calmly opened the door and walked outside. He was met with a challenging shout from one of the other rebels, but instead of responding, the young man simply opened fire.

Gunfire shattered the silence and shouts of alarm and outrage quickly joined the cacophony. Captain West watched the entire scene using penetrative radar.

It was like no engagement he'd ever seen. The young man simply continued walking forward, mowing down his fellow rebels without hesitation. Several of them tried to shoot back, but their panic made them reckless and most of the shots missed. By the time one of them managed to hit the target and send the enthralled young man crashing to the floor with several grisly exit wounds, seven rebels were dead.

"He's done," Loc said, before stooping to pick up another weapon. "Bring me the other one."

Lexi glanced at Captain West. He could see she felt the same confusion he was struggling with, but he nodded to her quickly. This was no time to disobey.

Lexi pulled the second captured rebel up, not so roughly this time, and Captain West felt an unfamiliar reluctance when he saw the terror in the young man's eyes.

"Shoot everyone still alive outside this room," Loc said, pointing to the door.

As soon as he spoke, all expression drained from the young man's face and he took the weapon willingly. This time, when he stepped outside, the remaining rebels started shooting immediately.

Captain West waited for the young man to fall, but the bullets didn't seem to hit anything vital. They sprayed the corridor with blood, but the rebel just continued walking and firing until the remaining rebels could no longer hide behind their makeshift defences.

This time the attacker took down another five rebels before a bullet finally caught him in the head.

Captain West stood stunned.

"Well?" Loc said, snapping him out of it. "Are there too many of them now?"

"Uh… no, sir," West said, feeling a little afraid himself.

"Then get moving," Loc growled. "And make sure you kill every last one of them."

"Yes, sir," West replied quickly, before turning to Lexi and motioning her forward.

She was clearly as unsettled as he was, but Captain West wasn't concerned it would affect her abilities. It wasn't clear what Mr. Breeden had just done, but whatever new Cosmotech technology he'd just witnessed, he doubted it was legal and could easily imagine Mr. Breeden wanting to keep it secret.

"*Just finish the mission in front of you,*" he thought firmly. "*And hope to hell he doesn't use whatever that was on you as well.*"

MOVING ELEVATOR, BAS QUIRAT - June 8, 2147 - 2.08pm

MIANA STOOD CALMLY NEXT TO KURT, HER EXPRESSION firm and her body ready for action – the complete opposite to what she felt inside.

Now that she knew the truth, or some of it at least, she should have felt better. She *deserved* to feel better. But even after Saadi had answered so many of her questions, she felt more lost than ever.

"*Am I supposed to be the Mahdi?*" she wondered. "*Am I the one meant to help Isaac save us all?*"

Saadi hadn't said it outright, but he'd certainly implied it and Miana was just beginning to realise that she didn't want to believe it. There were too many pressures on her already. Why did it have to be her responsibility? And what could she possibly do about any of this anyway?

If Saadi was right, they weren't just fighting some evil corporation here. They were battling an alien-run secret society with psychic powers who'd been planning their victory for thousands of years.

And yet, whatever their advantage, the forensic inspector in Miana knew she had to try. Millions of lives were at stake here and she had a duty of care, if not for the Lynt City residents she'd served for such a large part of her life, then for human kind in general.

251

Of course, at the same time the atheist inside her screamed that this was all superstition and religious manipulation. She was no Mahdi sent by Allah to aid the Messiah fight some final battle between good and evil. She was just a woman caught in the wrong place at the wrong time.

"And somehow the last to know about it."

She felt a touch on her shoulder and looked up to find Kurt smiling in his usual, reassuring way. At least he seemed to be coping with it all, which was no small thing given what Saadi had told them. *"Does he feel the same pressure as me?"* she asked herself, *"or is he faking it as well?"*

She could tell Kurt didn't like the idea they would be separated before the end, which was nice, but it only reinforced the idea that they had no control over what was happening to them.

Putting a hand on his, Miana offered him her best reproduction of a smile and then almost fell over when a distant *rumble* shook the elevator.

"What was that?" Kurt asked.

"They're in pursuit," Saadi said simply. "We must move quickly."

Miana would have liked more of an explanation, but before she could ask for one, the elevator doors opened and they were confronted with another room full of people. All of them wore white garments that looked suspiciously like religious attire and everyone stared directly at her.

"They think I'm the Mahdi," she realized.

"Come, please," Saadi said, leading them out into the crowd.

Miana followed quickly, not wanting to fall behind with so many unfamiliar faces surrounding her, and almost smiled with relief when she felt Kurt's hand close over her own.

The staring Quirations reached out and touched her as she passed, without any desperation or urgency, and the hope in their eyes made Miana feel sick.

"*I didn't ask for any of this,*" she thought, hating them even though she knew it wasn't their fault. "*I don't even know what they want from me.*"

Ahead of her, the apartment's front door was opened by one of the staring Quirations and Saadi led them outside. The crowd quietly followed them out and formed up around them like a protective cocoon with Saadi, Kurt, and Miana at its centre.

"What are they doing?" Miana whispered to Saadi.

"They will help us get where we need to go," he replied simply.

"And where's that?"

"The military transport hub."

"Military?" Kurt said, his frown echoing Miana's concern.

Saadi looked at him for a moment and then back at Miana.

"You need to escape the Bas Quirat and get into orbit," he said quietly.

"What's in orbit?"

"Isaac Taylor and Hani'ah Naziri," Saadi replied. "You will find them on an orbital space station owned by Cosmotech Defence."

Miana studied his face for a moment and could tell there was something he wasn't telling her.

"How do we get inside the transport hub?" she asked. "Won't it be guarded?"

"Of course," Saadi replied with a reassuring smile, "but as you can see, not all Quirations believe me to be the anti-Christ. We will find our way."

Miana glanced at the people escorting them, not wanting to catch their admiring eyes, and felt a new unease in her stomach.

"I don't like using people," she said quietly.

"These people are acting on faith, Miana," Saadi replied. "Would you deny them their beliefs simply because they make you uncomfortable?"

"I think I have a right to be uncomfortable," Miana shot back, her temper rising. "No matter what you believe, Saadi, I'm the one being manipulated here."

"That may be true," Saadi conceded, "but you now know more about the future than I do. Everyone here has made the choice to help in the only way they can. You must make that choice also, one way or another."

Saadi's words dampened the fires of Miana anger and she lowered her gaze. No matter how she tried to control things, they just kept slipping out of her grasp. Whatever happened next, they were now well and truly in Saadi's hands and, Mahdi or not, she had no choice but to trust him.

When she eventually looked up, she saw that the group had turned a corner and the corridor opened onto a large space. It had the look of a religious chamber and was almost full to capacity with people wearing similar robes to the Quirations that surrounded them. The crowd was split into a dozen or so neatly arrayed groups and passage between them was possible via a network of corridors made of intricately patterned tiles.

Staring around the colossal chamber in amazement, Miana was surprised to see that the ceiling far above them was completely open. The night sky shone through brightly, full of glittering stars, and a red streak that she'd never seen before glowed at the centre.

"*My God,*" she thought in fascinated horror. "*The Jupiter flare.*"

The red smudge was insignificant when compared to the great expanse around it, but when you considered the relative size it must represent...

"*How can we possibly do anything against that?*" she thought in despair.

Lowering her eyes with a shiver, Miana noticed that the Quirations who'd been escorting them were now breaking away in pairs so they could join several of the praying groups that filled the chamber.

She frowned in suspicion as their escort gradually thinned and leaned in to Saadi so her English wouldn't give her away.

"Where are they going?" she whispered.

"We will need a distraction to go any further," he replied, nodding toward an alcove on the far side of the grand chamber.

Miana looked at the alcove and saw an elevator door guarded by two Quiration soldiers, or possibly police officers. She turned to Saadi, about to ask him what kind of distraction he was talking about, when a loud Arabic voice suddenly echoed through the chamber.

"My Quiration brothers and sisters, you are being deceived!"

Miana turned toward the commotion and recognised one of the people who'd arrived with her. He was standing on the edge of a fountain with his hands raised above his head.

"Hani'ah Naziri is a false Prophet!" he bellowed. "She will not save us from the coming Apocalypse! She is a servant of Satan!"

The crowd around the speaker responded instantly with hissed reproach and demands for him to get down and be silent, but another of Miana's escort stood beneath him, pushing away anyone who came close.

"*This is a dangerous game Saadi is playing,*" Miana thought.

She could feel the atmosphere turning already and wasn't surprised when another loud voice echoed through the chamber from another direction.

"Hani'ah Naziri is not the Prophet you believe! The real Mahdi has come to avert the Apocalypse!"

It was another of Saadi's escorts and this one was standing on a bench at the edge of the chamber. This time, the crowd nearest to the speaker began shouting immediately and they surged forward to pull him down. The person meant to be protecting him was overwhelmed quickly, but before the speaker could be pulled down, several new voices echoed through the chamber.

"You are being deceived!"

"Hani'ah Naziri has poisoned your minds!"

Miana looked for them and saw people standing out from the crowd all around the chamber, each one preaching messages that clearly went against what the majority of the chamber believed.

255

As a result, Quirations all around the chamber began to strain forward to stop them or simply move out of the way so they would not be caught in the crush. In moments, the open space they were walking through became crowded with surging bodies and the noise grew quickly as screams and shouts joined the rebel preachers. Staring around at the growing chaos, Miana saw that only four of their original escort remained. One of them – a tall, thin man with a sharp, jet black goatee – leapt onto a railing not far from the guarded elevator and began to shout over the growing din.

"Hani'ah Naziri is the anti-Christ!"

Again, some of the nearby crowd surged forward to pull him down and the remaining escorts had to fight hard to push them back. Miana glanced at the elevator guards, who'd clearly noticed the commotion, and watched as they had a quick, whispered conversation.

"*One of them will come for him,*" she thought.

And a moment later, just as she predicted, one of the guards moved to arrest the tall speaker.

As soon as he left his post, Saadi pulled Miana and Kurt out of the crowd. The remaining guard immediately raised his weapon.

"Hello, Jaichim," Saadi said in Arabic, his arms open. "I have come for the visit I told you about."

"Teacher," the guard said, eyes wide as he looked apprehensively from him to Miana and Kurt. "I... is it really time?"

"It is," Saadi replied simply.

"I'm not sure..." Jaichim spluttered, frowning at the shouting, surging crowd behind them. "I mean, I wasn't ready for... I don't think I can let you through."

Miana saw the fear in his eyes and knew this wasn't going as Saadi expected.

"I understand your reluctance," Saadi continued calmly. "They have forced great fear into your heart."

"I am not afraid," Jaichim replied firmly, raising his weapon again.

"Please," Saadi said, lowering his arms. "Do not give in to your doubts, Jaichim. Your actions here will live on for generations. Listen to your heart. What does it tell you?"

Jaichim's face twisted in anguish. Miana could tell he respected and probably revered Saadi, but she could see the moral dilemma in his eyes. It was easy to talk faith and belief when there were no real consequences attached to them, but when it came to acting on that faith, things were very different. This was clearly a life or death decision for Jaichim and Miana could only hope his faith was stronger than his fear.

For several tense seconds, Jaichim's agonised expression flickered between terror and resolve, then he finally seemed to reach a decision.

"I'm sorry, teacher," he said, lowering his weapon along with his eyes. "I have failed you in our hour of greatest need."

"No, Jaichim," Saadi said, placing a hand on the man's shoulder. "You have triumphed when we needed you most. Now, take us to the launching bay."

"Yes, teacher," Jaichim replied, looking up with a new determination in his eyes.

"Come," Saadi said, motioning to Kurt and Miana.

Jaichim swiped his hand over the activation pad beside the elevator and the doors opened. They all quickly moved inside and Jaichim activated another pad on the inside.

As the doors closed, Miana caught a final glimpse of the turmoil outside. It was horrible. People were wrestling with each other, women were screaming, men were hurling their shoes and she could see several people with blood streaming down their faces.

"*What have we done?*" she thought in disgust.

When the doors cut off the terrible sound of rioting, Saadi spoke into the silence, as if hearing her unspoken question.

"Many more lives will be saved than those that may be injured or arrested today," he said quietly.

Refusing to look at him, Miana simply waited as the elevator took them up. She might be forced to endure her place in this madness, but she didn't have to condone it.

"*Just let there be a point to it all,*" she thought coldly. "*That's all I ask.*"

LOC BREEDEN SURVEYED THE MASS OF SHOUTING, fighting Quirations with a scowl.

Once he'd unleashed his psychic power and sent the Quirations best and brightest back at them, his team had fought their way here with a minimum of fuss. They'd even met up with the officers Captain West had sent up the central elevator shaft and were now closer to Miana than ever.

But proximity meant nothing when there was a thousand rioting Quirations between you and your target.

"Hani'ah you stupid fucking bitch," he thought bitterly. *"This is what you get for encouraging religion."*

Loc would have almost been impressed if it wasn't so frustrating. Miana was outmanoeuvring him in ways that suggested she'd either tapped into some incredible source of luck or, far more likely, was being helped by an unknown party with incredible foresight.

The second option made Loc think of Jemdek Aik, the rebel leader he'd talked with in the Dhal-Sim café.

Despite the Triumvirate's claim that Jemdek had pulled everything he needed from Loc's mind, he believed there was more to the rebels' source of knowledge.

259

"*Someone is feeding them information,*" he thought, before turning to Captain West. "Where are they?"

"They've entered one of the military access elevators with a Quiration soldier, sir. It stopped on the military transport hub less than a minute ago."

Loc felt a sudden chill. He couldn't afford to let Miana get away again.

"Can you shut down the hub?" he asked quickly.

"Not with our current level of access," West replied. "Quiration Military servers are protected by–"

"They're going to escape," Loc snapped, blood pounding in his ears. "Again! I don't care what you have to do, Captain. Get us up there, now!"

Captain West turned to the mass of people filling the chamber.

"We won't make it in time, sir," he said desperately. "If they have direct access to the flight deck, this crowd will–"

"Then mow them down!" Loc snarled.

Captain West didn't exactly flinch, but his eyes grew wider.

"Even if we did, sir," he said after a moment, "we're too far behind the target. And it might even make our progress harder. The Quiration police force will–"

"Argh!" Loc shouted, waving a hand in Captain West's face to shut him up.

What was he going to do? Even with all his power, he could never control this many people. And as much as he wanted Captain West and his team to shoot every one of these useless zealots blocking their path, he was well aware even Hani'ah couldn't conceal such an atrocity. Triumvirate connections or not, she would be forced to do everything in her power to stop him from leaving the Bas Quirat alive.

Clenching his fists in frustration, Loc realised that if he wanted to stop Miana, he would have to share their intelligence with the Quirations.

"*Damn it, there has to be another way,*" he thought with a grimace.

The last thing he wanted to do was hand his victory to Hani'ah, but he couldn't risk losing Miana again. The Triumvirate were already close to reconsidering his ascension and this would at least allow him to place the blame on the Quiration's Prophet if something went wrong.

It was the thinnest silver lining to what was turning out to be a stinking, noxious cloud of failure.

Gritting his teeth in frustration, Loc turned to Captain West.

"Alert the Quiration authorities," he said as calmly as he could manage. "Give them Saadi's location and make sure they know the information is genuine."

"Right away, sir," Captain West replied, looking relieved.

"Then we push through this mess," Loc continued firmly. "If they can at least hold Saadi and Miana for a few minutes, we might be able to arrive before this whole fucking mission turns to shit in our hands."

"Yes, sir," Captain West said with a nod.

Loc waited impatiently as his orders were followed and received some grim satisfaction when his security team finally charged into the rioting Quirations.

Progress through the mess of people was slow but steady, and yet avoiding being pulled into the seething mass of bodies was almost as difficult as smashing open a path that they could move through.

Whenever a Quiration was unfortunate enough to look him in the eye, Loc ruthlessly took control and made them aid in the push, and as they gradually moved closer to the elevator, he felt his temper smoothing.

"*This isn't over yet, Miana,*" he vowed. "*You won't get away so easily this time.*"

MIANA WATCHED AS THE ELEVATOR GUARD, JAICHIM, pulled aside a Quiration officer at a simple checkpoint and had a whispered conversation with him. The officer's face quickly went from confusion to ashen realisation then he let them through without looking any of them in the eye.

"Another rebel?" Miana asked when they were out of earshot.

"Another believer," Saadi replied quietly.

As they continued on, Miana found it hard to ignore the sudden change in architecture. Whilst the residential areas were full of brightly coloured details and the gleaming edge of extravagance, this place was clearly designed for a purpose. The hallways were sparse, clean, and functional, and the surfaces held no bright colours whatsoever. Only white, grey and the occasional gleam of brushed metal.

Their guide, Jaichim, led them through the sober corridors for several minutes before bringing them to a room filled with lockers. He swept his hand past several of them and they opened to reveal a collection of helmets, neatly hanging garments, and a dozen sectional pieces of body armour.

"Put these on," he said in Arabic, before striding back through the door and disappearing down another corridor.

Miana looked at Saadi for confirmation, but he was already at one of the lockers, industriously removing his clothes.

Moving to an open locker herself, Miana inspected a pair of thick, ribbed leggings and a zip-up jacket. Both were heavily padded and seemed to be made of several layers of material.

"They're orbital flight suits," Kurt said as he began to pull off his own clothes. "You need to be naked for the biological integration to work properly. It's a lot like a survival suit, really, just more expensive because it needs to hold up in the vacuum of space."

Miana heard a touch of excitement in Kurt's voice and looked up to find him naked from the waste up. She stared at his chest and stomach for a moment, well and truly distracted by the hard, rippling muscles, but quickly looked away when he reached down to pull off his pants.

Taking her own clothes off, she noticed that she felt less embarrassment than she should have, but still couldn't bring herself to look at Kurt when she was naked. She just quickly pulled on her leggings and jacket, and frowned when they appeared to be several sizes too big.

"I don't think–" she began to say, but when she clipped the two garments together at the waist, something in the material contracted and the sleeves and legs shortened to the correct length.

For a moment, an almost uncomfortable pressure squeezed at Miana's legs, arms, and torso then the material relaxed and she was left wearing a perfectly fitted jumpsuit.

"*Okay then,*" she thought, bending her arms and legs.

A large pair of boots waited at the bottom of the locker and when Miana stepped into them, they too vacuumed shut around her feet and ankles.

She looked at the strange sectional pieces of armour that were left, but had no idea what she was meant to do with them.

"Need help?" Kurt asked.

Miana looked up to find that he'd already put most of his on.

"Sure," she replied thankfully.

As usual, Kurt happily explained the purpose of each monitoring devices and section of torso armour as he helped her put them on, and Miana couldn't help smiling. Despite their situation, he just couldn't help but be himself.

When they were almost done, Miana looked up to see Jaichim standing in the doorway with half a dozen armed men.

"*He betrayed us,*" she thought in a panic.

But Saadi didn't seem concerned and when he walked up to Jaichim, they held a whispered conversation that clearly wasn't hostile.

As her heartbeat gradually slowed, Miana turned her attention to the men and women Jaichim had brought with him. They weren't aggressive at all. Quite the opposite in fact. Most of them were staring at her with the same looks of awe she'd received from the Quiration rebels earlier.

"*Not again,*" she thought, frowning as she pulled on her gloves.

"Put your helmets on," Saadi told them after a moment. "Jaichim will take us to the launching hanger."

Trying to avoid the Quiration's stares, Miana pulled on the helmet that came with her orbital flight suit and then followed Kurt out of the locker bay.

"It's not far," Saadi added when they were on their way.

The now familiar sensation of wearing a survival suit made Miana feel a little safer, but she still held her breath every time Jaichim made them pause at an intersection. Each time he seemed to have a quiet conversation with someone on the other end of a video call before moving on and Miana assumed they had access to the Bas Quirat's security system.

They managed to move through several corridors unmolested, but Miana jumped when a voice suddenly echoed down a side passage behind them.

"Jaichim!"

She expected the Quiration to turn toward the voice, but instead he continued on as if he hadn't heard anything.

"*Oh no,*" Miana thought, hoping they weren't in as much trouble as she suspected.

"Hey! Jaichim!" the voice called again, louder this time.

This time, Jaichim came to a reluctant halt and bowed his head in a way that made Miana's stomach clench. She paused uncomfortably beside Kurt while the officer who'd spoken appeared from the side passage.

"What are you doing?" he hissed at Jaichim. "Aren't you supposed to be guarding elevator seven? Why are you escorting a flight crew? I thought all launches were prohibited today."

Jaichim turned to confront the man and the look in his eyes sent a chill through Miana.

"Jaichim?" the officer said, frowning. "What's wrong? Who are—"

At this point, the officer saw Saadi's face and his eyes went wide.

"Saadi!" he gasped in recognition, but before he could do anything else, the corridor echoed with a loud *thwip, thwip!*

Miana saw the officer clutch at his chest and realised what had just happened.

"You shot him," she gasped.

The guard collapsed to the floor.

"Why did you do that?" Kurt said, confronting Jaichim.

"Shut up!" Jaichim snarled, pushing him away. "You think I wanted to kill him? He was a good friend."

"Please," Saadi said, stepping between them. "We must keep moving."

"I could have stopped him without anyone getting hurt," Kurt snapped, glaring at Saadi.

"It is done," Saadi said firmly. "And we must hurry."

266

Miana could see Kurt clenching his jaws in frustration and realised he was struggling with his temper as much as she was.

"He's right," she said, taking his arm and pulling him away. "There's nothing we can do about it now."

Kurt looked at her with a helpless expression that made her heart crumple in her chest, but he nodded reluctantly.

Feeling wretched, Miana followed the others down another corridor and was glad when they finally reached a large gateway that led onto the launching hanger Saadi had mentioned.

Miana gaped at the enormous space beyond it. The area directly in front of them was brilliantly lit and packed with fighter jets parked in four long rows. The jets were angled in toward two runways that ended in launch tunnels and punched through an enormous transparent wall. Miana assumed the wall was meant to seal the hanger from the low pressure outside, but it also allowed a spectacular view of the Marsian night sky.

There were dozens of technicians strolling amongst the jets and working at several heavy-duty maintenance bays and Miana hoped they weren't going to be caught up in whatever was about to happen.

Jaichim led them out into the hanger as if they were meant to be there, but just as Miana was about to step across the threshold herself, she heard a *thwack* followed by a meaty *thud*. She turned in confusion and saw one of the Quiration's who'd been escorting them had collapsed.

A rush of panic flooded through her and she heard Kurt shout something unintelligible, moments before something hit her from the side. Not sure if she'd been shot, Miana yelped in alarm as someone pushed and pulled across the floor. The next thing she knew, she was huddled outside the hanger entrance between Kurt and Saadi.

"Are you alright?" Kurt asked, his hands searching for wounds on her arms and legs.

"I… think I'm okay," Miana replied breathlessly.

She looked around in confusion and saw that Jaichim and the other Quiration soldiers had scattered to either side of the hanger entrance. She searched for the officer who'd fallen beside her, but he wasn't among them.

"Who's firing at us?" Kurt asked Saadi over the gunfire.

"Forces still loyal to Hani'ah," Saadi replied. "Someone must have warned them we were coming."

Suddenly Jaichim was crouched in front of Miana and his voice was full of urgency.

"You must get to a jet and taxi into the launching airlock one at a time. Do not hesitate. There are not enough of us to continue this fight and activate a double launch."

"We can't go out there!" Kurt snapped. "They'll cut us down in seconds."

"No, they won't," Jaichim said with a shake of his head. "We are not complete fools. We have been preparing for this day for months. Just be ready to move."

"What is he talking about?" Miana said to Saadi, her breath finally back.

"Just be ready to move," he echoed Jaichim's words firmly.

"No. I don't like being left in the dark," she replied. "Tell me what's going to happen."

"Dark is exactly what it's going to get," he said, glancing up at the hanger lights. "But don't worry, Miana, your helmet has active light-enhancement built into the viewing screen. You'll get out of this alive. Both of you."

The way Saadi said this made Miana pause for a moment and an ominous feeling joined the sickness in her guts.

"What about you?" she asked him.

"I'll be right behind you," he replied, but Miana sensed the hesitation in his voice.

"What about you?" she asked, louder this time.

Kurt looked at her in puzzlement and then turned to Saadi.

"What's going on?" he asked.

"I'm here to help you," Saadi replied cryptically.

"Like Naseem?" Miana said forcefully.

"Please, we must be ready." Saadi replied, looking away.

"Miana–" Kurt began.

"No!" she hissed at him, before returning her glare to Saadi. "You don't need to die here, Saadi. What do you know is going to happen?"

"Miana," Saadi said, looking her in the eye and placing a hand on her shoulder, "you know what's at stake. If there was any other way–"

"No! I don't accept that," Miana said, pushing his hand away. "There's *always* another way, Saadi."

"Of course there is," he conceded firmly, "but I have a duty, Miana, just as you once did as a forensic detective."

"That was *nothing* like this," Miana snapped. "I never expected to die fighting crime."

"But you accepted the possibility," Saadi countered. "You chose to put yourself in harm's way for the sake of the innocent. Are you telling me I shouldn't do the same for the sake of the entire human race?"

Miana felt a flash of frustration, but no answer came along with it and she turned away from Saadi in disgust.

"I do what I believe in my heart is the right thing to do," he added quietly, putting his hand on her shoulder again. "And what would we be if we did not act on our beliefs?"

At this point, the hanger suddenly went dark and Miana flinched. But the darkness only lasted a moment. When the light returned it had a green tinge that blurred slightly when she moved her head, but it was definitely enough to see by.

"Time to go," Saadi said, getting to his feet.

Gritting her teeth in frustration, Miana allowed Kurt to help her up. Saadi made them wait a moment as Jaichim and his men charged out into the hanger then he nodded to them and Kurt took her hand.

"Together," he said quietly.

Miana nodded grimly then they moved out of cover and followed Saadi toward the line of jets.

Gunfire and shouting followed them through the hanger and Miana watched as Jaichim advanced boldly on the attacking Quiration forces. There were already several limp bodies already sprawled in the distance and she was certain there would soon be many more.

Looking away as another surge of frustration washed through her, Miana saw that Saadi had stopped beside one of the fighter jets.

"You know how to fly one of these," he said to Kurt, more statement than question.

"Well... yeah," Kurt replied, sounding a little upset. "It's the same control configuration as a T10-Cesna."

"Then go quickly," Saadi said to him, "both of you in this one. I'll follow you shortly. Remember, Kurt, you must get to that space station and find Hani'ah Naziri."

"And fix what's been broken," Kurt said with a grimace. "I haven't forgotten."

"Remember," Saadi said, "to fix what's been broken and restore the balance, you must shatter the parts to save the whole."

"Shatter the parts, got it."

"It's important you remember, Kurt," Saadi said, offering him a hand.

"Don't worry, I will," Kurt replied, shaking his hand with a solemn expression.

Then Saadi turned to Miana.

"The Saviour needs your help," he said.

Miana hesitated, not sure if this was meant to be goodbye, then she looked him defiantly in the eye.

"I don't know what I believe, Saadi, but I respect your right to choose how you want to fight. Just know that when the time comes, I can only promise to do what *I* think is right."

"What else could anyone ask of a truly good person?" Saadi replied, before bowing low. "Farewell, Miana Raiken, champion of justice. Do not fear for Kurt, he may not have your wisdom, but he will find a way to do what needs to be done before the end."

"Hey," Kurt said, "I'm right here."

Saadi turned to him and smiled in a way that touched Miana unexpectedly.

"Good luck, Saadi," she said, tears welling in her eyes.

Saadi met her gaze one last time then he nodded once and turned to head for a jet on the other side of the runway.

Kurt looked like he wanted to say more, but instead he stepped up onto the jet's ladder.

"This way," he said, offering her a hand.

With gunfire still echoing loudly around them, Miana climbed to the top of the cockpit and saw that the only way inside was through hatches that led into two separate, pod-like cabins.

"Looks like we'll be separated sooner than expected," Kurt said with a hint of reluctance.

"Looks like," Miana replied.

Both hatches were already open and when Miana stepped into hers, she was surprised to find the cabin full of a thick, viscous fluid.

"Is… this right?" she asked Kurt.

"These jets are capable of manoeuvring at incredible speeds," he replied, "particularly when they get into the vacuum of space. If the cabin was full of air, the G-forces would crush us in an instant, but liquid doesn't compress, so even if the jet falls apart around us we won't feel a thing."

"That's… reassuring," Miana said with a frown.

She watched Kurt ease himself into the cabin in front of hers and then lowered herself into the glistening liquid. It closed over her like honey and felt stranger than she expected, but when she was fully immersed it was clear as the purest water. She could see the controls in front of her perfectly, without any distortion, and the only indication she was sitting in liquid was an unfamiliar resistance to any movement.

Running her eyes over the control panel, Miana saw that it was labelled in Arabic and was glad Kurt was the one in control.

"Buckle up," he said through her helmet intercom.

At the sound of his voice, a video feed appeared in her helmet's HUD and Miana saw Kurt reach across his body and pull a buckle at shoulder height down to a clasp at his opposite hip. He then repeated the motion in the opposite direction and Miana copied him with her own restraints.

After that, Kurt touched the control panel in front of him and an odd rumble moved through her as the jet's engines ignited.

A tinted radiation shield slid closed above her and Miana looked up to see the remaining bubble of air slowly disappearing. Outside the cockpit, the flash of weapon's fire was easy to see in the darkness, but it was also coming from the entrance to the hanger and so couldn't have all been Jaichim's rebel group.

"*Reinforcements,*" Miana thought, her anxiety rising.

"I don't like this," Kurt said beneath his breath.

"What do you mean?"

"They're not just going to let us just fly out of here. Even if Jaichim keeps those anti-aircraft guns offline, they're sure to send other ships after us. I can definitely fly this thing, but we won't last two seconds in a serious dogfight."

"Saadi seems to know what he's doing," Miana reasoned. "He probably has another team waiting for us in orbit."

"I hope so," Kurt said grimly.

Miana watched with growing trepidation as they taxied toward the launching tunnel and wished the jet would go faster. It took an agonisingly long time to get all the way inside then lights began to flash insistently and a pair of thick doors closed behind them.

They were now effectively locked inside a cramped corridor approximately one hundred metres in length with two slowly opening doors at the far end.

Miana could see starlight twinkling in the darkness beyond and felt a new rumble as Kurt opened the throttle. Her anxiety grew as their mounting thrust was held in check by some kind of locking bolts then a countdown appeared on the screen in front of her.

Miana didn't need a translation as she watched the countdown approach zero and she pressed her head back into the headrest, silently praying that Jaichim had managed to shut down the anti-aircraft defences.

As the countdown ended, Miana expected a jolt of acceleration, but was taken by surprise when the corridor simply flashed into motion without a hint of acceleration.

"*The liquid*," she thought in amazement.

A moment later, the dark Marsian landscape exploded into view and Miana stared around herself in amazement. The dimly lit horizon tipped downward as they accelerated up through the atmosphere and the stars began to grow brighter as the light pollution from the Bas Quirat fell away behind them.

As they rose into the night sky, Miana felt an exhilaration she wasn't expecting, but it disappeared when she remembered who was meant to be with them.

"Where's Saadi?" she asked Kurt. "Has he made it out yet?"

"Hang on," Kurt replied.

A view of the Bas Quirat appeared on the screens in front of Miana and she searched it for a second ship.

"I don't see anything," she said.

"I'll run a sensor sweep," Kurt added, "he might still be... oh no."

"What?" Miana said, her panic rising, "What is it?"

"The launching tunnel," Kurt said, his tone grim.

Miana focussed in on the launching tunnel they'd just exited and saw something dark rising from its end.

"It that... smoke?" she asked, dread prickling at the back of her neck.

"It's only coming from one of the tunnels," Kurt replied quickly. "He might still make it."

Miana felt a sudden hollow feeling in her chest. She wanted to believe that he would appear, just as Kurt hoped, but after everything the Quiraton had said...

"*What are you going to do, Saadi?*" she thought helplessly.

SAADI WATCHED AS MIANA AND KURT TAXIED TOWARD the launching tunnel. It was harder than he expected to let them go.

Miana truly was an impressive woman. Intelligent, insightful, and skilfully empathic. He still wasn't sure if she was the Mahdi, or if there was any truth to the prophecies at all for that matter, but he had no doubt she would do what was needed when the time came. The question was, would he?

Turning his attention to the hanger's control tower, Saadi saw that Jaichim and his followers were still fighting the Quiration forces loyal to Hani'ah.

"*Just as Naseem described,*" he thought with a chill.

He'd long pondered what it would feel like at the very end. His faith – which had guided him for so long now – was still strong, but there was fear as well. Believing something would happen and witnessing it in person were two very different things.

"*I don't want to die,*" he thought, genuinely surprised to hear the words appear in his mind.

He knew what was at stake. If he didn't do what needed to be done, the loss of life would be unimaginable. But the thought of dying seemed to activate some kind of inbuilt survival mechanism and as his fear grew, Saadi felt doubts he'd thought were long since conquered return with a new urgency.

What if he failed? Or even worse, what if the Divsek who'd spoken to Naseem was lying to them, just as the other Divsek had been lying to humans for millennia? What if the future he was fighting to protect turned out to be just as destructive as the one he was trying to prevent? What if he didn't *have* to die?

With each new doubt, Saadi felt his heart beating faster and his skin prickled with sweat.

"Not now," he said aloud, focussing fiercely on the jet's control panel. "I can't fail them now."

But his fear held him paralysed. Try as he might, he couldn't bring himself to make the next move. He willed his hand to reach for the control panel, to push the throttle forward and get his jet moving, but he could only stare at a blinking red display that showed the hanger's launch tunnel was now active.

He looked at it through his thick, cockpit window and saw that Miana and Kurt were locked inside and ready to launch. But even that certainty didn't help with the phantom terror that gripped him.

"*Coward!*" he berated harshly in his mind. "*How can you falter when so many have died for this cause before you?*"

But the words came with a sickness that made his breathing sharp and shallow. He closed his eyes, blocking out the future that raced toward him and wondered if this was how Abdul and all the others who'd sacrificed themselves already had felt before the end.

"*I can't do it,*" he thought incredulously. "*I don't want to die.*"

And as this new certainty tore his faith asunder and lay waste to all he'd worked for, despair flooded in to claim him.

Saadi let out a low moan as his mind flashed with accusations. Fear pounded through him from head to toe and yet, above it all, one question continually surfaced. How could he stop what was already in motion?

As his desperate mind searched for an answer, a sharp tone sounded in his helmet and a row of flashing red lights lit up at the edge of his control panel.

"It's happening," he thought, eyes wide.

He looked to his left, where the lights were indicating damage, and saw sparks exploding against his armoured cockpit. His mind flashed to the vision Naseem had shared with him and his eyes flickered to the hanger's entrance.

There he was – Loc Breeden – standing over several of Jaichim's blood-spattered followers and surrounded by what looked like Quiration citizens.

Saadi would have seen through the deception immediately, even if he wasn't already aware of it. The way they stood gave them away as easily as the way they held their weapons. These were hired killers. Thugs. Cosmotech Defence's most expensive attack dogs.

Several of them were firing at him, their weapons biting ineffectually at the jet's tough armour, while two more advanced on the hanger's control tower and Jaichim.

With Naseem's predictions once more coming to life before him, Saadi's fear seemed to choke in his throat and he turned back to his controls to find his weapons were now active.

They shouldn't have been. There were several contingency locks built into the jet and even more systems in the control tower that prevented any weapons being fired inside the hanger. But they were all disabled now. Jaichim had done his job and was expecting Saadi to do the same.

The thought sent Saadi's mind back to the moment he'd confronted Jaichim at the elevator and he remembered what he'd said to him…

"Do not give in to your doubts, Jaichim. Your actions here will live on for generations. Listen to your heart. What does it tell you?"

And Saadi suddenly realised that his fear had done more than paralyse him. It had silenced his heart. It had drowned his senses with doubt and cut him off from his greatest source of strength.

"*What is my heart telling me?*" he thought to himself.

And as the question was asked, an emotional plug seemed to open inside his mind. A familiar calm washed over him and his hand moved to the trigger cover that prevented him from accidentally activating his weapons. Then, almost without any conscious decision, he flicked it open.

A small barrel extended from the jet's nose, creating a secondary targeting screen in the cockpit window, and Saadi turned the crosshairs onto the area just in front of Loc's advancing mercenaries.

"I don't want to die," he whispered as he pulled the trigger.

The hanger floor in front of the soldiers lit up in a long line of exploding metal and although he couldn't hear the weapon's report from inside the liquid-filled cockpit, he saw one of the soldiers flying backward as shrapnel bit into his armour. The others ran for cover behind a line of jets.

Lost in an almost trance-like state, Saadi turned toward Loc and frowned when he saw one of the Cosmotech mercenaries crouching next to a small device on the hanger floor. He turned to where the mercenary seemed to be aiming it and saw the launching tunnel with Miana and Kurt still inside.

"*That's not meant for me,*" he thought quickly.

With an instinctive jerk, Saadi pushed the throttle forward and his jet smoothly accelerated into the space between Loc's soldier and the launching tunnel. He saw a blast of fire obscuring the tunnel's rear viewing panel for a moment – Miana and Kurt were finally launching – then he turned to Loc, expecting to be hit by whatever had been fired at him.

But all he saw was a blurred flash of curved light as the missile manoeuvred over the top of his cockpit and slammed into the launching tunnel behind him.

The blast lit up the darkened hanger with a harsh white light and Saadi felt his jet being rocked sideways by the resulting shockwave. His control panel lit up with damage indicators that detailed what

MARS - END OF DAYS

had been done to the hanger then the insistent alarm in his helmet changed to a more serious tone.

The first launching tunnel was now completely inoperable.

Quickly checking his active link with Miana's jet, Saadi breathed a sigh of relief when he saw that it was still in one piece. It must have been close, but Kurt and Miana had escaped before the explosion and were now rapidly rising into the sky above the Bas Quirat.

"*They made it,*" he thought with a flood of relief.

But he knew they weren't safe yet. He had to make sure neither Loc's nor Hani'ah's forces could use the second launching tunnel to follow them. Once they reached a high enough orbit, the jet's stealth technology would be enough to keep them hidden, but if someone followed them within the next few minutes they could establish a proximity lock and make them an easy target.

Turning his jet toward the second launching tunnel, Saadi selected a missile that would delay any pursuit.

"Good luck, Miana and Kurt," he said, before pulling the trigger.

Nothing happened.

"What...?" he gasped, glancing down at his controls.

His weapons were offline again. The access he'd been given by Jaichim had somehow been revoked.

"*No,*" he thought desperately, "*This wasn't meant to happen.*"

He turned toward the hanger's control tower and saw that the fighting had ended. Loc's mercenaries were now in control and Jaichim's body was slumped against a wall, his eyes blank.

"*What is happening?*" he thought quickly. "*Naseem said nothing about this.*"

For a moment, Saadi was confused and his doubts rose to take control once again, but this time he was ready for them. Instead of giving them any notice, he focussed in on his core, on his *heart*, and through his confusion, Saadi realised this was exactly what he was fighting for. Not for a certain future, but for an uncertain one. Not for one truth, but for many.

He was fighting for a world where a person's choices mattered and you were free to listen to your heart without fear of coercion or manipulation.

As the certainty took hold within him, Saadi realised that the choice was, and had always been, his and his alone. He may have surrendered to his fear for a moment, but when it truly mattered, in his moment of greatest need, his faith had returned to cradle him.

He turned to look at Loc Breeden and smiled as a feeling of unexpected bliss flowed through him. He knew now that the future they feared more than anything would never come to pass. Not because of his faith in the future that had been shown to him, but because of his faith in the people who were destined to shape it.

And with that, he returned his gaze to the second launching tunnel and pushed the jet's throttle to maximum. The acceleration was instant, blurring the hanger around him, and through his cockpit window Saadi saw the unopened end of the second launching tunnel rush toward him.

In the instant before impact, there was moment he was sure he saw Miana's jet through the hanger's enormous window, glistening in the distance as it rose into orbit, then the world came crashing in around him.

This time Saadi felt the impact with bone-shattering clarity. His jet slammed into the launching tunnel with enough force to split the cockpit around him and he felt something jagged spear into his leg. His vision flashed white and a screeching, crashing sound rushed in to fill the sensory void, but it all happened so fast that Saadi's brain wasn't able to process it.

The pain felt more like a conscious acknowledgement of injury than an actual experience of it and the violence was so overwhelming that he had no choice but to surrender to it.

For a moment, he wondered distantly why he'd been so afraid of this moment, then the world snapped back into focus and he was lying sideways in a twisted wreck that dripped with rapidly draining cockpit fluid.

The cabin had been torn open almost entirely from top to bottom and was surrounded by smoke and sparking debris, now exposed to the hanger beyond.

It was then that Saadi's pain receptors decided to explain the severity of his injuries. Agony rolled in to swamp his senses and although he desperately wanted to scream, to acknowledge what had been done to his body with all the strength he had left, all he could manage was a wheezing cough that hurt more than it helped.

He reluctantly turned his gaze downward and saw that just beneath his groin were two torn, bloodied stumps that pumped clouds of red into the pool of cockpit liquid still draining out around him. He closed his eyes to escape the terrible reality in front of him and hoped that death would come quickly.

"The illusive Saadi Khalil," a voice said from somewhere above him. "Ignorant tool of the betrayer. We meet at last."

With some effort, Saadi managed to open his heavy eyelids and saw Loc Breeden staring down at him with eyes that glistened with red fire. But he was not alone. Behind him, crowded like voyeuristic bystanders, were five hulking shadows with sunken eye sockets that glowed with the same red fire.

"Divsek," he murmured, before coughing painfully again.

"You know far less than you think," Loc growled, his voice sounding hollow, even this close.

"I have... faith," Saadi replied slowly.

"Faith," Loc said, the derision clear in his voice. "Faith is simply a human weakness to be exploited."

"No," Saadi disagreed as the pain in his chest grew sharper, "it is our greatest strength. If you had not misused it for so long, you might have seen how it could be used against you."

Loc remained silent for several seconds before speaking again.

"Tell me, Saadi, did your faith show you what was going to happen here?"

"I knew enough," Saadi said, before coughing up a thick spatter of blood. "You... clearly didn't."

"Your death was inevitable," Loc replied, waving his hand in dismissal.

"Yes," Saadi conceded, wheezing loudly, "but... my end... has served its purpose."

Loc darted closer at this and Saadi felt an explosion of pain as the barrel of a rifle was pressed against one of his bloodied stumps.

"Miana Raiken and Kurt Jones will die very soon," Loc hissed as pain shot through Saadi's torso.

"Is that... a prediction?" he asked between gasps, "or one... of Hani'ah's prophecies?"

In reply, Loc pushed the rifle harder and Saadi groaned in agony.

"Do not speak as if you haven't manipulated your own followers in the same way Hani'ah does hers."

"I gave them perspective," Saadi gasped, "and a choice."

"Choice," Loc said, pulling the rifle away with a grimace of distaste. "And how did that choice manifest, Saadi? In disobedience. War. Death. Mortal sins that will damn your followers for all eternity."

At this last comment, Saadi felt an overwhelming urge to smile and did so gladly.

"Nothing... is certain," he said, his voice weak.

"Wrong," Loc replied, lifting his rifle once more.

Saadi closed his eyes, still smiling, and the world exploded with the brightest light he'd ever seen. And as the light gradually faded to darkness, Saadi Khalil was content, for he knew that when it mattered most, he had chosen with his heart.

Loc felt the Triumvirate leave him with a jolt and was left standing by the jet's wreckage, holding a blood-stained weapon above the ruined corpse of Saadi Khalil.

They'd used him without warning again. Stepped into his body and finished off the rebel leader once and for all. Loc had no idea what they'd said to him, or if they'd said anything at all, for that matter, because after taking control, the Triumvirate had left him in darkness, waiting for what could have been his own death.

He wanted to be angry, he wanted to curse until he ran out of swear words, but he knew he'd failed them. Again. And the Triumvirate were unlikely to forgive the transgression twice.

"*I'm done,*" he thought helplessly.

He dropped the weapon to the wet hanger floor and waited for their judgement.

"*Just make it quick,*" he asked.

But instead, Captain West appeared beside him.

"The Quiration rebels are all dead," he said. "Miana Raiken and Kurt Jones have reached orbit. We lost their signal less than a minute ago."

Loc turned to him with a calm he hadn't felt since entering the Bas Quirat. He would have preferred to take some of the rebels alive, but the fighting had been fierce and although his team were instructed to avoid casualties, Hani'ah's forces had been given no such order. He could have stopped them, of course, but he'd been too preoccupied with getting to Miana to use his powers on them.

"You did all you could," he said quietly.

"Yes, sir," Captain West replied with a frown. "The Quiration forces are securing the hanger. They'll have questions…"

Captain West left the statement hanging in the air and the diplomat in Loc studied it like an oddity.

"Do I care?" he said out loud.

"Sir?" Captain West said, clearly concerned.

For a moment, Loc found the man's confusion almost funny and he smiled without saying anything. This seemed to disturb Captain West even further and he turned away to consult with the rest of his team.

Not sure what to do next, Loc allowed his gaze to take in the rest of the hanger. The lights had been restored and it was full of Quiration soldiers. As Captain West predicted, one of the military Commanders was striding across the hanger toward him and Loc could see the diplomatic look in his eyes. The Quirations clearly weren't concerned with the actions of his security team. They just wanted to contain this embarrassing situation.

"*And why not?*" Loc thought to himself. "*We found and neutralised the rebel terrorist, Saadi Khalil. What more could they possibly want?*"

"Loc Breeden," the Commander said in heavily accented English. "It is a surprise to see you here."

"I'm sure it is," Loc replied calmly.

"May I request that your security team relinquish their weapons to my soldiers? We have the situation under control."

"You do now," Loc said pointedly.

The Commander acknowledged the slight with a nod and a smile.

"My soldiers will escort them back to your quarters," he said.

"And what about me?" Loc asked, raising an eyebrow.

"The Prophet, Hani'ah Naziri, is ready to speak with you," the Commander replied.

"Of course," Loc said, certain Hani'ah would relish the opportunity to gloat. "Lead the way."

As the Commander turned, Loc met Captain West's gaze and nodded in response to his unspoken question. After nodding back, West instructed his team to hand over their weapons to the waiting Quirations and they were led away.

Loc watched them go for a moment and then turned to follow the Commander. They walked out of the enormous hanger and along several corridors before stopping in front of an open elevator. The Commander gestured for Loc to enter, but didn't join him inside.

Loc should have been suspicious, but he felt nothing. He wasn't even surprised when the elevator doors closed and a familiar pain pricked the base of his neck.

"*So it comes,*" he thought helplessly.

He wasn't sure how his dismissal would be handled, but he assumed it would end with his death. The Triumvirate certainly couldn't allow him to walk around with so many of their secrets.

As the pain in his neck increased, the elevator dissolved into shadow and Loc was left standing on a rocky floor, the stone cold and black beneath his feet. Three spotlights appeared in the darkness and Loc saw the Triumvirate standing only a few metres in front of him.

"Masters," he said calmly.

"You have failed us again," the Third began, just as Loc expected.

"Miana Raiken and Kurt Jones have reached orbit," he conceded. "The rebels seemed to know more than we anticipated."

"Saadi Khalil," the second said in a tone that was not as harsh as Loc expected. "He was a resourceful man."

"He was," Loc agreed, not sure what else they expected of him.

"We have another task for you," the first said, her expression as severe as ever.

Loc was stunned. He had not expected this.

"Of course," he said, trying not to sound eager.

"Isaac Taylor will be moved to Doctor Grayson's orbital station," the First continued. "Miana Raiken and Kurt Jones must not, under any circumstances, be allowed to approach the facility."

Loc couldn't believe his luck. The orbital station they were referring to was the most well-defended installations in the solar system.

"They'll never reach it," he said, as much a statement as it was a promise.

"Nevertheless," the Second replied, "the future is less certain than it has ever been. The Jupiter flare is all too real, Loc. They cannot be allowed to disrupt Isaac's work."

"I... understand," Loc replied, not sure that he did.

"There is much more than lives at stake here," the Third added with a scowl. "The plans you have helped cultivate will come to nothing if the Jupiter flare is allowed to reach Mars. Trillions in future revenue will be lost and Cosmotech's reputation will be destroyed."

"*Ah,*" Loc thought to himself. "*That makes more sense.*"

Grayson must have known the Jupiter flare was a possibility when he discovered a way to use the Vita Nova comet to terraform Mars. That meant his orbital station was some kind of contingency plan and if Miana Raiken discovered this, she might be able to prove Cosmotech had knowingly put Mars at risk.

"I understand," he said out loud, more confident this time.

"Consider yourself under the command of Doctor Grayson until you reach the orbital station," the Second said. "Once on board, he will be occupied with preparations and you will take over the security of the station."

"Of course," Loc replied.

"There is no room for error, this time, Loc," the Second added.

"I understand," he repeated quickly.

"No, I don't think you do," the Third said with a scowl. "For some time now, you have been closer to joining us than you may think. But after the way you handled Miana Raiken and the emergence of the Jupiter flare, we were forced to delay your ascension."

Again, Loc was shocked. Could this really be true?

"However," the First added in an uncharacteristically even tone, "we have not overlooked your successes, nor has our decision to let you join us changed in any way. You *will* become one of us, Loc Breeden. But first we must ensure the legacy that has won you a place alongside us does not fall to dust beneath your feet."

Loc couldn't believe it. The power he'd craved for so long was finally within his grasp and yet it almost didn't seem real.

"I will make sure it does not," he said firmly. "Miana Raiken will not be allowed to threaten our future."

"You must do everything in your power to ensure it," the Second replied solemnly, "for when this last mission is complete, your life will change forever, Loc Breeden."

"You will answer to no one," the Third added.

"You will be one of *us*," the First said with feeling.

"You will know everything that we do and you will command all the power we have accumulated over the centuries," the Second finished with a sweeping hand gesture.

"I'm ready," Loc replied, the hunger growing inside him.

"Yes," the Second said with a nod, "and this last mission will prove it, once and for all."

"Thank you," Loc said with more sincerity than he'd ever said those words.

Then the Triumvirate faded away and when the elevator returned, he stood in stunned silence for a moment. All the frustration, suspicion, and resentment he'd endured over the past few days was forgotten. Ultimate power was finally within his grasp and all he had to do was keep Miana from reaching one of Cosmotech's most secure facilities.

"She won't get anywhere near it," he thought with a grin. *"And when I join the Triumvirate, I'll make her pay in the worst possible way for putting my ascension at risk."*

When the elevator doors opened again, they revealed a large chamber that looked just like a throne room.

Not surprisingly, Hani'ah was sitting on the 'throne' at its centre and, despite her blindness, Loc put on his best diplomatic smile.

"Prophet Hani'ah Naziri," he said, striding forward and bowing low in greeting.

"You have failed," she said in Arabic, her tone cold.

"Have I?" he said, replying intentionally in English – he saw no reason to maintain diplomatic courtesies now, nor did he want Hani'ah to mistakenly think he had any respect for her. "Your rebel Saadi Khalil is dead. How is that a failure?"

"Miana Raiken and Kurt Jones are alive," she said with a disapproving frown that made her forehead ruby glint in the light.

"They are," Loc agreed with a shrug, "but they pose no real threat. That is, unless, you know something I don't?"

"They pose an unacceptable risk to the work of Isaac Taylor," Hani'ah snapped.

"Really?" Loc said with mock concern. "Is there a new prophecy I should know about? Please, Holy Prophet, share it with me."

Hani'ah fell silent at this and the two servants at her side glared at him with a venom he thoroughly enjoyed.

"Precisely!" a voice cut through the chamber.

Turning toward the familiar bark, Loc saw Dr. Grayson shuffling into the throne room.

"The matter is never final. Never final. Always in flux while the parameters refuse to be seen."

"Doctor Grayson," Loc said, not sure even this bumbling savant could ruin his good mood. "I understand we're relocating to your orbital station."

Dr. Grayson looked up at him in surprise and then frowned in irritation and turned to Hani'ah.

"Preparations have been made. You will accompany us to the station."

Loc knew that under any other circumstances, being ignored would have infuriated him, but the fact Grayson was giving orders to Hani'ah Naziri was amusing enough to make up for it.

"My escort is ready," Hani'ah replied simply.

Dr. Grayson's eyes went wide for a moment and he flinched several times before holding a hand up to his temple and speaking in a frantic tone.

"No, no, no! No escort. Only you. Your assistants if you must, but no escort. Quirations must stay here. Here!"

Loc laughed in the uncomfortable silence that trailed Dr. Grayson's words.

"It appears you're not as welcome as you think," he said to Hani'ah.

"Then we may leave at once," Hani'ah said, ignoring him.

Loc had to admire her composure. He'd expected Hani'ah to argue the point, but it was clear she had no intention of missing this opportunity to step into whatever mythical role she'd convinced her people to believe she represented.

"Good, only good," Grayson replied, before turning around and shuffling back the way he'd come. "Time is running down. Closer than ever now. Open, always open."

Loc watched him go for a moment and then returned his gaze to Hani'ah.

She was already stepping down from her dais, her servants still glaring at him.

"May I be excused, Holy Prophet?" he said with another mocking bow.

"I have had many visions of the future," she replied, her tone haughtier than ever. "But your success is not among them, Loc Breeden. Do not let your arrogance get in the way of your duty."

Loc knew he shouldn't let her feeble insult get to him, but with so much riding on his 'success', the last thing he wanted to hear was her negative portentous drivel.

"Watch your own arrogance, Prophet," he spat back, not hiding his contempt now. "Lest it condemn you before your 'divine' visions have a chance to save you."

"We shall see," Hani'ah replied simply.

"So we shall," Loc agreed as he spun away and stalked back to the elevator that had brought him there. "So we shall."

MARS ORBIT - June 8, 2147 - 3.42pm

ISAAC WAS FEELING NERVOUS, BUT ENERGISED.
Everything was happening so fast now and for the first time since arriving in this strange, parallel universe, he actually knew what was happening and what he had to do.

After their partial success in the Quiration laboratories, he'd spent a few hours supervising the removal of P.A.T.R.I.C. and had taken a final shower in his luxurious suite before being escorted to a large jet.

He was seated near the front along with Dr. Grayson, Loc, Hani'ah and her ladies in black. Loc's security detail sat in the rear section of the jet, but Dr. Grayson's burly security guards were nowhere to be seen. Neither were any other Quirations.

Isaac was surprised at that. He would have thought someone like Hani'ah would travel with an enormous entourage. On the other hand, Loc had certainly brought enough security to keep them all safe. Isaac wasn't sure how the politics of such an arrangement were meant to work, but he assumed the Bas Quirat had a pretty good relationship with Cosmotech Defence if they trusted them with their Prophet.

Putting the thought aside, Isaac looked out the generous window beside him and surveyed a spectacular view of the cosmos. It reminded him of the last time he'd been in orbit, back when his parents had taken him and his brother to Icarus – one of Mars' many orbital hotels.

His memories of that time were magical. They'd played zero-G Terran Wars – which he'd won, of course – stuffed themselves sick on the dessert buffet and even modified the hotel's telescope and named a twin star solar system they discovered by creating an anagram of their names – 'Sajisanoac One'.

It was a stupid name, but the memory still made Isaac smile and he would have happily stayed inside it if the Cosmotech space station hadn't just rolled into view.

"Woah," he said in unabashed amazement.

Loc had told him they were on their way up to one of Cosmotech's space stations, but he hadn't been expecting this. It was enormous!

The main structure seemed to be made of seven huge rings, the largest of which Dr. Grayson had said was just over two kilometres wide. The rings rotated around a complex axis of support struts capable of withstanding several billion tonnes of stress and the gradual decrease in their diameter made the whole thing look like an elongated cone with its sharp end pointed toward Mars.

Each ring spun at a different rate because their unique diameters required a different angular momentum to create the required gravity along its inner surface. Most were set to the gravity on Earth, but at least two of the rings were calibrated to the much lighter burden felt on Mars.

But most spectacular of all, above the highest, largest ring, was an almost invisible net of glistening cables that stretched out in a giant parabolic satellite dish, nine-hundred kilometres in diameter. And at its centre, a glistening cloud of ice particles swirled in a lazy tornado.

"Magnificent, isn't it?" Loc said from his seat beside Isaac.

Isaac turned to look at him. Something about Loc had changed since their visit to the Bas Quirat. He hadn't seen much of him since they arrived, but something had obviously happened. There was a distinct eagerness to Loc's behaviour that wasn't there before and yet his tone had an edge that almost felt... manic.

"It's amazing," he agreed carefully.

"My life's work," Dr. Grayson added in a spiteful tone from the seat in front of them, "realised within one of the largest structures ever constructed."

Dr. Grayson wasn't quite himself either. He hadn't had lone arguments since boarding the ship and, surprisingly, it worried Isaac.

"Your whole life?" he said, trying to coax a bit of conversation out of him. "The station is your design?"

"Oh yes," Loc said, answering the question for him. "There isn't a bolt, circuit, or fabricated surface that didn't require Doctor Grayson's signature."

Isaac noticed a slightly spiteful edge to Loc's tone, but decided he was probably just tired. He certainly looked it. Dr. Grayson, on the other hand, remained silent and Isaac decided he wasn't going to get anything more from him.

"That's... incredible," he said, trying to imagine how much time had gone into creating a space station of this size. "Are those ice particles I can see above the station?"

"Ionised particles of frozen ammonia, water and carbon dioxide," Loc corrected him. "They're from the tail of a hyperbolic comet called the *Vita Nova*. Before the threat of the Jupiter flare, Cosmotech Defence planned to capture as much of the tail material as possible and use it to saturate our atmosphere. If we can gather enough, the material will eventually terraform the planet."

Isaac frowned as he remembered what Anya had told him when her 'old man' persona, Dr. Haig, had been in control back at the Valles Dome planetarium. She'd described this situation almost exactly – a comet shedding ice across the solar system before the tail is ionised by a massive solar eruption. It was the perfect medium for a Jupiter flare.

"So… you're saying that space station is now one of the largest lightning rods in existence?"

Dr. Grayson let out a sudden, barking laugh.

"An adequate description, Isaac, yes."

Surprised he'd got a reaction at all, Isaac looked back out the window and stared at the station with a whole new perspective.

"*We're bringing the Jupiter flare straight to us,*" he thought with a chill. "*Straight to me.*"

"Don't worry," Loc said, as if sensing his anxiety. "If Doctor Grayson believes this will work then it will work."

"The prophecy will be fulfilled," Hani'ah added in Arabic, speaking for the first time since they'd taken off.

Isaac turned to look at her.

"*I hope it's that simple,*" he thought.

As he waited for Hani'ah to pick the thought from his mind, something caught his attention through her window. He focussed on it and decided it was some kind of lumpy black satellite.

"What about those?" he enquired, pointing as it passed them.

"Part of the station's defence grid," Loc replied casually. "They're equipped with a sensitive proximity warning system, to prevent any orbiting debris or small meteorites from damaging the station."

Isaac turned back to his own window and saw another one slide by on his side. This one was close enough to make out a sinister looking appendage on the underside.

"They're armed," he said with a frown.

"Of course," Loc replied, as if it were obvious, "they're equipped with lasers, rockets and an ingenious Gatling gun design that utilises its own explosive discharge to maintain its position while firing. This is a multi-trillion dollar installation, Isaac. We can't risk it being damaged by space debris."

Isaac wasn't sure how a Gatling gun would be effective against meteorites, but he supposed even Cosmotech Defence would have enemies. He also doubted Loc would admit the weapons might be used against anything other than harmless space junk and so he didn't bother asking.

He watched as several more of the menacing satellites slid by them and then returned his focus to the space station. They must have been approaching at a decent speed now because it just kept getting bigger and bigger. He'd always marvelled at the way his favourite science fiction movies used different methods to portray the scale of structures built in the vacuum of space, but none of it was as good as the real thing.

"*Wow,*" he thought to himself.

A short tone came from the intercom above him and a crisp voice suddenly filled the cabin.

"Please, secure your helmet. We are about to commence docking procedures."

Reluctantly pulling his gaze from the window, Isaac bent to grab the helmet beneath his seat and then placed it over his head. It slid easily into the locking mechanism at his jacket's neck and when he rotated it slowly, a faint *click* sounded in his ear and a cool stream of breathable air began blowing against his cheek.

He returned his gaze to the window and watched as the station began to slowly turn away from them. He could tell from the view that their jet was now heading for the largest ring and turning as it went so their roof would line up with the ring's outer surface. As it did so, momentum-induced gravity pressed Isaac gently into his seat and he directed his gaze down the outside of the twelve colossal rings that gradually slid into view.

The great, dark bulk of Mars slowly lined up beneath the rings and the frightening new perspective sent a wave of vertigo through him.

"*That's a long way down,*" he thought, before looking away and taking a deep breath.

A brief shudder passed through the jet when they made contact with the docking clamps and a green light appeared in the panel above Isaac's head. They were now safely locked to the outer hull and could remove their restraints.

"We've arrived," Loc said, sounding eager.

With gravity re-established, it was much easier to get up and move around the cabin. Hani'ah and her ladies in black moved to the exit first, then Dr. Grayson, Loc, and finally Isaac.

Loc took a moment to show Isaac how to tether himself to the exit rail, then a hatch in the ceiling opened with a *hisss* of readjusting pressures. A series of steps slid out of the cabin wall and Dr. Grayson led them upward, sliding his tether along with him. The stairs took them into a brightly lit airlock, just large enough to fit all six of them. Apparently Loc's security team would have to wait.

When they were all inside, an orange light on the wall blinked on and off and the hatch they'd entered through closed with a heavy *clunk*. Isaac heard the locking mechanism *whirr* as it ratcheted firmly into place then the orange light blinked off and a green one came on above the airlock's only other door.

Isaac saw Loc untethering himself and quickly did the same. Hani'ah was the first to sweep up another set of stairs that had just slid out of the walls and her ladies in black weren't far behind. Isaac waited impatiently for Loc to motion him forward then he followed with wide eyes and a pounding heart.

As he emerged into the space station, the first thing Isaac noticed was how the wide, incredibly long corridor curved gently upward in either direction. Once again, he had to readjust his perspective.

"I'm standing on the inside of the largest ring," he thought in excitement. *"This is so cool."*

A dozen or so people dressed in clean white lab suits waited in a neatly organised group and Isaac expected Dr. Grayson to address them – this was his station after all. Instead, he ignored them and turned to address Isaac.

"You will accompany me to the primary research platform," he said, before turning to Hani'ah. "Ms. Naziri, please allow my staff to escort you to the secondary platform. There you will be shown where the psychic connection with Isaac will be made. Until that time, they will cater for your every need."

Hani'ah Naziri bowed her head in acknowledgement then her women in black led her away.

"Loc Breeden," Dr. Grayson added, not looking at him, "you have other business to attend to."

"Of course," Loc said with another smile that, strangely, never reached his eyes. "Good luck, Isaac. I will be available if you need me. All you need do is ask."

Isaac was sure now that there was stuff going on he wasn't aware of, but this kind of drama was as foreign to him as Arabic, so he decided to leave it alone.

"Uh... sure thing," he replied uncertainly.

Loc bowed his head for a moment and then turned on his heel and stalked away.

"Come, there's not much time," Dr. Grayson said loudly, before striding off down the corridor and causing the welcoming committee to part quickly and form up behind him in a scramble. "I want the prototype unloaded and integrated into the station *immediately*. Did you received the design specs I sent you?"

"Yes, Doctor Grayson," one of the people following him answered smartly.

Isaac skipped a few steps in an effort to catch up with them and then settled into a fast walk near the back of the group.

"And the modifications I sent through are complete?" Dr. Grayson asked firmly.

"Yes, Doctor Grayson."

"I want three teams monitoring the set up," Dr. Grayson continued. "The first will…"

As the orders rapidly multiplied, Isaac tried to stay focussed, but it was hard when they were moving through such a new and interesting environment.

"*This place is amazing.*"

He'd thought the Quiration laboratories were bustling, but they were nothing compared to Cosmotech's space station. It was like a small city running at peak capacity. Everywhere he looked there were people moving with a purpose and every room and corridor they passed looked clean, ordered and, above all, deliberate.

When they eventually reached what Isaac assumed was the primary research platform, the group behind Dr. Grayson scattered to their various tasks, and he was left staring around himself in amazement.

The research platform was close to fifty metres across and had a bank of instruments down one side that looked suspiciously like the ones he'd taken apart in the Bas Quirat. These ones were being worked on by dozens of serious looking technicians and Isaac couldn't help but notice they were adding several components Dr. Grayson had brought with them.

On the other side of the platform, three holographic images hovered at eye level, each one bigger than Isaac was tall. He walked over to them, fascinated with the vibrant colours and detail in each, and realised they were near-perfect representations of planetary objects.

The most brilliant one on the far left was clearly meant to be the sun. It glowed a brilliant yellow, with surface convections etched orange and brown in amazing detail. From what Isaac could see, there were several areas of solar activity being monitored. Each one was traced in brilliant green and sprouted data panels that were filled with graphs and numbers.

It was like nothing he'd ever seen and Isaac couldn't help wondering what sun-worshipping civilisations from the past would think of such a detailed replication of their 'deity'.

The hologram next to it wasn't so bright, but it was just as recognisable. It was Mars without a doubt, with the Valles Dome, Lynt City and the Bas Quirat clearly marked and magnified.

As Isaac ran his gaze across the barren, storm-swept surface, he noticed a tiny version of Cosmotech's space station orbiting above the Bas Quirat. He gingerly touched the hologram with a finger and imagined an enormous version of it crashing through the station ring he now stood inside.

Smiling to himself, Isaac turned to the last and, by far, the strangest hologram. It glowed a brilliant white and looked, for all intents and purposes, like an enormous iceberg. Of course, most icebergs didn't seethe with hundreds of tiny volcanoes of escaping gas and ice.

"The *Vita Nova?*" he guessed as he stepped toward it.

"Correct," Dr. Grayson said, appearing suddenly at his shoulder. "The promise of life for so many and, at the same time, death for all."

Isaac wasn't sure he'd ever get used to the way Dr. Grayson seemed to appear and disappear without warning. At least he was in one of his more lucid moods.

"Where is it now?" Isaac asked.

"Passing between the orbits of Earth and Mars," Dr. Grayson replied, his eyes dull. "It crossed our current location several weeks ago, hence the volume of ionised particulate matter you witnessed on our approach."

Isaac stared at the holographic replica of the monstrous comet, not sure how he should feel about it. In one sense, it was a beautiful thing to behold and it demonstrated the infinite possibilities of the cosmic realm. In another sense, this was the very real harbinger of the Apocalypse – a reaper of civilisations and bringer of destruction on worldwide scales.

"How much time do we have?" he asked.

Dr. Grayson waved his hand at the image of Mars and it shrunk until they could see a visual representation of a slice of the solar system. Jupiter was shown at the very top of the map and a jagged, glowing line of red, much like a lightning bolt, stretched down toward the tiny representation of Mars.

The Jupiter flare was much closer than Isaac expected.

"A little over an hour," Dr. Grayson said dispassionately. "Enough time for a final test. We must ensure we can establish the connection before the Jupiter flare arrives. I don't want the initial power surge to destabilise the process."

"Initial power surge?" Isaac said with a frown. Dr. Grayson hadn't mentioned anything like that before.

"We have the most powerful energy production plants in existence on board this space station," Dr. Grayson explained, "but we still cannot simulate what approaches. However, if we detonate a large enough electro-magnetic pulse at the centre of the station, I believe it will provide enough energy to accomplish what we need."

"An electro-magnetic pulse?" Isaac said.

"One large enough to wipe out this station and the Bas Quirat beneath us as well," Dr. Grayson added.

Isaac's eyes went wide and Dr. Grayson's gaze settled on him for a moment.

"P.A.T.R.I.C. will absorb it all, Isaac," he said matter-of-factly.

"Yeah," Isaac replied slowly. "Sure it will."

"Now, I have some final preparations," Dr. Grayson said with a now familiar wave of his hand. "My staff will assist you with anything you might need. I will be back before it is time."

"Sure thing," Isaac said absently.

He watched the Doc walking away, mumbling to himself again, and wished he shared the man's confidence. Or if not that, at least his lack of anxiety.

"*I guess I'll just have to wait and see,*" he thought helplessly, before turning back to the holograms, "*and hope Hani'ah's prophecy is as rock solid as she believes.*"

ANYA DREAMED. SHE WAS LYING ON A BED THAT SHE'D chosen with her twin sister, Fayina, the week before their sixteenth birthday. She turned onto her side and saw Fayina sitting on her own bed and leaning against the wall.

She tried to get her attention, but couldn't make a sound. Fayina was talking quietly to someone on her data pad and although she glanced at Anya occasionally, she was clearly immersed in the conversation.

Anya tried to get up, but couldn't move her body.

"You're going to kill her," an unfamiliar voice said behind her.

The words sent a chill through Anya and she tried to turn toward the voice, but her body failed her.

"Your parents as well," the voice added.

This time Anya tried to protest, to scream her innocence in defiance of the faceless voice, but once again, her vocal chords refused to cooperate.

"You let a teenage crush come between you and your twin sister," the voice added in a derisive tone.

Desperate to face her accuser, Anya struggled harder, but could only stare at her twin sister, Fayina.

301

"You're going to kill them," the voice repeated cruelly.

Panic rose inside Anya and it grew until it almost strangling her. Then everything suddenly changed. Now, she was standing in front of a large window and staring into a gleaming, chrome-plated room with three trolleys at its centre. Each trolley held a lumpy silver bag – two large and one smaller – and Anya realised she was looking at her family. Her dead family in body bags.

"No!" she screamed in terror.

This time her voice echoed loudly off the window and she was able to move forward and hammer against the glass.

"They're not dead!" she screamed, hitting as hard as she could. "I didn't kill them!"

Each time her fist pounded on the glass, a larger-than-possible shudder vibrated through the chrome-plated room and the bags began to move on their trolleys. Realising what she was doing, Anya quickly stopped hitting the window, but one of the bags had already moved so close to the edge that it slipped off the trolley and split open to reveal the pallid, lifeless face of her father.

"Noooo!" she screamed again, raising her hands to her face and taking a step back.

The other two bags teetered on the edge of their trolleys and as Anya watched in horror another tumbled to the floor and split open, ejecting the ragdoll corpse of her mother. Her eyes were clouded and dead, but they still somehow locked onto Anya, and their silent accusation tore at her chest.

Sobbing desperately now, Anya pressed her hands against the glass and could only watch as the last bag began to slide inevitably from its perch.

"Fayina!" she screamed desperately.

Not wanting to see her sister's dead body, but unable to look away, Anya was taken by surprise when the bag broke open and a bolt of red light flashed out from the darkness within.

She turned from the glass, momentarily blinded. When the harsh glow faded, the trolleys and dead bodies were gone.

In their place was Anya's reflection. Her true reflection. Four people, each inhabiting the same body, but with the distinctive look of the personas she'd created to cope with the loss of her family.

"Ianka!" she said, hammering on the glass again. "Celia! Dr. Haig!"

But none of them seemed to hear her. Only Fayina was aware of Anya's presence and she scowled at her with a hatred she'd never confronted in this way.

"Do I really hate myself so much?" she asked, tears rolling down her cheeks.

"You have reason to hate yourself," the strange voice said from behind her.

Spinning around in alarm, Anya stumbled back when she saw five shadowy figures towering over her. They were shrouded in darkness apart from five sets of glowering red eyes and, behind them, a flickering light glinted off wet, cave-like walls. Anya's darting eyes searched for any detail that might explain what she was seeing and she eventually realised the walls were encrusted with veins of red crystal.

"You caused the death of your twin sister, Fayina, and your parents," one of the figures said in a thick, deep voice.

"It wasn't–" Anya began, but she was cut off by Fayina's harsh voice.

"Yes! I was too stupid, selfish, and *horny* to see that she needed me. I killed her."

Anya turned to Fayina, expecting to hear the others disagree, but they remained silent and simply stared into the distance as if she wasn't even there.

"What would you do to save your sister?" the dark figures asked.

"There's no way–" Anya started to say, but again, Fayina cut her off.

"Anything!" she shouted. "I would do *anything* for her!"

Anya looked at Fayina and then back at the dark figures, and couldn't help imagining them grinning in the darkness.

"There is a way, if you would hear it," one of them said, with none of the sadistic pleasure Anya imagined.

"Tell me," Fayina growled.

"Isaac Taylor," the voice replied.

"Isaac?" Anya said at the same time as Fayina.

"What does he have to do with anything?" Fayina added with a frown.

"He is different," the voice explained. "You know this. You have sensed it."

Anya knew it was true. She'd known it from the first time she'd seen his aura. But what did that have to do with what was happening to her now?

"Tell me how he can help my sister," Fayina demanded.

"The difference you sensed in Isaac is far greater than you think," the voice continued, ignoring her outburst. "He is not from this reality. He came here by accident and is now working with Cosmotech Defence to open a portal that will take him back to his own reality. He is consumed with returning home to his twin brother, Jason."

Anya couldn't believe what she was hearing. Could this really be true?

"What are you talking about?" Fayina snarled.

"A cosmic event approaches," the voice answered patiently. "You know of it already."

"The Jupiter flare," Anya said at the same time as Fayina.

"It will provide the power Isaac needs to open his portal," the dark figures added. "But it is a power that can be used for so much more."

"More?" Fayina said. "What do you mean, more?"

"Time," the voice explained, "is but one of the many dimensions that shape this reality. It may appear constant and immutable, but it is not. The same mechanism that will allow Isaac to move between realities can be used to link different moments in time."

Fayina gasped, as surprised as Anya.

"Are you saying I can go back and save my sister?" she asked.

"If you know how," the voice replied. "Yes."

"*You* know!" Fayina snarled, slamming her fist into the window that separated them. "Tell me how! Tell me now!"

Anya couldn't bring herself to believe such a thing was even possible, but the fantastic promise lit a spark of hope deep inside her.

For a moment, she was glad Fayina was here to speak for her.

"You will be granted the knowledge you seek," the voice replied calmly, "but there is a price."

"*Of course there's a price,*" Anya thought, realising where this was going.

"I told you I would do anything," Fayina growled.

"Even take a life?" the voice boomed.

Anya's eyes went wide at this and even Fayina seemed taken aback.

"You want me to kill someone?"

"Yes," the voice replied. "At the right moment, you will intervene and they will die. When this is done, you will be shown how to save your sister."

"No!" Anya shouted. "I will never take a life, even if it means my sister will be saved."

"How do I know you can even do this?" Fayina demanded.

"You will be provided proof before the price must be paid," the voice promised.

Anya still didn't quite believe this was anything more than a twisted nightmare, but it felt real enough. She wanted to think even Fayina wasn't capable of killing someone, not even in her worst frame of mind, but to save her sister…?

Even locked away from her personalities, Anya could feel the same longing Fayina must be experiencing and knew it might be enough to make her pay the price.

"Who?" Fayina asked simply.

"Does it matter?" the voice asked in reply.

Fayina paused for a moment and Anya could see her jaw muscles working as she wrestled with the decision.

"No," she said after a moment.

"Then we have a deal?" the voice asked.

Anya hammered on the glass again in an effort to wake her other personalities so that Fayina, the worst aspect of her, would not be the one to make this decision. But they continued to stare blindly through her.

"Yes," Fayina said at last, glaring through the glass with a determination Anya found all too familiar.

"No!" she said, hammering on the glass again. "You can't do this, Fayina! I won't let you."

But the psychological embodiment of Anya's rage and guilt wouldn't even look at her, and for the first time Anya wondered if Fayina even knew she was there.

"Then it is done," the dark figures said behind her. "You will now awaken inside a space station. A guide will appear to show you the right time and place, and who you must kill. Remember, only when you have completed your task will you be reunited with your sister."

"Just... promise me my sister will survive," Fayina said grimly.

"Your sister will live," the dark figure replied solemnly, its eyes flaring bright red in the darkness.

Anya felt more helpless now than when she'd first lost control of her own body. But beyond her desperation, a traitorous hope had insinuated itself at the back of her mind. What if the mysterious figures were telling the truth? What if she could save her sister and be rid of the anger, guilt, and loneliness that had made her create so many personalities?

It was a tantalising thought, despite being selfish and wrong, and Anya didn't know how to feel about it. But either way, she seemed to be stuck as an observer and could only hope that Fayina would refuse to commit murder when the time came.

"*You can't save a life by taking one,*" she thought to herself, not sure she even believed it.

Fayina awoke with a start and sat up to find herself on a bed in a white room, surrounded by medical equipment.

"So, it wasn't just a dream," she said quietly.

"No," a strange voice answered. "It wasn't."

Fayina leapt into a crouch and scanned the room, but there was no one else there.

"Who was that?" she snarled. "Show yourself!"

"Do you see the glasses on the bedside table?" the voice asked.

Fayina glanced to the side and saw a set of clear glasses within arm's reach.

"What about them?"

"Put them on and you'll be able to see me."

Fayina picked up the glasses carefully and glared at them in distrust. She knew Cosmotech had all kinds of freaky technology. Who knows what these things might do to her?

"Why would we bother tricking you? You've been under our control for some time, Fayina. You know why you're here. Put them on."

Fayina bared her teeth in anger, but knew the voice was right.

As soon as the glasses slid over her eyes, a figure appeared at the end of her bed. He was short, hunched, and his long, greasy hair was pulled back from eyes that flickered around the room constantly.

"Who are you?" she said with a frown.

"Unimportant," he said with a dismissive wave of his hand.

"Then how do you know what I was dreaming?"

"You were told to kill someone," the man said simply. "This is your target."

Another figure appeared beside him. A woman, much taller than he was, who was wearing a long, white robe and a small ruby that glimmered at the centre of her forehead.

As Fayina studied the beautiful face, she realised her eyes were clouded. She was blind.

"Who is she?"

"The woman you will kill to save your twin sister."

Fayina felt her heart skip a beat.

"So it's true? You can really send me back?"

"Of course," the man replied, "but… not until this woman dies."

Fayina noticed his reluctance and felt an all new level of distrust.

"You're asking a lot for very little assurance," she growled.

"And you're free to decline," the man replied with a scowl.

"I was told I would see proof," Fayina countered.

"And so you will," he replied. "Very soon, I can assure you of that."

Fayina already knew she would do whatever he told her to, if only for the smallest chance that his mad claims might be true, but something inside her didn't want to give in so easily. She gritted her teeth, trying to think of some other way she could ensure she wasn't walking into a trap, but nothing presented itself.

"Where do I go?" she asked eventually.

The man grimaced, as if he'd been hoping she would disagree.

"Not far," he said, shaking his head and still not looking at her. "The glasses will light the way and provide all the security access you'll need. There are clothes hung next to the door. Put them on and you'll blend in."

Fayina got up from the bed, conscious of a dull ache in her limbs, and touched the clothes he mentioned – white pants and a knee length lab coast. She would never choose to wear something like this on her own, but they looked official enough to blend in with whoever else might be working on the station.

Beside the clothes was a small pistol in a torso harness and Fayina took it out and turned it over in her hands. She'd never killed anyone, despite wishing death on many, but this would certainly make the job easier.

"Now, I must leave you," the crumpled man said with a spiteful edge. "Everything you need to complete your task will be provided via the glasses. If you're caught or killed our agreement is nullified. As soon as you complete your task, the glasses will show you a route to safety. There you will find several staff making preparations for your journey back to your sister. You will only hear from me again when it is time to act."

Fayina glared at him.

"You'd better not be lying," she growled. "Or I'll find you, whoever you are."

At this, the old man finally looked at her and Fayina found his haunted gaze hard to meet.

"Truth is both the key and the cage," he said in a hollow tone.

Fayina frowned at the cryptic remark, but before she could say anything else, the old man disappeared and a map of the space station appeared in the upper right corner of her vision. The route she was meant to follow was marked as a green line and a small counter advised her it wouldn't take long to reach the targeted location.

The information should have sparked a comment from Dr. Haig, or Ianka even, and for the first time Fayina realised how quiet they'd been.

"This will be easier without them," she growled dismissively as she began to undress.

But something inside her knew it was a lie. It was a frustrating irony. She hated them all so much and knew what she planned to do would go easier without them whining for her to stop.

And yet... she wanted to hear their voices anyway. She wanted to shout them down and force her decisions on them just like Anya had done to her so many times in the past. But most of all, she didn't want to do this alone.

"Screw them all," she said forcefully.

The words echoed through her mind with the satisfying heat of anger and Fayina's resolve solidified. No matter the cost, she was going to save the innocent twin she'd betrayed so many years ago.

"No matter what," she promised herself quietly.

MARS ORBIT - June 8, 2147 - 4.12pm

KURT STARED UP AT THE GLOWING RED STREAK THAT dominated the star-filled expanse above them. The Jupiter flare was still a long way off, but it held the malicious promise of cosmic, inter-stellar violence and Kurt was embarrassed to find that he was actually excited.

He'd seen the impending disaster first hand and so he knew how destructive the Jupiter flare could be, but the thrill-seeker inside him was enjoying the immensity of it all. And he still had hope. He didn't know how they were going to stop it, but they'd managed to get this far, hadn't they? Surely it couldn't end badly when they had an alien from the distant past on their side… could it?

And who could forget the whole nation of people who believed they would succeed. That had to count for something, right? Their belief might be reserved for Miana, but that was fine by Kurt. He didn't fancy himself anyone's Messiah and, to be honest, he had faith in her too. Maybe not the same kind as the Quirations, but if he could choose anyone to face the end of the world with, it would be the woman sitting behind him.

"Have you worked it out yet?" she asked through the helmet intercom.

Kurt guiltily returned his attention to the map in front of him.
"I... think so," he replied after a moment. "The Quirations use a different co-ordinate system, but I'm pretty sure I can take us to the station Saadi was talking about."

Miana didn't reply to this and Kurt silently admonished himself for bringing up Saadi.

"So... what are we going to do when we get there?" he asked.

"I don't know," Miana replied quietly.

"They're not just going to let us come aboard," he added.

"You're probably right," Miana agreed.

Kurt waited for her to say more, to validate his faith in her, but she stayed silent.

"*It's times like this I wish I did believe in God,*" he thought glumly.

They flew on in silence for a few minutes until a glimmer of light caught Kurt's attention.

"I think I see it," he said, before making his viewing screen zoom in on the sparkle.

The station was still a long way off, but with magnification it was possible to make out a series of rings arrayed in a cone formation that pointed down toward Mars.

"It's a big installation," he said, studying the image. "I'm not even sure where we should try and dock with the thing."

"The largest ring," Miana said.

"As good a place as any," he conceded. "It looks like there's already another–"

But before he could finish, an alarm began blaring and his console lit up with warning beacons.

"What's that?" Miana asked.

"Oh shit," Kurt swore, realising what the console was displaying. "Shit, shit, shit!"

"Kurt, what–" Miana began.

But there was no time to explain. With a hard yank on the joystick, Kurt pulled them into a violent turn that blurred the stars around them. Then he activated the jet's nitro thrusters.

As they shot away from the distant space station, the g-forces they experienced were incredible, but they felt nothing inside their liquid-filled cockpits. The sensation of going nowhere made Kurt panic for a moment and he tried to find out how to display which direction their imminent destruction was approaching from.

"What's going on?" Miana said sharply.

"Someone fired on us," Kurt replied, studying the missile trajectory that blinked onto his screen.

"Fired on us?" Miana said, her voice tense. "Who?"

"I don't know," Kurt snapped as he turned them again so they were angled directly away from the missile.

Miana didn't say anything more and Kurt was glad. He was fluent when it came to speaking Arabic, but reading it was another matter entirely and he didn't need the distraction.

After a few false starts, he managed to make the viewing screen project where the missile would intercept with them and felt a chill when he saw it was seconds from blowing them to pieces.

"Fuck!" he swore, before pulling them into another hard turn.

The stars blurred around them again and Kurt saw a flash from the corner of his eye as the missile scoured within inches of their right wing. He quickly pulled them out of the turn, certain the missile wouldn't take long to recover, and searched his console for some way to stop it.

"*Come on, come on,*" he thought desperately. "*This is a military jet. There has to be something that can take the missile out.*"

Not surprisingly, there were already several glowing icons that offered a response, but in his excited state, Kurt was finding it hard to work out what they meant.

He eventually decided to activate an icon that looked like a missile itself and saw several new missile trackers appear on his viewing screen. They were shaped like small rockets and as they approached the missile accelerating toward them, each one turned from green to red.

"*They're arming,*" Kurt thought with wide eyes.

He held his breath as they closed on the missile and was surprised when the icons split into a cloud of tiny pixels at the last moment. He twisted in his harness to see what was happening and was just in time to see a small fireball light up the darkness of space. Then there was nothing.

Turning back around, Kurt saw a small Arabic symbol flashing on the console and realised it was letting him know that the missile had been destroyed.

"Holy... shit..." he gasped, taking a much needed breath.

"Is it over?" Miana asked, her voice tense.

"I hope so," Kurt replied with feeling. "I don't know how many more of those we can handle."

"Where did it come from?" Miana asked. "We were still so far away."

"I'm not sure," Kurt said, his mind racing with possibilities, "but I have a hunch. Hang on a moment."

Cutting the engines, Kurt allowed them to drift as he accessed the computer in his flight suit. He still had a copy of the Cosmotech database they'd stolen back in Lynt City and so it only took a moment to find information relating to the space station they were trying to get to.

As he suspected, there were security files that outlined a spherical grid of armed satellites.

"I knew it," he said, shaking his head.

"Tell me," Miana said grimly.

"They've got a grid of armed satellites surrounding the station. Each one has lasers, missiles, Gatling guns, and the best tracking systems money can buy. We can't get within five hundred kilometres of the station without setting one of them off. We'd already be space dust if it weren't for the advanced defence systems in this jet."

Miana remained silent and Kurt didn't blame her. He'd thought their new psychic powers would allow them to easily fight back against Loc and his Cosmotech cronies, but they were useless against this kind of deadly machinery.

"We'll think of something," she said eventually. "We have to."

Kurt turned to look at the distant gleam of the space station.

"I hope you're right," he said, "because something tells me we just lost our element of surprise."

COSMOTECH ORBITAL PLATFORM - June 8, 2147 - 4.25pm

LOC STORMED THROUGH THE SPACE STATION WITH Captain West and his security team trailing close behind him.

He hated this place. Not only was it full of the kind of scientific eggheads that he actively avoided, but he also held no real authority here. Dr. Grayson ruled his trillion dollar orbital platform with an iron fist and Loc didn't have to read anyone's mind to know the Cosmotech employees stationed here didn't hold any fear in reserve for the likes of him.

Striding to a halt at the station's main security centre, Loc waited a moment as he was identified and then strode through the enormous vault-like hatch that opened before him. It was time to put aside his irritations and focus on what the Triumvirate had tasked him with.

"*Miana isn't getting anywhere near this station,*" he thought determinedly.

Despite the obvious attention being diverted to Isaac Taylor and the approaching Jupiter flare, there was still a considerable number of security staff on duty. The centre of the room was dominated by a partially exploded scale hologram of the station, upon which several staff seemed to be running diagnostic checks.

317

Around them, the walls were covered with video feeds and more holographic displays. Whatever he might be, Grayson wasn't sloppy when it came to security.

"Good evening, Mr. Breeden," the security centre's manager said briskly. "My name is Eléna Montoya. Doctor Grayson has informed us of your intentions and I've upgraded your security status accordingly. Your teams' as well."

Loc didn't bother with a reply, he simply turned and nodded to Captain West.

At his gesture, the Captain and his team quickly dispersed amongst the local Cosmotech staff and held quick, whispered conversations before taking over at several computer stations.

Eléna didn't seem at all phased by his team's actions and, rather than protest, she offered Loc her own seat.

"You'll be able to monitor your team and all security systems from here, Mr. Breeden," she said politely. "If you require any assistance or refreshments of any kind, please ask."

Loc offered her a slightly longer glance this time and felt a grudging respect. This woman clearly understood the chain of command and might even prove useful once this was over and he'd joined the Triumvirate.

"*Soon*," he thought as he sat in her chair.

He began by running through the systems that were currently monitoring the station and was honestly impressed. He'd seen many during his career with Cosmotech Defence, but this was by far the most elaborate. No doubt due to Grayson's obsessive compulsive personality.

"Sir," Captain West said, his tone grabbing Loc's attention.

"Speak," he commanded quickly.

"One of the defence satellites was activated less than ten minutes ago."

"Is it Miana?" he said, his hope rising.

"The vehicle signature matches the craft they stole from the Bas Quirat."

Loc frowned. He wanted to be pleased, he wanted to accept the confidence that assured him Miana would never make it through the station's formidable defence grid, but the bitter taste of experience wouldn't let him.

"What happened?" he asked calmly.

"The grid launched an EVO tactical missile, sir, but the craft deployed counter measures and escaped without damage."

Loc clenched his fist in frustration. If he weren't so anti-religious, he might be willing to believe there was some supernatural being protecting Miana and Kurt.

"I don't want to wait for them to make another attempt," he said firmly. "Can we target them from here?"

"No, sir. Their craft is equipped with stealth technology that the station can't penetrate. But I can take a team of jet fighters out to the grid perimeter. We have scanners capable of triangulating their position."

Loc smiled.

"Do it," he said, wishing he could be there when Miana finally succumbed. "I want them blown from orbit, Captain. No excuses this time. Don't come back unless Miana Raiken is dead, or you are."

"Yes, sir," West replied quickly.

Loc watched him go and wondered what he would do with Captain West when this was over. Although he'd shown no hesitation, he'd witnessed Loc's psychic power in the Bas Quirat and was therefore a liability. The Captain wouldn't dare jeopardize himself before Miana was dealt with, of course, but his loyalty could no longer be guaranteed.

It was a shame. Despite West's abject failure at stopping Miana up until this point, he was still one of the most useful assets Loc had ever commanded.

"*We'll see,*" he thought, turning back to his console. "*For now, it is enough that he kill Miana and assure my ascension.*"

STAGE 7: JUPITER FLARE APPROACHES MARS

June 8, 2147 - 4.28 pm

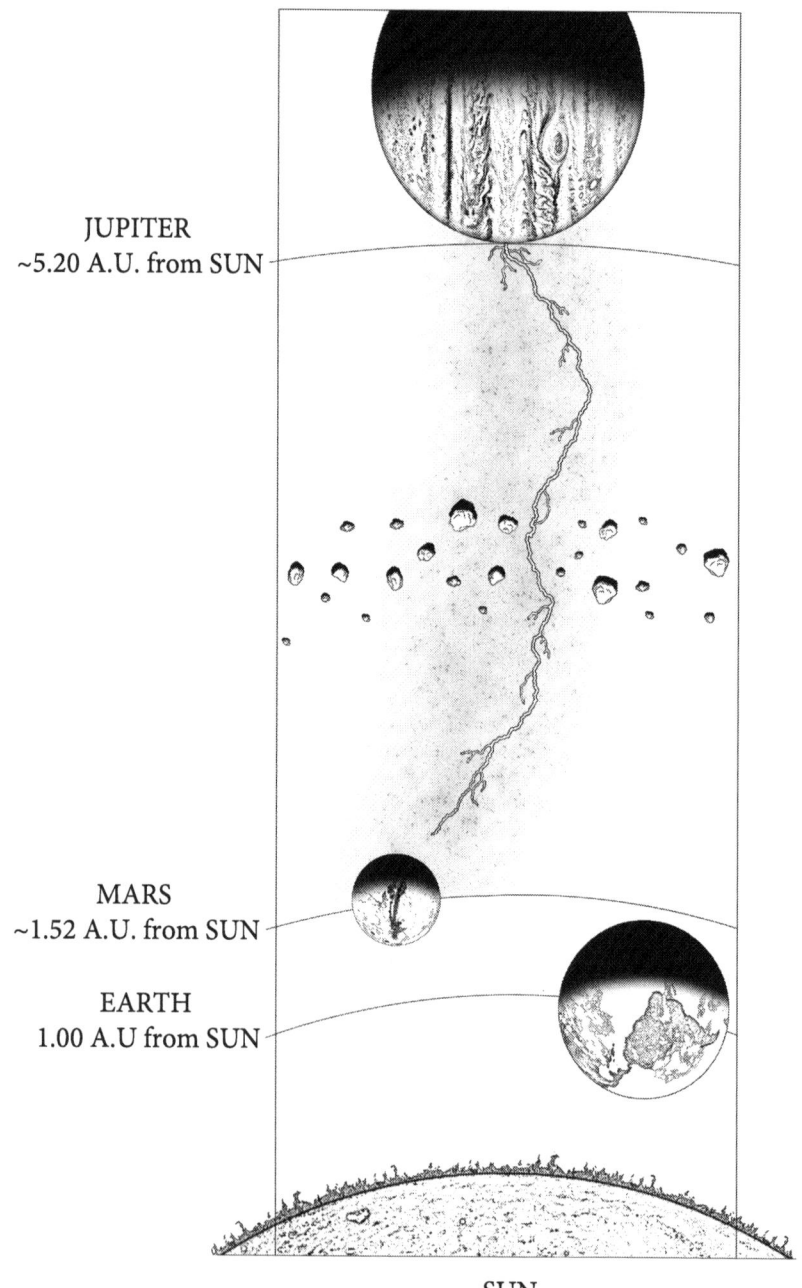

JUPITER
~5.20 A.U. from SUN

MARS
~1.52 A.U. from SUN

EARTH
1.00 A.U from SUN

SUN

1 Astronomical Unit (A.U.) = ~149.6 x 10^6 km

COSMOTECH ORBITAL PLATFORM - June 8, 2147 - 4.28pm

ISAAC STOOD ON THE SMALL, CIRCULAR DAIS AT THE centre of the primary research platform. He wore his trusty skull cap and when he turned, he could see the wires that trailed out behind it curving up toward a concave collector that towered over him like a giant hairdryer.

Through the vast, transparent ceiling above, the Jupiter flare glowed angrily in one direction while Mars loomed large below the space station in the other. He didn't want to think about what would happen if one reached the other, but couldn't help imagining the planet as a giant, rust-coloured infant, cowering behind its mother in fear.

With his heart beating a frantic rhythm, Isaac held the rail surrounding his platform in a vice-like grip. He didn't like Dr. Grayson's plan to detonate an E.M.P. device at the centre of the space station. He was confident P.A.T.R.I.C. could absorb that much electromagnetic energy – they'd virtually verified it twice already – but if they were wrong...

"This entire station, including all the systems keeping us alive, will be fried," he thought with a shiver. *"And I won't be saving anyone if I'm dead."*

"You will not die today, Isaac Taylor," Hani'ah's translated voice spoke confidently in his ear.

Isaac craned his neck to look straight up through the ceiling and then focussed on the secondary research platform on the far side of the space station. He could barely see Hani'ah across the large gap, but her white-clad form was easier to spot when he found the two dependable shadows waiting either side of her.

"I hope you're right," he replied, out loud this time.

"I am," Hani'ah said firmly. "Your destiny is close to being fulfilled, Isaac. You should be rejoicing."

"I think I'll wait until it's done before celebrating," Isaac added sourly.

He still wasn't used to Hani'ah reading his thoughts. In a way, it was similar to what he already did with Jason, or used to at least, but there was a big difference between sharing every thought with your twin brother and sharing them with the spiritual leader of a nation of Islamic Quirations, let alone a female.

The fact their telepathy worked over such a distance was a good sign. They needed a clear psychic connection if they wanted Dr. Grayson's plan to go off without a hitch.

"I have a suggestion," Hani'ah added after a moment.

"Go ahead," Isaac said.

"The Game," Hani'ah continued, "let me start the process this time. Rather than beginning with a simple image, I will create one as complex as I can handle. Then, when you take it from me, our psychic connection should be boosted to the appropriate levels almost instantly."

Isaac nodded as he thought it through. It was a good idea and one he would have thought of himself if he weren't so used to taking baby steps with Jason.

"Definitely worth a try," he replied.

"We're ready," Dr. Grayson said, appearing unexpectedly at Isaac's side.

"Oh, right," Isaac said with a nervous smile. "Time to get this show on the road, huh?"

"Indeed," Dr. Grayson said, his eyes studying the device that towered behind Isaac. "Are you ready, Ms. Naziri?"

"I am," Hani'ah replied simply.

"Then we will begin phase one."

With his heart beating faster again, Isaac waited as P.A.T.R.I.C. was brought online. He could see some of the graphs coming to life on the screens arrayed around the platform, but didn't bother to read them. There were more than enough people monitoring them already.

"Phase two," Dr. Grayson said after a moment.

As soon as the station's formidable power grid was connected to P.A.T.R.I.C., Isaac's psychic connection with Hani'ah solidified into a clear presence in his mind. They were now being fed enough electricity to run a small city.

Isaac waited for Dr. Grayson to speak again, but when he looked over, the scientist was slumped and quiet. He also trembled slightly, as if he were reluctant to continue.

"Doc?" Isaac said hesitantly.

"Of course," Dr. Grayson said abruptly, flinching upright. "Let... let The Game begin."

Isaac frowned, but Hani'ah was already crafting her psychic image and so he turned his attention to the world being created in his mind's eye.

It began with Hani'ah herself, standing tall in her usual white robes, with her arms spread wide and her head tilted upward. Then beneath her feet, marble tiles appeared and began to spread outward before cascading down a set of intricate marble steps that looked just like the throne room where Isaac had first met her.

As soon as the marble steps were finished, Hani'ah's twin ladies in black appeared at her side, kneeling demurely with their eyes downcast. Then the floor swept further outward in a rush, creating the enormous throne room in a splash of imagination that leapt up marble pillars and archways like self-aware paint.

In seconds, the entire throne room was rendered in spectacular detail and Isaac found himself wondering once again if he'd underestimated Hani'ah's ability.

"Are you ready?" she asked with just a hint of pride in her voice.

"I'm ready," Isaac replied, his nerves giving way to a competitive tension. "How about you, Doc?"

"In your own time, Isaac," Dr. Grayson replied from somewhere behind him.

"Right," Isaac said, taking a deep breath.

As he let the breath out, he took Hani'ah's image into his mind and allowed the Quiration architecture to settle into place. Hani'ah was clearly more familiar with the throne room than he would ever be, but he refused to omit any detail, unwilling to lose The Game before they even had a chance to begin.

"You're doing well," Hani'ah coaxed him. "Keep going, Isaac."

With a frown of determination, Isaac focussed on recreating her image in perfect detail and eventually felt the mental load fall away.

"*I did it*," he thought happily.

Now that he had a moment to study what he'd seen, Isaac realised just how beautiful the throne room was. Hani'ah's imagination had included more detail than Jason had ever been able to create and, for a moment, Isaac wondered who designed it.

"The design is my own," Hani'ah said in response to his unspoken question. "It was gifted to me in a vision."

"It's amazing," Isaac said, feeling a little awkward acknowledging Hani'ah's visions when he still found them so hard to believe himself.

"It is your turn, Isaac," she reminded him.

"So it is," he replied with a smile.

Now that he was in his element, Isaac's heart was finally beginning to slow down and, as he began to flex his own imagination, he felt much calmer.

First, he surrounded the throne room steps with Quiration soldiers. He knew their uniforms weren't quite right, but after adding some weapons and plenty of beards, they looked fearsome enough. He then added two lines of Quiration women, like the ones who'd greeted him on his arrival to the Bas Quirat. They all wore colourful, silken garments that flowed around their feminine bodies with the same allure Isaac remembered, but he made sure there was no skin showing. The last thing he wanted to do was offend Hani'ah.

As an afterthought, he added Loc and his team of Cosmotech security on one side of the throne room and placed Dr. Grayson with his own serious black-suited bodyguards on the other. He then made the two groups face each other with the animosity he imagined they would show if they weren't consummate professionals.

When he was finally done, he glanced at one of the graphs measuring the amount of electricity their psychic connection was drawing from the station.

"Woah," he said beneath his breath.

Hani'ah had been right. With a single psychic exchange they were already drawing close to the station's maximum energy output.

"Detonation in three…" Dr. Grayson said.

"Wha-?" Isaac spluttered, panicking when he realised what was about to happen.

"I'm ready," Hani'ah said firmly.

"Two…" Dr. Grayson added.

Isaac held his breath as Hani'ah began the difficult task of taking the new image he'd created. It wavered for a moment as she tried to include Loc, Dr. Grayson, and their small armies, but they soon stabilised and Isaac couldn't help noticing the Quiration uniforms flickered into much finer, more correct, detail.

"One…"

Isaac looked up at the EMP device floating at the centre of the station.

"Detonate," Dr. Grayson finished simply.

With a much dimmer flash than Isaac expected, the EMP went off and a shockwave of optical distortion exploded outward. As it rippled through the station itself, Isaac closed his eyes and focussed on the image Hani'ah was still attempting to take from him.

He waited for a sign it had all gone horribly wrong – a scream, a crackling spark, maybe a sudden drop in background noise as the station's life support systems failed – but there was nothing.

After a few seconds, he gingerly opened his eyes, hoping his other senses weren't lying to him.

"Huh?" he grunted in amazement.

The research platform was thankfully intact and all the electronics seemed to be working fine, but outside the station was another matter entirely.

Between himself and Hani'ah, at the very centre of the space station's largest ring, there was a shimmering hole in space. Its edges were traced in a shifting silver light that seemed to pulse in a strange rhythm. Through it, the other side of the space station had been replaced by stars that looked familiar but somehow... different.

It was just like the experiment back in the Bas Quirat. The psychic connection they were sharing through P.A.T.R.I.C. had created some kind of hole in space and it was changing the view of anything behind it.

Looking around the research platform, Isaac quickly confirmed that the people around him weren't frozen in time like before, then he turned to look down the inside of the station's rings.

"*What on Mars...?*" he thought with a gasp.

There were more of the strange holes forming below them and, through these, sections of Mars were now coloured a brilliant green instead of the dusty brown he was familiar with. The holes themselves didn't seem stable and they disappeared almost as rapidly as they appeared, so the glimpses were only momentary, but there were a lot of them. Isaac didn't know how far out from the space station they were appearing, but some looked like they were a long way away.

With an excited chill, he turned toward the approaching Jupiter flare and wasn't surprised to find that it too was being partially obscured by the strange holes in space.

"*That's strange,*" he thought with a frown.

Through the holes that obscured it, he expected to see more unfamiliar star formations, but instead he saw glimpses of another glowing red light, as if there were two Jupiter flares following slightly different paths through space.

"It's working," he heard Dr. Grayson say in a hollow, almost frightened, tone.

Not sure what that actually meant, Isaac returned to his psychic link with Hani'ah and saw that she'd managed to take the rest of the image from him.

"The prophecy will be fulfilled," she said in a calm voice.

Isaac had heard the words before, but this time he was surprised to find that he actually believed them. If they could absorb the power of such a large E.M.P. without even the slightest damage to the station, then surely the destructive energy from the Jupiter flare could also be stopped.

"Are you ready, Isaac?" Hani'ah asked, interrupting his thoughts.

"I'm ready," he said, with feeling.

"Then let us meet our destiny together."

FAYINA STRODE THROUGH THE UPWARD-SLOPING corridors with a scowl she didn't try to hide. It appeared she was, in fact, on an orbital space station somewhere above Mars. She could see the rusty glow of her home planet through the occasional viewing panel and it provided a stark contrast to the gleaming crimson of the Jupiter flare that sparkled in the other direction.

"*Not my problem,*" she thought, ignoring its fiery glow.

The strange man she'd seen upon waking had also been right about her uniform and security clearance. There were people everywhere, rushing around the station on mysterious errands, but none of them paid her any attention. Which was good, because she was not in the mood to talk.

She followed the steady, green navigation line being created by her glasses around another corner and was confronted with an airlock that led onto a connecting walkway. These short, mostly transparent tunnels seemed to link the main sections of the space station's largest ring.

The first set of doors slid open soundlessly ahead of her and locked into place behind her just as quietly. When the second set allowed her out onto the walkway, she saw a few white-clad employees halfway along staring expectantly upward.

Frowning in suspicion, Fayina looked up through the thick tube of reinforced resin that surrounded the walkway and was just in time to see something flash at the centre of the station. A second later she felt a pulse of energy wash through her and something silver appeared where the detonation had occurred.

It was vaguely circular, but the edges constantly rippled and changed as if the whole thing was made of fluid.

"Strange," she said in confusion.

And something else wasn't right. Like a bizarre optical illusion, the silver-edged hole seemed to act like a window that allowed her to see through other side of the space station.

Another unexpected flash of colour caught her attention and Fayina turned to look down the space station's rings. I seemed there were more of the silver-edged holes appearing between the space station and Mars, but it wasn't the anomalies that had drawn her eye, it was green forests, blue oceans, and white streaks of cloud that she could see through them.

"*What the fuck is going on?*" she thought with a frown.

"*We're seeing through time,*" Dr. Haig answered.

The voice took Fayina by surprise and she felt a strange mix of relief and irritation. The last thing she wanted to do was deal with her other personalities, but if Dr. Haig was right then at least it meant she was doing the right thing.

"Proof," she said quietly.

"*What's going on?*" Ianka's voice asked sharply.

Fayina scowled, her relief swamped by anger.

"I should have known your silence was too good to be true," she growled.

"*Where are we?*" Celia whined.

"You wouldn't believe me," Fayina replied.

"*Please,*" Dr. Haig added in his frustratingly calm tone. "*Tell us what you're doing, Fayina.*"

"What you never could," she growled, turning back to the floating green line that led across the walkway.

"*Or never* would, *more likely,*" Ianka growled back.

"Shut up, all of you!" Fayina snarled beneath her breath.

The outburst made the gawking employees turn to look at her, but Fayina acted like they weren't even there and entered the far airlock before they could say anything.

"*Don't ignore us,*" Ianka snapped in her most irritating tone.

"*Where's Isaac?*" Celia asked reproachfully.

"He's here," Fayina replied, hoping it would at least shut Celia up. "He's safe and working on a way to get back to where he came from, okay? So forget him. He doesn't need our help."

"*He still owes us a considerable sum of money,*" Ianka reminded her firmly.

"*Are you wearing glasses?*" Celia added. "*Where did you get them?*"

"Shut up," Fayina hissed as she exited the other side of the airlock.

"*You know more about Isaac, don't you?*" Dr. Haig said slowly.

"What do you care?" Fayina snarled beneath her breath.

"*Please,*" Dr. Haig replied. "*This is important.*"

The others remained silent this time, as if urging Fayina to answer. She didn't feel like sharing, not with so much at stake, but if she didn't give them something, she was certain their incessant whining would only get worse.

"I don't know much," she said reluctantly. "He's from another reality, or something. I think he's working with Cosmotech on a way to get back to wherever he came from."

"*How?*" Dr. Haig asked.

"Who cares? They're using the Jupiter flare somehow."

"*Is he working with the man we saw at the Lynt City precinct?*" Dr. Haig pressed.

"How should I know?" Fayina replied.

"*You've been awake longer than us,*" Ianka accused her. "*What happened while we weren't here?*"

"Nothing," she snarled.

"*That man didn't have Isaac's best interest in mind,*" Dr. Haig added.

"He'll be fine," Fayina replied. "This is about me, not him."

"*What is?*" Celia asked.

Fayina ground her teeth, but stayed resolutely silent this time. She'd tried to do the right thing, but it was clear that no explanation was going to shut them up.

Returning her attention to the green navigation line, Fayina rounded another corner and stopped when she saw that it led to a dead end. For a moment, she thought she'd been betrayed and rage rose within her, then she noticed the navigation line was outlining an open vent.

"You're kidding me," she said quietly.

"*Are we going in there?*" Celia asked, sounding scared.

"*Tell us what you're doing!*" Ianka demanded.

Keeping her mouth firmly shut this time, Fayina crouched down and quickly crawled into the vent. She expected to make a lot more noise as she made her way through it, but the vent was well built and barely made a sound.

The others continued chattering as she followed the navigation line around two corners before stopping in front of another vent, this one firmly closed.

Looking through it, Fayina saw a large open platform with a high, transparent ceiling. There were more Cosmotech employees here, all concentrating on complicated work stations, but what immediately drew her attention was a woman surrounded by a soft red glow – the one she was here to kill.

Her target was seated near the centre of the platform in a large, slightly reclined chair with some kind of device strapped to her head. There were two other women standing either side of her dressed in black from head to toe. Only their eyes were visible through narrows slits in the fabric, but Fayina knew right away that they held a special relationship with the woman she was here to kill.

"*What are you going to do?*" Ianka asked in her most commanding tone yet.

"*Who is she?*" Celia added. "*She's gorgeous.*"

"*She's psychically connected to someone,*" Dr. Haig said, sounding fascinated. "*Her aura is brilliant.*"

Fayina wasn't interested in reading the aura of a woman she was about to kill and so she focussed instead on a commotion coming from one of the many work stations.

A white-clad employee was pointing up at the transparent ceiling and Fayina ducked her head so she could see what he was pointing at. She expected it to have something to do with the 'other' Mars that was appearing through the strange anomalies, but instead she saw twin Jupiter flares getting brighter by the second.

"There's two of them," she said, feeling breathless. "And they're headed straight for station."

"*Time is running out,*" she heard Dr. Haig say.

And Fayina knew he was right. If she wanted to see her sister again it was now or never... but she'd been told to wait for a signal.

"Fuck," she swore beneath her breath.

Patience was another skill Fayina had never learned and the knowledge she would have to listen to the others throwing questions at her, even for another minute, made her fists itch. They wouldn't understand what was going to happen until it was over. Only when their sister had been saved would they accept what she had to do.

"It just better happen soon," she mumbled, watching the approaching flares anxiously. "I want this shit over and done with."

MARS ORBIT - June 8, 2147 - 5.31pm

KURT WAS STARTING TO LOSE HOPE. HE KNEW THEY couldn't come this far and just give up, but there was no way they were getting to that space station in one piece. They could always make a suicide run and fly straight through the space station's defence grid, but Kurt didn't want to mention it in case Miana decided it was their only option.

The thought triggered another wave of depression and Kurt focussed on a blip that had appeared on his radar.

"Oh great," he said, his stomach sinking even further.

"What is it?" Miana asked.

"They've sent someone after us," he replied, running his eyes over the information his scanners were feeding him. "They're jets. Armed. At least as good as ours, but probably better. There's no way we're getting past them, Miana. We might not even get away."

"Damn it, it can't end like this," Miana snapped, her frustration clear.

"I was just thinking the same thing," Kurt replied, "but what the hell can we do? That station is probably the most well-protected installation in the solar system. We're not going to get inside it Miana. No way in Hell."

"Hell doesn't exist," Miana said coldly.

"Neither does the Apocalypse, remember?"

Miana remained silent at this and Kurt mentally kicked himself. However bad things were, his negative attitude wasn't going to help.

"Look, our only option here is to retreat and hope they don't follow us," he said. "We won't last more than a few minutes against them. I'm no fighter pilot."

Again, Miana didn't say anything and Kurt could feel the tension building.

"The Jupiter flare is almost here," he added grimly. "We might already be out of time."

"Then our only option is to engage them," Miana replied firmly.

Kurt blinked in surprise and suddenly felt dizzy. Somehow he knew this was always going to end in a suicide run, but hearing Miana say it was more frightening than he expected.

"Look," he said, feeling a little desperate. "I *really* don't think that's a good idea, Miana."

"Do you have any others?" she asked calmly.

Kurt gritted his teeth in frustration.

"No."

"Then it's our last and only chance."

Kurt shook his head.

"You know, for someone who didn't like Saadi charging to his death, you're showing a serious lack of concern for what is essentially an identical course of action."

"Fly straight at them," Miana said, ignoring his comment. "Straight back toward the defence grid and straight through it."

Kurt stared up at the space station glistening in the distance and felt an unfamiliar fear clutch at this stomach. He usually enjoyed the rush that came with imminent danger, but this was nothing like what he was used to. There was no calculated risk here and the inner voice he relied on to avoid serious injury and death was screaming at him to turn around and get out of there.

"I know I'm asking a lot, Kurt," Miana added quietly, "but time *is* running out and we can't just leave. We both knew our lives would be put on the line at some point and if this is the only path available to us, then it's the one we have to take. Don't you agree?"

Kurt remained silent himself this time. He'd always wondered how he was going to die. Would it be a spectacular fall in an underground chasm? A heart attack while leaping out of a stratospheric balloon? Sitting alone in a retirement community, reminiscing about his crazy adventurist life over hot chocolate?

All three options sounded desirable in their own way, but could they really compare to a beautiful woman – who he suspected he'd fallen deeply in love with – asking him to rush headlong into overwhelming odds for the hope they might save the entire planet?

"Alright," he said with a smile. "I'll take this one, last, stupid risk with you, Miana. But you've got to promise me something."

"What?"

"If by some miracle, or prophecy, we actually survive what's coming, you owe me an expensive dinner," he said.

"What?" Miana repeated, her tone more incredulous this time.

"And a kiss," Kurt said, the fear making him reckless. "I've been wanting to kiss you ever since we crashed into that cave back on the planet. And besides, I think you owe me one."

Miana went quiet for a moment and Kurt wondered if he'd pushed it too far.

"I promise," she said eventually. "An expensive dinner and a kiss."

Kurt could hear the warmth in her voice and knew he'd been right to ask. Miana felt something for him too. It was exactly what he needed and the knowledge sent a rush of energy through him.

"Right," he said with a grin. "That's settled then. Let's give these bastards one last run, hey?"

Turning them toward the oncoming jets, Kurt slowly opened the throttle and focussed on the blips lighting up his radar.

"*Now I just have to work out what to do when we reach them,*" he thought with a frown.

He'd got the hang of the jet's defence systems at least, but now he needed something to attack with. After a quick search, he found the right Arabic symbols and took a moment to assess the jet's hardware. "We've got our own missiles," he said as the incoming radar blips began to blink red – the jets were nearly in range. "Okay then. Let's see how they like being on the receiving end for once."

Pushing the throttle all the way forward, Kurt waited until the targets stopped flashing, signifying they were now in range, and then pressed the trigger. A puff of gas appeared at their wing and Kurt watched as three missiles shot away from them, one for each of the jets rushing toward them.

An alarm sounded as the enemy launched their own missiles and, at the last moment, Kurt pulled them into a sharp turn and activated the defence mechanism he'd used earlier. The cockpit lit up briefly as each of the incoming missiles detonated in space then three streaks of light flashed past them as the enemy jets screamed by.

"Yes!" Kurt shouted when he realised they were still in one piece. "That's the first obstacle down."

He turned back to the space station, trying not to think about its formidable defence grid, and paused when a bright flash obscured it for a moment.

"What was that?" Miana asked in his helmet.

"I don't know," Kurt replied, "but it definitely came from the space station."

He used the ship's cameras to zoom in and the image shimmered as if seen through an atmospheric heat haze.

"*That's shouldn't happen in space,*" he thought.

Blinking in confusion, Kurt almost missed something silver that appeared ahead of them and barely had time to make another sharp turn before it whipped by them.

"What... did you see that?" he asked Miana.

"Not really," she replied. "It was moving so–"

But before she could finish, another flash of silver appeared in their path and Kurt pulled them in the other direction to avoid it.

This time, he was able to make out a large ring of rippling silver.

"What is that?" he wondered aloud.

"Oh my God," Miana gasped. "Look down."

Kurt assumed she meant he should look at the planet and so he spun the jet until it came into view above them.

"Oh shit," he swore.

There were more of the strange silver rings appearing in space between them and the planet. But that wasn't all. When seen through the silver rings, the planet was no longer the barren, reddish-brown they were used to. Instead it was green. Even blue and white in places.

"Is that what I think it is?" he asked.

"The same planet from our vision," Miana replied, confirming his fears.

But before he could say anything else, another alarm sounded and Kurt glanced at his display to find the jet's they'd just passed had fired on him again. He quickly activated the missile defence system, but a flashing Arabic symbol informed him that something was wrong.

"Oh crap," he said quietly.

"What is it?"

"I thought we were okay, but they must have damaged us on our last pass," he replied. "We can't stop those missiles. Hang on!"

Realising it was a useless suggestion in the safety of their liquid-filled cockpits, Kurt pulled them into another sharp turn and fought back an urge to swear again. There was no way they could outrun the missiles now and they were coming in fast. He began to flip and turn, trying every tricky manoeuvre he could think of, but the missiles easily followed him through each one.

More of the silver rings began to appear ahead of them and Kurt was forced to fly around them, ruining several of his manoeuvres and allowing the missiles to get closer.

"I think this is it!" he shouted desperately. "I'm sorry, Miana. I was really looking forward to that kiss!"

He wanted to say more, to tell her exactly what he felt, but it was too late. The missiles had caught up with them. He pulled them into a final, desperate spin, expecting to be blasted into a million pieces any second, and flinched when one of the missiles exploded behind them.

For a moment, he thought they'd been hit and simply didn't feel it inside their liquid-filled cockpits, but no alarms appeared to suggest death was imminent. He craned his neck to see the damage for himself and saw a large silver ring rapidly disappearing behind them.

"The missile hit it," he said breathlessly.

"What?" Miana asked.

"I think… the missiles hit one of those holes in space," he explained breathlessly.

With a renewed spark of hope, Kurt quickly turned them toward another of the strange silver rings. The second missile was still hot on their tail, but this time, he was able to use his flips and spins to angle their jet in behind the silver ring just in time.

He waited for the flash that would signify the missile had exploded in space, but this time there was nothing. He glanced at his radar, but the missile had disappeared from view.

Frowning hard, Kurt craned his neck to search for any sign they were about to be blown apart and jumped when another alarm sounded.

"*They've fired another missile,*" he thought instinctively.

But when he looked at the radar, the missile was actually ahead of them and moving in the same direction.

"What the hell?" he said in confusion.

But before he could say anything else, the missile locked onto them again and tried to turn in a tight circle, which only made it slam into the edge of another silver hole in space. The detonation was brief and violent, and as it momentarily lit up the darkness of space, something clicked into place in Kurt's mind.

"It went through," he gasped.

"What?" Miana asked.

"The missile," he replied, louder this time. "Miana, I think I finally have a plan."

"Tell me," she said in her usual blunt manner.

Kurt thought about it for a moment – he could be wrong, after all – but it wasn't like they had any other choice. It was either this, or a suicide run straight into more missiles.

"I'm… not sure I want to say it out loud," he said after a moment. "Do you trust me, Miana?"

"Of course," she said, with a speed that made Kurt wish he could kiss her right now.

"Then since we're about to gamble with our lives, I'd like to do it my way if that's alright with you."

"Will it work?" was all she asked.

"I have no idea," Kurt replied honestly, "but it's better than flying straight through a defence grid. And if it does work, we might actually get to the station before the Jupiter flare does."

"Then do it," Miana replied firmly.

Kurt smiled. Something about her trust gave him more energy than any of the thrill-seeking stunts he'd tried in his professional career.

"Once we're inside the station," he told her, "and we *will* get inside, we'll see what Saadi meant about us splitting up. But until then, you're with me and I'm not going to let anything hurt us, okay?"

"Okay," Miana replied.

"And don't forget that kiss," he said finally.

"I won't," Miana replied with a laugh. "Let's just get this done so it makes a difference."

"You got it," Kurt said with another rush of energy. "Let's go save the world."

CAPTAIN WEST FOCUSSED ON THE SHIP FLITTING AWAY ahead of him. Miana Raiken should have been dead several times over, but despite the fact Kurt Jones was clearly untrained in zero-G combat, there was no denying he was still one hell of a pilot. He took just enough risks to stay out of Gatling gun range and was using the silver-edged anomalies being created by the space station as the perfect cover from missiles.

"Phelps, hang back inside sector eight-four-two," he ordered. "I'm going to try and herd him toward you. Halley, stick with me, we'll probably have to do this together. Missiles clearly aren't going to end this. We have to get in close."

"Affirmed," they both replied.

Frowning in determination, West flew hard and fast, not willing to give Kurt a second's advantage. His tactics slowly began to close the gap, but there was soon another problem.

"Captain," Lexi said, "he's heading deeper into the anomaly field."

West glanced at their location relative to the space station and saw that she was right. It almost looked as if Kurt was intentionally heading for the most concentrated area of anomalies.

"*What is the fool doing?*" he thought in frustration.

343

For a moment, he contemplated breaking off the pursuit and simply waiting for them to be blown apart like the missiles had been earlier, but he knew it wasn't an option. Mr. Breeden would never forgive him if Kurt somehow managed to manoeuvre his way through to the station and after seeing what his employer was capable of...

"Stay on them," West ordered sharply.

And so they followed Kurt deeper into danger and immediately found it harder to gain ground. The anomalies were appearing at random now, sometimes right in their path, and West had to spend a considerable amount of mental focus on simply avoiding them.

He noticed a particularly large anomaly had opened ahead of them and tried to anticipate which angle Kurt would use to avoid it, but the fool didn't seem to see the approaching danger.

"*Wait,*" he thought in confusion, "*what's he doing?*"

The hole in space shuddered as Kurt flew toward it and its jagged, silver edge cut in and out faster than he would ever be able to compensate for. But Kurt didn't turn away. He just kept straight on as if he were playing some kind of cosmic game of chicken and expected the anomaly to disappear just before he reached it.

"What is he doing?" Halley shouted, echoing West's thoughts. "He's headed straight for it!"

West felt his chest muscles tighten as the distance between Kurt's jet and the anomaly ran down and wondered if their mission was about to end sooner than he expected. But at the last possible moment, the hole flickered wider instead of disappearing and rather than exploding into pieces, Kurt's jet shot straight through the silver hole without a scratch.

"They went through," Phelps said, sounding shocked.

"Do we follow them?" Halley asked quickly.

Captain West hesitated, a little shocked himself. Clearly these strange holes in space were not what he'd thought. But should he send his team through? What were they risking here? Was this mission worth his team's lives?

"Yes," he said firmly. "Go, go, go!"

Following his own orders, Captain West accelerated toward the anomaly that had swallowed Kurt's jet and saw Halley lining up just in front of him. The anomaly's jagged silver edge tore in toward them, looking far less stable than it had only a moment ago, but West knew there was no backing out now.

"Punch it!" he shouted as they closed the last few hundred metres.

Halley's jet reached the anomaly first and West was sure she would scream through it just as Kurt had. But at the last moment, the hole's edge flickered inward, just far enough to clip her wing.

In a moment that seemed to stretch into eternity, West watched Halley's jet being torn apart in the strangest way possible. Where the anomaly's silver edge touched it, parts of the jet seemed to rust in an instant, while others crumpled and twisted in on themselves, shearing off the wing. But it didn't tumble away from the jet, instead it became transparent and plunged straight *through* the cockpit as if it had somehow become intangible.

As his eyes widened in horror, the wing suddenly re-materialised and was locked into place at a bizarre angle, rupturing Halley's cockpit violently and spewing red-stained liquid out into the vacuum of space. The rear engines exploded a moment later and flames leapt forward with a vengeful hunger, engulfing the entire, twisted wreck in an intense fireball.

In a sudden, glaring flash, time returned to its normal pace and Captain West heard himself scream as the ragged silver edge tore toward his own jet. There was no time to turn away from his imminent death and so he instinctively closed his eyes and waited for the inevitable.

"Aaaaaaarrrrrgh!"

Expecting sudden pain as his life was torn from him, West was surprised when nothing happened. His eyes flickered open again and he saw something that he didn't, at first, believe.

Through his cockpit window, Captain West stared down at a Mars that looked nothing like the one he remembered.

Somehow his rusty, arid home had been transformed into one covered in oceans, forests, and an atmosphere thick with water-laden clouds.

"*Where the fuck am I?*" he thought in a panic.

His shock was interrupted by an alarm that warned of an imminent attack and, almost without thinking, West activated a counter measure and pulled his jet into a sharp turn.

A moment later, something exploded off his left wing – a missile – and as he completed his turn, he saw his attacker, Kurt Jones, accelerating away.

"*Sneaky bastard!*" he thought with a grimace.

He quickly moved back into position behind Kurt and realised there were anomalies here as well. From this side, however, the parts of Mars he could see through them were dusty brown, just as they should be.

"*I can get back,*" he thought with a touch of relief.

He turned to where the space station should have been, expecting to see it too through one of the anomalies, and noticed something else instead.

"*Another Jupiter flare?*" he thought incredulously.

This one traced a very different pattern through the cosmos and it wasn't as bright as the one he'd studied earlier, but it was definitely headed for the fertile planet below.

"*This place has its own Apocalypse on the way,*" he thought numbly. "*I have to get out of here.*"

Returning his gaze to the icon that tracked Kurt and Miana, West saw they were still heading straight through the field of anomalies. As expected, it was possible to see glimpses of the space station through the silver holes in space and the sight made him finally realise what Kurt was doing.

"*Of course!*" he thought.

If one of these holes could bring them here then another could just as easily take them back, and if they flew through one much closer to the space station, they could bypass the security grid altogether.

It was a desperate, even courageous move and it fitted Kurt's psych profile perfectly. But what worried West more than anything was the ominous feeling that it was going to work.

"Fuck," he swore sharply.

He couldn't afford to fail this mission, not if he wanted to survive the day, and so he bared his teeth, pushed his throttle all the way forward and headed into the anomaly field once more.

As the two ships moved closer to the space station, the anomalies became more numerous and Captain West found them harder to avoid. He barely missed one that flickered out of his way at the last moment and realised it was only luck that was getting him through now, not skill.

Suddenly it was Kurt who was in his element and Captain West who was at a disadvantage.

A new alarm sounded in his ears and West looked down to see a countdown had appeared on his screen.

"*Not good,*" he thought, shaking his head.

The countdown was based on a simulation Dr. Grayson had provided them with and it indicated the Jupiter flare was now minutes away from reaching the space station.

Captain West took a moment to calculate his current progress and realised that at this rate, even at maximum acceleration, they would only just make it to the station before the Jupiter flare did.

"*This is a suicide run in more ways than one,*" he thought.

It was the only explanation that made any sense. There was no time for Kurt to dock with the station and nothing they could do even if they did somehow manage to bluff their way on board.

The only viable plan of attack was to get past the defence grid on this side of the anomalies, fly back through one of the holes in space, and then use their jet like a missile to take out the station.

"Lunatics!" West growled.

He didn't know how Dr. Grayson and Isaac Taylor planned to save Mars from the Jupiter flare, but if this place was truly a glimpse into Mars' past then their failure was certain to have devastating consequences. Whatever Mr. Breeden might have against Miana Raiken, West had to do everything he could to stop the second Jupiter flare from reaching the planet.

Resigned to the fact his chance of survival was now as slim as his chance of success, Captain West focussed on closing the gap between himself and Kurt.

With each second, the anomaly field grew thicker around him and he knew it would soon became impossible to avoid them. Kurt began dealing with the problem by darting through the holes rather than avoiding them, but each time he did, the perimeter defences around the Cosmotech space station activated.

Captain West watched the approaching missiles from the corner of his eye, coaxing them in toward the target, but with so many anomalies in the intervening space, every one of them exploded before they could hit home.

He began to duck back through the anomalies himself and felt a traitorous urge to end the pursuit and simply fly to a place of safety. But two things kept him on Kurt's tail. The first was the knowledge he would be condemning his own world to death if he didn't stop Kurt from attacking the space station. The second was that he was now so deep in the anomaly field that there was no guarantee he would even make it out alive if he did cut and run.

On several occasions, he managed to get Kurt in his sights and fire off a quick burst of gunfire, but before he scored a hit, Kurt simply darted through another anomaly and disappeared from view.

Grinding his teeth in frustration, Captain West flew around another hole that had swallowed Kurt and was caught by surprise when a much smaller one appeared ahead of him. He pulled his jet into a spin, hoping it would slide right by him, but it was too close. He didn't even have time to scream as the silver edge tore through his ship.

Nothing happened.

"*What?*" he thought with a shudder.

Breathing heavily, Captain West realised that somehow the anomalies were no longer dangerous. He knew too little to speculate on why that might be the case, but it made him wonder if it meant the two times being connected by the anomalies were somehow becoming one.

"*Are they beginning to share the same space?*" he thought incredulously.

The thought frightened him more than anything that had come before and his eyes flickered to the countdown that glowed on his control panel. It was now well into the final minute.

"*This is it,*" he thought, locking his jaws for the final push.

He knew there was only one chance to stop Kurt. To do any real damage, they would have to enter the space station's rings and head for the infrastructure at the top. And if the anomalies were no longer affecting their jets then neither would it affect his missiles.

As Kurt flew into the smallest of the station's rings, Captain West manoeuvred himself into position and roared a final, desperate battle cry as he fired his full complement of missiles. The flickering light of their exhausts headed straight up the centre of the space station toward their target, but West's eyes focused instead on the fearsome red glow of the twin Jupiter flares that loomed beyond them.

In a flash greater than anything he'd ever seen, the two colossal lightning bolts impacted with the parabolic mesh that flared out above the space station and began to jump its way downward in a sizzling fire of energy.

"*They're not going to make it,*" he thought in a mix of horror and relief, "*but neither am I.*"

His cockpit window automatically increased its tinting to cut out some of the glare and Captain West almost laughed at the absurdity. Nothing would keep out the glare he would experience in a few short moments.

349

He watched in amazement as the red energy began to collect at the centre of the space station like a tiny red sun and glanced at Dr. Grayson's countdown. It had now passed zero and was counting into the negatives.

"*That's it*," he thought with a small hint of triumph. "*They didn't make it. They're as dead as I am.*"

He looked back up at the intense glare of the Jupiter flares and focussed in on Kurt's jet, which was now a mere shadow against the flaring red light. A final flare of hatred washed through him and then the shadow of Kurt's jet suddenly fell to pieces.

For a moment, Captain West thought his missiles must have reached their target and his hatred changed to a surge of vindication, but the icons tracking his weapons were still visible.

Suddenly, West realised what was really happening.

"*They've ejected...*"

The thought hit him with a shock that held him momentarily paralyzed and he could only stare in horror as the empty remains of Kurt's jet and his missiles plunged into a sphere of red energy that was now growing within the centre of the space station.

"*I have to-*" he thought, snapping out of his shock, but it was already too late.

This time, as the red fire rushed forward to engulf his ship, Captain West's scream didn't last long. And as his body was shredded to atoms, his last thought was of his own failure.

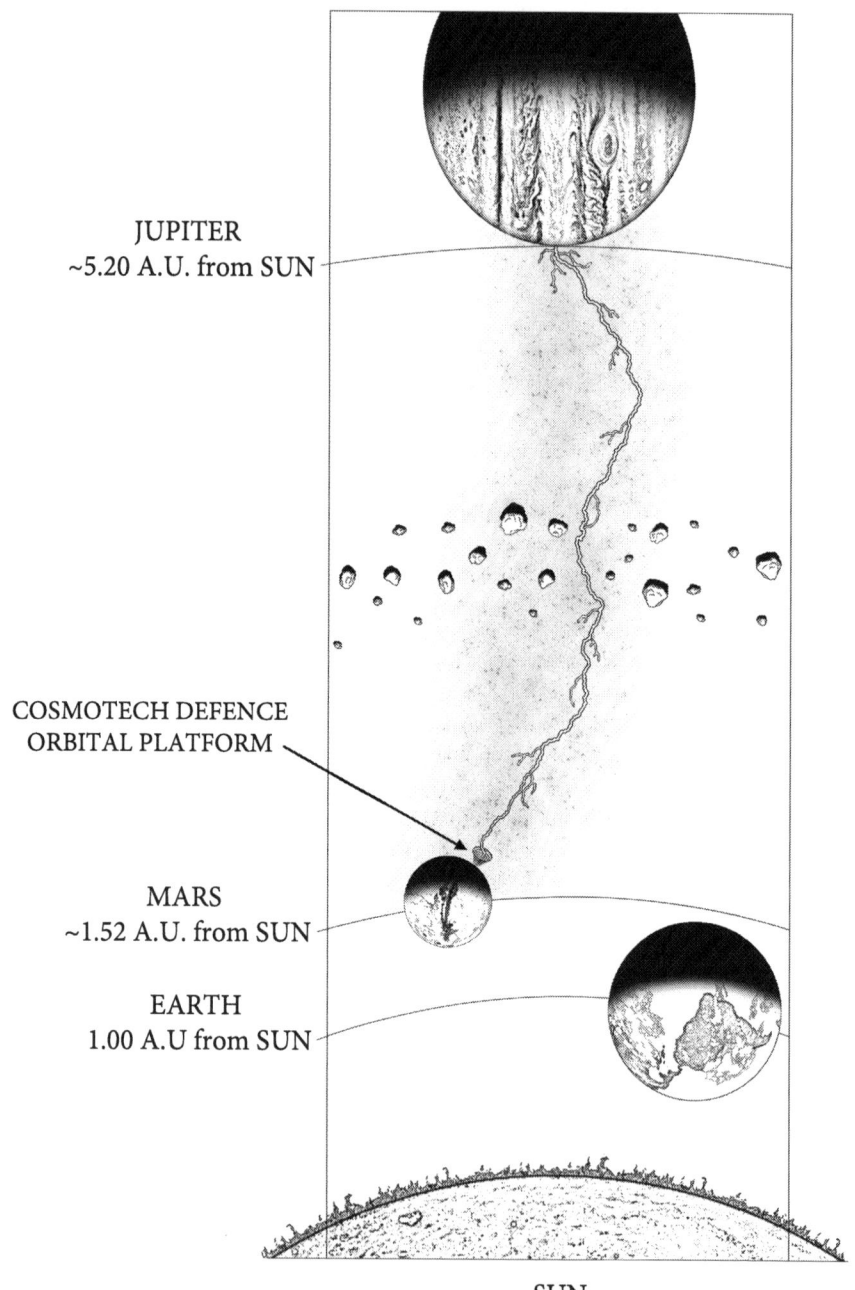

JUPITER
~5.20 A.U. from SUN

COSMOTECH DEFENCE
ORBITAL PLATFORM

MARS
~1.52 A.U. from SUN

EARTH
1.00 A.U from SUN

SUN

1 Astronomical Unit (A.U.) = ~149.6 x 10^6 km

COSMOTECH ORBITAL PLATFORM - June 8, 2147 - 5.58pm

ISAAC COULD FEEL IT COMING. IT WAS LIKE A TINGLING sensation in his head that had just became strong enough to detect.

He turned to look up at the approaching Jupiter flares and was just in time to see them close the last few thousand kilometres and slam into the colossal satellite dish that waited above the space station like a giant shield.

The twin bolts hit the parabolic dish at separate locations, but rather than smash straight through it as Isaac would have expected, the sizzling energy spider-webbed down the metallic mesh toward the centre. The central point was suspended not far above the station's largest ring and when the energy reached it, an intense magnetic field funnelled the energy into a large torus.

The giant, donut-shaped torus grew rapidly as the energy circled through the centre and flowed back out around the sides, until a gleaming vortex appeared beneath it, creating a pulsing sphere of red energy directly between Isaac and Hani'ah.

It was like a tiny red sun had been formed at the centre of the space station and as the incredible phenomenon manifested, Isaac felt an overwhelming torrent of power surge into his psychic connection with Hani'ah.

Like oxygen feeding a fire, the power made their psychic link explode brighter and Isaac could barely find the breath to gasp as his perspective grew beyond anything he'd ever imagined.

For a moment he assumed his mind would be swept away and his body cast into oblivion. No nexus of human minds could possibly contain such power. And yet, whatever Dr. Grayson had done to enhance P.A.T.R.I.C., the delicate psychic balance that Isaac held with Hani'ah remained stable. Calm even.

He still didn't know what was causing the silver-edged anomalies that surrounded the station, or why they seemed to be linked with another version of Mars, but if such a connection could be created then surely it meant he would be able to return to his own reality. And, even better, the Jupiter flares from both worlds were clearly going no further. All they had to do was hold this psychic connection long enough and he would simultaneously save two worlds and be reunited with his brother.

"*This is going to work,*" he thought in excitement. "*I'm actually coming home, bro. I'm finally coming home.*"

APPROACHING ORBITAL PLATFORM - June 8, 2147 - 6.00pm

MIANA SCREAMED AND COVERED HER FACE AS THE Jupiter flares' energy flashed toward them. An alarm began echoing through her helmet and she sensed movement, but the fiery death she expected never came.

When she opened her eyes again, an Arabic word she didn't recognise was flashing brightly on the console. She quickly moved her focus to the cockpit window, but didn't know what she was seeing. The chaotic blur that seemed to rush past her was like nothing she'd ever seen and it took her grasping mind a moment to realise what it was.

"*We're crashing into the space station,*" she thought in shock.

As she finished the thought, the confusing blur came to a sudden stop and was replaced by billowing smoke and sparking debris. She searched beyond the mess for some kind of reference, but could only see an empty floor that ran all the way to some distant walls.

"What... happened?" she said out loud, her mind still reeling with shock.

"Miana?" Kurt said through her helmet intercom. "Are you okay?"

"Kurt?" she said, realising for the first time that he was nowhere to be seen. "What did you do?"

"I ejected us both," he replied. "Did you make it into the station?"

"*I should have known he'd try something like that,*" Miana thought, before adding out loud, "I think so."

It looked like the spherical cockpit she'd entered back in the Bas Quirat was also an escape pod. Kurt must have ejected them before the Jupiter flare could vaporize them and sent them crashing through the ceiling of the station's largest ring.

Miana felt sick. As far as she could see there was no one else around, but it didn't mean her entrance hadn't injured anyone.

"*I hope not,*" she thought. "*Unless that person was Loc Breeden.*"

Looking up, she expected to see a gaping hole where her escape pod had just crashed through the ceiling, but some kind of temporary bulkhead was already closing over it.

"Where are you?" she asked Kurt. "I can't see you anywhere."

"I… don't know," he replied, and for the first time Miana detected a hint of pain in his voice.

"Are you okay?"

"I'm fine," Kurt replied, a little too quickly for her liking. "Now let's get you out of that pod. Do you see three Arabic symbols on the dash?"

Miana didn't think he was fine at all, but she looked for the symbols without comment and found them in a vertical line at the right hand side of her screen.

"Green ones?" she asked.

"Green is good," Kurt replied. "It means the atmosphere outside your pod is safe. Now, touch the bottom symbol."

Miana did as he asked and another tone sounded in her helmet, moments before a series of bubbles traced a line around the centre of her pod and it split open, spilling the liquid that had cradled her out onto the floor. The harness holding her in place detached a moment later and Miana awkwardly climbed out of the wreckage.

She now had a much better view of the room she'd crashed into and couldn't help noticing that everything was stained with a harsh red light.

"*The Jupiter flare,*" she thought instinctively.

She couldn't see what was going on outside because of the damage her escape pod had done to the ceiling, but it was clear the Jupiter flares had reached the space station and were going no further.

"*They've contained them both,*" she thought. "*For now.*"

"Are you out?" Kurt asked.

"Yes," Miana replied, looking around again.

"Me too. Better keep your helmet on for now," Kurt advised. "Then we'll be able to communicate with–"

Suddenly a harsh static cut him off and Miana frowned.

"Kurt? Are you there, Kurt?"

"He's dead," a familiar voice replied.

Miana felt a sudden chill in her stomach.

"Who is this?" she asked.

"You don't recognise me?" the voice replied in a mocking tone. "I think I'm actually offended."

The chill in her stomach began to spread outward and Miana felt her fists tighten.

"Loc Breeden," she said slowly.

"Well *done*, detective," he replied wryly. "Now, please remain where you are. You have illegally invaded sovereign territory. Cosmotech Security will be with you shortly."

"Kurt?" Miana said loudly. "Can you hear me, Kurt?"

"I told you, he's dead," Loc replied, the pleasure in his voice clear.

At his words, Miana felt a sudden, crushing weight on her chest and couldn't breathe for a moment.

"*No, it's not true,*" she thought fiercely.

She pulled a deep breath in through her nose to calm down and ignored the pain that rasped down her constricted throat. She couldn't afford to break now. Kurt was as resilient as it was possible to be and with the psychic powers he now possessed, it would be foolish to think Loc had killed him so easily.

"Listen to me, Loc," she said as she headed for the nearest exit. "You've been lied to."

"People lie to me all the time, detective," Loc replied calmly. "The real trick is recognising the truth among those lies."

"Then I hope you've worked out what's really going on," Miana said quickly. "This station wasn't designed to stop the Jupiter flare."

Before Loc could answer, two large, heavily armed security officers appeared in the doorway ahead of her. Neither looked willing to discuss the situation.

Miana stopped in her tracks and slowly raised her hands.

"It's over, detective," Loc said simply. "Please, take off your helmet."

The two security officers advanced with their weapons raised and Miana reluctantly did as Loc asked. As soon as she did, her lungs filled with acrid smoke and she coughed loudly.

"You have an uncanny knack for ruining my plans," Loc continued calmly, "but I honestly respect your tenacity. It's a shame I won't get to do this myself. Kill her."

The officers hefted their weapons to follow the order and Miana's heart leapt with panic. But before they could fire, her lips moved of their own accord.

"Lower your weapons."

The security officers did so immediately.

Miana was shocked. Someone had just spoken through her and the sensation took her back to her final encounter with Mr. Drevit – Loc's assassin. She wasn't having an out-of-body experience this time, but somehow she knew that the Divsek who'd hitched a ride in her mind had just spoken on her behalf.

As soon as the officers lowered their weapons, Miana heard Loc's sharp intake of breath.

"What are you doing? I said shoot her! Kill her, now!"

But the officers remained still, calmly staring at Miana with emotionless expressions.

"Take me to Isaac Taylor," she said, again without any conscious intention. "Do not let anyone stop us."

The officers turned toward the entrance they were blocking and promptly marched through it.

Miana wasn't sure if the Divsek was about to take control of her body as well, but after a few seconds it appeared she was supposed to follow the security guards on her own. But she didn't want to do it this way. Every moral instinct she had refused to accept that controlling people was the answer to an evil that did the same.

"Stop!" she said loudly.

The security guards actually paused at her command and Miana was surprised.

"No," she said firmly, refusing to move and hoping the Divsek realised she was trying to communicate with it. "Not this way. If you're going to use your power to help me get to Isaac then do it without hurting anyone."

Again, Miana waited for the Divsek to ignore her request and simply take control, but after a few moments, it was only her voice that was co-opted.

"Very well, Miana," it said, before addressing the security officers again. "Take me to Isaac Taylor. Protect me from anyone trying to stop us, but do not kill them."

Miana noticed the statement didn't preclude violence altogether, but she decided not to push it. Moral objection was one thing, but getting to Isaac was important and if the restrained use of force was necessary, then so be it.

"Thank you," she said quietly, before moving to follow the security guards.

"What do you think you're doing, detective?" Loc snarled.

"What you can't," Miana replied firmly.

"You'll be gunned down without warning!" Loc promised.

"We'll see," Miana replied, before talking to one of the security guards. "Can you jam Loc Breeden's signal."

"Yes," one of them answered.

"Then do it," Miana said. "I don't want to listen to him anymore."

The security officer consulted a small panel on his forearm and when Loc didn't speak again, Miana nodded.

"That's a victory, at least," she said beneath her breath, before addressing the security officers again. "Get moving."

The officers immediately did as she commanded and Miana found herself thinking of Kurt again. Whether they saved the world or not, if Kurt wound up dead she wasn't sure it would be worth it.

"*I just hope he's okay,*" she thought with a frown. "*If Saadi was right then the planet is depending on more than one of us succeeding.*"

FAYINA SQUINTED UP THROUGH THE VENT AS THE Jupiter flares were diverted into the slowly growing sphere at the centre of the space station. She couldn't imagine what kind of technology was funnelling so much power into such a beautiful and apparently non-threatening form.

Shaking her head in dismissal, she turned to the woman she was there to kill and wondered what role she was playing in all this. Whatever it was, she was showing clear signs of distress and Fayina could only assume the device she was hooked into was to blame.

For a moment, she contemplated asking Dr. Haig about it, but was interrupted when the mysterious man who'd appeared earlier flashed into view on the other side of the vent.

"Now!" he shouted. "You have to do it now!"

Fayina's heart pounded faster as adrenalin rushed into her veins and she returned her gaze to the woman in white with a new resolve.

"Fuck it!" she snarled, before leaning back and kicking open the vent.

A few scientists stationed nearby noticed her incursion, but they didn't seem to know what to do and were too far away to do anything anyway.

Ignoring them, Fayina raised her pistol and sprinted toward her target, ready to do what was necessary to save her sister. But before she could get close enough, she was surprised when the two women in black at the target's side shot forward in a blur.

Not ready for the attack, Fayina quickly found herself locked in two vice-like holds.

"Get out of my way!" she shouted, trying to push them off.

But they wouldn't let go. These women, whatever they might look like under their full-body coverings, were incredibly strong. And Fayina could see from the fire in their eyes that they were passionate too. They weren't going to let her kill the woman in white while they were alive.

"Fine," she snarled, before headbutting the closest one in the face.

As her forehead smashed into nose cartilage, Fayina felt the woman's grip weaken and quickly wrestled her arm free so she could elbow the other one in the throat. The woman reeled away, making a desperate choking sound, and Fayina thought that might be it for her, but despite the obvious pain she was in, the woman barely paused before throwing herself forward again.

"*They're crazy,*" she thought to herself.

The woman she'd headbutted was also attacking again and Fayina happily allowed her rage to take over. She had no reason or desire to kill these women, but they were in her way and she wasn't going to let them stop her.

With extreme prejudice, she slammed a fist into the midsection of one, while the other clasped onto her leg and bit down hard. The pain lit up brighter than the red glare that coloured everything around them and Fayina used her other leg to stomp on the woman's head.

She felt teeth ripping free and a pain that suggested flesh had gone with it then the woman's head hit the floor with a loud *crack!* Fayina knew it might very well mean she was dead, but the other one was attacking again and so she was soon too busy to care.

She felt fingernails tearing at her eyes and lashed out with her fist again, hitting the woman in the same spot. She heard a croaking groan as the wind was knocked from her attacker and used the moment of respite to stand tall and grasp the woman's neck in a guillotine choke.

The woman in black fought back, kicking and clawing at anything she could reach, but with the rage flowing strong now, Fayina felt nothing. She simply forced the woman's head down to her chest and squeezed her arms tighter until the struggling ceased.

She held on for a few seconds, just to make sure, and then dropped the limp body with a snarl. She looked around, expecting to see someone else coming at her, but the scientists were simply staring at her with various looks of shock and horror on their faces.

Ignoring them all over again, Fayina looked for the pistol she'd dropped and then snatched it off the floor before walking purposefully toward the woman in white. The Jupiter flare made her robes look like they were already soaked in blood and Fayina felt nothing as she stepped in close and pressed the barrel where she knew the heart would be.

Upon contact, the woman's eyes flickered open to reveal the milky white corneas of a blind woman.

"Limadha la 'araa hdha?" she said in Arabic, but Fayina didn't understand.

"I'm sorry," she said, tears of rage and guilt suddenly clouding her vision, "but I have to save her."

Then she pulled the trigger.

The woman's body jolted violently as the projectile punched through her chest and Fayina felt the shock and confusion of her other personas as they suddenly awoke within her.

"*What did you do?*" Celia asked breathlessly.

Leaving the question unanswered, Fayina stepped back and looked around for some indication of what she was meant to do next. She'd done what they wanted. Now she needed, *desperately* needed, to be given what they promised her.

"I did what you asked!" she shouted at the gaping scientists. "Tell me what to do next! Where do I go?"

In response, a savage pain ripped through Fayina's temples and she barely managed to cry out as she fell to the floor, her limbs suddenly weak.

She tried to get up and fight whatever it was that was hurting her, but it was impossible. Even her eyes remained unresponsive and she could only stare across the floor toward one of the women in black she'd knocked out earlier.

"*What's happening to me?*" she thought, her rage swamped by fear.

"*What did you expect?*" Ianka's stern voice demanded. "*What could have possibly made you kill?*"

"*What did they promise you?*" Dr. Haig asked in his irritatingly calm voice. "*Who were you trying to save?*"

Fayina didn't want to tell them. She knew it would help them understand, but now that she'd been tricked, that she'd *failed* them, she couldn't bring herself to say it. As much as she hated her fellow personalities, she didn't want them to suffer the despair she was now feeling.

A figure appeared at the corner of her vision, standing just close enough to see, and Fayina realised it was the man who'd guided her earlier.

"I'm… sorry, Fayina," he said with a sincerity that sounded almost sarcastic. "I know you're feeling betrayed, but you should know that what you've done will ensure your sister will have never died."

"*Our sister?*" Celia cried. "*What is he talking about?*"

Fayina felt tears streaming from her frozen eyes and desperately wanted to believe him, but this wasn't what she expected. This wasn't what she'd been promised.

"Everything will soon be over," the figure continued with an edge of regret. "The past we know will soon be wiped from existence and our suffering… our suffering will have never been."

"*You were trying to save Fayina?*" Ianka said sharply. "*How could you be so gullible? So stupid!?*"

"*I don't know,*" Fayina sobbed, trapped within her own mind again. "*I don't know.*"

"Don't blame yourself," the figure said as it gradually faded. "There was nothing any of us could have done differently."

Despite the man's sincerity, his words echoed hollow in Fayina's ears and she knew now that she'd made a terrible mistake.

But there was nothing she could do about it. She was helpless. Merely an embodiment of Anya's guilt and rage, trapped in the recesses of her own mind. And she deserved it. She deserved to suffer for the life she'd just taken. She deserved to die.

ISAAC TORE HIS GAZE FROM THE SPECTACULAR FLOW of energy at the centre of the station and glanced at the graphs being displayed around the platform. The numbers were incredible. The Jupiter flares were feeding immense amounts of energy into the ball of plasma at the centre of the space station, but it was being consumed in equal measure by the strange anomalies his psychic connection with Hani'ah was creating.

Turning to look at Mars, Isaac saw it was now completely covered by forests and oceans. But that wasn't all. The new terrain was also partially transparent and it allowed him to see the more familiar version of Mars as well, as if both now occupied the same space.

For a moment, he wondered how the bizarre illusion was being created. Was he seeing another reality now connected to their own? And if so, did it mean he could get back to his own reality and to Jason? Did it mean there were other realities he had to sift through before finding the right one? How many of them were there? Was it even a finite number?

Trying not think about the implications of searching an infinite multiverse of possibilities, Isaac focussed on the fact that whatever was happening, it was drawing more energy from the Jupiter flares than they were feeding into the station. Whether he managed to get back to his own reality or not, it seemed more and more likely that the planet below them was going to be saved.

"How are you holding up, Hani'ah?" he asked, more for his own benefit than hers.

He expected an optimistic comment – Hani'ah's reservoir of faith seemed endless – but instead he began to see things he didn't expect. The mental image they shared was suddenly invaded by flashes of movement. There were glimpses of faces he recognised – Hani'ah's ladies in black and...

"Anya?" he said in confusion.

The visions were blurred as if seen in fast motion. Fast, *violent* motion. And whenever Anya appeared, she was snarling and attacking in a way that could only mean one thing.

"*Fayina's in control,*" Isaac thought. "*But... why am I seeing this?*"

Concerned for the delicate psychic balance they were maintaining, Isaac tried to take more of the image he was sharing with Hani'ah. It shimmered and faltered, just like it did when she'd struggled to take it from him, but he soon managed to get it under control.

"Hani'ah," he said when it felt stable, "are you okay? What's happening over there?"

But again, in place of a response he saw Anya's face appear as if she were standing right in front of him.

"Why didn't I see this?" Hani'ah said finally.

Then Anya's face twisted into a snarl and something bit into Isaac's chest. He gasped in shock and clutched at his heart, but before he could even wonder what had caused the pain, something else hit him. This time the sensation was purely psychic and it shattered the image he'd been sharing with Hani'ah like a brick through glass.

The psychic link they'd been sharing whiplashed into Isaac's mind and he tried to cry out, but couldn't make a sound. Instead, his legs give way beneath him and he barely managed to grasp the rail in time to stop himself falling to the floor.

"*Something's happened to Hani'ah,*" he thought in a panic.

He wasn't sure how he knew, but he was certain of it, and now the immense power they'd been funnelling through their psychic connection was backing up in his mind.

The mental pain was excruciating. Isaac's burning eyes flickered up to the cause of his agony and he felt a whole new terror when the sphere of red energy grew noticeably larger. Now that his psychic connection with Hani'ah had been lost, the amount of energy he was capable of consuming was a dripping tap compared with the ocean of power being funnelled into the space station.

He could already see the excess energy breaking through the magnetic containment field. Arcs of red lightning speared outward to ground themselves on the station and explosions of glass and torn metal began to blossom into space.

Isaac heard some of the technicians lining the research platform screaming in panic then an evacuation alarm split the air. He turned his gaze down again, hoping to find someone who could help him, but the technicians he saw were arguing heatedly and pointing wildly at him and the growing ball of plasma. Others were running for the exit, their faces twisted with terror, and Isaac would have gladly joined them if he'd had the strength.

He searched for Dr. Grayson, certain at least that he would know what to do, but the doctor was standing motionless at the edge of the platform.

"*What's he doing?*" Isaac thought in confusion.

Dr. Grayson seemed completely unconcerned with what was happening around him. He just stared up at the growing ball of plasma with a look of resignation on his face. Perhaps he was experiencing shock or was simply lost in another of his strange mental episodes, but either way, Isaac quickly realised he wasn't getting any help from that direction.

He turned back to the pulsing ball of plasma and tried to fight the immense storm of energy being forced into his mind. But it was useless. There was just too much to handle on his own. They'd tried their best and they'd failed, and now he would never see Jason again.

"*I'm sorry bro,*" he thought helplessly. "*I thought I could do it without you, but I was wrong. I'm so sorry.*"

KURT WAS IN SERIOUS TROUBLE. HIS ARM HAS BEEN badly slashed and broken when his escape pod crashed into the space station. His flight suit automatically tightened a tourniquet above the wound to prevent him from bleeding out, but the broken bone was causing a grating pain that wasn't getting any better.

He knew he should be glad his plan had worked at all, but it was hard to feel positive when your arm felt like it was being stabbed repeatedly with a hot knife.

At least he'd managed to get out of the wrecked escape pod. He should have known his radio link with Miana wouldn't work inside the space station – Cosmotech Security had dealt with that quickly – but he wasn't ready for Saadi's prediction to come true so soon.

He desperately wanted to find Miana and make sure she was okay, but for once he had his own mission to complete.

"*Yet another thing I have to take on faith,*" Kurt thought with a grimace. "*Looks like Saadi might make a believer out of me after all.*"

Bracing his broken arm with his other hand, Kurt lurched toward the doors that led out of the room he'd crashed into and leant against the wall beside them.

371

He knew from the moment his radio transmission was cut that Cosmotech Security would be coming for him.

"*I have to be ready,*" he thought determinedly. "*They won't give me a second chance.*"

And, just as he expected, two security officers with rifles burst through the doors almost as soon as he reached them. One of them immediately turned to check the room's corners, swinging his weapon toward Kurt, and they locked eyes.

Almost without thinking, Kurt used the connection to project what he now thought of as his 'psychic self' along it and into the officer's mind. The results were instantaneous.

"Stop where you are," he said loudly.

The officer complied straight away, freezing where he stood, and the second officer spun toward his voice and fired a single round.

Kurt felt something push against his uninjured arm and heard a *ping* that he hoped meant the shot had ricocheted instead of punching through his flight suit, then he moved his gaze from the first officer to the second.

Again, they locked eyes for a moment and a second psychic connection was made.

"Freeze!" he said loudly.

The second officer complied just as easily as the first and Kurt breathed a ragged sigh of relief. He then looked down at his shoulder and was relieved to find no hole in his flight suit, just a shiny scar of paint-stripped metal where the projectile had impacted.

Shaking his head and silently thanking his luck, Kurt returned his gaze to the waiting security officers.

"Tell me how many security officers are coming for me," he ordered.

"Three teams, six officers," the first one replied in a monotone.

"*Shit. I've got to be quick,*" Kurt thought with a frown, before adding out loud, "Where can I find Hani'ah Naziri?"

"Hani'ah Naziri is located on research platform Beta," the officer replied. "Twelve hundred metres spinside."

Kurt assumed the officer meant the direction the station was spinning. Twelve hundred metres also didn't sound very far, but when you had six of the solar system's highest paid security officers on your trail, nothing was straightforward.

"Take me to her," he said firmly, "and let me know when a security team gets close."

At his command, the officers began striding across the room and Kurt pushed himself off the wall to follow them. He tried not to jolt his arm as he walked and made sure the officers stayed between him and the path ahead, not ready to put himself in harm's way just yet. He also kept glancing backward, hoping another team wouldn't catch up with them from behind.

When they were through the far doors, they headed down a short corridor that opened onto a large open park. There were trees, gardens and even some sculpted, grassy hills, but the scenery was ruined by a fiery red light that seemed to illuminate everything.

Kurt looked up at a transparent ceiling no more than twenty metres above them, expecting to see the Jupiter flares, and gaped instead at a giant sphere of red energy. He had no idea what was happening, but the view was as breathtakingly beautiful as it was terrifying.

The enormous accumulation of energy *thrumm*ed through his body at an uncomfortable frequency and Kurt wondered how the space station was bleeding away its destructive potential.

"*As long as it keeps doing it,*" he thought with a shudder.

Returning his gaze to the park ahead, he saw that one of the officers in front of him had stopped.

"What is it?" he asked quickly.

"A security team is approaching," the officer said.

"Shit!" Kurt swore reflexively, before focussing on the entrance at the far side of the park.

The doors were already opening and, just as the first two had done, two more security officers charged through with their weapons at the ready.

Kurt tried to look them in the eyes, hoping the psychic connection would work at this distance, but nothing happened. Either they were too far away or they weren't looking directly at him.

At that point, a rifle barrel from one of the officers flashed and Kurt heard the insistent *SSsszzzz* of a bullet whizzing past his head.

"Shit!" he swore again, before diving behind a thick bench beside the path. "Take them out!"

The officers under his control opened fire immediately and the *CRACK-CRACK* of their weapons frightened Kurt in a visceral way that left his bowels feeling weak. The exchange lasted only a few seconds, however, because his protectors didn't move into cover. They simply stood where they were and before Kurt could even catch his breath, the head on one of them snapped back and the officer tumbled to the red-stained grass with a large hole in his helmet.

"Shit," Kurt swore for the third time, realising he probably should have told them to defend themselves.

A moment later, the second officer thudded to the earth.

"*What the fuck do I do now?*" he thought desperately.

Did he dare raise his head and try to establish another psychic connection with the attacking officers? How much time would he have before they managed to put a bullet in his brain?

"*Not enough,*" he thought with a cold certainty.

He could hear them approaching now, their boot steps ringing on the cobbled pathways, and the tension in his stomach screwed tighter.

"*Just do it,*" he told himself. "*Move! Before they get too close!*"

But his legs wouldn't obey. Something in him simply didn't like his odds of survival.

In desperation, Kurt thought about shouting his surrender and hoping it would give him the precious time he needed to make the psychic connection, but before he could try it, an alarm split the air and a light began blinking high on the wall behind him.

Kurt stared at it in confusion for a moment then something crashed into the garden beyond his hiding spot. The noise it made was incredible, like a scream made entirely of smashing glass and tearing metal. At the same time, a powerful wind roared into life around him and Kurt instinctively grabbed the bench with his good arm to avoid being swept out of cover.

The wind ripped and tore at him, making him snarl with pain, but his good arm held and he was even able to turn his gaze up to the shattered ceiling and the pulsing red sphere that raged beyond it.

"*It's larger,*" he thought with a chill.

Then a blinding bolt of red lightning snapped out to ground itself on the station and Kurt realised what had just smashed through the garden's ceiling.

"*It's out of control!*"

The station's counter measures quickly began to close the hole that allowed the garden's atmosphere to escape and, for a terrifying moment, Kurt imagined himself being pulled out and plunged into the centre of the raging red inferno.

But the counter measures were effective. In seconds, the wind that pulled against him was gone and he fell back to the garden path with an agonising jolt.

He took a quick moment to breathe, hoping the security officers were doing the same, and then risked a quick glance over the bench. The damage was incredible. A large crater had been gouged out of the grassy hills and several small trees were on fire.

It took a moment to find them, but the security officers were now sprawled against the far wall, as if they'd been thrown there by the lightning bolt. One of them didn't seem to be moving and, judging by the blood spatter on the wall behind him, Kurt assumed he was dead. The other was struggling to his feet, looking groggy and hurt.

Seeing his opportunity, Kurt leapt out from behind the park bench and sprinted toward them, pausing only to scoop up a rifle that thankfully hadn't been sucked into space.

He then stood over the surviving officer with the rifle held firmly in his good arm.

"Freeze!" he yelled over the blaring alarm.

The officer grimaced in pain as he turned to look up and Kurt met his gaze gladly. The psychic connection was instantaneous.

"Are there any other officers nearby?" Kurt asked quickly.

"No," the man replied in a monotone, the pain now gone from his face along with all other expression.

Kurt was surprised. He thought Loc would have been pressing his advantage.

"How far away are they?" he asked.

"There are no more security teams headed to this location."

Again, Kurt was surprised.

"Why not?"

"They're being diverted to intercept Miana Raiken."

"Oh no," Kurt said with a sinking feeling.

He looked back across the ruined gardens and wondered how long it would take to reach her, but an image of Miana's disapproving face appeared in his mind. She wouldn't be happy if he abandoned his own mission to help her, no matter what danger she might be facing.

"Damn it, Miana," he muttered, before reluctantly turning back to the security officer. "Take me to the Beta research platform. Quickly!"

The officer struggled the rest of the way to his feet and then limped back through the doors he'd entered through. Kurt followed him closely, acutely aware of a new tightness in his chest, and tried not to think about Miana.

"*I just hope she's alright,*" he thought with a grimace.

COSMOTECH ORBITAL PLATFORM - June 8, 2147 - 6.15pm

DR. GRAYSON STARED AT THE UNSTABLE ACCUMULATION of energy that raged at the centre of the space station. It was finally time. All the work he'd done to betray his own species was coming to fruition and there was nothing anyone could do to stop it.

His demons had won.

He felt he should be doing something, perhaps rebelling against them in this final moment on behalf of all those that were about to be wiped from existence, both past and present. But he knew it was pointless. He couldn't prevent this any more than he could prevent his own suffering. Better to let them both be wiped from existence once and for all.

It was strange. Here, at the end of all things, Dr. Grayson had long feared how his demons would rejoice. He always imagined their hateful voices laughing and baying at him until their screeches reached an agonising crescendo that would only end when his eardrums burst. But they were uncharacteristically quiet.

He should have been glad. After decades of incessant mental torture, now that he'd accomplished all that his demons demanded of him, Dr. Grayson deserved this terrible silence.

But it only reminded him of what he'd done. All he wanted now was for it to be over as quickly as possible.

"*I deserve nothing,*" he thought sadly.

Without needing to look around, Dr. Grayson knew his staff were abandoning their stations and heading for the nearest escape pods. He'd tripped the alarm himself not long ago and officially approved a full evacuation. Their desperate flight would do nothing to save them, of course, but it would give them hope in their final moments, something he'd always been denied.

Standing at the edge of the primary research platform, he watched as the plasma sphere's event horizon gradually, inexorably destabilised. He felt a dull ache each time a lethal bolt of plasma snapped outward and ploughed into his perfectly designed space station, but little more.

"Not long now," he whispered.

He could sense the imminent and irreversible loss of containment approaching and closed his eyes as the final seconds bled into a past that would soon be gone forever. But instead of a final all-consuming surge of red energy, a voice hissed sharply in his head.

"*Stop her!*"

"What?" he gasped, his calm crumbling into confusion.

"*Do not let her create a psychic connection with Isaac,*" another voice roared.

"*Kill her!*" a third added.

Dr. Grayson felt the cold chill of shock wash over him. It should have been over. What was happening? Why were his demons tormenting him with doubt when they'd already won?

He looked around the platform, searching for the cause of their ire, and saw a woman with glowing red eyes striding toward Isaac.

"What are you doing?" he screamed, stumbling into a run. "Get away from him!"

The woman turned toward him and Dr. Grayson recognised her immediately. It was Miana Raiken, the one he'd been warned about. The one Loc Breeden should have killed many times over.

"Why is she still alive?" he whined as he ran toward her. "Why is she here? Why isn't it over?"

Caught in a chaotic rush of adrenalin and urged on by his demons, Dr. Grayson curled his hands into fists and launched himself at Miana. But before he could swipe at her glowing red eyes, she darted out of the way and he was suddenly stumbling to the floor.

The next thing he knew, his face was being pressed into the platform with his arm twisted painfully behind his back. He could feel Miana's breath against his ear and realised she was saying something, but he couldn't hear her. His demons were baying crazily in his head, screaming and hissing at him to fight his way free and kill Miana whatever the cost.

Their voices cut into his psyche with an agony that should have dulled after so many years of abuse and in animal desperation Dr. Grayson fought against the grip that held him.

Miana was strong, too strong to break her hold, but Dr. Grayson kept fighting until he felt the bones in his upper arm give way with a sudden *snap-snap*. The agony it produced seared like a branding iron across his mind, but even that couldn't drown out his demons.

The broken bones did take away Miana's leverage, however, and as she lost her secure hold on him, Dr. Grayson tore his way free.

Ignoring the terrible, grating pain, he scrambled to his feet and backed away from her, cradling the arm that now hung limp at his side. He saw her lips moving as she again tried to speak to him, but the voices were louder now than they'd ever been.

"*Kill her!*"

"*She must die!*"

"*Do not let her live!*"

"*Kill! Kill! Kill!*"

Dr. Grayson screamed in agony and clawed at his ears with the hand that still worked. He wanted desperately to do what they commanded, just as he'd always done, but he knew he couldn't kill Miana. He couldn't kill anyone.

He knew because he'd tried to kill himself so many times before today and it just wasn't in him to take a life. Not even his own, wretched version of one.

He stared into Miana's glowing eyes as the voices grated incessantly at his ears and began to sob as he realised it wasn't over. It would never be over. All his work, his torment and pain, had been for *nothing*.

"You promised me!" he screamed at the demons. "You promised!"

But as usual, they ignored his cry and attacked with renewed vigour, mercilessly urging him to do what they wanted, unwilling to relent.

And it was at that point that Dr. Grayson had a moment of clarity. If was as if the weight of physical and mental pain was so great that he'd reached the very limit of human suffering. And at the very precipice of his agony, he felt a strength flow into him that he'd never experienced before.

He screamed as the epiphany took shape, pouring all his fear, anger, and despair into the sound, and as a desperate resolve hardened in his mind, he turned from Miana and ran.

Miana watched the screaming, sobbing man run away from her with a mix of pity and disgust. She had no idea who he was, but the man was clearly insane. Whether it was due to the chaos happening all around them or something more, she couldn't tell, but she was glad he was leaving. Somehow, he'd resisted the Divsek's psychic control and that made him the first real threat she'd encountered.

The rest of her journey through the station had been littered with short clashes with security and it was only by using the Divsek's powers that she'd managed to make it this far. The destabilisation of the red sun at the centre of the station had certainly helped, but she didn't think the advantage was worth whatever might come next.

Focussing once more on why she was here, Miana turned to Isaac. She could already see he was in a lot of distress and felt compelled to call out to him as she approached.

"You're not alone, Isaac."

As soon as she spoke, Isaac looked up and when their eyes met, Miana felt a sudden rush of mental pressure close over her mind. She stopped in her tracks, overwhelmed by the sensation of *weight* that now pressed against her mind and felt a sense of connection with Isaac that was almost as embarrassing as it was strange.

"Who... are you?" he asked slowly.

"A friend," she replied – or the Divsek did at least. Given the sudden turmoil in her mind, Miana doubted she would have been able to speak for herself.

"A friend?" Isaac said with a frown.

"I'm here to help," the Divsek added.

At the news, Isaac looked both relieved and confused.

"You can help me stabilise the Jupiter flares?" he asked.

"Not stabilise," the Divsek replied, "only slow the unravelling process. The balance must be restored from the other platform."

This time Isaac glanced upward and looked frightened in a way that echoed through the strange connection they now shared.

"Hani'ah is dead," he said, his expression grim.

"There is another," the Divsek replied. "If we can hold on long enough, the balance *will* be restored."

Miana immediately thought of Kurt and hoped the Divsek was referring to him.

"Who's Kurt?" Isaac asked.

Miana was shocked. He'd picked the name directly from her mind.

"Another friend," the Divsek replied simply. "He will succeed, Isaac. And you may still make it back to your brother."

"Wait, how do you know my name?" Isaac asked with a frown. "And how do you know about my brother?"

"I have seen much, Isaac, and you shall too before the end. But there's no more time for explanations. We must concentrate if we're to hold the end at bay."

Miana doubted Isaac would be satisfied with the response, any more than she would have been, but he seemed willing to take it on faith. For now.

"What do you need me to do?" he asked.

"The Game," the Divsek replied.

"You know about that too?"

"I do," the Divsek replied, "and we will now play for the fate of the solar system."

"If you say so," Isaac said, "shall I begin?"

"No," the Divsek said. "I will begin, Isaac. If you truly want to change things, you must first see what has come before."

Miana wasn't sure what the Divsek was referring to, but she soon got her answer when the research platform disappeared around them and she was suddenly standing on the edge of a mountain.

It seemed the Divsek planned to show Isaac what it had shown her and Kurt back in the alien cave and Miana was glad. She hadn't been looking forward to explaining that particular truth.

As the vision rolled forward, Miana settled into the spectacle and found her thoughts once more returning to Kurt and what was expected of him.

"*Come on, Kurt,*" she thought to herself. "*We're counting on you.*"

KURT FOLLOWED THE LIMPING SECURITY OFFICER through the space station, cradling his broken arm and trying not to let the fleeing people unnerve him. Most of them were clogged around stairways that led down into the floor and, presumably, escape craft.

It would have been so easy to join them, to escape this crimson-lit nightmare and continue living. But Kurt knew there was no way he could abandon Miana now. Not when they'd come so far.

At least the general panic meant they weren't being delayed. None of the fleeing employees gave them more than a terrified glance and Kurt found that he was grateful. He really didn't want to find himself in another firefight.

As they continued on, a few more lightning bolts crashed into the station, but they were far from where Kurt and his psychically enslaved security officer were running. They also seemed to be coming at more infrequent intervals and Kurt hoped that was a good sign.

With his arm aching and fear broiling through his mind, Kurt felt like they ran for an eternity before the security officer finally came to a stop.

"Oh God," he said, staring at another nightmarish scene.

The second research platform was bigger than he expected. It was also empty apart from the woman Kurt was there to find and three bodies strewn at her feet.

Hani'ah Naziri was hard to miss. She was slumped in some kind of chair at the centre of the platform with a complicated-looking device strapped to her head. It trailed dozens of wires that stretched up to a strange device above her, but the strange contraption quickly lost its intrigue when Kurt saw a large red stain at her chest.

"*She's dead,*" he thought with a cold certainty. "*What the hell am I meant to do now?*"

Two of the bodies slumped at her feet wore black Quiration burkas and a third was dressed in what looked like a Cosmotech uniform. Kurt couldn't tell if they were dead, but the question quickly lost importance when he recognised one of them. It was the same woman Cosmotech were trying to capture in their Lynt City offices. Her name was simple... sounded Russian...

"Anya Polovski?" he mumbled. "What're you doing here? And why are you wearing a Cosmotech uniform?"

Not sure how to even guess at an answer, Kurt nevertheless knew she was somehow mixed up in this mess. And given Hani'ah's condition, he could only hope she was the one Saadi had been talking about.

He quickly turned to the officer he'd brought with him.

"Watch the entrance to this platform," he ordered. "Uh... both of them. Don't let anyone inside."

The officer raised his rifle to do as commanded and Kurt quickly moved to Anya's side. For a moment he looked up at the pulsing red sphere of energy. It didn't seem so volatile now, but even as he hoped it meant something was going right, another bolt of lightning speared out to crash into the space station.

"Shit!" he swore as the station shuddered beneath his feet.

Again, he felt an urge to get the hell out of there, but there was no turning back now. If his platform was going to be hit then it was going to be hit. He had other things to worry about.

Turning his gaze to Anya, Kurt carefully knelt down beside her and gently turned her head upward. Her eyes were open at least, but she didn't react to his presence or touch. It was only when he pressed his ear against her mouth and heard the faint rasp of air that Kurt knew she was alive.

"Thank God," he sighed in relief. "I don't know what I would have done if you were dead."

Shifting into a more comfortable position, Kurt placed Anya's head in his lap and looked into her eyes. They didn't seem focussed on anything and only seemed to move in response to him moving her body.

"Um... I need you to wake up, Anya," he said, hesitantly. "I don't know what's going on here, but I was told that you – well, I think Saadi meant you – are the only one who can restore the balance. Don't ask me what balance we're talking about here, because I have no idea. But if it *is* you, then you broke something... I'm guessing. Look, either way, you have to fix it."

Feeling a bit stupid now, Kurt stared at Anya's blank expression and felt frustration roll through him.

"Okay, look," he said slowly. "I'm going to try something that could help you and, believe me, I'm only trying to help here, okay? So if you wake up, don't... hurt me, or anything. Alright? I know you can be quite violent... when the need arises."

Again, Anya gave no indication she'd heard him or understood anything he was saying.

Kurt sighed.

"Okay, here we go."

Turning her head slightly so he could look her straight in the eye, Kurt allowed his psychic self to flow out of him as he'd done several times now. The connection wasn't as immediate as he was used to, but he did feel something behind her eyes. There was a presence that felt somehow… jagged. Or shattered. It wasn't whole, that was for sure, and there was plenty of emotion mixed in for good measure. Anger, fear, guilt, curiosity…

"*Could you be what's broken?*" he thought with a frown.

Not sure what to do next, Kurt tried using his psychic influence to gently bring the pieces together. At first it seemed to work and he was able to bring two of them so close that they almost seemed to fit together, but as soon as he tried to bring in a third, one of the pieces he'd already moved pulled away from him, as if it didn't want to be near more than one other piece at a time.

He tried the same thing several times, starting with different pieces, but they all acted the same, refusing to be brought together with more than a single other piece.

"*This isn't working,*" Kurt thought to himself.

In frustration, he tried to take a mental step back, but something stopped him. He frowned and tried harder, pulling away from the shattered presence with all his psychic strength, but the more he pulled, the harder he seemed to be held in place.

Feeling a little panicked now, Kurt twisted and turned his psychic self, trying to tear his way free, but the more he struggled the deeper seemed to go. He noticed that the pieces he'd been moving were now forming up around him and as he moved into their centre, everything seemed to fade into shadow around him.

Kurt struggled harder, certain this couldn't be good, but the darkness was overtaking him too fast. In moments, his psychic self was completely swallowed and all connection with his body and the outside world was gone.

Kurt blinked. Suddenly he was standing in a small room with gleaming metal walls. He looked down slowly and saw Anya lying on the floor not far in front of him, curled into a foetal position.

He instinctively knelt down and placed a hand on her shoulder. She looked different to the woman he'd found lying at Hani'ah's feet. Her clothes were no longer that of a Cosmotech employee. Instead, they looked more like a military uniform.

Her eyes were also focussed on nothing, but here, they were also filled with a fear that twisted her expression with anguish.

"Uh... Anya?" Kurt said hesitantly, his voice echoing strangely in the metallic room.

"She won't help you," a voice said behind him.

Kurt shot to his feet and spun around to find himself facing another woman.

"Anya?" he said uncertainly.

She looked... exactly the same as the woman cowering behind him, but somehow different. Her longer hair was tied in a sensible looking bun at the back of her head for one thing, and she wore a grey skirt suit with sensible black shoes and a crisp white blouse, which went nicely with her stern expression.

"Who are you?" another voice asked.

Kurt spun again, certain he couldn't have missed a third person, and was confronted with another version of Anya. This one was dressed much more fashionably, in clothes that reminded Kurt of Yasmin. Her skin was also tanned and smooth and her face was painted expertly as if she were about to head out to a dance club. Her expression also looked quizzical and, for some reason, Kurt immediately caught himself doubting her intelligence.

"You're here to help, I hope," another grating voice added.

Kurt turned again, completely confused now. How could he have missed a fourth person? He'd turned around completely almost twice now.

This one didn't look much like Anya, because it was a man. A much older man, in fact, who wore a lab coat over a neat brown suit. He was also slightly hunched and not so slightly wrinkled, but his expression was calm and gentle at the same time.

"Uh, yes," Kurt said hesitantly. "I'm here to help."

"And how do you propose to do that?" the stern woman asked.

Kurt had to turn around all over again to look at her and found that he was completely confused now.

387

"I don't really know," he admitted, "but it has something to do with fixing something you broke."

"There's nothing broken here," the stern woman replied smartly.

"Are you kidding me?" the attractive one gasped. *"Everything* is broken!"

Kurt turned toward her and again lost sight of the stern woman or any of the others. It was the strangest sensation. He knew he was surrounded by four separate people, but no matter how he tried, he could never see more than one of them at the same time.

"Um... I don't even know where I am," he said slowly.

"You're out of your mind," the old man replied, making Kurt turn to him again. "And inside ours. Although I'm not sure how that can be."

"I think I do," Kurt said with a frown, "but it's complicated."

"Well, spit it out," the stern woman demanded.

Kurt turned to look at her and saw that she had her arms crossed over her breasts and was now wearing an even more disapproving expression.

"Uh, I have... sorry, I was *given* a kind of psychic power," he explained. "It lets me..."

Kurt paused, not sure how to explain his particular talent.

"Control people?" the old man finished for him.

Kurt turned to him in surprise.

"Well... yeah," he replied. "How did you know that?"

"We've witnessed it first hand," the stern woman answered.

"It's what got us into this mess," the attractive one added.

Kurt closed his eyes, unable to keep up with the strange sensation of turning toward each person.

"This is too much," he mumbled.

"How about now?" the old man asked.

Frowning in suspicion, Kurt opened his eyes to find himself staring at a mirror. Behind his own reflection, he was able to see all the different versions of Anya, although none of them were standing close together.

He began to instinctively turn around, but quickly stopped himself. He didn't want to risk going back to seeing them all separately.

"That's... better," he said slowly, "and it makes a kind of sense, really."

"In what way?" the old man asked.

Kurt stared at him for a moment as his thoughts aligned.

"I'll try to explain, but first, can you tell me how you got here? The Cosmotech space station, I mean."

"We were following a boy," the stern version of Anya said.

"Isaac Taylor," the attractive one added.

"We were attacked and sedated," the stern version continued, giving the younger version a disapproving look. "When we regained consciousness a man in the employ of Cosmotech Defence tried to take control of us with the same psychic power you claim to possess. Only his attempt to control us had an unexpected result."

"Our parent personality was imprisoned," the old man finished.

"You don't know that," the stern woman snapped.

"Parent personality?" Kurt asked, confused now.

"We are one mind, split into many," the old man replied.

The words hit Kurt like the answer to a complex mathematical equation.

"You're schizophrenic?" he said.

"We are multiple personalities," the stern woman corrected him, "kept in check by our parent personality who has been absent since we were attacked."

Kurt's eyes went wide as he contemplated what they were saying.

"And what happened after the attack?"

Anya's personalities turned to look at the woman cowering on the floor behind Kurt.

"Who is she?" he asked.

"She is our guilt," the old man replied.

"She is our rage," the stern woman added.

"She's our sister," the attractive one finished.

"I don't understand," Kurt said slowly.

"She's been in control ever since our parent personality was taken from us," the old man said.

"She killed someone," the attractive one said sadly.

Kurt thought about the bodies he'd found lying beside Anya and the footage he'd seen of her in the Cosmotech offices at Lynt City.

"I think I know who you mean," he replied slowly, thinking hard. "So... how do we find and free this parent personality?"

"Don't you think we would have do so already if we knew?" the stern woman snapped.

"Of course," Kurt said, raising his hands in a placating gesture. "I just... I think I'm here to help you fix this, so... any information you can give me would be... useful."

"I don't see how you can do anything," the stern woman replied, crossing her arms again.

Kurt could see he wasn't going to get any answers from Anya's personalities and so he paused to think about his predicament for a moment. None of this was familiar to him, but there was a strange logic to it all. Rules that he could use to his advantage, if he could only work them out.

He stared at the mirrored surface that allowed him to see Anya's multiple personalities. Without it, he couldn't see more than one of them at a time. What part of Anya did this represent?

"*Wait a minute,*" he thought. "*What was it Saadi said? Something about shattering the parts... or something. To restore the whole. That's it. Shatter the parts to restore the whole.*"

Slowly, Kurt reached out and touched the mirrored surface.

"What's behind this?" he asked.

"Behind it?" the stern woman said with a frown. "Nothing, it's a mirror."

"We don't know," the old man corrected her.

"Really?" Kurt said slowly, feeling like he was finally getting somewhere. "Well... in the absence of any other ideas, I think it's worth finding out. What do you think?"

He pushed against the mirror, hoping it would give a little, but the surface was hard and didn't budge. He looked at his fist for a moment and wondered if he was going to feel anything in this psychic form. He could still feel the sting of his broken arm, but it otherwise worked fine in this strange mental landscape.

"*Worth a try,*" he thought with a shrug, before slamming his fist into the mirror as hard as he could.

Thankfully, there was no pain whatsoever and a slight shudder did roll through the mirror from the point of impact, but it was far from a shattering blow.

"Damn," he said with a frown. "I'm not strong enough."

He glanced at the reflection of Anya's personalities.

"Do you think you could help?" he asked. "Something tells me this could provide an answer or two."

The personalities looked at each other for a moment then the old man shuffled forward and smacked his own hand against the mirror. His feeble hammering did even less than Kurt's.

A moment later, the attractive one stepped forward as well and, after studying herself for a moment, ran a finger gently over the makeup under one eye.

"How about we do it together?" she said.

"Good idea," Kurt said, "On three, okay? One, two, *three!*"

This time all three of them hit the mirror together and it shuddered much more noticeably.

"It's still too strong," he said with a sinking feeling.

"Oh, for pity's sake," the stern version of Anya said, rolling her eyes. "If we're going to do this, let's do it properly. As hard as you can everyone! On my count, hitting on three. One, two, *three!*"

This time, when they hit the mirror it flexed even further, but still didn't shatter.

"Again!" the stern woman demanded. "One, two, *three!*"

They all hit it again, but the mirror simply flexed and held strong.

"One, two, *three!*" the attractive one shouted, and they all hit it again.

Kurt watched the ripples distorting their reflections and knew it wasn't going to be enough.

"Okay, wait," he said, holding up his hands.

The three personalities quickly stepped back from the mirror and Kurt looked at the reflection of Anya's final personality.

While they'd been hitting the mirror, she'd moved out of her foetal position and was now sitting up and hugging her knees. But apart from the change of position, it didn't look like she knew what was happening.

Kurt stared at her for a moment. He wanted to talk to her directly, but doubted she would respond if he didn't turn away from the mirror. He didn't want to, just in case he couldn't turn back, but after a few moments of thinking he reluctantly turned away.

The first thing he noticed was that all the other personalities vanished as soon as he lost sight of their reflections then he stepped forward and crouched next to the one version of Anya he hadn't heard from yet.

"I know you feel bad about what you did," he began gently.

She flashed him a fiery look at this, but her anger didn't last and she quickly looked away again.

Kurt immediately felt sorry for her. The Divsek had clearly known Anya could be manipulated into killing and didn't care that she might not cope with the emotional consequences.

"You were being manipulated," he continued calmly. "You were being used. I don't know what you were promised, but the people who used you have been doing it to others for years. Centuries, actually. Everything they did to you, everything they told you, was all a carefully calculated fiction designed to bring you to this place and *make* you do what you did."

The woman huddled before him didn't react to the words, but Kurt could tell she was listening.

"But you don't have to accept it," he continued. "You can fight them. You can make up for your mistake by making sure they don't get what they want."

This time, Kurt finally saw a change in her. She looked away from him and her muscles tensed, as if her anger was growing.

"That's right," he continued carefully. "You don't have to take this lying down. Or sitting down for that matter. We need your help! Are you going to let those bastards win?"

At this, the woman turned to look at Kurt with such rage and anguish in her eyes that he quickly got up and stepped back. She glared at him as he went, her eyes filled with an indescribable fury, then she suddenly leapt to her feet and ran at him with her fist raised.

Not sure how his coaxing had gone so horribly wrong, Kurt cringed away from the blow, but instead of hitting him, Anya's enraged personality sprinted past and with a roar that seemed to contain all the guilt, anguish and self-loathing that characterised her, she smashed a fist into the mirror.

Kurt turned in time to see the mirrored surface shudder violently and distort the reflection of Anya's other personalities until they were almost unrecognisable. Then the gleaming surface shattered into a million sparkling pieces.

Behind the glittering carnage, Kurt glimpsed a bright, glowing figure that was far too bright to look at and raised his hand to block out the glare. With the movement, another psychic rush came over him and he felt himself moving backward.

The glare behind his hand quickly faded and when he lowered it, he was surprised to find himself back in the space station, holding Anya's head in his lap. He blinked in confusion, not sure what had just happened, and hoped it meant Anya, the real Anya, was now free.

He felt a sudden urge to drop her and get some distance, just in case, but managed to hold the urge in check. This was it, make or break. If he'd done what Saadi meant him to do, Anya would wake up and help him save the planet. Otherwise…

"*She'll beat seven shades of hell out of me,*" he thought, feeling a little sick.

The tension grew as Anya's vacant eyes slowly focussed on him, but there was no anger in them now, only relief and tears that welled up almost instantly.

"Thank you," she said softly, her eyes glistening.

"Is that...?" Kurt said hopefully.

"It's me," Anya replied with a smile. "The parent personality."

"Oh, thank God," Kurt said, returning her smile with a relieved grin. "I just... to be honest, I'm just making this up as I go."

"Well, it's working," she said, moving to sit up.

Kurt helped her gingerly.

"I don't think it's over yet," he added as Anya slowly got to her feet.

"No," she replied, her face growing serious, "You said something about fixing what was broken."

"Well... yeah, but I thought that was you."

"Not just me," Anya said, turning toward the slumped form of Hani'ah. "I have to fix what I did."

Kurt frowned.

"Uh, I'm not sure that can be fixed." he said slowly.

"We need to help Isaac," Anya said, hobbling to Hani'ah's side in a way that didn't seem to match any wounds Kurt had noticed. Her voice was gruff too, and weak, as if she were suddenly old.

As he frowned in confusion, Anya studied the device strapped to Hani'ah's head.

"He was sharing some kind of psychic connection with this woman," she said in her strange voice. "When we killed her, the balance was broken."

"Balance?" Kurt said excitedly. "That's what Saadi said I had to restore."

"Saadi?" Anya said, turning to him with a stern expression straight from the personality he'd met in her mind. "Who is Saadi? And what are you talking about? You said you would explain."

"I did," Kurt said, taking a step back, "but... well, it might take a while. If I'm thinking what you're thinking, you plan to take Hani'ah's place, right?"

"If it's possible," Anya replied with a nod.

"Then let's get started on that and I'll tell you everything I know as we go. I don't think time's on our side here."

"Yes, you're right," Anya replied briskly. "You'd better talk fast."

"Oh, don't worry," Kurt replied with a grin. "If there's one thing I know how to do, it's talk."

LOC CHARGED ACROSS ANOTHER CONNECTING BRIDGE. His journey from the Security centre had not been an easy, but at least he no longer had to push past people rushing to evacuate. All the Cosmotech employees were now gone and he was alone in the presence of the angry red eye that pulsed at the centre of the station.

Given he was wearing the most advanced zero-G survival suit available, Loc wasn't concerned with the possibility of being flung out into space. But if one of those lightning bolts hit him directly...

"*Keep it together*," he thought firmly, ignoring the gruesome image that rose unbidden in his mind.

He knew he should probably be evacuating with everyone else, but he couldn't afford to leave just yet. Not before he located Dr. Grayson and determined whether there was any way to salvage this clusterfuck of a situation. The Triumvirate would never accept excuses with so much at stake.

Of course, if the situation did prove to be irredeemable then Loc also wanted to know if there was at least enough time to kill Miana Raiken.

"*That bitch has crossed me for the last fucking time.*"

397

The only consolation so far was that he finally knew how she'd corrupted Mr. Drevit and stolen from Cosmotech's Lynt City offices. Miana clearly had the same psychic powers as he did. He didn't know how she'd acquired them, but he assumed the geologist, Naseem Indari, had something to do with it.

"*No wonder the Triumvirate wanted him dead,*" Loc thought grimly.

Sprinting across another walkway, he was just about to activate the connection lock on the far side when a crimson flash lit up the door frame. He spun around, fearing the worst, and was just in time to see a red lightning bolt cut through the walkway behind him. It melted and tore through the structure like the flimsiest plastic sheeting and Loc fell back in alarm, stumbling hard into the connection lock.

"Fuck!" he swore, barely catching himself before falling flat on his arse.

With a snort of disgust, he tore his eyes away from the shattered walkway and was about to keep going when he noticed Dr. Grayson through the connection lock's viewing panel.

"*Finally, you old bastard,*" he thought to himself.

For some reason, Grayson was hunched over a device at the centre of the room and was working on it so feverishly that he didn't even notice Loc's entrance. As usual, the pompous prat was arguing with himself, but there was an unfamiliar manic edge to his voice that kept Loc from getting too close.

"Doctor Grayson," he said loudly. "What are you doing? What's going on with the Jupiter flare?"

Ignoring him completely, Dr. Grayson continued working on the strange-looking device, occasionally hitting it with a tool.

Loc took a cautious step closer and slowly reached out a hand to touch his shoulder.

"Doctor–"

But before he could finish, Dr. Grayson spun round with a wild look in his eyes and hefted the tool in his hand as if he were about to attack.

"It should already be over!" he screamed, as Loc stumbled back. "They said it would never have been! They promised me!"

Taken by surprise, Loc didn't know what to say. He'd always known Grayson was insane, but not this kind of crazy. The man was acting completely unhinged. And if the station's architect was mentally absent, what realistic chance did he have of salvaging anything?

"What are you talking about?" he said, ignoring an urge to simply get the hell out of there. "Who promised it would be over?"

"They're not alone," Grayson snarled, before his face suddenly twisted with anguish and he turned back to the machine he'd been working on.

"Who's not alone?" Loc said firmly. "And where's Isaac?"

"I told them I couldn't kill, I *told* them," Grayson rambled as he attached a thick power cable to the machine. "I did everything they asked. They promised me!"

"Who promised you?" Loc said, grasping Grayson's shoulders and spinning him round. "Tell me what they promised you!"

"The voices!" Grayson screamed, his eyes darting wildly around the room, as if trying to escape his head. "They won't let me stop. Won't let me rest. Won't let me *die!*"

Loc realised then that it was hopeless. Dr. Grayson had gone to a mental place that he couldn't return from without serious medication. And Loc knew better than most that there was no reasoning with a madman.

"Tell me where Isaac is," he said harshly, squeezing his suit's augmented fingers hard enough to ensure Grayson felt pain. "How do we fix this?"

For a moment the pain seemed to focus Dr. Grayson and his wild, roaming eyes snapped into focus.

"They lied to you too," he hissed accusingly.

The words surprised Loc enough to make him let Grayson go and the old man darted back to his machine and pressed a final piece into place.

"They lied to us all!" he screamed as the machine began to emit a loud electronic whine.

Not sure what was about to happen, but certain it couldn't be good, Loc stepped back instinctively and was just in time to avoid a sizzling red lightning bolt that smashed through the ceiling and pinned Dr. Grayson to the side of his machine.

Through his heavily tinted helmet, he saw the old man's skeleton outlined clearly against his luminescent skin, then the suicidal fool exploded into a million wet pieces.

At that point, the lightning strike's shockwave hit Loc and he was thrown backward into the wall behind him. Without his survival suit he would have surely been injured, if not killed, but as he collapsed awkwardly to the floor, Loc felt nothing.

He quickly picked himself up, still a little stunned at Grayson's drastic departure, and saw a warning in his helmet that indicated the air around him was rapidly getting thinner. He looked up and saw a ragged hole in the ceiling that was sucking a cloud of debris and unrecognisable body parts out into space.

His survival suit automatically had already detected the change in pressure and activated his magnetic boots, which allowed Loc to stare up at the breach in safety. He waited a moment for it to be sealed by the station's counter measures, but after several seconds he knew something was wrong.

"*Automatic repair isn't functioning,*" he thought to himself. "*I've got to get out of here.*"

Turning to the connection lock on the far side of the room, he moved as fast as his heavy, magnetic steps could go. It was closed tight to prevent the pressure breach from spreading through the station, but with a quick authorisation code, Loc was soon on the other side.

He had no choice now but to abandon the station. He still didn't know what Grayson was talking about, but the scientist's madness was indication enough that remaining even one more minute on this station was a bad idea.

He quickly activated a map in his HUD to find the nearest escape craft and was taken by surprise when a familiar pain blossomed at the base of his neck. It was more intense than usual and Loc fell to his knees as the psychic connection with the Triumvirate was made.

In a painful flash, they appeared within the empty corridor, standing shoulder to shoulder and wearing grim expressions.

"Masters," Loc said in reluctant greeting.

"You cannot evacuate, not yet," the third said simply.

"The station is compromised," Loc replied. "Grayson is dead. What else can I do here?"

"Go to the primary research platform," the second replied. "Kill Miana Raiken."

Loc liked the sound of that, but at the same time it made him suspicious.

"Why does she matter?" he countered. "This whole place is going to be destroyed when the Jupiter flare–"

"Don't think!" the third snapped. "Time is running out and your place among us will be forfeit if your final task remains incomplete. You *must* kill Miana Raiken!"

Loc gritted his teeth in frustration.

"What about Grayson?" Loc snarled. "He said I was being lied to and I know he's privy to more information than I am. What was he talking about?"

"Doctor Grayson was clinically insane," the first answered this time. "You already know this. He served his purpose many times over, but was always at risk of the kind of psychosis you just witnessed. Don't let his failure pull you down as well. Not when you've almost proven your place. When you're one of us, you will be given all the knowledge and power you crave. You will answer to no one, Loc Breeden, not even us. But you have not proven yourself yet. This final task *must* be done."

Loc knew they were asking him to ignore the suspicions they themselves had created, but it was clear the Triumvirate needed him now more than ever. There was no way to prove they were lying to him, but neither had they ever lied to him before. Not once in the many years he'd worked for them.

But now they were asking him, Loc Breeden, to act on faith. It would have been funny if the stakes weren't so high.

"Of course," he said, getting back to his feet. "I serve the Triumvirate and always will."

"Very good," the second said with a nod. "Now go. Quickly."

"And do not fail," the third hissed.

And then they were gone.

Loc clamped his jaws with a new determination and ran. This was it. This was his chance to finally become one of the most powerful humans in the solar system. And all that stood in his way was Miana Raiken.

"*Time to die, detective,*" he promised coldly.

MIANA WATCHED FOR A SECOND TIME AS MARS WAS destroyed by Jupiter flares. She expected it to be easier to watch since she knew what was coming, but it wasn't. The vision of a vibrant Mars being torn apart made her sick with sadness and watching the present version being assaulted in the same way left her breathless.

The only thing that helped was the knowledge that one hadn't actually happened yet and could still, hopefully, be changed.

When the devastating images were finished, Miana found herself back on the research platform, staring at a pale Isaac Taylor. He didn't look good. There were dark rings under his bloodshot eyes and his body language screamed fatigue.

"What… was that?" he gasped, leaning hard against the railing.

Miana opened her mouth to answer, but the Divsek took control of her vocal chords again.

"The world below as it once was," it said in a solemn tone. "And the past as it currently stands."

"As it currently stands?" Isaac said, squinting in irritation. "What's that supposed to mean?"

"That it can be changed," the Divsek replied. "As it already would be had I not intervened."

403

Isaac gave Miana a momentary look of disbelief.

"I... saw some of it before," he said, blinking slowly. "When I first came here."

"The transition to this reality opened your mind to many things," the Divsek replied.

"You know about that?"

"I do."

Miana didn't know what they were talking about, but she kept silent. This clearly wasn't about her.

"What were those... creatures in the cave?" Isaac asked, referring to the hulking, chanting shadows. "I've seen them before as well."

"They are the reason you are here," the Divsek replied. "They are the Divsek."

"The Divsek," Isaac said with a frown. "Who are the Divsek?"

"That will take more explanation than we have time for," the Divsek replied. "But you will have your answers, Isaac. First, there is more you must see."

Isaac's eyes widened at the news and he quickly looked away. He obviously didn't want to see any more and Miana couldn't blame him. She knew what it was like to have everything you thought you knew about the world pulled into question.

For a moment she even thought Isaac would refuse, but after a few seconds he pushed himself back from the railing, took in a deep breath, and looked at her again.

"Alright," he said determinedly. "Let's get it over with."

At that moment, Miana felt a tide of admiration for Isaac. No one could know how they would react when faced with such horror, but as bad as he might look, Isaac was brave enough to push on.

She felt the Divsek preparing to create a second set of visions in their minds and realised she was excited. This was more information than she'd been provided with so far and she still had many questions of her own.

She slowed her breathing as the research platform began to fade around her, but before anything could take its place a sudden pain stabbed at her temple.

She flinched and blinked in shock, realising her psychic link with one of the security officers had disappeared. She turned to the entrance he'd been guarding and saw a large, armoured figure standing over his body with a rifle pointed in her direction.

Reacting instinctively, Miana dived to the floor and heard a projectile *hiss* overhead. She knew without a doubt there would be more to follow and so she immediately scrambled up and dove for the cover of a workstation.

More projectiles *pinged* off the floor behind her, but none of them bit home. When she was in cover, she saw the other security guard running from the far entrance, but before he could launch a counter attack, a loud voice echoed through the chamber.

"Stop where you are!"

The security guard came to an immediate halt and, before Miana could react, a puff of red mist exploded from the back of his helmet and his head snapped back.

Again, Miana felt a sympathetic pain in her forehead and was forced to close her eyes. In the darkness behind her eyelids, she saw a ghostly image of the armoured figure striding toward her and realised she was seeing the platform through Isaac. Somehow the psychic connection they shared was more than she expected.

In the pale, ghostly image, she tried to make out a face behind the helmet's screen, but Isaac seemed to recognise the wearer before she did.

"Loc?" he said in confusion. "What are you doing?"

Miana felt a cold hand close over her heart.

"*Not him,*" she thought. "*Not now.*"

"Hello, Isaac," Loc replied calmly. "As you're probably aware, the station is under attack. Several terrorists have managed to bypass our security defences and I'm afraid one of them is Anya Polovski. She murdered Hani'ah Naziri, Isaac."

"I... know," Isaac replied hesitantly.

"Another has come to assassinate you," Loc continued smoothly. "Her name is Miana Raiken."

Miana felt Isaac's surprise through the psychic link and knew she couldn't afford to let Loc control the situation like this.

"He's lying, Isaac," she said quickly. "You know I'm here to help."

"Don't believe her," Loc added loudly. "Whatever she's told you, her goal is to destroy this station and end any chance you might have of getting home to your brother."

Miana frowned at Loc's words. She didn't know anything about Isaac trying to get back to his brother, or that he even had one, but if it was true then she couldn't ignore it. Particularly now that Loc was using it against her.

"Whatever you need to do to get back to your brother, Isaac, we can't do it if this space station explodes," she said.

"More lies," Loc replied loudly. "I'm the only one trying to save this station and all those still aboard and that will only happen when you and your terrorist cell are dead."

Miana could tell through the psychic link that Isaac didn't know what to believe. He clearly didn't want to accept Loc's story, but she could sense a hint of doubt that wasn't there a moment before.

"If I die, you save nothing," Miana snapped.

"Another threat, terrorist?" Loc replied.

Miana clamped her teeth in frustration.

"I told you before, Loc, you're being manipulated. You don't understand what's–"

"If anyone is being manipulated," Loc interrupted her smoothly, "it's Isaac. He's risking his life to save our planet and get home to his own reality. All you want to do is use him as a weapon against Cosmotech Defence."

Miana felt a surge of anger at the blatantly manipulative lie and tried to suppress it before Isaac's doubt was fuelled any further.

"Do you even know who you're fighting for?" she asked.

"Spare me your bullshit, please," he replied in a derisive tone. "I've heard more than I can stand. Surrender now and you have my word you will not be harmed."

Miana could feel the situation moving out of her control and tried to think of something that might swing the momentum back in her favour.

"Like the Cosmotech officers you just murdered?" she asked.

"Are you referring to the ones you were controlling with your mind?" Loc countered. "That's what she does, Isaac. Psychically controls the innocent and uses them to fight her battles. Those poor bastards killed seventeen civilians and six security personnel on their way here. Did she tell you about that?"

Miana was prepared for the lie, but Isaac clearly wasn't. His shock was obvious and strong.

"Don't listen to him, Isaac!" Miana cried. "You know I'm not who he says."

"I… don't think she's a terrorist, Loc," Isaac said slowly. "She was helping me control the Jupiter flares."

"Are you so sure?" Loc replied in the same calm, convincing tone. "Or was she preparing your mind for control? What fanciful story was she telling you before I got here, Isaac? What was she *showing* you?"

This time, Miana wasn't sure if the lies were having any effect on Isaac because his doubts seemed to be weakening their psychic link. She was losing her connection with him.

"What... about doctor Grayson," Isaac asked, clearly hoping a third party might help clarify things. "Where is he?"

Through Isaac's eyes, Miana saw Loc's expression firm and knew this might be of help to her.

"He's dead," Loc replied flatly. "One of Miana's friends killed him."

"That's a lie!" she yelled, every forensic instinct in her certain of it. "Tell Isaac what really happened to doctor Grayson, Loc. Tell him the truth!"

"He was shot in the head by a terrorist insurgent," Loc countered firmly. "Isaac, you knew what a brilliant man he was. He designed this entire space station. It was no coincidence Miana had him targeted him for assassination."

"Your lies are going to catch up to you, Loc," Miana warned, again trying to remain calm. "There are forces at work here that–"

"Enough!" Loc snapped, cutting her off, "I'm sorry, Isaac, but Miana Raiken has been committing crimes against Cosmotech Defence for decades. I know you don't have all the information, but I simply can't afford to let her get away again."

At this, Miana heard his boots approaching her position. She looked around for a place to retreat, but there was nowhere to go. He was going to walk right up and shoot her point blank.

"*What do I do?*" she thought desperately.

"*Face him,*" the Divsek spoke in her mind.

"*Are you serious? He'll shoot me,*" Miana replied.

"*I will keep you safe,*" the Divsek added.

"*Like you did with Naseem?*" Miana asked, feeling a little wretched even as she thought it.

"*Please, Miana,*" the Divsek replied calmly, "*you must stand and face him. It is the only way this will last long enough for Kurt to restore the balance.*"

At the mention of Kurt, Miana felt her heart skip a beat and wanted to curse out loud. She couldn't be sure the Divsek meant to manipulate her in this way, but it was hard to think otherwise.

"*Alright, fine,*" she thought, closing her eyes and steeling herself. "*I've trusted you this long. I guess I shouldn't stop now.*"

"*Thank you, Miana,*" the Divsek. "*I promise this will all be over soon.*"

"Yeah, yeah," she said beneath her breath.

Every protective instinct screamed for her to run, but instead Miana firmed her jaw and pushed herself up off the floor. As she rose in front of Loc, she saw his expression twitch into a grin and knew he wasn't going to hesitate. This was it. She was finally giving her life to this bizarre cause.

Then her vocal chords once more worked of their own volition.

"Throw the weapon away," she said clearly.

Loc's arms jerked in response and the weapon he'd been holding clattered noisily across the floor.

His smug expression went from satisfaction to shock in an instant.

"How did you-?" he began, then his eyes flashed red and his face twisted into a snarl of outrage. "Betrayer!"

Behind Loc, five looming figures seemed to materialise out of the air and Miana took a frightened step back. Their eyes glowered angrily, almost the same colour as the Jupiter flare, but the rest of their hulking bodies remained shrouded in shadow.

"*The other Divsek,*" she thought with a chill, then the one inside her mind spoke again, "Welcome, brothers."

"You are *nothing* to us," Loc snarled in reply. "Tell us why you have done this. Tell us why you are jeopardizing our world's only chance for salvation."

"You know why," the Divsek replied with Miana's voice. "You believe what you've seen was a solution. I have seen beyond that solution to even more dire consequences."

"Lies!" Loc screamed. "Your visions are flawed. Twisted by a false ideology!"

"My ideology comes from my visions," Miana's Divsek replied firmly, "not the other way round."

"Then they are aberrations of a sick mind," Loc countered.

"No. The sickness is yours, brothers."

Loc took a jerky step forward at this, as if barely restraining himself from physical attack.

"You would condemn an entire world to death for the chance of saving a species as undeserving as humans?"

"The fact you believe I fight for the humans shows just how much you misunderstand me," Miana's Divsek replied sharply. "Have you forgotten the first tenant of our faith. *All* life is sacred! Who are we to choose the survival of one form over another?"

"*We* have the weight and wisdom of ages," the Divsek replied. "*You* are but a child with a broken mind, seeing phantoms of the imagination in place of truth."

"My visions do not always come to pass, that is true," Miana's Divsek admitted. "But that is because I see *beyond* the choices that seem to blind you. I see more than one truth!"

"Blasphemy!" Loc screamed.

"No!" the Divsek in Miana's mind snapped back. "If you succeed in saving what was, you doom the future *forever!* Let me show you, brothers, please! Our world cannot be saved, but in time the humans will repopulate our planet. They will bring *new* life."

"Enough lies!" Loc roared. "You talk of dooming the future, but it is your interventions that threaten the rightful timeline. We will not allow you to condemn the past to ruin. Today your blasphemy ends, betrayer."

As Loc spoke, the eyes of the dark figures behind him blazed suddenly brighter and Miana felt an almost physical pressure close over her mind. She waited for the Divsek inside her to fight back, to say something more and convince its brothers to keep talking, but Loc's voice boomed through the research platform instead.

"Stop breathing!"

As soon as the words registered in her mind, Miana felt her chest muscles constrict and the air paused in her throat.

"*No,*" she thought helplessly.

She wanted to breathe, *needed* to breathe, but she couldn't find the will to even try. She could feel the Divsek fighting against the psychic pressure that was literally suffocating her, but it seemed as helpless as she was.

"You've lost your faith," Loc said, striding toward her and bringing the hulking, shadowy figures with him, "and all the power that comes with it."

Miana tried not to panic, knowing it would only make her oxygen need spike, but even that seemed beyond her control. Her heart thumped faster as adrenalin was dumped into her veins and all she could do was fall to her knees.

"As you fade into nothing," Loc continued, standing over her now, "know that it was not us, but your own misguided ideology that defeated you."

Shadows swirled at the edge of Miana's vision, making the figures behind Loc seem to grow even more frightening, and she realised that it was over. The psychic connection with Isaac was nearly gone now and the throbbing pain in her temples assured her that unconsciousness was close.

"Let go," Loc said, for the first time not unkindly. "Trust in your brothers. Let us save the future you fear."

And Miana gave up. Her fight was over, one way or another, and yet instead of regretting the fact that Isaac would be overwhelmed and the Jupiter flares set free to ravage the station and the planet below, she found herself regretting the kiss she would never receive.

"*I'm sorry, Kurt,*" she thought in despair. "*I tried…*"

Isaac watched the confrontation between Loc and Miana in stunned disbelief. He had no idea what was going on. The images Miana had shown him were shocking enough and made her worth listening to, but after Loc had intervened, all that was thrown into confusion.

For a moment, he'd almost accepted that Miana really was some kind of crazy, psychic terrorist, but then Loc's eyes had blazed red and he'd changed in a way that was more frightening than anything he'd accused Miana of.

And to make matters worse, the psychic pressure from the Jupiter flares was building again. Whatever Miana might or might not be, she was helping him control the massive amounts of energy being forced into his mind and Loc's actions were ending that assistance.

"You have to stop," he gasped, barely able to get the words out.

But Loc didn't give any indication he was listening.

"Please, stop," Isaac said through gritted teeth. "She was helping me!"

But Loc just ignored him again and another wave of psychic pressure closed on his mind.

He saw Miana fall to her knees and the psychic link they shared became almost too weak to sense. He groaned in pain and gripped the railing with trembling hands, trying to think of something that might help, but it only reminded him of how useless he really was without his brother.

"Jason was always the one with the answers," he thought with a grimace.

He missed his brother so much. He knew he'd never created anything of real value without Jason's help and it was becoming painfully clear that the same rules applied here. He couldn't do this on his own any more than he'd done anything else.

"I'm sorry I never thanked you, bro," he thought wretchedly. *"You were always my better half."*

The regret washed through him like a fever and Isaac imagined he could feel the point at which his mind would finally give in. He had no idea what would happen, but from the pain he was experiencing, he assumed his brain would simply melt in his skull.

Of course, it was just as likely the Jupiter flares would break free from their containment and obliterate him along with the space station in a sudden, fiery explosion. He only hoped the end would be quick. After all this effort and pain, Isaac just wanted this nightmare to be over.

He felt his muscles tense as he prepared for whatever ending he was destined to endure, but was surprised when a familiar voice spoke suddenly in his mind.

"Isaac? Can you hear me?"

412

As soon as the words registered, the psychic pressure seemed to fade away and Isaac was left blinking in shock. For a moment, he thought it was his brother and felt a surge of irrational hope, but then his groping mind realised the psychic connection he'd held with Hani'ah was back in place.

"Anya?" he said hesitantly, as his memories stepped forward to recognise the voice.

"*It's me,*" she replied in his mind.

Isaac was once again left dumbfounded and he took a moment to reply.

"*What... are you doing?*" he asked, in his head this time.

"*Trying to make up for what I did,*" Anya replied grimly.

Isaac's memories flashed back to the images he'd seen just before the psychic connection had been severed.

"*Is Hani'ah...?*" he began, but was unable to finish the question.

"*She's dead, Isaac,*" Anya replied, her voice filled with regret. "*I killed her. I'm so sorry. Fayina took control and there was a... someone promised her I'd see my twin sister again if...*"

Anya's voice trailed into silence.

"*You have a twin sister?*"

"*I did,*" Anya replied.

"*Did?*" Isaac thought with a frown. "*What do you mean? Is she alright?*"

"*It... will take a while to explain,*" Anya replied.

With the mention of time, Isaac remembered Miana and looked at her with a feeling of dread. She was still kneeling in front of Loc, but her face was dangerously pale and her lips had turned blue.

"*It'll have to wait,*" he said quickly. "*Do you know a woman named Miana Raiken?*"

"*She's not breathing,*" Anya replied, just as quickly.

"*You can see her?*"

"*Through your eyes,*" Anya confirmed, "*but I can... feel it too. What happened?*"

Isaac took a deep breath.

"*She was helping me control the Jupiter flares,*" he explained, not sure how much to tell her. "*We were sharing some kind of psychic link, but Loc Breeden – he's the guy standing over her – he's controlling her somehow. I… don't know what to do.*"

Anya remained silent for a moment and Isaac imagined he could feel her thinking the problem through.

"*Tell her to breathe,*" she said after a moment.

"What?" Isaac said out loud.

"*Trust me, Isaac. Just tell her to breathe, quickly!*"

Isaac frowned. He didn't know how that was supposed to help, but at this point, he was willing to try anything.

"Miana?" he said loudly, "You have to breathe, Miana. Breathe!"

He felt silly saying the words out loud and didn't expect anything to happen, but to his surprise Miana reacted immediately. It was as if he'd cut an invisible rope around her neck and she fell forward, choking in air as her oxygen starved lungs tried to fix the imbalance.

Relief flooded through Isaac and he could tell through the psychic link that Anya felt the same.

"No!" Loc screamed, spinning toward Isaac with literal fire in his eyes. "Stay out of this, Isaac!"

As he spoke, Loc's eyes blazed suddenly brighter and the fire seemed to spew forth in a red wall that rushed toward Isaac.

He raised his arms instinctively and partially turned away, but rather than physical pain, something slammed into his mind with a force he'd never experienced. He fell backward with a yelp, smacking his lower back into the railing behind him, and then stumbled to his knees.

"*Isaac! Are you alright?*" Anya said, her voice barely making it through the ringing pain in his mind.

"What… was that?" he gasped as it gradually faded.

"*Some kind of psychic attack,*" Anya replied. "*I felt it too, although not as bad as you probably did.*"

"It hurt like hell," Isaac groaned, grimacing as he slowly got back to his feet.

He looked around the platform, expecting to see some kind of damage, but the red fire that had rolled over him hadn't left a mark. He turned back to Miana, who still lay gasping on the ground, and saw Loc lifting an armoured leg high in the air above her.

"No!" he cried out in alarm, realising in horror that he was going to stamp it down on her head.

But before Loc could land the crushing blow, Miana held up a hand and barked in a gravelly, but distinct voice.

"Stop!"

Loc froze with his boot hovering threateningly above her head.

"Impossible!" he screamed. "You have no power over us!"

"Not... on my own," Miana replied, turning her head and revealing eyes that glowed far brighter than Loc's, "but I am no longer alone."

For a moment, Isaac wondered what she was talking about and then... he *felt* it.

"*The Jupiter flares*," he thought, staring up at the pulsing energy construct above them.

A portion of the incredible energies being drained by his psychic link with Anya was somehow being funnelled into Miana.

"*She's using it to overpower Loc,*" he thought in amazement.

When he turned back to Miana, she was slowly getting to her feet.

"It's time for you to see what I've seen," she said, confronting Loc face to face.

"Lies!" Loc snarled defiantly.

"Be silent!" Miana snapped and her eyes blazed brighter for a moment, causing Loc to stagger backward and bring his hovering boot down hard. "There is *no* more time for denial!"

Then she turned to Isaac.

He took an involuntary step back as her blazing red gaze locked onto his.

"It is time for you to see the truth also, Isaac Taylor."

Nodding uncertainly, Isaac flinched when Miana's eyes flashed again, but instead of a rolling wall of red flame the light caused a shadow to appear in the air behind Miana. It was taller and much larger than she was, but its body was completely bathed in shadow so that all he could see was an outline.

Like Miana, its eyes also blazed with red fire and Isaac got the distinct impression they were looking right at him.

"I am a Divsek, speaking through the body of Miana Raiken. And these," she said, gesturing toward Loc, "are my brothers."

The air behind Loc shimmered as if seen through a heat haze and five new shadows appeared. These were much larger than the one behind Miana, but their fiery eyes were not as bright.

Isaac stared at the strange, nightmarish figures for a moment and realised he'd seen them before. It was only for a moment, but these were undoubtedly the shadows he'd seen standing behind Hani'ah when they tested P.A.T.R.I.C. in the Bas Quirat.

"We are from the planet you see below," Miana continued, bringing his focus back to the figure looming behind her. "A living version of Mars that existed many millions of years ago."

As she spoke, the research station faded away and Isaac found himself standing on the edge of a cliff again, staring out across a vibrant, green landscape. At first he assumed it was the same place Miana had shown him before, but as his roaming eyes picked out new details in the landscape, he realised there were differences.

The most obvious were the forests, which were clearly older. At regular intervals, thick, powerful trees that towered to impossible heights emerged from the dense canopy and between their colossal branches, Isaac could see beautifully crafted habitations strung together like enormous vines. Even from this far away, he could see they were teeming with intelligent life.

Along with the giant trees, the rocky hills that occasionally broke through the canopy were not the simple, if elegant sculptures he'd seen earlier. These were carved into enormous castle-like structures and their intricacy rivalled even that of the Bas Quirat.

As Isaac gaped at them in wonder, his eyes caught a glimmer of light coming from the rivers and he saw that these too looked as if they'd been sculpted. They glittered with crystalline structures that seemed to funnel the water into small inlets and larger lakes with their own strange, crystalline cities. Tiny motes of light and shadow moved within the glittering structures and Isaac knew they too were full of intelligent life.

There was so much to see that he felt overwhelmed for a moment and it was a comfort when Miana spoke again, only this time in his mind.

"*In the absence of the Jupiter flare, our world thrived,*" she said solemnly. "*Under the Divsek's guidance, sentient races were shown how to connect, integrate, and work together in ways that advantaged all living organisms.*"

Isaac felt a sense of warmth and compassion along with the words and the cynic in him wondered if such a utopia would ever be possible in a world with humans.

"*But this perfect world was not destined to last.*"

At this point, the sky changed from brilliant blue to star-filled darkness. The forests, mountains and rivers took on an almost magical appearance as artificial lights glimmered within the alien cities. But it was not the only light Isaac could see. There was something else casting a flickering glow across the landscape.

He turned to the stars for an explanation and found there were more than he expected. Most of them seemed to appear and disappear like glitter falling through the air, but some streaked across the sky before winking out.

"*Meteorites,*" he thought in realisation.

For some reason, there were millions upon millions of tiny meteorites burning up in Mars' atmosphere. But even this strange phenomenon couldn't explain the flickering light that covered the landscape.

Looking up further, Isaac turned to the part of the sky that was partially obscured by the mountain behind him. It was here that the night sky was the brightest and as he watched in ominous anticipation, an enormous, blazing white shape began to emerge from the summit.

417

"*Oh no,*" he thought in recognition.

"*The Vita Nova,*" Miana confirmed in his mind. "*It has passed through our solar system several times, but its unique trajectory has only created the possibility of a Jupiter flare on two separate occasions.*"

Isaac watched wide-eyed as the full majesty of the comet was revealed and it began to ponderously cross the sky. It was moving so slowly that it was hard to accept it was travelling at thousands of kilometres every second, but its crawling speed only reinforced how enormous it actually was.

"*The Vita Nova was never destined to intersect with a planet,*" Miana continued, "*but by preventing the first Jupiter flare from ever touching our world, my brothers will unwittingly place it directly in the comet's path.*"

Isaac followed the sparkling object until it reached the far horizon and gradually began to disappear from view. Then an intense orange light silhouetted the entire horizon.

"*It's reached the atmosphere,*" he thought in horror.

A moment later, the orange light blazed into a sudden flash of white and Isaac was forced to turn away. When the light eventually faded, allowing him to look again, he saw a colossal shockwave rolling over the horizon. It blasted across the landscape with incredible speed and smashed apart the intricately carved mountains he'd only just been admiring, tearing enormous chunks of rock from their spectacular facades and sending them tumbling through the air.

The shockwave then swept across the forests, flattening all but the largest trees and shredded the vine-like cities as if they were no more than brittle leaves. But it was the crystal cities straddling the lakes and estuaries that were hit the worst and as the water feeding them was blasted with the force of the most violent hurricane, they shattered into sparkling dust.

Isaac trembled in abject horror, and yet despite the terrible carnage he was witnessing, he knew this was only the beginning.

The ominous certainty churned unpleasantly in his gut and when he returned his gaze to the horizon, he saw a harsh orange glow was now outlining the mountains. As he watched, the light seemed to grow in intensity then the horizon itself began to lift into the sky.

Frowning in confusion, Isaac couldn't work out what was happening until he saw the orange light appear through cracks in the rising horizon.

"*Oh… jatz,*" he thought with a chill.

The distant landscape was literally cracking apart as a planet-shattering earthquake forced its way out from the point of impact. What he saw rising above the horizon was the loosened bedrock exploding into the atmosphere in a seismic wave of destruction.

A cold hand closed over Isaac's heart. Whereas the initial atmospheric shockwave had merely pushed things over, smashed them, or thrown them into the air, the destruction now rolling toward him was beyond comprehension.

A giant curtain of bedrock rose into the night sky like a perfect tsunami and, beneath its colossal shadow, the mountains and forests were smashed apart like delicate porcelain. The terror in Isaac's chest spiked as the wall of destruction rushed toward him, but before it could reach the mountain he was standing on, the image suddenly went dark.

"*Destruction will be total,*" Miana said solemnly in the darkness. "*All life on this world will be extinguished. And yet the consequences do not end here.*"

From the darkness, stars began to appear around Isaac and he realised he was now floating in the vacuum of space. He looked around, searching for anything familiar, and found it looming not far beneath his feet. It was the unmistakable, half-illuminated planet Earth.

"*Not only will the Vita Nova destroy our world,*" Miana continued, "*but the shrapnel it casts out into the solar system will eventually find its way to Earth.*"

The fear in Isaac suddenly grew colder. At first, he didn't see any sign of what Miana was talking about then he noticed a shadow passing across the portion of Earth that was lit by the sun.

Just like the Vita Nova, the colossal chunk of Mars moved at barely a crawl, but Isaac knew it must be travelling at an incredible velocity to move even that fast. He followed it with his eyes, unable to look away, until the giant rock reached Earth's fragile atmosphere and disappeared in a flash of bright white light.

From this new vantage point, Isaac could see the pressure wave it created rolling through the cloud-filled atmosphere with a violence that must have been terrible on the ground. Then the colossal rock hit the Earth's surface and another, brighter flash blazed across the heavens. When it eventually faded, a circular curtain of material could be seen rising out of the atmosphere. It was an incredible sight to behold and Isaac felt he could now fully appreciate the terrible carnage he'd just witnessed on Mars.

When the growing edge of the impact crater finally ran out of energy, a moon-sized circle of destruction was left on the planet's surface and, inside it, a bubble of seething, red-hot gases rose up like a blister.

As Isaac watched in horrified fascination, the glowing cloud rolled out beyond the edge of the crater and slowly began to consume the Earth.

"In a single day," Miana said grimly, "vaporized rock the temperature of the Sun's surface will completely cover the planet. It will burn every forest, boil every ocean and sterilise all life on the planet. Even down to the smallest microbe."

As she spoke, the Earth began to look more like a ball of fire than one of water and continents, and just when Isaac thought he couldn't bear to see any more, the image changed.

Now he was standing on a hell-like plain of fire, surrounded by charred rock cut with glowing veins of red. Above him, thick black clouds churned in violent motion, spewing fireballs and meteorites down like rain to smash into the charred surface. In the distance, bubbling lakes of molten material gushed across the landscape and screaming tornados of fire and smoke danced above them in tortured lockstep.

It was the most inhospitable place Isaac could imagine and yet the most frightening thought was that this could actually be Earth's future.

"*As with our world,*" Miana continued, "*destruction will be total. But even worse than the destruction of our two planets is the fact that neither will ever recover to a state that can sustain life.*"

This final revelation hit Isaac like a sledgehammer and Miana pounded it home with one, final sentence.

"*Life will never gain a foothold in this solar system.*"

With those words ringing in his ears, the nightmarish image faded away and Isaac was once more back in the space station.

He turned to look at Miana, but found her once more focussed on Loc, just as the Divsek behind her was focussed on its brothers.

"You have now seen what I attempted to explain to you, so long ago. Can you understand now why I could not let you go through with your plans?"

"What you have shown us is fantasy," Loc replied, though his voice had lost its manic edge. "If what you say is true, we would have seen it ourselves."

"Your vision is clearer than mine," Miana's Divsek conceded, "but even together you cannot see beyond a moment as critical as this. That is my gift, or my curse, as you call it. I have the ability to see beyond the temporal waypoints that block your visions."

Isaac saw the shadowy figures behind Loc turn to one another, as if conversing silently amongst themselves, but they didn't take long to once more turn their blazing eyes on the Divsek behind Miana.

"No!" Loc barked. "We cannot risk our home on fantasies when so much is at stake."

"Your home is not important," Miana countered. "It is *life* that we ultimately serve! Not any one version of it."

"Do not preach your perverse ideology to us!" Loc roared. "It has poisoned your mind and twisted your visions into worthless nightmares. We will never follow you, tainted one. Betrayer! Blasphemer!"

"Accept the truth!" Miana screamed back at him, her eye blazing red.

This time, Isaac saw a pulse of red energy explode from her eyes and when it reached Loc, one of his hands blazed into flame and he staggered backwards, barely managing to stay on his feet.

The fire didn't last long and when it went out, Isaac saw that the glove of his survival suit had been burned away. The flesh, however, seemed fine and there was a ring on one finger with a large red stone that blazed with the same light burned in Loc's eyes.

"Is that it?" he snarled. "Is that all you have, little brother?"

"No," Miana replied calmly. "That was only meant to weaken you. Whether you believe my visions, or not, you have used humans for the last time."

And with that, the eyes of both Miana and the Divsek behind her blazed the brightest Isaac had yet seen.

"Release Loc Breeden!"

This time, the ring on Loc's finger didn't burst into flames, it exploded, shattering the gemstone into a puff of red dust. Loc's blazing eyes opened wide in disbelief and then he stumbled forward as if an invisible leash had been cut.

Behind him, the shadowy forms of the Divsek suddenly grew more distinct.

"Turn around," Miana commanded.

Loc stared at her with wild eyes, clearly no longer in her control, but he eventually did as she asked. When his gaze finally rested on the looming figures behind him, he shrunk away from them in fear.

"Here are your true masters, Loc Breeden," Miana said coldly. "Here are your manipulators. They have been controlling your every decision and whatever they may have promised you, you were never more than a tool to them. An expendable pawn in a game you were never meant to know existed."

"No!" Loc screamed. "This is all a lie!"

Miana turned to the Divsek looming over Loc.

"Sound familiar?" she asked.

But the Divsek could no longer reply. Without Loc Breeden as their mouthpiece, the shadowy forms could only rage silently, their eyes blazing in anger as they desperately tried to take back control.

Through his psychic connection with Miana, Isaac could feel their clawed mental hands desperately reaching for Loc, but it was hopeless. With the amount of power flowing into Miana from the Jupiter flares, the smaller Divsek was easily able to keep them at bay.

"You have no more power," it told them through Miana. "Loc Breeden is now forever free of your so called *guidance*. And for the first time in his life, he will make a decision based on truth rather than lies."

Miana returned her fiery gaze to Loc.

"Loc Breeden," she said firmly.

Reluctantly, Loc turned to face her, his eyes filled with fear.

"Your decision is simple," she continued grimly. "You will either stay here and help us make this right, or you will go and face whatever future awaits you alone."

Loc stared at Miana, clearly searching for words, then he turned to Isaac with a look of such despair that it made him want to look away.

"*What would I do?*" he thought wretchedly.

Loc blinked slowly, as if he'd finally reached a decision, then he abruptly broke into a run and headed for the exit.

Isaac watched him go with a mix of pity and disappointment. It was clear he'd never met the real Loc Breeden, but he honestly liked the man he'd met in Lynt City.

Turning back to Miana, he found her standing in front of the five larger Divsek, her eyes blazing bright.

"I will not forgive what you have done, or what you were planning to do," she said quietly, "but I will promise to rectify it. May you find peace in the world beyond, brothers."

Then she waved her hand in a wide arc and another pulse of red light surged from her eyes. This one seemed to shine directly through the shadowy figures and a strange groaning noise cut through the air as they faded away.

When they were gone, Isaac realised he'd been holding his breath and so he let it out in an explosive sigh.

"That..." he said beneath his breath, "was intense."

He looked at Miana and unconsciously straightened his back when she turned to him, trying to hide the fear from his face.

"You have no reason to fear me, Isaac," she said with a smile. "But it is time for you also to make a decision."

"Me?" Isaac said uncertainly. "What do you mean?"

"You've seen what will happen if this timeline is erased," Miana's Divsek said calmly. "You were meant to be the unknowing architect of its destruction. As such, you are the only one who can save it."

"I... don't understand."

"This space station was not created to facilitate Cosmotech Defence's terraforming process. It was created solely to interface with P.A.T.R.I.C. and allow the Divsek to create a connection between our past world and this one. Two very distinct points in time."

Isaac glanced up at the twin versions of Mars that turned below the space station.

"*The Divsek promised they could do the same for me,*" Anya said in his mind, her voice filled with regret and anger. "*When I killed Hani'ah, they said I would be taken back in time so I could prevent the death of my sister.*"

Isaac closed his eyes for a moment. He could feel the sadness that came with the words and found it hard to bear.

"Is that even possible?" he asked, directing the question to Miana.

"With the power you now command, there is much that is possible," she replied.

"*It's okay, Isaac,*" Anya added. "*As much as I want my sister back, the past is the past. And after what I've done... I wouldn't deserve such a chance anyway.*"

Isaac knew he probably shouldn't, but he couldn't help feeling pity for Anya. He didn't know what he'd be willing to do if he were in her situation and it was Jason's life on the line, but he doubted he'd be strong enough to avoid such a potent temptation. Even if it meant taking another person's life.

"How will connecting these two timelines destroy this one?" he asked Miana with a frown.

"This space station isn't simply draining the Jupiter flares of their energy," the Divsek explained, "it is also drawing the Jupiter flare from my time into this one. If none of its energy ever reaches my home planet, a time paradox will occur that will very quickly end the existence of this timeline. But not before the destructive force of the first Jupiter flare is spent in a future that no longer exists. Our world will be saved, only to be destroyed thousands of years later along with Earth and all chance of life in this solar system."

Isaac shook his head in astonishment. It would have been a brilliant plan if it were not for the 'consequences' Miana's Divsek had shown him.

"So, what's the hold up?" he said determinedly "We obviously can't let that happen. How do we stop it?"

Miana remained silent for a moment.

"You still have a decision to make, Isaac," she said grimly.

Isaac frowned.

"What decision?" he asked.

In reply, Miana gestured behind Isaac and he turned to find a ghost-like figure looking lost and wearing a ridiculous-looking device on his head.

"Jason?" he said incredulously.

"Isaac?" Jason replied, looking up at him. "Oh my God, it worked! Tracy, it worked!"

"Tracy?" Isaac said with a frown. "Who's Tracy?"

"Oh…" Jason said with an awkward smile. "Uh, just a friend, I guess. I… couldn't do it without you, Isaac. So I got some help."

Isaac felt a momentary stab of jealousy and was immediately embarrassed by it. How could he feel that way after all the help he'd been given?

"I hear you, bro," he said, attempting a smile. "I think I probably needed more help than you did. But… how are you doing this?"

"I worked it all out, Isaac," Jason replied, sounding excited. "The experiment threw you out of dimensional phase with our reality. P.A.T.R.I.C. forced too much power into our psychic link and the excess energy altered the dimensional vibration of your molecules. With nowhere else to go, you were spat out in a reality that matched your new dimensional frequency."

"So… are you saying I can get back?"

"Hell yes!" Jason said with a laugh. "Especially with all that energy you're hooked into. I don't know what's going on over there, but your psychic signature is lit up like a Christmas tree! What is that?"

"It… might take a while to explain."

"Well, I don't know how you're doing it, but by my calculations, you've got more than enough psychic energy to alter your dimensional frequency back to normal and get you home."

Isaac felt a sudden chill douse his excitement. He turned to Miana and the Divsek.

You still have a decision to make, Isaac.

"Isaac? Are you okay, bro?" Jason said. "I don't think we should waste any time here. I'll feed you the dimensional frequencies that match our reality so you can tune the phase-shift cycle feeding your skull cap. It took me a while to work out how to do it, but it should be a cinch for you."

Isaac turned to his brother with a heavy heart.

It wasn't fair. He was being asked to sacrifice everything that meant anything to him for the sake of a reality he didn't even know existed a few days ago. He knew he would never willingly condemn all life in this solar system, but at the same time it felt as if the very nature of the decision meant he had no real control over his answer and it made something inside him rebel.

"*Isaac,*" Anya said in his mind. "*I know better than anyone how important Jason is to you. Fayina meant the same to me. You owe nothing to our reality and I know this decision isn't mine to make, but... all I can say is that life without your brother isn't the end you might think.*"

Isaac could sense the truth in Anya's words, but he still wanted to go home. He wanted to leave this decision, this world, this entire experience behind him and return to everything he knew. To his twin brother, Jason, and the special connection they'd shared since birth; to cities and cultures he was familiar with; to his home.

But even as he contemplated being back where he belonged, somehow Isaac knew the satisfaction would be short lived. Whether it was a day, a week, or years later, he would eventually question whether his happiness had been worth the price. And just like the decision he had to make now, there was only one answer.

"Um... bro?" he said slowly.

"We don't have much time, Isaac," his brother prompted him in the stern fashion he knew he wouldn't miss.

"Believe me, I know," Isaac said quickly. "I just... I can't come home."

Jason looked shocked for a moment and then he frowned and shook his head.

"What are you talking about? There's no need to worry. This is going to work, Isaac. I'm sure of it."

"I know it will," Isaac said. "It's just... I've found myself in the middle of something big. Even bigger than getting us back together."

"Bigger than us?" Jason replied angrily, although Isaac could hear the desperation in his voice. "What could be bigger than us?"

"How about the fate of all life in the solar system?" Isaac replied.

Jason remained silent for a long moment, as if unsure how to respond, then he spoke with a tone Isaac had never heard him use before.

"You're serious, aren't you?"

"For once... yeah, bro. I am."

"I can't believe it," Jason said, throwing his arms in the air. "I let you leave this reality for what, only a few days your time? And you go and grow up on me."

"I'm sorry, bro," Isaac said with feeling.

Jason smiled sadly.

"Me too, Isaac. But I trust your judgement. I always have. No matter what I might have said."

"And I couldn't have done any of it without your brains," Isaac countered. "You always did the hard thinking and came up with the important answers."

"Ha! I could easily say the same thing about you," Jason replied.

Isaac smiled, genuinely this time. Who could have guessed he'd feel closer to his brother than ever before and all it took was moving to another reality?

"We'll work something out, bro," he said firmly. "I may not be able to get back today, but you've *got* to hear what happened to me over here."

"You better believe it," Jason replied with a grin. "I've got a few good stories of my own."

"For once," Isaac joked.

"For once," Jason agreed with a nod. "Alright, Isaac. I guess... I guess I'll catch you later then. Good luck with saving the solar system. I... I love you, bro."

"I love you too, bro."

As Isaac watched Jason's ghostly form fade away, tears filled his eyes and a hole seemed to appear in his chest that he wasn't sure he'd ever be able to fill.

Wiping his eyes self-consciously, Isaac turned back to Miana.

"Decision made," he said with a smile he no longer felt.

"Thank you, Isaac," Miana said, and for the first time her eyes weren't filled with red fire. This wasn't the Divsek talking.

"*Yes, thank you, Isaac,*" Anya echoed in his head.

"Don't mention it," he said weakly, with a wave of his hand. "I'm kind of attached to this timeline now. I don't think I could bare to go back knowing this one didn't exist anymore. So... how do we go about saving it then?"

With a smile, Miana's eyes flashed bright again and Isaac knew he was talking to the Divsek once more.

"You must release the power of the Jupiter flare into the past," it said.

"What?" he replied. "You mean I have to intentionally destroy your world?"

"You must allow destiny to unfold as it was meant to," the Divsek countered, "so an entire solar system might continue to serve the sacred tenant of life."

"And what about this timeline? If I release the Jupiter flares, won't both worlds be hit?"

"No," the Divsek replied. "My brothers may have meant to end this timeline forever, but by creating this space station they have unwittingly helped to save it. To ensure enough energy reaches my world, all of the Jupiter flares' remaining power must be directed to the past. Even the one in this time."

"Then I get to at least save one world?"

"*And an entire solar system,*" Anya added in his mind. "*don't forget that.*"

"Well, I guess that'll have to do," Isaac replied.

"Are you ready?" the Divsek asked.

Isaac took in a deep breath and shrugged.

"As I'll ever be," he said, feeling a little lightheaded. "Let's save the solar system."

LOC STUMBLED THROUGH THE SPACE STATION, feeling numb. His mind reeled with what he'd just witnessed, but he couldn't make sense of it yet. All he could think about was getting off this cursed space station.

"*I have to get away,*" he thought desperately.

His survival suit alerted him that a nearby escape pod was available and he pulled himself out of his reverie long enough to activate the entrance. A hatch in the station floor hissed open immediately and Loc wasted no time scrambling down the stairs and into the main passenger space.

There was room for eight people, but with no other life signs within range, the escape pod allowed Loc to start the ignition sequence. The hatch he'd scrambled through quickly closed behind him and he collapsed into a seat, allowing his suit to automatically lock him in place.

As the escape pod prepared for launch, a short countdown appeared in his helmet's HUD and Loc stared down at his now ungloved hand where his red-stoned ring used to be.

It had all been a lie. The Triumvirate were nothing but a figment of his imagination. A carrot on a stick designed to make him willingly dance on the end of someone else's strings.

That crazy bastard Dr. Grayson had been right.

"Fuck," Loc swore savagely, slamming his fist into the seat next to him.

He wondered if the same, maddening sense of betrayal he felt now was what had driven the old man to suicide.

"*No!*" he said firmly in his mind.

He wasn't going to let this end him. Like any fucked up situation there had to be an advantage he could find.

As his mind turned away from his betrayal and clicked into a more familiar gear, Loc began to realise there was an opportunity for *great* advantage. If the Triumvirate no longer existed and never had in any real, physical form, then Cosmotech Defence was now leaderless. There was now a power vacuum in place the likes of which had never been seen in human history. And Loc Breeden was in the perfect position to take advantage.

He was already one of the most powerful people in the organisation. Even Dr. Grayson, one of the most irritating obstacles to his ascension, was now dead and gone. All he had to do was return to Lynt City, consolidate his power base, and come up with a fiction that would convince the rest of the organisation to fall into line. Then he would effectively become the Triumvirate himself.

"*Yes,*" Loc thought with a shiver.

It was perfect. After so many years of playing the role of dutiful puppet, Loc would finally be the one pulling the strings. And it would be so easy. Given their obvious need to remain in the shadows, never making any personal contact with anyone, it would appear as if nothing had changed. No one would have any reason to doubt the new orders delivered by Loc Breeden, the Triumvirate's most trusted diplomatic liaison.

He would have to broker some serious renegotiations following the absolute disaster that was the *Vita Nova* terraforming initiative, but that would be a simple matter after what he'd just been through. In fact, he was already looking forward to the challenge.

Loc smiled as the escape pod's countdown fell to zero and almost laughed as he felt it break free from the space station. It almost felt like he was being reborn and as his brave new future came into focus ahead of him, Loc realised this was how it was meant to be all along.

Through the escape pod's small strip of window, he watched the harsh red glow of the Jupiter flares slowly fading away. Now that he was off Grayson's wretched space station and away from the terrible truth he'd been forced to witness, Loc felt anger join his determination.

"Miana Raiken," he thought with a grimace. *"So much of this is her fault."*

He probably should have thanked her while he had the chance. After all, her actions had been instrumental in removing the Triumvirate and ensuring his ascension to the most powerful position in the solar system. But instead, he wanted her to suffer more than ever.

"After I take over Cosmotech Defence, we'll meet again," he promised in his mind. *"And there will be nowhere you can hide from me, Miana. When I find you, I'm going to enjoy taking you apart, piece by piece. You're never going to fuck with me or my plans again!"*

As he finished his curse, the escape pod began to shudder with the violence of re-entry and a harsh orange glow obscured the small strip of window.

Loc gritted his teeth as the atmosphere screamed past the escape pod and felt a light jolt as the stabilisers kicked in to slow his descent. When the pod guided him safely to the planet's surface, another jolt shook the cabin and Loc's survival suit indicated that he had touched down.

He quickly pulled off his harness, eager to begin the next phase of his career, and moved to the pod's main computer terminal. It took a moment to activate the communication array then he allowed his survival suit to sync with the host program and use it to send out

433

a distress signal. He knew it would call a Cosmotech security team to his location and he would be on his way back to Lynt City within the hour.

As he waited for a response signal, he accessed the emergency suit next to the computer console and took its glove to replace the one that had been burned off earlier. When he was done, he looked to see if a response signal had come in yet.

"*Nothing?*" he thought angrily.

He impatiently refreshed the system-sync and re-entered the command, but again, there was no response.

Slamming his newly gloved fist into the wall beside the computer panel, Loc snarled at it.

"What the fuck are they doing? Someone is going to pay for making me wait."

He quickly commanded the host program to search for other escape pods in the area and watched as a topographical map was constructed in his helmet's HUD. The map pulsed outward from his pod as the sensors searched for recognisable signals, but it soon became clear that no other Cosmotech craft were in range.

Loc frowned. There was something strange about the terrain around his escape pod.

"*Where did I land?*" he thought in irritation.

Confident at least that his survival suit could deal with whatever he might find, Loc activated the escape pod's main hatch and waited as it opened to reveal the terrain outside.

"Oh… shit!" he swore in terror.

It was green. Luscious, rich, and thick. It looked like his escape pod had crashed into a forest and as much as Loc wanted to believe it was some kind of arboretum within Lynt City, or even the Bas Quirat, he knew it wasn't.

"*I'm on the wrong Mars,*" he thought in horror. "*On the way down to the planet, I must have travelled through one of those damned time vortices.*"

He quickly stepped out of the hatch and looked up into a bright blue sky that was even close to the right colour. There was also an evil red glow that could be seen floating far above and he realised that the space station was still there.

"*If I can just get back into orbit, I might be able to–*"

But before he could finish the thought, the red glow in the sky suddenly charred brighter.

"No, no, NO!" Loc screamed in desperate realisation. "I'm not meant to *be* here!"

But his protests went completely unheard and he could only watch in mounting terror as the Jupiter flare speared down through the atmosphere, getting brighter and brighter as it came. Crackling thunder followed it down, getting so loud that Loc's helmet had to muffle the sound to avoid injury, but he could still feel it in his bones.

Loc knew he was in danger, knew he was probably about to die, but he was frozen where he stood, unable to move.

Then the Jupiter flare hit the planet's surface.

The impact must have occurred somewhere far beyond the thick forest that surrounded Loc, but it lit up the canopy in a harsh silhouette against a brilliant white sky. Another roaring sound soon joined the rolling thunder and it seemed to free Loc from his stasis, allowing him to turn and dive for the safety of the escape pod.

In a panic, he managed a single step, but just as he leapt for his life, a colossal shock wave slammed into him with more force than he'd ever experienced. Pain seemed to smash his entire body at once and, in a violent instant, he was lifted off his feet, swept across the small clearing, and slammed into the trunk of a large tree.

The force of the shockwave then flung him up into the air and he travelled several hundred metres before his upward momentum finally began to ease.

This time Loc's survival suit hadn't protected him completely. He felt several agonising breaks as he tumbled downward and shock once more swamped his senses, leaving him feeling weak and cold.

His survival suit reacted quickly by injecting him with a blood protein stabiliser and a powerful local anaesthetic. The concoction took effect almost immediately and with pain no longer blinding his senses, Loc awoke into a raging, sonic nightmare.

The air around him screamed as it tried desperately to fight against the incredible shockwave that forced it through the atmosphere.

At the same time, debris from the shattered planet hammered against his armour with a constant grating *hssssh* interspersed with the occasional bullet-like *ping*.

But worst of all was the roar of the approaching Jupiter flare.

The stabilising jets in Loc's survival suit tried in vain to keep him oriented in the same direction, but the atmosphere they were trying to push against was full of turbulence. He continued tumbling through the sky, helpless and terrified, and could only catch a glimpse of the monstrous red tornado as it scoured across the landscape toward him.

"I'm going to die," he thought with a strange certainty.

It was an odd feeling, knowing his death was imminent. And here, at the very end, for the first time in his life, Loc found himself wishing he believed in something.

The thought made him laugh. A cruel, desperate laugh that defied the reality screaming toward him. Then the red fire surged through the atmosphere and engulfed his completely, turning Loc's laughter into a scream.

The world disappeared in a flood of intense red light and all-consuming pain, and Loc Breeden, last of the Divsek's human pawns, passed on to the world beyond.

KURT PACED AT THE EDGE OF THE PLATFORM, FEELING completely useless. He'd already done everything he could think of to help. The two unconscious women he'd found wearing Quiration burkas were now safely on their way back to Mars in an escape pod. Luckily, he still had the Cosmotech security officer under his control, or it would have been a long and painful task, given his broken arm.

The much trickier detail to deal with was Hani'ah Naziri. Kurt knew all too well how the Quirations would react to the death of their prophet. He'd witnessed their zealous behaviour first hand and knew it wouldn't be pretty. But he believed he'd come up with a solution that would minimise the pain for everyone.

There was no way to hide her death, that much was clear. Hani'ah Naziri was perhaps the most famous person on Mars. So, if he couldn't conceal her death then the only option left was to make it a death the Quirations would accept.

It wasn't as difficult as it sounded. She was an honest to God martyr, after all. And if everything went according to plan, her death would come at the cost of saving *millions*.

437

He knew it would work. The Quirations would never choose to believe their Prophet had died due to a simple bullet to the heart when they could believe she'd saved their planet. All they needed to do now was actually save said planet.

Kurt still wasn't sure how that was going to work. He trusted that Miana and this strange woman, Anya, knew what they were doing and so the most useful thing he could do now was make sure they had a way off the space station if everything went to plan. Cosmotech Defence weren't likely to be very accommodating if they were captured on board.

And so, with the security officer's help, he'd managed to gain access to the station's main computer. There were plenty of classified systems he would never be able to hack, but a map of the station was easy enough and so he had that displayed on one of the enormous viewing screens already.

From there he'd found a ride waiting for them at the security transport terminal. The security officer still under his control had enough access to operate at least two of the jets and it made Kurt feel incredibly grateful. He really didn't like the idea of using an escape pod. They would be far too easy to find for one thing, and if they were intercepted, they would also be helpless. What he needed was a way to reach Mars' surface undetected so they didn't have to explain what had happened here today. At least not before they were ready to.

But that was it. That was as much as he could think to do and now all he felt was anxious.

For what felt like the hundredth time, he turned to stare at Anya and look for some sign they were winning. She'd been talking to herself for some time now, or perhaps to Isaac, but Kurt had stopped listening when the conversation had become technical. Dr. Haig, one of Anya's many personalities, certainly seemed to know what he was talking about.

From the look of it, she still wasn't doing, or saying, anything interesting and so Kurt turned back to the communication grid he'd been working on and continued trying to find a way to talk to Miana.

Suddenly he felt a change in the air.

He looked straight up, sure it had come from the energy construct at the centre of the station, and was just in time to see it dissolve and blast down toward the planet.

"*Is this good or bad?*" he wondered, following the colossal red lightning bolt with wide eyes.

The sight of the Jupiter flare roaring into the distance was awesome enough, but when it struck the planet Kurt felt as if he'd been dunked in an icy pool of water. The incredible amount of energy being transferred to the planet was *devastating*. Shockwave after shockwave coursed outward from the point of impact and even from this far away, Kurt could see the rocky surface breaking apart as the Jupiter flare ripped deep, glowing gashes across the planet.

For a moment he could only watch the carnage unfolding beneath them, then his senses returned to him in a rush and he spun toward Anya.

"What happened?" he asked loudly, racing over to her. "Did you lose control?"

"It's okay," Anya replied calmly, although she looked as if she was concentrating hard. "This was deliberate. We're directing the Jupiter flares down to the past version of Mars."

"What?" Kurt said. "Why?"

"It's the only way to save all life in the solar system," she replied. "Don't worry, there'll be time to explain later. Which is more than I could have said a few minutes ago."

Kurt stared at her in disbelief, but decided not to interrupt her with any more questions. He was alive, after all, and Anya seemed confident that this was deliberate and they still had things under control.

He turned back to the raging river of energy that streamed through the space station and followed it down to the planet once again.

Somehow, the knowledge it was only the past version of Mars that was being destroyed didn't make him feel any better. He'd seen that world through the eyes of its inhabitants and couldn't help but mourn their terrible loss.

As he watched in awe and wallowed in guilt and sadness, the carnage seemed to continue for an eternity until the Jupiter flares feeding into the station from deep space began to grow thinner. After only a few minutes, the diminishing flow seemed to reach a critical point and, abruptly, the colossal lightning bolt faded away.

Kurt blinked in surprise. The change in illumination was stark. Whereas moment ago the research platform had been awash with harsh red light, now it was made up of greys, whites and silver. And everything seemed to be tinged with an odd blue colour.

He knew it was probably just an after-effect of seeing so much red light, but it still felt strange.

"Is that it?" he asked Anya.

She looked at him with old, tired eyes and Kurt knew she was going to speak with her old man voice.

"That's it," she confirmed.

"It didn't seem to go on for very long," he said uncertainly.

"Time has been dilated via the transition between worlds. The Jupiter flare experienced by the past Mars would have gone on for many hours."

Kurt turned to what was left of the planet she was talking about and could easily believe it. The surface was a fiery mess. He could see earthquakes and violent volcanic activity still tearing the landscape apart and there were several glowing scars left by the passage of the Jupiter flare that could almost have been the birth of the Valles Marineris Canyon.

As he surveyed the destruction, the temporal hole in space that allowed them to see it slowly began to close and the terrible image gradually faded from sight. As the present version of Mars took its place, Kurt imagined he could see some of the destruction mirrored in geographical features forever locked within the planet's bedrock.

"We just killed an entire planet," he said quietly.

"And saved an entire solar system," Anya added.

Kurt turned to her and saw that she was taking the device she'd used to psychically connect with Isaac off her head.

"So that's really it?" he asked. "It's over?"

"It's over," she confirmed, sounding like her parent personality again.

"Do you know what they're doing over there? Is Miana okay?"

"She's fine, Kurt," Anya said. "And she's looking forward to seeing you again."

A sudden need to go to her rolled through Kurt and he turned to the console he'd been hacking with a desperate frown. The communications network still wasn't connected.

He quickly turned back to Anya.

"Do you... know how to contact the other research station?" he asked.

In reply, Anya hunched forward and her face became haggard once more as her old man personality took over.

"That shouldn't be a problem," she said, shuffling toward the console.

She mumbled to herself in the old man's voice for a moment as she pored over the controls then she tapped on the control desk, ran through a quick sequence of commands, and an image appeared on the large screen above it.

"Miana," Kurt said, recognising the figure standing a few metres back in the image.

Miana turned toward the camera transmitting the image with a look of surprise. Then she recognised Kurt and the way her face lit up made his heart leap with joy.

"Thank God you're not hurt," he said in a rush.

"I wish I could say the same about you," Miana replied.

Kurt glanced down at his immobilised arm.

"Oh, that," he said, looking back at her, "it's nothing. I'll be fine. But before we do anything about it, first we have to get off this station."

"You sound like you have a plan," she said with a smile.

"You know me so well," Kurt replied with a grin. "I'll send you a map. Follow the co-ordinates to the security terminal. We're taking a jet out of here."

"Another good plan," she said simply. "I look forward to seeing you in the flesh, Kurt. I have a promise to keep."

Kurt felt another thrill at the thought of locking lips with her. It felt like he'd wanted to kiss her forever.

"I better get moving then," he said with mock excitement that almost, but didn't quite, match the actual feeling that pounded in his chest.

"See you soon," Miana finished with a smile.

As the image winked out, Kurt felt a rush of exhilaration that almost took away the lingering pain in his arm.

"Right, let's go," he said, turning to Anya.

"I'm staying," she replied abruptly.

"What?" Kurt said with a frown. "What are you talking about?"

"I committed murder, Kurt," she replied simply. "I have to face the consequences."

"Are you insane?" he said incredulously.

Anya gave him a stern look and Kurt realised who he was talking to.

"Oh, right. Look, forget I said that. But you *can't* stay and face the consequences, Anya. The Quirations will crucify you. Possibly *literally*. You do know who you killed, don't you?"

"No," Anya replied. "But it doesn't matter. What matters is she's dead because of me."

"Hang on a minute, didn't you just say a minute ago that the entire solar system is alive because of you?"

"Yes, but–"

"Well there you are then," Kurt said firmly. "And don't forget, you were being manipulated by evil aliens, or indigenees, or whatever you want to call them. The Divsek. They made you do it, Anya."

"I wanted to do it," she replied quietly.

Kurt looked at her with his mouth open.

"Okay," he said slowly, "we've all done things we regret in the past few days. Hell, I've broken so many laws there's probably a system-wide manhunt with my mugshot being used to train up bounty hunters. But it's the context that counts, Anya. We saved *millions* of lives here today, not even taking into account what you just told me."

Anya turned away, looking more distraught than ever and Kurt got the impression she wasn't going to budge.

"Look," he said, lowering the volume a little, "the Quirations are going to want an explanation that makes sense here, don't you think? And if you ask me, there are only two that will cut it. The first is that a crazy infidel from the hostile world outside their beloved Bas Quirat killed their even more beloved Prophet. Now that would stir up a hornets' nest in ways I don't even want to imagine. They'll probably declare war on the rest of Mars and all those lives we just saved will be lost in a senseless bloody conflict."

Anya didn't say anything at this, but Kurt could tell she was listening.

"*Or,*" he said with feeling, "you can let go of your guilt for the good of everyone we just saved and let the Quirations believe that their prophet sacrificed herself to save everyone. She'll become a Holy martyr in the best traditions of their faith and her followers will forever remember her as the Prophet who saved their world. Tell me, Anya, which do you prefer?"

"They're both lies," she replied bluntly.

"Exactly," Kurt said, flinging his good arm up in the air. "Do you really think they'll accept the truth? Even if they understood it? We're talking *legends* here, Anya! This day is going to be spoken about for *centuries!* Whatever the Quirations choose to believe happened here, it's almost guaranteed to be something grand enough to fit the persona they've worshipped for *generations*. Are you getting what I'm saying here?"

Anya looked at him with a piercing gaze that Kurt found hard to match, but he held it anyway. This was one argument he couldn't afford to lose.

"I get it," she said with a nod.

"Then which is it going to be? Are you going to salve your conscience and risk that *your* truth will be twisted into a monster beyond your control? Or are you going to make this right some other way and let the Quirations come up with their own truth?"

Again, Anya looked at him with a severe expression.

"Tell me, Kurt, what is your profession?" she said sternly.

"Uh… I'm an adventurist," he replied, a little surprised at the question. "A sports guide… in a way."

"Really?" she said with a raised eyebrow. "Well you appear to have a rather advanced understanding of Quiration psychology."

"I've… um, met many of them in my travels," he replied uncertainly.

"And bedded quite a few, no doubt," Anya said, more statement than question.

At this, Kurt truly didn't know what to say, but Anya didn't allow the silence to go on for long.

"Very well," she said. "I will put my needs aside for now. But if this turns into something my admission can help, I won't hesitate to turn myself in."

"That's fair, that's fair," Kurt said, relief flowing through him. "I know I can't ask for anything more."

"Well," Anya said, a small smile on her face. "If we're going to get out of here before your Quirations or Cosmotech find us, we'd better get moving."

Kurt returned her smile thankfully.

"Sure thing," he said, turning toward to the exit. "You don't have to tell me twice."

COSMOTECH ORBITAL PLATFORM - June 8, 2147 - 7.32pm

MIANA ALMOST SKIPPED THROUGH THE SPACE STATION as she followed the map Kurt had sent to her. It was over. They'd done everything that was required of them and, somehow, they'd actually won.

She would have broken into a run if she could, but Isaac was understandably fatigued and he already trailed behind her, so she tried to keep her elation separate from her pace.

"So…" he said wearily, "what happens now?"

Miana turned to look at him and felt the Divsek rise up and take control her vocal chords. She didn't know how long it was planning to stick around in her mind, but this was one question she was happy to let someone else answer.

"Now you create your own future," the Divsek replied as Isaac caught up with them.

"And… are your brothers gone for good?" he asked.

As they moved on together at a much slower pace, Miana felt the Divsek's sadness flow through her. It was clearly still upset about what it had been forced to do.

"I do not know if they will return," it answered eventually, "but they have no reason to linger. I believe they will fade into the world beyond."

"And… what about you?" Isaac asked hesitantly.

This was a question Miana would have liked to ask herself and so she listened carefully for the answer. As much as she appreciated what the Divsek had done for them, she didn't particularly like the idea of having an alien presence lurking at the back of her mind and able to take over her body with a thought.

"I have accomplished what was needed," the Divsek replied simply. "I am no longer needed and so I too will fade."

Miana was relieved with the answer, but also a little embarrassed that it made her so happy.

"To the world beyond," Isaac said quietly.

"Yes," the Divsek replied.

Miana found it heartening to hear the Divsek talking as if there was no doubt some kind of existence waited beyond death and it made her wonder if there were any beings in the universe that didn't believe something similar.

Isaac, on the other hand, remained silent for a long moment and Miana found herself wondering what he was thinking. Of all the people who'd been manipulated by the Divsek, he was perhaps the one forced to give up the most.

"Can I ask you a question?" he said after a moment. "The Divsek, I mean."

"Of course," the Divsek replied.

"Have you… looked any further in this timeline?"

Again, Miana found herself eager to hear the Divsek's reply, but this time it remained silent much longer, as if it were deciding whether or not to answer.

"I have seen much, Isaac Taylor," it said eventually. "But there would be no benefit to life in sharing it."

"There might be a benefit to me," Isaac offered with a grin.

Miana smiled as well and she could tell the Divsek was also amused.

"You are an intelligent, compassionate being, Isaac," it replied. "I have no fear for your future and neither should you."

This seemed to satisfy Isaac, but Miana found she was a little disappointed. After all that had happened and the uncertainty she was going back to, any knowledge that might help her navigate life a little easier would be invaluable. But at the same time, her instincts told her it wasn't that simple. They'd already seen how visions of the future could be changed. Who could tell what they would do to their own future if they ended up knowing too much?

Knowledge might be power, but it also came with responsibility and Miana felt like she'd had more than her fair share of that lately.

"And now, it is time for me to leave you," the Divsek said solemnly.

Isaac looked at her with a tired smile and simply nodded, but Miana felt suddenly unsure.

"Now?" she said in her own voice, "but Kurt will want to talk to you. He'll have so many questions."

"And you will discuss them together," the Divsek assured her, "in ways that will take you much further than the answers could ever accomplish."

"I... thank you," she said quietly, "for all your help."

"And thank you for yours," the Divsek replied. "Both of you."

And with that, Miana felt something leaving her. It was subtle and came with only the faintest shiver of recognition, but one moment she could feel a distinct presence in her mind, and then it was gone.

"It's gone," she said in a whisper.

Isaac looked at her with a sad expression and Miana saw her own longing mirrored in his eyes.

"Come on," she said with a smile. "They'll be waiting for us."

Isaac nodded, returning her smile with the best his tired face could manage, and they continued on through the space station.

Miana brooded on everything the Divsek had told her and what they were going to do when they got back to Mars, but as soon as they reached the security terminal, everything else seemed to fall into irrelevance. Because there, standing next to one of the entrances that Miana assumed would lead down to the jet he'd prepared for them, was Kurt.

At the very first sight of him, Miana felt a powerful emotion gush forth inside of her and her eyes filled with tears. She strode faster, desperate to touch him and feel his arms around her.

Kurt looked up as she approached and his smile lit up the security terminal like the Jupiter flare never could. Miana skipped a few steps, intending to plunge into his arms, but at the last moment she saw panic in his eyes.

"Broken arm!" he blurted, raising his good arm in warning.

"Oh," Miana said, feeling stupid as she slid to a halt. "I totally forgot, I'm so–"

But before she could finish, Kurt reached up with his good hand, placed it against the back of her neck, and pulled her into a long, passionate kiss.

Miana closed her eyes as their lips locked together and felt a desperate hunger take hold of her. She brought her own hands up to clutch Kurt's raspy chin and run her fingers through his hair, and for a long, blissful moment, nothing else mattered. All she knew was Kurt and the kiss she never thought she would get to have.

After several seconds that Miana knew was burned deep into her memories, Kurt reluctantly pulled away and Miana took a step back.

"That," Kurt said, grinning from ear to ear, "was totally worth the wait."

Miana laughed with a giddiness she knew probably made her sound decades younger, but she couldn't deny that he was right.

"We did it, Miana," Kurt said, stroking a hand down her cheek. "We actually beat Loc and saved the planet."

Miana placed her hand over his and lowered her head.

"One of them," she said quietly.

For a moment, Kurt placed his forehead against hers then he pulled away and lifted her chin so he could look her in the eye.

"I don't know about you," he said with a smile, "but I could really, *really* do with some sleep. And that's not going to happen until we get back to the surface. So how about we make a move, huh? We can debrief on the way home."

Miana looked at him for a long moment, savouring the feeling of just being in his presence again, then she nodded once.

"That sounds like a great idea," she said with a smile.

MARS ORBIT - June 8, 2147 - 7.47pm

ISAAC SAT IN ONE OF THE JET'S PASSENGER SEATS, staring down at the planet that was now, at least for the foreseeable future, his new home. It was a strange thought and he doubted it would properly sink in for a while, but at the same time he was content. Tired, perhaps, exhausted even, but content.

It was funny how saving a planet from destruction could bring you closer to that planet. It was also nice knowing millions of people were getting on with lives they may not have had without him, even if they'd probably never know it.

It was different to the faith that had been placed in him by Hani'ah and the Quirations, or even the strange man who'd kidnapped him in Lynt City. That belief had felt fake. Fraudulent even. But this was something far more powerful. What he felt now was a belief in himself. Not in his intelligence or his technical ability, but in his humanity.

When it came to the crunch, he'd made the right decision and now, looking back on how hard it had been, Isaac was even more certain he'd done the right thing. He still wanted to find a way back to Jason and his own world, if that was at all possible, but the drive wasn't so desperate anymore.

There would be plenty of time to work on it, after all, and besides... something about experiencing so much without his brother had sparked a feeling inside him that Isaac had never felt before. He wanted to explore this new world on his own; go on a few more adventures without the safety net of his brother there to catch him when things got tough; find out what else he was capable of.

He was certain any achievements would be severely limited without Jason's ability to help him understand things so easily, but on the other hand, it wasn't like he was alone.

He turned to look at Miana and Kurt, the two strangers who were probably more responsible for saving this reality than he was. They sat in the pilot and co-pilot chairs at the front of the jet, talking quietly and holding hands in a way that made Isaac smile. It was nice seeing a couple so much older than he was acting like teenage lovers. It gave him hope for his own future relationships. He had no idea what they planned to do once they reached the planet's surface, but he got the feeling these were two genuinely kind people who would never willingly abandon him.

And then there was Anya. Isaac turned to look at her and saw that she too was staring out the window with a faraway look on her face. He certainly owed her a debt and not just the considerable sum of money he'd contracted for her services.

Anya and her many personalities had helped him through possibly the most emotionally draining and physically dangerous time of his life. It only seemed right that he should be there to help her work through all the things this catastrophe had forced her to confront. And to *do*.

Isaac felt a wave of sadness roll through him as he thought about Hani'ah. She was a remarkable woman, whether she'd been manipulated by the Divsek or not. It was a shame her life had to be lost in the process of fulfilling her own prophecies.

But Isaac didn't blame Anya. She'd been manipulated worse than any of them. And as he contemplated her situation, Isaac realised that he wanted to know more about this sad, fascinating woman.

No, it was more than that. He wanted to *be* more to her. After all they'd been through and all she'd helped him accomplish, they shared a powerful connection that couldn't be denied. And the fact she'd lost a twin sister only made that bond stronger.

Isaac could all too easily imagine what it would be like to know your twin had died and left you alone in the world. At least he knew Jason was still alive. And yet despite her loss, Anya had found a way to move on with her life, to become stronger. It wasn't the way most people might have chosen, but who was he to say there was anything wrong with it?

Isaac sighed. There was so much to work through, for all of them.

After everything that had happened, he expected this to feel like an ending of sorts. But it was almost the exact opposite. The last few days had included more abrupt and serious changes than most people went through in their entire life, and yet he got the feeling there was much more to come.

Turning back to his own window, Isaac stared out at the infinite cosmos that glittered in a shining arc above the great brown curve of Mars.

"I just hope that whatever happens, I do you proud, brother," he thought to himself.

And then he smiled, because he knew that, wherever he was, Jason was probably thinking the very same thing.

THE END

What is the System Series?

The System Series is an ever growing set of stand alone novels by Kynan Waterford, based on the planets in our Solar System. Each story is written in a new universe with new technologies, new characters, and all new adventures. So stay tuned for *Earth - Singularity*, coming in 2017, and make sure you get the whole set!

Jupiter - Illusions of Faith and *Pluto - Secrets Within* are **available now** as e-books on Amazon.com and as paperbacks from **www.kynanwaterford.com.au**

A note from the author.

So, there you have it. My first two-novel story! I hope you enjoyed Mars in its entirety and that the wait for Part Two was worth it. I certainly enjoyed playing in a world that is not too far ahead of our own. As usual, I couldn't resist throwing in some aliens, a few serious mental issues, and a little psychic-powered time travel to boot. But what's a good sci-fi story without such fantastical elements?

I have to admit, I found it a real challenge working with so many important characters this time, but looking back, I couldn't imagine losing any of them. It's truly strange how the creative process works sometimes. In the beginning of a book, you have so much control and can make things up willy-nilly. But as the book progresses, we authors find ourselves more and more at the mercy of the characters we create and the worlds we create them in.

I wouldn't have it any other way, of course, but if you're wondering how I come up with all this stuff, I really have to place some of the blame on my fictional character's shoulders. Am I allowed to do that? Oh well. Too bad, I just did.

For those who know me only as an author, you may not be aware that I became a father for the first time in 2016. Little Rowan was born a few weeks early, but he is a very healthy and, these days, very happy little boy.

Watching a new life come into this world was an amazing experience that has changed my perspective in so many ways that I knew were coming, but could never fully anticipate.

I already had a healthy respect for women, but now I have an even deeper sense of just how amazing they are based on what they go through before, during, and after childbirth.

Cassandra, you are incredible. Not only have you created the most special thing in my life (I love you Rowan!), but you are an amazing mother, have supported me tirelessly since I first embarked on my sci-fi writing career, and have continued to love me for the weird, silly, serious, nerdy and creative man that I am.

Special thanks to my father, Colin, who inspired so much of this book and taught me what it means to be a man as well as a father to my own family. And trust me, he know's a thing or two after raising ten children (yes, you read that right, *ten children!*). I know I speak for all of my (many) siblings when I say that your love and your example has made an incalculable impact on our lives. Thanks for everything, Dad. Be assured your legacy will live on.

And for fans of my work, just a little heads up... 2017 will involve a lot more than just *Earth - Singularity*. I've been lucky enough to catch the eye of a very talented and driven man, Scott Brewer, (Google him) and I'm now helping to turn his sci-fi movie (being shot in 2017) into a novel. So expect some very cool sci-fi costuming, movie cameos, Pop Convention awesomeness and more in the coming year.

If you'd like to follow all the nerdy fun, make sure you follow me on Twitter *@KynanWaterford*, Instagram *@kynan_waterford*, like my facebook page *@KynanWaterfordAuthor*, or sign up to the newsletter on my website www.kynanwaterford.com.au

There'll be plenty of behind the scenes pics, videos, and short stories from the sci-fi universe we'll be creating, so stay tuned.

Until next time, wishing you and your imagination all the best,

Kynan Waterford

Printed in Australia
AUOC02n0256270317
284204AU00002B/2/P

9 780992 565565